HALO

Book Four of the "Celestial Creatures" series.

Olga Gibbs

Angry Bear
PUBLISHING

Halo.

Published in 2020 by Raging Bear Publishing.

A CIP catalogue record for this title is available from the British Library.

Paperback ISBN 978-1-9164710-30
Cover design by Perie Wolford.

For upcoming publications visit www.OlgaGibbs.com

Men talk of heaven –
There's no heaven but here;
Men talk of hell –
There's no hell but here;
Men of hereafters talk of future lives –
O, love,
There is no other life but here.

Omar Khayyam

CHAPTER 1

The jagged air slides into my throat, ripping my lungs with its small spiky tips. It tastes of mildew and soil, and stripped of the oxygen.

I feel cold, yet burning at the same time. The chatter of my teeth is an erratic tune to the wringing twists of my muscles.

I try to open my eyes but my lids refuse to obey. I try to lift my right arm, then the left, but I don't feel any movement in my muscles or in the air around me.

Restrained in my movements, unable to breathe, surrounded by the darkness and fed on the air with the taste of the soil, the fear of being buried alive makes the decision for me, releasing the panic, that presses on, eroding reasoning and I begin to scream.

But the longer I scream, the harder my panic whips at me, as I feel the vibration of my lungs and my throat, yet can't hear a sound. I can't hear my own scream.

My voice bounces in my head, but produces no more than a muffled whisper, which then dissipates, absorbed by the soil, confirming my worst fears.

My eyes are burning and blind, producing the moisture, which runs down my cheeks in slow and sluggish streams. The moisture is too hot and too thick to be tears and I scream again, riding another wave of fear and agony.

I scream, and for the first time I truly wonder if I'm dead, if that's the way of angelic death, as my imagination draws vivid images of my dead and decomposing body, seeping the last of its blood into the greedy soil, sentenced to spend an eternity there.

Suddenly, another thought punches at me and I choke on my scream: "*Jess!*"

"Uriel, Uriel", a soft voice calls my name in a whisper, and at first I think it's my head had finally gave up on me, when I feel a soft breath on my face, followed by another murmur into my ear: "Uriel."

It's me. Someone's talking to me. Someone sees me.

Then another thought comes with relief, "*Maybe I'm not dead.*"

"Yes, yes! It's me", I breathe out. But I don't know if I was heard, as my voice is barely a whisper of a wind and my words are a soft rustle of leaves in a tree.

"Please don't scream again, Uriel", the voice whispers, "otherwise they'll come sooner, don't speak and don't struggle. You won't get free but your essence would grow weaker with your every move."

The soft fingers brush my hair as the lips kiss my earlobe: "You have to stop struggling if you want to live."

I begin to cry.

"*I am not dead. I am not dead*" is the only thought I'm able to form in my mind, as the sweet relief and hope whirl within.

"I'm not dead", I whisper, seeking confirmation of my hope.

The body leans closer to me and I can feel a strand of hair tickling my lip.

"What?" It rustles.

"Am I dead?" I push out of my throat, louder this time.

"What? Um, no", the voice stumbles. "You're not in Udhad, if that's what you're asking."

I try to move again but to no avail. I try to open my eyes but my lids are refusing to lift.

"Why can't I see?" I whimper.

"Wait."

A few seconds later a hand lifts my chin and a damp cloth touches my face. The cloth reeks of mildew, stale water and dirt. It comes to my face three, four times, with water splashing between the touches.

"Try now, but don't force your eyes if they don't want to open."

I can't afford not to force. Forcing and pushing through pain is the only way forward, I've learnt this by now. I have survived by pushing through, by forcing my body and my mind.

There's never another way out of Hell. It's the only way out.

My eyelids are still heavy but the lock, the glue, that was holding the lids together is off, and after a few more minutes of struggle I feel my eyelids rising, cold air touching my eyes.

But I can't *see* any light. Mindful of the earlier warning, I swallow my panic and my screams.

"I still can't see", I stammer, objecting weakly.

"Give your eyes time to adjust. It's dark in here."

The owner of the voice is right, and after a few more minutes of straining into a dark void, I begin to make out a faint outline of a figure in front of me.

"Who are you? Where am I?"

The body has an outline of human forms and proportions. A weak, flicking light lies on his shoulder, illuminating the left side, while keeping the face in the darkness.

The body stands on the ground and I'm level with it.

I must be standing up.

But I don't feel the weight of my body on my feet. I don't feel my muscles at all.

"Where am I?" I ask again, louder this time, but what I've intended as a demand comes out like a plea.

"You're in Wusuru Asar."

"Where's that?"

The darkness is silent and the outline is immobile.

"Hello? Are you there? Did you hear me? Please answer me. Where am I? Where is Wuru-sulu?"

With subsiding panic, the strength of my voice is growing, and with every new word I utter, my determination to fight returns.

"Um... In Arllu. It's Wusuru Asar", the voice corrects me.

Like I give a shit how to pronounce my latest lock up!

So, I'm in Hell...

The last word is more apt than I would've wished.

The damp air rides its wet fingers under my tunic. The armoury corset around my waist feels light and empty.

The person was right earlier: the longer I stare at the dim outline in front of me, the more my eyes adjust and the clearer appears the body.

The body is human and slim, draped in dark rags that hang on the skinny frame in raw edges. The hair is shoulder length, although it's impossible to tell the colour.

"Who are you? What's your name? Who will come? Who are "they"?" I ask, but I think I can guess who "they" are as I remember Butcher's face inches away from mine, with the hilt of his sword sticking from the middle of my chest.

"My name is Shana", the voice answers, "I was born here and I live here, working for *them*."

For the second time she doesn't assign them a name, but I don't press. Arllu is Baza's playground, and with Butcher in tow, it can only be them.

"Why can't I move?" I ask after a moment of silence.

The light footsteps slide sideways. A hand gently pushes my head upwards, holding it in place, waiting for me to see something.

For a few moments, I can't see anything but the darkness above, until the hand nudges my head further and a glint of a dim light slides off a shiny rope, wrapped around my wrists and my arms, which are pulled above my head.

The rope is dark, sleek with some substance, and as thick as my arms.

I narrow my gaze on the rope, *feeling* rather than seeing something, when another glint of the dancing light brings the clarity of the image and the shock of realisation with it.

The rope is suspended off the dark ceiling and wrapped around my wrists. Its shiny skin ripples in rhythmic movements and, watching closer, I can see the endless amount of dark teeth, like roots on the ivy, sunk into my white skin.

I'm choking on my horror and my screams, but I can't stop watching the skin of the "rope" rippling in waves as it sucks me, I can hear its gluttonous gulps.

I want to scream and rip my arms at my shoulders, just so I can get away from it, I want to shake off the parasite, but I no longer have a control over my body.

I retch, needing to relieve myself, but I'm no longer human and even bile doesn't come to my calling.

The soft whimpers come from my sore throat and I begin to cry.

"Oh no, Uriel. Not again. You have to stop."

The hand brings my head down.

"You can't do this. You can't cry or you'll lose more blood."

So my earlier tears are blood...

I know that I need to be shocked at another disclosure, but my quota for shock in a lifetime must have been used up.

"Help me", I whisper. "Help me, please, Shana. Please. Help me."

My voice grows louder and more desperate with every word, hotter and more urgent.

"Please, help me. Please, Shana. Please, I beg you!"

I scream and cry into the silence that doesn't answer. Shana doesn't answer, but in all fairness, I'm not sure what I'm asking her to do.

Of course, I want to be free, free from this paralysing hungry creature, from this cell, from this place, I want to run away, but I am happy to accept another offer of freedom. Anything would be better than the wait and the knowledge of where I am and what is coming.

A fast and painless death would be the biggest mercy anyone could give me right now and I know I will never receive it from Baza. I've seen plenty of his world and his rule to know that a fast death would be the last thing he would plan for me.

"Please, Shana, please."

"I can't do it, Uriel", her soft voice eventually stammers. "Stop asking me, *Sar*. Please, stop asking me and stop crying. I can't do it for you, but if you continue, they'll come and they will hurt you more. Please stop screaming. You are inviting punishment upon both of us. "

"Please, Shana. Help me. I beg you. Help me escape, kill me, do anything you want just don't leave me here."

My bloody tears stream down my face.

The numbness of my hanging body, of my frozen muscles, of my fuzzy head and hazy vision, the heavy lids, filled with sticky blood, which is no longer human, and the creature above that sucks me dry. If all of this is not the epitome of Hell, then I don't know what is.

"I can't do what you're asking me, Sar, it is an impossible ask. No one would risk granting you your wish against Lord's orders, and there's never a way out of here, not the one you're asking for."

The damp cloth smelling of dirt comes to my face.

"You will lose your sight if you continue to cry", she says next to me after a moment of quiet, as the cloth travels over my eyes.

"And what? What if I lose my sight, so what? What's the point? What difference would it make? I will die here soon enough. I will die and no one would know where I am and what has happened to me. Jess would be alone, truly alone. She'll be waiting for me and I won't come. This would be the end, the end of me, and the end of her. Nobody will come as nobody knows where I am, not Rafe, nor the brothers or Sam..."

I fall silent with a new sudden thought.

"Unless he knows where I am, because he is the one who sold me out", I mutter.

I bark a coarse laugh.

"Don't go anywhere. I'll be back", I mimic Sam's last words to me.

"Don't go anywhere, little gullible girl. Stay right here. Butcher is on his way", I mumble low.

I cough a sad laugh.

"Very fitting, serves me bloody right. That's exactly what I deserve. Thinking I was something special, thinking I could be loved, thinking I could take these assholes down and survive in their world, maybe even live. How sad... But look what I've done! Look what I've done to Jess! I've turned my beautiful sweet sister into an animal, a monster who eats lizards, and who will remain the monster forever.

"I thought I was special. I thought I had finally found my place, thought I could be the change, thought I could make it in here. I thought I was strong to bend this world, but instead the world has bent and broken me...

"I'm just a human, a stupid human who doesn't know shit, doesn't know a single thing about this world, yet thought she could outrun it. Naïve, dumb, stupid... A human, who singlehandedly ruined Uriel, had achieved something that not Baza or Mik'hael have managed to accomplish in all their lives."

I huff.

"I wonder if I would go to Udhad when they kill me or somewhere where humans' souls would go?" I muse. "But am I human? Or will I see real Uriel in Udhad? What she will do to me for killing her soul, her essence, her legacy? But no matter what she does, it would be the perfect punishment for everything I've done and ruined."

I quieten for a moment, but the silence is too sticky, suffocating me, so I continue speaking, needing to say something, anything, just so I can hear human voice, not feeling alone and buried.

"She is not gonna be pleased... But maybe he'll lock me here for eternity. He promised it already... Sold me out just as Rafe warned he would... Good job at least I've sent Rafe away, to Jess. He'd keep her safe... for a moment, before her world would collapse on top of her too..."

My thoughts skip from person to person, vocalising them as they come, as I begin talking to myself, finally losing my mind.

CHAPTER 2

A key rattles in the distance, then turns, followed by a swing of blunt metal on its hinges.

Shana's little body scatters sideways, disappearing into the shadows.

"Here is our undefeated Uriel. The conqueror of the lands she has no business to be in."

I recognise Butcher's voice before I hear the screech of his leather tunic, accompanying his movements.

The sizzle of hot metal dipped into cold water sounds closer, followed by another heavier this time, screeching swing of another metal door.

The sounds of prisons. They're all the same...

A pair of heavy boots marches over pressed dirt, coming into my line of vision and stopping in front of me. They are a black lace-up military grade pair favoured by Butcher.

The weak light has gone duller, obstructed by the large frame.

"Don't mind me, girl, I just came to check on you."

The boots walk a circle around me. His incoherent mumbling travels with him, his head is drawn up. Knowing him, he is admiring the creature, maybe congratulating it on a job well done.

The boots are back in front of me, having completed the 360 degree tour.

A hand, sealed in a leather glove, comes under my chin, lifting my head.

The Butcher's large face is an inch away from mine and the scent of his musky sweat and the scent of his leather are added with the heavy odours of my dungeon.

I drop my gaze to his chest. Even in this darkness, his necklace of human teeth glows with the whiteness of his trophies.

My tooth will be there soon, probably in the middle, and every time he'd go to a Hell pub with his mates, he'll show everyone the tooth he pulled from the mouth of Uriel... Maybe he'll even get a drink on a house for that...

"Still alive? That's good. I can't afford you dead before the big execution."

My head is turned side to side by his sure hand, my eyelids are pulled up.

"It won't be long now, little Uriel."

With it, he lets go of my head, which flops back onto my chest.

The earlier sounds of his arrival echo in reverse within my earthy tomb with his departure, before the silence hangs over my cell again.

"Uriel...Uriel..." I mumble into the dark silence, repeating his last word to me.

And for a moment I don't even know what I'm trying to say, before an unexpected wave of raw and burning hate swallows me and I begin to yell.

"God damn you, Uriel. God damn you, all of you, all of you and all of your Heavens and Hells. You, An, rot in Hell too, you old bitch; rot and die, just like I will", I roar.

Paralysed by the parasite around my wrists, I can't move.

My voice and my bloody tears is all that is left of me, but even that is absorbed by the greedy soil.

"Rot in Hell!" I roar.

I lost it and I know it.

The guilt for what I've done rips at me. The guilt for what had happened to Jess, who will be left forever as an animal, stranded alone in Hell, the guilt for everyone, who stuck their necks out for me. For beautiful and loyal Domiel and Dumah, who would be dead and extinguished soon just like their useless leader, the fearless brothers, who were screwed by the Heavenly powers before but now will be done for sure, and I would be the final nail in their coffins, for Tabby, who's already dead because of me.

Their faces are a morbid parade in front of my eyes.

I've over-played my hand.

The girl who decided to play the heavenly games she knew nothing about and, absolutely logically, had lost.

But I can't blame just myself. I need to share the weight of this guilt before it breaks me.

"What sort of mother are you, An?" I scream at the soil under my toes, but I can no longer see it as my eyes are covered with dark red film. "Letting one child of yours kill the other? Aren't you embarrassed at how you've raised them? Aren't you ashamed? Another shit mother has screwed up her children."

I laugh. I laugh and I can't stop.

But soon the hysterical laugh turns into the howl, and the howl turn into sobs and cries, but eventually, even those are gone. The answering silence weighs heavier than the screaming condemnation ever could.

"All that I wanted was to protect myself, my sister", I say, explaining myself to an invisible accuser and to my guilt. "I wanted to protect her home, her life for her. I wanted to protect the children of my neighbours, the children on our streets, my friends who would sell their souls to Scouser just to survive, survive in a world that hates them, amongst parents who never wanted them."

"The way to Hell is paved with good intentions", auntie's Pat favourite saying comes to mind.

If only she knew...

I weep. I sob, listening to the sound of the fat bloody drops of my tears hitting the ground.

The light footsteps rush over the pressed soil floor.

"You need stop crying, Sar. It will start hurting soon."

Shana's soft hand lifts my face and the cloth glides, cleaning the blood, which has already begun to crust over.

"Thank you, Shana."

Even if she can't free me, I understand that she showed me as much kindness as her fear allowed her.

"You're welcome, beyelai Sar. Would you like a drink of water? I was told you were human once."

"That would be great, thank you."

She gently lays my head onto my chest and disappears into the shadows.

A few minutes later, her soft hand lifts my chin up and the rough metal edge of a bowl touches my lips.

The water sliding into my throat tastes and smells of a stale puddle, which sat stagnant for a few months, before becoming a home to tadpoles and algae. But it's nice to feel the cool of water in my raw and burning throat, nice to feel something human, including Shana's touch.

"Thank you", I say after the empty bowl is taken away from my lips. "Why are you doing this?"

"What, beyelai Sar?"

"Why are you being nice? Haven't you heard the Butcher? I will be executed soon, and your niceness is wasted on the dying person."

Shana holds my chin with one hand, while the other is sliding over my face with a cloth, cleaning up the remnants of blood.

The outline of her slim shoulders rises as she shrugs.

"Butcher? Oh, you mean Asmodeus", she says. "But even if so, it is virtuous to show kindness to someone in their last moments of life. It's hard and lonely to die, no matter where you are, probably just as hard and lonely as to live in here."

"You live here? Where?"

"There." I feel the movement of air, as she waves her arm sideways.

"The corridors in Wusuru Asar go for a while. We live in them. Istana babá lives in Wusuru and lived for as long as our Elder can remember. I was born in Wusuru."

Istana babá...

There's something familiar about it, about that name, somewhere I've heard it before, but I can't put my finger on it.

"What is this place? Wusuru..."

She quietens for a moment before answering.

"This level of Arllu, Wusuru Asar, is for the traitors of the Lord."

"Which Lord?" I ask in a whisper, knowing only one "Lord", thanks to my mother.

"Lord of Arllu."

"Ah, him... okay."

I have to say, it's a relief.

"So, I'm a traitor of the Lord Baza?" I ask, but I don't need her answer. "Sounds about right. Are there many "traitors" in here?"

"In this corridor you're the only one. But there are many traitors in many other corridors."

"So, I've got a private wing of the prison all to myself? Nice."

I quieten and so does Shana.

But I don't like the silence of this earthy tomb. The silence here doesn't ring like a silence of an open space. This silence suffocates.

"So what are you doing here? I mean working..."

I want Shana to talk. I want to feel her touch; I want to hear her voice. I don't want to be left alone in the darkness of this cave, paralysed, with my own thoughts and guilt. I'm grateful to her for her time and kindness.

"I serve five corridors", Shana answers, "this one and four more. I look after the traitors of the Lord, making sure their essence or bodies don't escape, before the Lord had bestowed his rightful punishment upon them."

"Sure, sure", I say. I want to nod my head but my muscles are not controlled by me. "The rightful punishment and bestowing are very important."

"Um", I say, thinking what else to ask or say to keep the conversation going. "Do you like it in here?"

I inwardly cringe at my question. Typically British, I'm asking how she likes her working conditions and feeling a question about the weather is ready to slide off my tongue next.

"I don't know", she answers and I feel another shrug of her shoulders. "As my father once said: "The slaves have no voice, therefore shouldn't have an opinion."

"Slaves? Are you a slave?"

"Yes", she says, calmly and matter of fact.

"For our disobedience we were dishonoured and cast down by the Goddess of Ama -Arhus, who had declared that we should beseech our new Lord and master for his forgiveness, and we could achieve it only by submitting ourselves to him, our lives and our freedom, submitting the lives and the freedom of our children to him too", she recites someone else's words, the words which were drummed into her head over time.

Slaves... Another empire, which was built on the lives and bones of slaves.

But Shana's mentioning of the Goddess had finally flicked the proverbial switch, lightening the light bulb above my head, bringing with it the memory of the moment when I heard the word "istana" first time.

The glamorous event of gold, glitter, crystal and champagne at Baza's, the ball given in my honour, gorgeous Sam, sealed in impeccable tux, the tables, filled with food from gazillion courses and Sam, leaning into me, his bright blue eyes on me, his breath stroking my ear, moving my hair, sending happy and excited tingles over my body, and following my gaping gaze to the waiters with rice paper-thin, butterfly wings behind their backs, telling me that they were left behind in Arllu as a collateral by a Sumerian Goddess.

"Your goddess sounds like a gigantic bitch", I state.

The gasping and then the silence scream pretty clear of Shana's shock and the obvious conclusion that she has never heard such heresy, and I'm about to apologise, when her soft voice begins to ring with a quiet laughter.

The key scrapes the keyhole in the distance and the metal door cries on its hinges.

Shana lets go of my face and my head flops onto my chest.

The dirty and bloodied cloth drops to the ground with a wet splosh, as Shana scatters into the shadows.

The sizzling of the metal comes next before the heavy steps strut over the pressed ground, each one supported with a squeak of the leather.

The dark boots come and stand in front of me.

Their owner doesn't say a word, but he smells different to Butcher. The body bends over and for a fleeting second, I see a bare arm and shoulder, covered with black leather tunic, the face of the Butcher's minion, before he scoops the bloodied cloth off the ground and straightens.

I can't see, but I think he inspects the cloth for a few moments, before he turns, marching towards the direction Shana had run to.

It doesn't take long to find out his intentions, as after a few long minutes of silence, the corridor erupts with Shana's screams.

They're long and agonising, ringing in the depth of the earthy cocoon, and although most of the sound and intensity of the screams are lost, swollen by the soil, the pain and torture in them is obvious and clear.

"No!" I scream at the soil at my feet.

"No! You, bastard! Don't! Don't touch her! Don't you dare touch her!" I roar at the ground.

But I am ignored, and Shana's screams keep on ringing.

"Leave her alone! It's my fault, all my fault. Take it out on me!" I roar.

How much do I want to rip the parasite above me apart, finding the freedom to repay this bastard for every one of his deeds, coin for his coin, blow for his blow and punch for his punch. How much I regret not sinking my knife into him earlier, how much I wish I had my powers in me to make it better and right again, to fight one more day, even for one person.

"Don't touch her!" I scream with her and she screams with me, but eventually, her crying ceases. Not a whimper comes to me.

Oh god, he killed her. He killed her.

I can't believe it and I struggle to accept it. The punishment for the "offence" of a damp cloth is beyond disproportional. The brutality of it is utterly savage.

The heavy steps of the minion press the ground.

His smell is next to me again.

"Pig. Dirty fat pig", I hiss at the soil, "I hope you will rot in Hell one day. I hope the lakes of Hinnom will toast you like a marshmallow, before Udhad comes calling next, and I will be there, waiting for you, and your master won't help you there."

"Stupid wardum", the boots answer. "*This is* Hell and I'm not the one who is rotting in here".

The right boot disappears from my line of vision, and the next moment, my stomach ruptures with the excruciating pain, as the force of his enraged kick swings me on my "rope".

"Say hi to Udhad and Uriel from me. By the time I get there, you'll be long gone."

Laughing, he walks out of the cell, locking the door behind.

CHAPTER 3

I t takes me a while to learn how to breathe again and to gulp a splinter of stuffy air, bringing it into my lungs, to stop myself swinging, and to settle the pain, shredding at my insides.

When my breathing settles enough to talk, I call into the silence: "Shana. Shana. Sha-a-a-na-a."

But there's no answer.

Oh, no! No, no.

"Shana, please answer me", I call again. "Please. If you don't want to talk to me, it's fine. But please say something, just so I know that you're alive. I *need* to know that you're alive."

"Please. Oh, god, please be alive", I mutter. "Please, please."

I've killed another one. Another one is dead because of me.

But before I dive into another bottomless pit of the familiar self-loathing, the slow, tripping footsteps sound down the corridor, trudging closer, taking long and exhausted breaks in between.

"Shana", I breathe out.

I hope it's her. It must be her, as there's no one else is left here but us.

"Thank god, you're alive. I'm so happy you're okay."

As her tripping footsteps shuffle closer, I whisper: "Please, Shana, don't come near me. No! Don't. I don't want him doing it to you again. Stay away."

But soon, I can feel her body next to mine and I can hear her laborious wheezing next to me.

"Even if I stayed away, it won't change the disciplining ordinance, Beyelai Sar", she says. "He will come and beat me later. I'm scheduled for another appointed beating in two bêru."

"What? What do you mean "scheduled for another beating"? In what perverted place are there "scheduling" of beatings?"

The notion of booked in to a diary, regular beatings doesn't fit into my head.

"Is it him who's doing it?" I ask. The cruelty of one monster minion seems more plausible. "Then you need to tell someone! I don't know, your elder or Baza, whoever. What the hell!"

Shana's soft hand comes over my chin, raising it up. The cloth comes next.

"You've bled again", she tuts at me. "I've told you, you're losing the life source."

I didn't know I was bleeding through my eyes again, but I can't afford to risk the Baza's minion returning and beating the crap out of her, because of me.

"Shana, don't. Get your hands off me. Don't touch me."

But she ignores me, as she's wiping my face.

"My grandmother told me that we shouldn't fear death. She said that our life is what we should fear. She told me that Ishtar is waiting for her children beyond the veil, to grant wings to everyone who had suffered through this life and this master, to grant wings to everyone, who accepted their fate without objection. She said that those wings would be the most beautiful wings the world would have ever seen, that the wings would rise every istana out of the dark corridors and into the light, into the wide blue skies where Ishtar would meet us and we'd join her in her throne room. That's what she had told me and it's what our elder tells us too."

She stops speaking, gathering her breathing.

"But sometimes, when my *ikstaya* would get really sad or angry after her appointed beating, she would tell me another story, a story she called "Dakha-las": the prophecy that was told before her time but is forbidden to tell now, the story of another Goddess coming to free us, of the Goddess who will take us to the surface and into her heavens, the Goddess who will teach us how to fly again."

"Um", I utter. I don't know what should be an appropriate response to this trip down the memory lane or what supportive words I should say after she has shared the story of their forbidden prophecy.

"That's sound like a good plan, to grow wings, beyond the veil... The freeing Goddess sounds nice too."

During one of my history classes I read a quote that stuck with me, the quote that had angered me then as it had reminded me of my mother, of her obsession and hate: "Religion is the opium for the masses, but it eases their suffering."

Back then, I couldn't see past the word "opium". I couldn't understand how the hateful lies can help or ease anyone's suffering. I didn't understand the meaning of the quote. I saw it as another justification and validation of my mother's favourite obsession.

But now, looking at Shana's dark face, listening to her laborious breathing and feeling her sympathetic hands on me, for the first time I really understand what this saying means, what the author was trying to say with it.

Believing in these stories helps slaves to survive.

These stories are the heavenly "fuel" that gets them through, powers their lives forward, giving them hope, a hope for fairness in another world, when they can find none in the present, a hope for a better life somewhere, "past the veil".

The promise of peaceful and lush afterlife is what helps them endure the horrors of their everyday lives.

To appease the rebellious ones, these bullshit prophecies are invented. The prophecies of a "freedom bringing Goddess", the one who'll free them, of the one who will change their lives on this plane; the one who will stand up for them, delivering the vengeance, equality, fairness and justice. The generations are born and die, waiting for the fulfilment of these prophecies, living in hope.

But this hope and these stories are all that they have. I understand this now.

"You have to stop losing blood. The *panta-ku* is already feeding off your essence, bounding and paralysing you", Shana says. "You couldn't afford to lose any more of it."

After a few minutes of silence her voice rustles again.

"May I ask you a question, Beyelai Sar?"

"Sure."

"What are you doing in here? Why are you in Arllu?"

I keep quiet for a moment, thinking how to answer.

I'm in Arllu because I needed an army, but I'm in this cell because someone has sold me out. The search for allies has led me here, forcing me to trust random strangers, strangers, one of whom has betrayed me, sold me to Baza. But it might not have been a stranger...

I knew that I could trust only a few, but the mistrust runs deeper now. However, how can the honesty hurt me when I'm already betrayed?

"I came here to convince some angels to join me and come with me to Uras."

"And they have refused your offer, binding you to these tunnels instead?"

She sounds perplexed by my journey and I understand where she's coming from, but I know exactly what has happened to me. I know I was betrayed, the only thing that remains a mystery is as to by whom.

It could've been anyone in the room. I didn't know any of them, was meeting them all for the first time.

But if I am to be honest with myself, and I must, I can't exclude Sam or Rafe. Either one could've been the one who betrayed me. My latest predicament is the glaring evidence of my inability to play celestial games and navigate this world's murky waters.

There's a lot more I don't know. Some of the politics of these worlds still elude me.

"Someone did. But I don't know who", I answer eventually.

"If I can ask another question, Sar?"

"Sure", I answer. It's not like I have anywhere else to be.

"I don't want to offend you with my ignorance, Beyelai Sar, but who are you? I've heard them calling you "Uriel" when you were brought, so that's what I've called you, but I have never seen an angel like you in these tunnels. You have *four* wings and they are so large. Never have I seen wings as large as yours, Sar, let alone the four. What sort of angel are you,

Beyelai? You've said you don't reside in Arllu, but where did you come from?"

"You don't know who Uriel is?" I ask in turn.

It's not me being big-headed, but so far, in this angelic world, everywhere I went, I didn't need to introduce myself, or who I have become.

"No", she mumbles. "Please forgive me, Beyelai Sar. We were cast down with our beliefs, which are different to our current master's. I know nothing of the world outside of Arllu. Now and again, I'd see different banished angels bound in here, but nobody I've seen is quite like you. On your arrival, Asmodeus Sar himself had visited Wusuru Asar. He had instructed our Elder to provide you with a vacant tunnel, away from other *"bound"*, and we were issued with a large list of instructions directly from him. Our Elder was spoken to, so you must be *jeruuno-sur*, the big deal..."

"That's who I am. I'm always the big deal, it seems."

I don't know how much is safe to share with her. How much I can tell her about Uras or Sarukh. The on-going trend clearly demonstrates that I have shit judgement of people or angels, and need to keep my mouth shut as I'm betrayed too often. But what I'm about to share is not a secret, although her presence and our conversation might provide an answer.

"I'm Uriel, a daughter of An, sister of Mik'hael and the ruler of Uras. I'm The Harbinger of Doom, The Keeper of the Gates", I begin, but I slam my mouth shut, stopping myself.

How pretentious.

These titles sound hollow in this dark cave, while their bearer is swinging off the ceiling by the feeding parasite and is about to be executed.

"Uriel lives in Uras, a castle suspended high up in the skies of Sarukh", I start again.

"Uras", Shana repeats, mulling on the word. "That sounds nice. What does Uras look like?"

"It's a white castle, surrounded by the open blue sky. The rooms and corridors there have no ceilings, so angels fly wherever and whenever they please."

"Oh."

A little breath of wonder escapes her throat.

"Is the sky really blue?" she whispers.

"Yes."

"What about the sun? How does it feel? How does it look? Is it really as warm as they say? I've heard it's so warm that animals lay beneath its rays."

"Yes, the sun is bright and yellow. It's very warm, almost hot in summers. It rises every day and set every night, and when it rises and sets, the sky turns the most beautiful colours: orange, red, purple, blue..."

"Have you seen a sunrise or sunset?" she whispers in awe.

"Of course, many times."

"I haven't, ever. No istana ever saw it", she says, falling quiet for a moment.

"And no istana ever will."

I feel like I ought to say something inspirational to her, something like "the sky is the limit" or "if you dream it, you can make it", or some other nonsense, but not only it would sound empty, coming out of my mouth, but locked up in this cell, I am the last one to preach affirmative willingness and positivity.

"Are there many prisoners in these tunnels?" I ask her, changing the subject.

Shana releases my chin and my head flops.

"Many. Although I don't know for sure, but why would you need to know?"

"I suppose you're right. Not like I can do anything about it."

CHAPTER 4

The key scratches the lock again, followed by another swing of the metal door.

I have another visitor.

This place is getting busier with every passing hour. Butcher is probably making a quick buck by selling tickets to a willing audience to have a glimpse at the last Uriel, imprisoned by the Great Baza, before she is extinguished for good.

The gliding footsteps, which could only belong to a woman and pretty one for that, the one who's aware of her beauty and impact it has on people, so she had perfected that slow and sensual walk over the years, sound next.

The noise of a hot metal in cold water sizzles later.

The dim light fills the cell, lighting the floor of the pressed dirt under my gaze.

Following the noises, Shana performs her rehearsed drill and scuttles into the shadows.

I swing on my rope, my toes barely touching the pressed ground, when the light and slow stride reaches me, and my nose invaded by a sensual smell of the familiar sweet perfume.

The sensual scent is unmistakable. I know it too well. I've smelt it before and now I want to kick myself for not trusting my gut earlier, for giving people second chances, for allowing others to sway me, and as a result, getting me screwed because of it.

The elegant black flat shoes, bare of any decorations, come into my vision.

"I should've thought it was you", I say, looking at her polished shoes. The weak light glimmers on their patent leather. "Once a bitch, always a bitch or as my nan used to say: "The snake never changes its skin. It regrows the same bitchy skin back".

The crystal musical laugh twinkles in my tomb, before it dissolves, swollen by earth. Her good mood doesn't vanish easily.

"I love your little human sayings. They're highly amusing. I'll try to remember this one."

I'm weak and dry from blood loss, but courtesy of Shana's earlier drink, I gulp a few times and a small spit flies out of my mouth, landing perfectly on a toe of a Lis' shiny shoe.

"Pagru di mursu sadhu", she hisses. "Dirty animal! Zu ku Damu!"

I laugh and then tut at her: "Are you kissing your mother with that mouth?"

I laugh some more. The little pleasures in life, they're the sweetest.

I expect Lis to hit or slap me. I expect her to storm off, but she doesn't do either. She doesn't leave, her shoes remain under my gaze and her hands, and shoes, don't connect with my body.

I sigh. She is here to chat. Ignoring her would only prolong our tet-a-tet.

"Now, as you have demonstrated that it was you, I guess you want me to ask "why"? Why such a kind and lovely person like you, has committed such a dirty and treacherous act. Is that what you're here for? For the final hair braiding and girls' heart to heart?"

"You're not that dumb for an animal."

"Oh, thank you, Your Royal Highness. Sorry, can't bow at the moment, neck kinda doesn't move."

She laughs and takes half a step closer. Her hand reaches to my chin, lifting up my head, and her strong perfume invades me, engulfing my nose and my head.

"You know, with the amount of trouble it causes you to lift my head, you could've unstrapped me so we could have our conversation", I say, rolling my barely moving eyes above me at the dark parasite-snake. "And it would've saved me from smelling your perfume. Seriously, girl, where did you find that cheap crap? It stinks of a prostitute."

She doesn't answer me, doesn't say a word but her harrowed eyes and shallow breathing betrays her rage, making me happy for a fleeting second.

Her golden wings shimmer in a dim light behind her.

"So? What do you want?" I ask her as she says nothing, still holding my chin.

"To see you, watch you being reduced to the animal that you're, and yes, make you aware of the one who betrayed you. I'm already a hero in Arllu, a legend in a making amidst my kind. Once you're executed, I will be written into the Celestial history as the one, who brought down the Infinite Uriel. "Onoskelis – the angel, who had achieved the impossible", she recites as if reading a newspaper headline.

"The angel who achieved something that neither Mik'hael or Baza could do", she adds.

"Um... Congratulations? What do you want from me? A parade in your honour? Or for me to throw you a party? If you haven't noticed, I'm a bit tied up at the moment with other engagements."

If I could shrug my shoulders, I would. But ignoring me, Lis continues.

"When Sam came to me, asking me all these questions about my fall, mumbling something about the redemption, the second chances, chances to return into Sarukh, I knew it had something to do with you."

The breath catches in my throat at the mentioning of his name.

No!

My tongue refuses to obey me. My voice is not mine to control.

I swallow.

I try again, and eventually, I manage to push out: "Sam... Is he in on it too?"

I've succeeded keeping my voice even, pushing down the rising metallic taste of hate with the bitter tinge of betrayal, which both taste so familiar.

My head swims, as my mind is busy blocking the thoughts from forming and the feelings from coming forefront. The embarrassment, guilt, shame, sorrow are mixed with a deeper layer of despair and mourning.

They press at a thin barrier, nudging and pushing. They scream at me, mocking me, demanding to be acknowledged.

I don't manage to ignore them for long, with the guilt breaking through first, as it turns out, it was never far away.

Rafe had told me not to come here. He warned me to stay away from Sam. He was right all along: these angels are fallen for a reason. I should've stayed in Uras, with my sister and tried my chances against Mik'hael on my own.

But as much as the rational part of my brain understands and accepts that this wishful thinking plans would've never worked out, my guilt refuses to let it through.

The worse still is that I've ruined Jess' life too. With my arrogance and ignorance, I dragged her into this celestial mess. I've turned my beautiful, sweet little sister into a bloodthirsty animal. I've brought her to Hell and abandoned her here, leaving her in the care of the angel who had *turned* her into the monster.

I was pressing my advantage, was pushing for reckless decisions which I thought would lead to a win, even when I was told time and time again, about the dangers of the world which I wanted to change and bend to my will.

Lis is quiet. I feel her studious gaze on me, as her fingers hold my chin. I want to see her face better too, yet the shadows of my underground cave hide her eyes and her features.

"Sam is going to die and it all will be because of you", she says.

"What?"

"He is going to die", she repeats slower. "Baza had sentenced him to obliteration through beheading, following dissolution in Hinnom for conspiring against the Lord of Arllu."

For a second these words spin on a loop in my head, without registering.

Their meaning is faint and elusive. But when they do sink in, relief, followed by happiness, lift me, bringing with it only one thought and it's a selfish one: "It wasn't him".

This thought goes on a loop in my head. It takes me a while to swim through happy waves of relief, towards Lis' voice, and when I do, I wish I was still in the depth of my happy denial.

"...His sentence will be carried out soon", she continues, "more than likely after your execution. Baza's Council have unanimously found him guilty of treason against Arllu, but even that vote was just a pro-forma: Baza doesn't need anyone's opinion on handling issues within his domain. Nobody would be allowed to tell him what to do. Yours and his executions are purely for show..."

"I thought you liked him", I interrupt her, and judging by the silence following my question, she knows who I am talking about.

"I do. I did, but he made his choice. He chose the weak, pathetic human over his kind", she starts and I hear hysteria, hate and *sorrow* in her voice. "He turned his back on his kind and Arllu. His path in Arllu was clear. He was destined to be Baza's lieutenant, Baza's confidant, and I would've been if not for you."

The longer she speaks, the louder and angrier she grows. Her hate towards me is palpable, eclipsing her emotions.

"We would have made a brilliant couple, a power couple. We would have been feared and revered. Many doors would have opened for us. We both could have had future. But you... *You!* You've ruined it all", she screeches the last sentence, her hate vibrating her throat.

She stops and I can hear her shallow breathing as she gathers herself.

"I would never have missed that kind of opportunity, little pet. If I didn't take it, someone else would have."

She calls me a "pet" as my old neighbour used to, but coming out of Lis' mouth, this word doesn't carry any adoration, but is full of repugnance.

"An opportunity like this will make a name for me. I will get a seat at Baza's Council. The perks from what I have done will be coming my way for many *GA*. I will be written into history of Arllu and *Dingir-Ki*. The generations after me would know my name above Baza's. Long after I'm gone, angels would be asking one another: "How had she succeeded in capturing the Great Uriel?" and "How canny and smart she must've been?" But what they won't know, is how easy it was to capture Uriel. How easily played the Great Uriel was, how dumb she was to understand what she had done", she huffs.

She falls quiet for a moment before she continues again.

"Sam has made his choice. He was careless and fell for a human. He disobeyed and failed his Lord, and if that wasn't enough, he took the enemy's side in the longest running dispute of *Dingir–Ki*. He co-conspired to free the fallen, by that act alone, betraying and weakening Arllu. He had invited the Sarukh *sadhu* into Apkallu. The amount of his treachery is truly great. No way in Arllu, his deeds would have been forgiven or excused. He and everyone else, who swore the oath of An to you, are going to die."

I swallow.

It is one thing to prepare for death, knowing that your mistake had cost you your life and it's another to know that your mistake had cost them theirs. Indirectly, I've killed them all. By inviting them into the fold and playing the leader I couldn't be, I've signed their death warrant.

"But what's about you?" I ask and my voice is no longer even. It's shaky and coarse. "You have sworn the oath of An to me. You have pledged your Qal to me. You have pledged to stand with me in the name of An. I know what it means to swear this oath, these oaths are sacred..." I press. I need to expose her. She is either going to die with us or she will show me the way out.

I see the dark outline of her head shake, followed by a soft chuckle and a tut.

I don't like it at all. I am about to be told that I was swindled.

"Poor, simple human", she says and softly laughs.

That's it. I was duped.

"Was it a crossing of the fingers behind the back jobbie?" I ask.

"No", she says. "I didn't need to do any of that. I was honest in my oath and I've kept it. I am standing next to you, am I not? Look."

She waves her hand at herself and me and laughs again.

"Here's the "standing next to you" part."

"There were more parts to that oath, more than this one. What about your Qal? It's mine. You've pledged it to me", I whisper with dry lips.

"Yeah", she stretches, "that one is not very straight forward, but if you die tonight or tomorrow, extinguished into Udhad, then technically speaking, there will be no Uriel for me to uphold my oath to."

My breath leaves me in a puff. I feel defeated.

"You, nasty little piece of work", I hiss. But my hiss and my bounded state are not threatening and Lis laughs again, her laugh is gloating and pleased.

"I guess your promiscuous friends are in on it too?" I ask, resigned. I want to know how deep the cut her knife has left in my back is.

"Ah," she answers and dismissively waves her free hand. "They couldn't care less. They are not the kind to pay attention to small print. They came because I promised them a great show and they got it. They wanted an evening of entertainment and they received one. More than that, they'll get a great boost to their social standing, a boost by association. Can you imagine the stories they'd be able to tell at dinner parties? They were there when the history was made. They have witnessed the last minutes of Uriel."

Her laugh rings with soft crystal bells and I want to punch her. I want to shove her laugh into her throat until she chokes on it.

"I would have imagined their social calendars are exploding right now, but I have to say, I haven't seen them since that meeting", she adds, musing. "Oh, well, wherever they are, I'm sure they are enjoying it as much as I am."

"You would subject your friends to the oath you never planned to fulfil yourself?" I hiss.

"They're not my friends", she cuts me off. "And what is there to "fulfil"? Soon you will be another page in the ancient history."

"You forgot about Rafael, you stupid bitch", I say, laughing too, although I can hear the desperation in my broken voice. "You swore your Qal to him too, and he's not here. He is not imprisoned. He owns your sorry arse now, with your pathetic life, your essence and the essences of your "not so much friends". He owns you with all of your backstabbing crap."

I feel the soft movement of air, as she nods her head.

"I understand how you would see it as an issue, but trust me, pet, it's a miniscule issue indeed, which won't be an issue for long. Any and all loose ends will be tied, one way or another. Seeing his big wet cow eyes, with which he was glaring at you, I'd bet he is not far from the tower", she says, contemplating. "I don't think he would have left his "Lazarus project" behind, and now, as Baza has sent the search party for him already, it would be only a matter of time before he is found, and once it has happened, he and everyone with him will follow your journey through Wusuru Asar, then swiftly executed."

"For Arllu sake, *sadhu*", she suddenly screams. "You honestly should've learnt the world in which you've decided to play. You only have a few *immu* before *you will be no more*. There will be no you, no oath. If you ask me, it was an extremely jejune move on your part. You can't even begin to contemplate the essence you've extinguished with your move and the worlds you've brought to their knees."

She quietens again and when she speaks a moment later, her voice is soft and dreamy.

"You can't even imagine how big your execution is going to be. Baza had sent for every malakhim into Apkallu, suspending the harvesting. So, I suppose, if you look at it from this angle, your death would allow humanity to survive... for another day or so. But then, Hell will break loose over Apkallu."

"I can't claim the credit for it", she adds. "It was Baza's pun. He had shared it at the Council. Clever, is it not?"

Lis' mood swings like a pendulum. She is chattier now.

"We'll move full trot to conquer Apkallu, Baza had said. Mik'hael doesn't care what happens to it and with Uriel gone, Apkallu is ours. We can take it and do with it as we please. Baza seems to think that even the formality of contractual agreement over the soul proprietary would not be required any longer. "Harvest away", he said." Lis' voice deepens, as she swings her arm, imitating Baza.

"By the way, the invitation to your execution was sent to Mik'hael too, and if rumours are true, he is coming. Can you imagine? The Lord of Sarukh, The son of An, the ruler of Daanom is coming here. Because *we* have something that he doesn't have, and *I* made it possible. I did it! The little ol' fallen me", she giggles again. "I might even get my pardon, although I doubt I'd take it. Life in Arllu is far too much to my liking..."

Lis goes on and on, rambling about the preparations for my execution, as if they are preparations for a coronation or a jubilee, but I don't listen anymore.

I'm lost in this bad dream.

The surreal reality of it raises its ugly head against my memories of my old home, the street I grew up on, my neighbours, auntie Pat, my human memories with a human normality of it all, while bound by the bloodsucking parasite, in the underbelly of Hell, I am about to be executed by the Lord of Hell himself, as the "Lord of Sarukh" comes to watch my last moments.

When these moments descend, I feel disjoined from reality, disconnected, in disbelief at the life I'm living. It feels like a dream, a cartoon or a joke. The craziness of it is truly unbelievable, and the realisation of my new life versus my life before takes me by surprise.

My arrival into Arllu and my capture had spelt death to more people than I would have thought. It's not just me and Rafe, but Jess, both brothers and *everyone* who pledged their loyalty to me. Everyone. But even that is not all.

Not once have I thought or contemplated that my life, *Uriel's life*, is the only shield that stands between humans and Baza.

My head spins, probably from the blood loss or maybe from Lis' cheerful proclamations and unbelievable world updates, the world which is shoved into my face yet again, and its undeniable connection with the world of normal people, who are going about their nine-to-five lives, not realising the existence of this world.

I knew of the dangers of my death, but I didn't think it would be an "open season" on Earth. I don't know why I didn't think of this, and that makes me angry, angry with myself, with the snake wrapped around my wrists and the snake standing in front of me.

Baza is there, hunting Rafe, Domiel, Dumah and Jess and it wouldn't take him long to find them.

Maybe Jess is already dead. She doesn't hold titles and there's no need for her public execution.

As this realisation punches at my head, my bloody tears begin to roll again.

"Oi", Rage hisses at me, furious and hateful, "*are you going to roll over and cry? Bitch about unfairness of life? Since when any of that has helped you? Since when was submitting yourself to people or circumstances an option? Since when was crying about things a solution?*"

The hate that I feel, the pain, the anger... They burn inside me, hurting more than the parasite or Lis. They scorch my lungs and my heart, and I need to release them before they char me out.

"Lis, come here", I whisper, "I have a secret for you, but you have to promise not to tell it anyone. It's about Sam."

I say the only name she would care about.

The bloody tears have finally stolen my sight. I'm blind again.

"What?" she bristles.

"You need to know this, Lis. It's my last secret, the secret I haven't told anyone."

She shuffles closer.

"Come closer. It's about Sam. Come. I'll whisper it to you."

She pinches my chin, bringing her face closer to mine.

"Closer", I whisper.

She turns her head. The wispy hair around her ear tickles my nose. The warmth of her body brushes my face. Her perfume is overwhelming this close.

I say the word I know she would want to hear, one name that would bring her closer.

"Sam..." I whisper and I cry. I'm weeping now, "Sam..."

"What? What?!"

She brings her head closer. The soft skin of her ear is under my lips and I feel its soft velvet as I brush it. I can taste her skin, but it's buried under the taste of my own blood, my lips are covered in it.

"Sam..."

I say it and my lips kiss her ear, moving over it, wetting it with my blood. I feel the pulse of her heart, drumming at the thin skin on her neck.

"Sam..." I sob.

I take another breath and my chest jumps with two babyish sobs, short like hiccups.

I open my mouth and, pushing my body forward with my toes, I close my teeth over her soft neck.

CHAPTER 5

My teeth sink deeper and, suddenly, I break her skin and begin to taste the copper of her blood.

She screams, pushing at me, but I don't let go, my jaw is locked. I swing my leg, hooking it around her hip, anchoring her close.

My teeth are the only weapon left to me.

Bound and blind, I have nothing else at my disposal to do the reprisal I need to do, and she's the only one I can do it to. She's not the greatest of evils, but she'll have to do.

Her blood runs into my mouth.

It's thick and rich. Its smell and flavour are retch-producing and overwhelming. I want it out of my mouth. I want it gone. I want to spit it out, but I'm afraid to open my mouth and to lose my prey. So instead, I lock my jaw tighter, feeling her straining tendons under my tongue.

Her screams ring bright, but they toll in vain. Nobody comes to her rescue: not Shana, nor Butcher or his minions, and nobody will. Nobody is going to save her, just as nobody is going to save me. We're both going to die in here.

Her blood fills my mouth to the brim.

It begins to spill, running down her white neck and down my chin. The blood stains her pastel blue blouse. The fat bloody drops fall to the ground, staining her polished shoes.

But not all of it escapes my mouth.

It begins to trickle into my throat, and against my will, the muscles on my neck tighten, pushing the blood down and I swallow, once, twice.

Repulsed by the blood's warm thickness, I want to vomit, but I push the reflex and blood down, swallowing both, keeping my teeth in her soft flesh.

She struggles next to me. She screams and flays her arms, pushing at my shoulders, wrestling against my hold, so I nudge harder, throwing my other leg around her and locking my knees at her waist, and my teeth around her throat.

I'm drinking her blood now and I force myself not to think about it.

I don't concern myself with what I am reduced to, what monster I've become. I close my blind eyes to it, refusing to care about any of it. My mind, like my jaw, is locked on the one, single, animal need to finish it, to balance the scales even a little bit, to take one of *them* with me to Hell.

In this world, I'm surrounded by monsters. I've turned my sister into a one, so what if I became one? What is another monster in this Hell?

My throat muscles move, pushing Lis' blood down my throat and into my stomach. I gulp her blood, while she's screaming, thrashing next to me.

What does this blood drinking matter if I'm already dead?

Suddenly, through her thrashing, through her screams and my retching gulps, the darkness surrounding us bursts with a startling light.

Through the red veil and closed eyelids, I feel, I *see* the light – the white, iridescent, blinding light that fills the cave and the air around. The light is blinding and it hurting me.

I don't know what the origin of this light is or what it might mean, but like a wild animal who is afraid to lose its last bone in the cold of starving winter, I pull Lis' body closer, sinking my teeth deeper, refusing to let go or surrender my prey to anyone, no matter who or what it might be.

With every urgent gulp, the light grows brighter, reducing Lis' screams to the weak whimpers.

I gulp faster and hungrier.

Something's happening. Someone must be coming.

A busy chatter of many voices rattles inside my head.

Relaxed, they talk and laugh like a pleasant crowd at a dinner party. But suddenly, the hum of their voices rush forward, encasing me as if I have opened a door to that party hall, and then shoved into that crowd.

I slow my manic gulps, straining my ears. But although I hear the voices in my head, I can't hear anything with my ears. The earthy tomb is as silent as usual.

The voices continue their conversations.

I begin to separate the conversations within the busy chatter of a train station. Five, ten, maybe more, conversations go on simultaneously, and judging by the background noises, the conversations take place in different locations.

It's no longer feels like train station chatter. It feels as if I was connected into a telephone network, listening to every ongoing conversation.

The female voices laugh and cry, complain and gossip. The male voices mumble and yell, negotiate and demand, and suddenly through this busy veil, I decipher a familiar voice, Butcher's, which clips short and barking instructions at someone.

An unexpected warm ball ignites in the pit of my stomach with the bursting heat of a shot of vodka. The heat is growing, spreading up my torso and down my legs.

The liquid fire heats my legs and my feet, engulfing my arms and my bound hands. The fire rises up my throat, and I lift my head up, in a desperate attempt to avoid it touching my head, but I fail and the fire engulfs the whole of me.

I open my jaw and I scream.

I no longer hold Lis' body with my legs and my teeth. Her body falls to the pressed ground with a thud.

But I don't care about her. I don't listen to her fall. I don't care if she's alive or dead. The heat inside my body grows, pushing at my skin, whispering something to the white light around me, as if the heat and the light need to join, to immerse in one another, and my skin is in their way, obstructing their happy reunion.

My closed eyes are burning from the heat inside and the blinding light around. My skin and my body are ablaze.

Strung and pulled by the wrists, torched and burned, I twist and I scream.

The sudden deep explosion answers my calls.

It erupts above me, rocking the ground under my feet, vibrating the air, sending shock waves through my body, and suddenly, unsupported, I fall to the ground, showered with warm blood and pieces of warm, still pulsating, body.

The voices of the idle chatter are still busy, unaffected or unaware of the blast, rumbling inside my head and the blistering light is still around me.

I raise my head.

Warily, I crack my eyelids open, but immediately slam them shut at the bright light and pain.

A heartbeat later, I take another deep breath and I open my right eyelid, as I lift my head. The bright light floods my vision but I force my eye to stay open, waiting for my vision to adjust.

Eventually, through the thinning red veil and against the white light, I'm able to make out brightly illuminated walls of the packed soil of my cell, a dirt floor and a wall of thick, grey steel, prison grade bars past the corridor, further away.

I pull my numb hands underneath myself, but my hands slide.

I drop my gaze to the ground.

The packed soil is covered with red and black blood, the shreds of the black skin and grey muscles of an animal.

I jerk my hand away from the black and grey mess, but the soil is covered in it and I have nowhere else to rest my hand.

The bits of the animal are torn, probably from the earlier explosion. Its black, excreting skin is covered in a millions of small suckers, like on the bottom of octopus tentacles, but these suckers, although having a round base, have now lifeless, roots, which are like white worms, protruding from the centre of each sucker.

The remains of the parasite are gruesome and morbid, yet fitting to my surroundings.

Lis' body lies on the ground, at the entrance of my open cell. The clothing on her right side is soaked in her blood, and the large gash of a torn wound is evident on her neck, stark against her now white, pale, skin.

I turn my head, blinking through the white haze.

My cell is an open alcove, a dug out in a wall of dirt with a narrow corridor past it.

The corridor stretches to the left and to the right of my cell, and at the furthest right end stands a young child, a teenager, with gaunt face, slim frame and twigs-like arms and legs, poking past the dirty rags she calls clothes.

It must be Shana.

"Shana", I call but my voice is coarse and quiet.

The voices inside my head carry on their busy chatter. I try to dislodge the rocks in my throat and block out the voices, but I wonder if I've broken something, as the voices don't quieten and my voice doesn't get any louder when I call to her again.

"Shana. It's okay. It's me, Uriel. You don't need to be afraid."

I turn and rise, first to all fours and then upright. My hands slide in the bloody hellish mess, but I force myself to ignore it.

As much as the light has changed the appearance of the cell and the corridor, it hasn't changed the smell of my prison.

I tread around Lis' body, through and around pieces of the black parasite, and out of my cell, towards the wall of metal bars.

I lay my hand on the bars. I try to rattle the wall, but the metal barred wall is solid.

I turn and look at my cell.

My cell is a hole, dug out within the earthy wall. There are many more earthy alcoves like this, dug out along the same wall, stretching to the right and left, through the length of the corridor. I thought the metal bars were protecting my cell, but these bars segregate the entire section of the underground prison, closing off the long corridor with over a dozen, currently empty cells.

Shana's earlier comment about the entire corridor being allocated to me makes sense now.

I shuffle closer to an empty alcove, a cell, to the left of mine.

I walk and the light travels with me.

The round alcove of a pressed earth looks identical to mine, apart from a living, thick, black snake hanging off its ceiling, wriggling and twisting impatiently, waiting for the next prisoner.

CHAPTER 6

I walk towards the cell I was held in.

With every passing minute I feel better and calmer.

The bleeding from my eyes has stopped. The only reminder of my earlier blinding tears is the blood crusting over my cheeks.

I move and rotate my shoulders, gingerly at first, but my body doesn't hurt any longer, responding to me as it should, as if the earlier paralysis brought by the monster had never existed.

I lift my arm and inspect it.

The bright white light is me. It's fused in me, within me, blasting out of my every pore, surrounding me in a cocoon of glorious light.

It's ten times brighter than my usual pearly glow, but I don't feel shock at this knowledge.

My wings open and I don't feel any pain there either. I turn my head, inspecting my glowing purple wings, the damage done by the lizard and the Butcher's goon is gone.

The chatter of the voices in my head hasn't dissipated but has gone duller, as if someone had turned down the volume on an annoying radio.

The corridor and the alcove in front of me are full of white light, and when I walk from alcove to alcove, inspecting the empty cells, the light travels with me.

Shana's gaze follows me too. Her eyes are shielded against my light by her hand.

The dark circles rim her eyes. Her skin is white and ashen, blue veins seeping through the translucent skin.

Under the guise of inspecting the cells, I finally come closer to her.

"Shana, it's me, Uriel, remember? You don't need to be afraid. I promise not to hurt you."

Her gaze bounces off me, off my face, darting behind my back, ogling my glowing wings and the light around me.

Ignoring my "firefly" external state and "telephone exchange" in my head, I come closer to her. But the closer I come, the deeper she pushes her small body into the wall.

"Shana, I need to get out of here. Do you understand me? Do you hear me? I need to get out."

I need to get out of this corridor before anyone discovers dead Lis or my freedom.

But I'm not going to the surface. I came here because I needed an army in order to survive and that hasn't changed. I can't come out of these tunnels empty handed. Running away will not solve any of my issues.

I keep gliding towards her, and when there's only a yard if left between us, suddenly, she drops to her knees, promptly following it with a full flop to the ground onto her front.

In the bright light of my body, I see two see through, veiny small wings behind her back.

She lies on the pressed ground, her legs together and her arms spread wide. The defenceless obedience and submission scream through the readiness of her pose.

I shuffle closer, but she doesn't move. Her face is buried into the floor. Her body is unprotected, open to anyone's will.

Standing above her, I can hear her shallow breathing, as I feel the frightened tension resonating off her.

"Shana."

I crouch next to her and I touch her shoulder. Her body jumps up as if it's electrocuted, but she remains in her submissive pose.

... Ready to receive a punishment...

I kneel next to her, gently stroking her shoulder.

"Shana", I call again. "Shana. Look at me."

Her head lifts, moving towards my voice. But she refuses to meet my eyes, her gaze fixed to the dirt floor in front of her.

I pinch her chin.

"I order you to look at me, Shana", I call.

Reluctantly, her dark eyes meet mine.

"You need to get up, and I want you to answer every question I ask you. Do you understand me?"

With large bulging eyes, hypnotised and locked on my wings behind me, she nods and unsteadily rises. I rise with her.

"You need to help me to get out of here, and you have to come with me. Butcher might come any moment, and if they find this." I nod my head behind me, towards my cell with the bodies of two dead parasites, one of whom is Lis, "I will not be able to protect you. I have no weapons to fight and protect myself, let alone you, and if I die, you will die too. Butcher is not going to forgive this. He won' be asking whose fault it was. He'll kill you. So, come on, girlie, think fast. How do we get out?"

But she just stares at me.

I can't leave her behind. Not only will they kill her, but I need her help to get out of "Wusuru", wherever this hell hole might be.

I let go of Shana's arm and stride towards Lis' body.

I kneel next to her, rummaging through her pockets, looking for a key.

But the two pockets of her skirt are empty.

I turn her over. Her arms flop around, and something big, chunky and out of place catches my eye.

I take her hand.

A massive man's signet ring sits on her thumb. The ring is big, cut out of a single black stone. Its polished sides shine like an onyx. The top flat surface of the ring is carved.

I tug the ring off Lis' hand and stride to Shana.

"What is this?" I shove the ring under her nose.

She drops her gaze, staring at the ring in my fingers.

"Shana, come on. Do you know what this is?"

"Yes", she stammers, her voice is barely a whisper. "It's the opener to the seal of the lower levels of Arllu."

"Would it open this section then? To get out? Is that how she got in?"

She nods.

"Come on." I grab her hand, tugging her towards the wall of metal bars.

Just under the wall, I let go of her, and armed with the black ring, I look for the door and for the lock.

But I can't find either.

I run my hands over the bars, stroking them. I kneel when feeling the bars around the bottom. I reach on my toes when I search high, but the bars don't have any hinges.

"What the hell. Where is it? It must be here, it must", I mumble.

"Are you the Goddess?" Shana rustles behind me.

"What?" I ask absentmindedly, preoccupied with my search.

I glance at her, but quickly turn away, too busy looking for a door, while crawling on my knees, stroking the base of the metal bars.

"Are you the Goddess? You must be the Goddess. Your wings are the biggest I've seen. You are glowing. You freed yourself from Gertüs Peluş, and it has never been done. It's simply unheard of. Asmodeus came to see you, and he never visited any other prisoner."

She falls quiet.

"Are you the Goddess from the prophecy? My ikstaya's prophecy?" she asks.

I glance at her again.

She stands there, motionless, expectant and completely useless, so without thinking and just in order to encourage her cooperation, I drop "Yeah, sure. That's me, darling. The goddess from your prophecy. Now, can you please help me to find the lock, the door, something? Do you know where it is? I can't feel or see anything..."

But she doesn't answer, and as the silence hangs longer, I pause the stroking of the metal and turn my head to Shana, watching her lightened face, her eyes open in wonder with a smile over her lips.

At this moment, it's clear that I've stumbled on new information.

Working this angle would ensure complete, voluntary and *eager* cooperation. This angle could bring masses of istana under my flag and to my shores. This angle would bring loyal to the point of fanaticism followers, fuelled by the promised path out of slavery, who would die with a smile on their lips for me. These followers would fight until their last breath for me and our journey. They would not be bystanders or cheats, they would be believers! They would be loyal fighters and soldiers.

Isn't that what I came here for?

But the lie tugs hard at my heart. The ethical dilemma sours my discovery.

I know I'm not the prophesised Goddess, they're waiting for. Hell, I don't even believe in Gods or prophesies.

I am a con artist and a charlatan, who would claim to be saviour and God, while leading the enslaved out of their Egypt, all to his own end goal.

Shit!

I can feel a strange metallic flavour under my tongue. The lies do taste bitter.

Right now is my chance to set the record straight. I can tell her that I'm not the Goddess, she was waiting for. I can tell her all of that... and I would never see my sister again, Rafe or Sam, leaving everyone, who pledged to me, to rot and die in the mouldy corridors of this hell hole.

"Can we please pause the chit-chat for a spell and concentrate on getting out? Can you help me or not? Do you know how this key works?" I bristle at Shana and kick at the metal bars.

"I beg your forgiveness, Beyelai Sar. I don't. Asmodeus and his angels use these keys, and I don't know how it works. The door opens for us only once in seti bêru. It opens when we are escorted from our homes into corridors, before we start our service, and a few times if we're called into the main hall, but we never have a control over this wall or its door."

"How did she get in?"

I nudge my head towards Lis' body.

"How do they bring in angels? How did this asshole, who hurt you came in?"

I kick at the wall again.

"Argh! There must be a way in and out!"

I reach up, stroking the bars under the low ceiling, progressing towards the corner, when the stone ring on my thumb vibrates, pulling my hand right as if drawn by a magnet. I let my hand glide, following the increasing pull, when the ring slams into an inconspicuously looking metal bar.

At the contact with the ring, the bar lights up and the ring sinks into a suddenly soft metal with a sizzling hiss I had heard prior to every visitor into my cell.

The thin rays run to the left from the bar, illuminating bars further away, carving out a lit up outline of a door, which protrudes forward.

A soft metal click sounds and the door nudges open.

I pull the door wider and take a step out. I'm desperate to be out, to be past these bars.

I turn to Shana.

"Are you coming with me?"

She nods.

"Okay, then." And I nod to her.

Before I look for a way out, there's one thing I need to do.

"Earlier you've said there are new prisoners in Wusuru. Do you know where they were taken?"

"I don't know for sure, but I think it might be Mitish's and Sarin's corridors. At the last meeting in the Great Hall only they and I were left behind to issue new instructions, Beyelai Sar."

She suddenly pauses.

"*Mammí Barragal*", she adds, looking directly into my eyes. Her voice is a reverent whisper when she smiles, giving me a small slow bow, and I know that I've just been assigned another great title.

"Where are the Mitish and Sarin's corridors? Do you know?"

"Oh, yes. It's not far at all. Only they are in opposite directions."

"Excellent. Let's go and see... say Mitish first. But, please, let's move it."

I'm not going to run away from these corridors.

Instead, I'm going deeper into them, as deep as I need, to get my army back.

CHAPTER 7

We walk down narrow and low corridors, taking turn after turn in the dark underbelly of Hell, and Shana is leading the way, her small veiny wings bounce in front of me.

The tunnels of pressed earth are dark and claustrophobic. They smell of mushroom spores and mildew. The moisture seeps off the ceiling, dripping in dull heavy drops to the dirt floor, and slides in thin streams along the walls.

I keep my head down for fear of scraping the ceiling with my head.

"I knew you'd come", Shana says suddenly. "Once my ikstaya had told me of the prophecy, I knew that one day it would come true and you would come. My ikstaya would never have lied to me. She said that the Goddess would be glorious, that she would shine of the blinding light and she would lead us out of the tunnels. She said that the Goddess will free us all. Ikstaya had said that she only wished she'd live long enough to meet the Goddess."

I listen to Shana's wonderment as I walk.

Being a con artist is not advisable for anyone with any scruples, and I have to bite inside my cheek to stop myself from turning around and telling her the truth.

"But my ikstaya is now gone", Shana adds quietly. "She waited for you, but you didn't come."

There's blame in her voice too.

"Many have died waiting for you. Why didn't you come earlier? What took you so long?"

I am blamed for not fulfilling the promises, which were not mine to keep.

I spin her to face me.

"Shana, I am here now, in my full godly glory, as ordered. Your ikstaya called and I came. It took longer to find you but I am here now, leading you out of the corridors as you and your ikstaya always dreamt."

I growl and turn away from her.

She doesn't point out that she's the one who is leading the way.

My body is still aglow with the white light and my head is full of voices, although both have dimmed a bit, but what hasn't eased, is the guilt that prods at me.

I hope Rafe managed to escape and is alive. I hope they didn't catch him. I hope he is with Jess. I hope she's safe.

But for how long?

What's happened to the angels that pledged to me?

I hope they're alive, because if they are dead, all that I've done was for nothing.

"Do you spend all of your lives in these corridors?" I ask Shana.

Luckily for me, Shana doesn't hold grudges.

"We are assigned a corridor when we reach ten GA, *Mammí*, and we serve it until we die or transferred into another corridor."

"Do you ever leave your corridor?"

"No, Mammí. We're not allowed."

"What? Like never?"

"No, Mammí. Never."

"So you live in the corridors forever, just like that?"

I'm finding it difficult to wrap my mind around an existence like hers, where one is born to be locked away for the rest of one's life, with the prisoners he's guarding, while being guarded by the prisoners of his own. It's questionable who is the real prisoner in this set up, whose sentence is harsher, that of an angel, who lived and enjoyed his life or Shana's and her kin, who were born underground and would die there, without seeing the sky, finding freedom to live their lives with an ounce of enjoyment, every day of their lives serving the master.

"Yes, Mammí."

"Tell me about yourself", I ask, slowing down next to her, matching my steps to hers.

"I was born here, in Wusuru Asar, thirteen sammu bêru ago. I never met my mother or my father. I don't know who they are or if they are still alive. My ikstaya is the only one I've known. I met her by accident when I was five sammu and I began my training within the corridors."

"What do you mean "by accident"? She's your relative. Why didn't you meet her earlier?"

Shana sighs.

"When istana are born, they are removed from their mothers and given into *guleesh*, where old istana who can't fulfil their duties in the corridors, are given responsibilities to look after new istana. Because there are one old istana for hundreds of newborn, many don't survive past their first sammu. Masters say that this is the way of nature, and that only fit and healthy istana should be kept. The Elder says that Masters don't need weak istana as we have a job to do, and nothing should distract istana from their duties to their Lord."

"I'm surprised that your *Lord* even allows you to have children", I growl through my teeth.

Of course I knew that Baza isn't a nice guy, no one gets to the position of the Lord of Hell by doing good deeds, but these details add the depth to the picture of his reign.

"Once in sammu, all males and all females of a breeding and bearing age are called upon into the Great Hall and demanded to copulate. I've heard that Asmodeus himself supervises it and that the ones who can't or refuse are beaten to death within the Hall, in front of everyone. Masters say that it's our duty to procreate for the Lord."

I feel as if I'm been punched in a gut. The air leaves my lungs and the tunnel ahead tilts.

After a pause, Shana adds "The next time they call, I will have to go too."

She falls quiet and I don't know what I want to do more, hug her, promising that everything will be okay, or strangle Butcher and Baza with my bare hands.

I regret asking her. I don't know what I can possibly say to make her feel better. Her life is beyond any "tomorrow will be a better day" nonsense. Istana's life had remained like this for generations, and doesn't appear to be changing any time soon. My tongue doesn't allow me to deliver anymore lies to her, no matter how small. I've lied plenty already.

"I was told that istana who successfully delivers a baby is given an extra bowl that day at dinner and is allowed to rest until the bleeding subsides, before they are sent to resume their duties."

"Baza is generous", I huff under my nose.

"Tell me about the corridors, Shana. Are there many of them? Is it hard to look after one?"

I'm trying to change the subject to distract her and myself.

"It is hard to look after a *full* corridor, Mammí", Shana answers, slightly brighter, "but if the corridor is half full or empty, then it's easy. Apart from keeping the gertüs peluş and prisoners alive, providing them with water and monitoring them, we spend most of our time keeping our assigned corridors tidy. Masters said we should take a pride in the appearance of our corridors. When we're allocated a corridor, we are given tools to keep it clean, like a broom and rake, sometimes a bucket and a cloth. The responsibility with many prisoners is greater. If any of them die prematurely, we are ones who receive the punishment, that's why I like the empty corridors.

"How many corridors are there? Many", she continues. "Everyone over the age of ten *sammu bêru* is assigned a corridor, and there are hundreds of us. The corridors of Wusuru are vast and they run for a great distance. Some hold the angels that were bound here for sammu-GA. A few generations of istana have changed in those corridors, looking after those angels."

"You said you and Mitish, and another guy were given new prisoners?"

"Yes, we were, Mammí. Usually, we are summoned into the Great Hall only for breeding or to be given a new set of instructions. But I've heard that sometimes, a few istana are summoned into the Hall prior to a big execution, but Arllu haven't had one in a few GA. You're the first."

How nice! I am special after all. But now this "special one" needs to find her small army and rescue them from Hell. Easy-peasy...

Before the final turn, a wave of cries rushes forward.

It rings brighter with every new step. The cries are weak, heated and urgent, mixed with delirious whispers. It is the suffering of many voices.

Shana stops in front of a wall of thick grey metal bars, identical to the ones which were separating my imprisonment corridor.

"Here", she says, pointing to the wall. "That's Mitish's corridor."

I push the stone ring higher on my thumb and march to the bars.

I start from the top left corner of the bars and sure enough my hand is pulled towards the fourth bar, which lights up, and once the ring sinks into a suddenly soft metal with a sizzling hiss, the door forms within the bars, giving a soft click of its readiness.

I push at the door and we step into a dark corridor of pressed dirt.

These narrow hall and carved out alcoves are identical to the ones I was locked in, but unlike my corridor, here every alcove is occupied by a body, suspended off the ceiling.

The delirious voices of prisoners' cries, whimper and mumble incoherent nonsense. I hear a cough and retching down the hall.

I come to the closest alcove, my body illuminating a prisoner within.

He has been here for a while.

His body is covered in tattered shreds of decayed rags that years and years ago someone would've called clothing. Now, the rags cover only a few inches of his malnourished, grey body, which is suspended off the ceiling on a snake. He is male. His grey skin is stretched over his bones and his long grey hair covers his face.

He is not the new addition to Baza's judicial system I'm looking for. He has been here for a while.

I walk into the next alcove.

There's another old man who hangs off another parasite.

My back tenses at the fear that it might be a trap. I'm about to turn to Shana, demanding to know what game she's playing, when I walk into another cell and my heart drops at the sight of one of the fearless warriors brothers with bright blue wings.

I don't remember his name. He was the quieter one out of the nine. During the meeting, he sat behind, watching and listening as Sabrael quizzed me. Now he swings off the ceiling, his wrists bound by a parasite, his feet barely touching the ground.

The beautiful caramel skin has faded, turning grey, his hair losing its lush black colour, as if the parasite sucked out colours out of him. His two large cornflower blue wings hang behind his back, shrivelled and pathetic like two deflated birthday balloons.

I cross the open threshold, coming inside his cell.

In an abused haze, he mumbles something incoherent. His head is slumped onto his blood-soaked chest, and coming closer, I see blood, running out of his eyes in two fat streams, down this face and onto his shirt.

I reach out and prod the snake's black skin with my finger, pulling the finger away quickly. I'm afraid and repulsed by the snake, of what it is and what it can do.

The snake's skin is cold and slippery and it doesn't react to my touch, deep in its fruitful hibernation.

I prod at it again, longer this time, but the snake ignores me.

I reach out, grabbing the body of the snake, squeezing it in my grip, strangling it, forcing it to let go of the angel, but instead of hurting the unvexed, sleeping parasite, my actions hurt the angel, as he throws his head back and roars in agony up to the ceiling.

His scream is answered by rushed footsteps.

"Shit!"

I have no weapons, no swords to cut the snake or defend myself from whatever is hurrying my way.

"Shana?" A male voice begins. "You're not supposed to be here. What are you –"

The rest of the sentence is never produced, as he comes into the cell and sees me.

The male is older than Shana but not by much. Just like her, he is scrawny and malnourished. His thin frame is covered with a dirty sack, which serves him as his clothing, tied around his waist with a thin rope, unravelling at both ends.

Our gaze meets for a second, before his shocked gaze begins a rapid dance between my glowing state, my shimmering wings, the empty corridor behind him and the metal wall of bars past Shana.

"Mitish, the prophecy is true", Shana says.

She rushes, coming to stand in front of Mitish's confused face.

"This is *Mammí Barragal*, the Goddess from the sky our Mother Ishtar had sent to free us and to give us an eternity of flying in the blue sky on our new wings. She has come, Mitish! She has finally come!"

But either Mitish has never heard of Shana's ikstaya prophecy, or he is harder to impress, but he scrutinises Shana for a few moments, before he pulls his gaze to me and without a word, takes a step backwards.

"You", I hiss, running up to him, closing the distance between us in a flash.

I grab the fistfuls of his grey sack in my hands.

"You're going to stay here and you're going to be quiet. If you're open your mouth and try to scream, I'll kill you. You try to run away and I'll kill you. You try to get Asmodeus, I'll kill you. So I suggest you stand there, next to Shana, and keep your mouth shut."

Still holding him by his dirty sack, I push him towards Shana.

"Here. Stand there and be quiet, otherwise it will be you who'll be swinging off this thing." I point to the parasite.

I spin around, looking for anything I can use as a weapon, to pry the angel out, but I see nothing.

"You, Mitish." I turn to him.

"Shana said you use tools to clean these corridors, rakes, brooms or something. Where is it? No. Actually, come with me. You're going to show me and I'll keep an eye on you."

I grab him by his shoulder and shove him out of the cell.

I glance over my shoulder.

"Shana, you're coming too."

Mitish doesn't say a word, darting skittish glances at my glowing hand holding his shoulder.

"Where to?" I ask.

Without a word, he points towards one end of the corridor.

As I walk with Mitish towards where he pointed, keeping his bony shoulder in my grip, my light illuminates each cell in his domain, and each cell is occupied.

My feet are slowing by each arched entrance to the cells, and when I spot familiar faces or familiar clothing, I have to clamp my mouth shut against my cries that are pushing to get out.

I see another warrior brother, a slim woman with gorgeous blonde hair, in a familiar floral dress, a small female in the black tunic of Ophanims. She was one of the four, expelled from Sarukh by Mik'hael for the treason of saving Uriel's essence and now she's punished once again, for siding with Uriel.

I feel sick at the sight of this gruesome show and from understanding that they are here because of me.

But not all who pledged are here. I would need to find the rest of them. I'm not leaving them behind.

"There", Mitish says, pointing at a narrow opening, which reaches to my waist in height, looking more like an entrance into an animal burrow than a door into a room.

"Get in!" I bark, shoving him at the opening and once he crawls through, I follow.

The narrow and short bottleneck opens into a small cubbyhole, a dugout within a wall of dirt. The cubbyhole is barely bigger than a kitchen cupboard, and just about tall enough for me to stand.

A broom with a long handle, a rake and a metal pole are leaning in a corner of this cubbyhole, and a rag is spread on the floor against the opposite wall.

Without taking a step within the cubbyhole, I reach out and scoop the three tall handles with my free hand. I can do something with it, especially with the metal pole, but just in case, I'm taking it all with me.

"Your *kuustra* is bigger than mine", Shana's voice stretches sourly behind my back, and I spin to see her face poking through the rabbit hole.

"You can sleep with all of your body on the floor. Lucky!" Shana grunts.

My gaze darts between the cupboard's floor and the young man in front of me.

I know I'm not brilliant at math, but I truly fail to see how a man even as scrawny as him can fit into this kitchen cupboard to sleep. Unless he curls up like a cat into a tight ball, but how many of us can sleep like that?

"My body doesn't fit on the floor of my *kuustra*", Shana huffs.

"You sleep here?" I ask Mitish.

But as if given a vow of silence, he doesn't answer so I look at Shana.

"How can you sleep here? It's so tight."

"That's not tight. His *kuustra* is twice the size than mine", she answers. "I always knew you were the Elders favourite", she says to Mitish.

My question of disbelief falls on the deaf ear of their everyday life, of normality of it, and currently I don't have time to explain my confusion.

"Go", I say, shoving Mitish towards the opening.

He climbs out of his cubbyhole, and once his slim body is through the hole, I drop on all fours and climb after him, clutching my tools in my hand.

The bottom half of my body is still inside the bottleneck, when Mitish's form dives towards me, his scrawny fist hitting my hand, which is holding his tools.

He hopes to overpower me but he is too untrained and too weak to fight, or even to begin to understand how to inflict the most damage.

But I know.

With my free hand, I grab his ankle and yank it, hard. Losing his balance, he falls, his head hits the ground with a thud.

In a few rushed moves, I'm out of the cubbyhole and next to him, and while still on all fours, I jam my elbow into his solar plexus with all of the force of my annoyance. He doubles over, whimpering and rolling on the ground.

"Try this one more time, matey, and you will be dead", I hiss.

I want to kick him as well, but I manage to restrain myself.

Huffing and out of breath, I rise to my feet, scanning Shana, who stares at me with her wide open, scared eyes.

I rest the broom against the wall and, with one swift kick, I brake the wooden handle, cracking it at the base. I lift it to my eyes, inspecting with satisfaction, a sharp end of the wooden pole, and I repeat the same with the rake.

Nice.

Now I have two sharp weapons.

I scoop Mitish off the ground next, yanking him to his feet.

"Come on, idiot. I've got things to do but if you try this crap again, I will test the sharpness of my new instrument on you."

I hold him tight, not planning to let go any time soon.

Shana follows behind me with her short steps.

The Hispanic warrior angel hasn't disappeared. He is still swinging off the ceiling and feeding the parasite.

"Okay. Both of you, go there", I say, pointing to the furthest corner of the blue-winged angel's cell. "So I can see you", I add, barking at Mitish.

He plods into the corner, nursing his midriff.

I walk a few steps to one side, then a few steps to the other, inspecting the snake.

I hope it will work. I don't know how I managed to explode my parasite, but it had demonstrated one thing clearly, these things can be killed.

"Okay, okay", I mumble, mindful of my earlier attempts to strangle the thing.

I choose a wooden pole with the sharpest end. I lay the metal pole and the other wooden stake on the ground nearby, glaring at Mitish as I bend down.

"Okay."

A deep breath, and after a huffy exhale, I jam the sharpest shard of the pole into the black sleek skin.

Instantly, the angel roars as if I've jammed the rod into *his* body.

Panicked, I yank the rod out, and immediately, his screams are echoed with monster's shrills, and the angel drops to the ground with a thud.

I hadn't given a thought before about how much time I would have for my rescue mission, if anyone would be expecting Lis or how long would it be before her disappearance is discovered, but this unplanned angelic bawling, in the depths of the earthy corridors, is most definitely going to bring visitors.

I'm running out of time.

I jam my sharp stick again into the snake's black wriggling body, then I scoop the other two sticks, walking around the body on the ground, towards Shana and Mitish.

"Shana, please check on him. Find some water, give him a drink and wipe his face. Look after him basically, just as you did so wonderfully for me."

I smile and stroke her cheek.

"You", I bark at Mitish, "with me."

I'm used to pushing and dragging him around, so I scoop a fistful of his rag by his shoulder and drag him out of the cell with me.

I do the same slaughter dance with my sharp pole in every cell, stabbing at the black parasite and releasing a bound angel, and soon the screams begin to ring in the earthy corridor at regular intervals.

Every time a new body drops to the ground, I step out of the cell and yell towards the end of the corridor, where I've left Shana: "Shana! Here's one more needs water and your help."

By the time I am finished, I got into the swing of it, jamming my sharp, now drenched in a black blood, pole decisively.

I counted twenty one cells in total, now each holding a freed angel and one wriggling, abandoned and dying monster.

CHAPTER 8

The phone exchange in my head buzzes with the usual calm chatter when suddenly, Butcher's voice comes to the forefront, barking at someone, issuing a clipped order to check on the screaming in sector "One-zero-four", to seal off the corridor and nullify it and all its residents if required. They don't have time to "piss about with dead treacherous animals".

His instruction is answered by a cavalier bark of a sycophantic voice and I almost expect to hear the click of heels over my radio.

...And that's what the end will look like.

As much as I expected it to happen, I haven't come up with a plan for this eventuality.

My eyes dance around the dark corridor of pressed earth.

I have two istana of questionable loyalty, twenty one comatose angels and no way to transport or hide them in this place.

"You, move."

I nudge Mitish towards his rabbit cubbyhole.

"Shana!" I call. "Leave everything and come here. Now!"

I jog towards Mitish's sleeping quarters, dragging the young male with me. The poor guy is like a ragdoll, dragged back and forth by me, but after his stunt, it's either this or death.

With my mind, I search within the phone exchange, for the answering male voice, but I can't find it. I'm sliding from conversation to conversation, I even manage to find Asmodeus voice, directing the training of his new recruits, replacing the few I've slaughtered, but I can't find the man, who was ordered to come here.

"Get in!"

I shove Mitish head forward into the rabbit hole he calls a home.

"Shana", I say, swinging my hand towards the opening, inviting her in, and without arguing, she nods, crawling into the room, and standing outside, I hear another round of her complaints.

"Shana, shush!" I hiss into the opening.

The voice of the Butcher's minion is nowhere to be found, but amongst the tangled mess of conversations, Baza's deep warm baritone of Father Christmas comes through, having a casual conversation with someone, bragging about "the first in the history of *DINGIR–KI* Lord of Arllu, who brought down one of the Sarukh *melam sahu*".

As much as I'd like to hear more of his conversation, I have more pressing issues. Someone is coming here and I can't allow them to find me.

I crawl into Mitish's cubbyhole, gripping my homemade weapons.

My plan is a bold gamble. But scaredy cats don't survive long in this Hell.

My plan is devised on a hunch that the coming minion would need to investigate the parasite mass release, before running away, crying to his boss, explaining the issue. I don't expect to see bravery from the minion, when the boss is not watching.

The three of us are tightly packed in the cubbyhole like commuters on a train bound south out of London at rush hour.

Mitish shifts next to me. His gaze darts between me, the hole's entrance and his feet, and following another suspicion, I bend over, scoop the rag off the floor and rip a strip off it.

With wide open eyes, Mitish watches my manipulations.

"No offence, mate, but I don't trust you, Mitish. After the stunt you pulled earlier, I hope you understand."

I swing the piece of fabric in front of his eyes.

"I need you to take this piece and tie it around your mouth. Now."

Mitish's eyes bulge and he shakes his head "no".

Not enough space...Oh, well...

I swing my leg back as far as the small cupboard allows, immediately shooting it forward, the knee first.

My knee connects with his groin. He opens his mouth to scream, but before his scream has a chance to ring, I shove the waddled piece of fabric into his mouth, and when he falls to his knees, I cover my hand over his mouth, taking a step around him, pressing his head to my stomach.

In the distance, the sizzle of the lock is followed by the screeching swing of the gate.

A few steps march down the hall, stopping abruptly.

He is here and he is alone. That's good.

"What in Arllu?" a voice calls.

"Mitish!" The male roars. "Mitish, *irtu etu dalkhu*, what's going on here? Where are you, good for nothing, lazy slave?"

The feet walk down the corridor, with the sound of short spells of silence, stopping by the cells, inspecting my handy work.

"Mitish! Mitish, you useless frog."

The feet march to our cubbyhole with a decisive purpose.

"Not a sound," I say, bending over, mouthing it into Mitish's ear.

"Are you there, slug? Sleeping, huh? Wait 'til I bring your flogging forward or issue the second one this month. What's going on in your sector?"

The feet are approaching and the voice grows louder.

I turn again, pressing my back against the wall, to the left of the opening, dragging gagged Mitish with me.

I put my finger over my lips, telling Shana to be quiet.

But there's nowhere left to go. There's no space to hide in this broom closet, but to be fair, I didn't plan to survive by hiding.

The shuffle of a body dropping to his knees sounds outside the hole.

"Just for this crawling alone you will get an extra flogging, rat", the voice hisses outside.

I push with my wooden stick at Shana and she squeezes her body deeper into the wall. I drop to my knees and push Mitish away from me. Even if he decides to scream now, it will not change a thing

The head pops through the hole, and spotting Shana it begins: "What are you doing here? You're dirty, little..."

His head swings to take in everything in the cubbyhole, turning until his gaze finds me, his eyes bulge in disbelief.

"What?.." he begins.

His hand, which is already in the cubbyhole, drops down his body, looking for a weapon, but I had my weapon at the ready first, so I strike first.

I swing my sharp wooden stake in the tight area of the burrow, jamming it sideways into the minion's neck.

His eyes open wide at the impact. His throat gurgles for a bit, his hand aimlessly stroking his body, and without finding his weapon, he gives another strangled hiss and drops to the ground.

I rise to my feet, and stepping with one foot on his head, I yank my stake out.

I glance around the cubbyhole.

Shana stares at me with her big eyes. Mitish has stopped screaming and struggling against his gag, and now with bulging eyes, matching Shana's, his gaze pinballs between me and the body on the ground, and I begin to worry that his eyes will roll inside his skull and he will pass out.

"I warned you", I say, pointing my stake at him.

A pitiful piglet's squeak escapes him.

I turn to the body, blocking the entrance, and the exit.

Like Winnie the Pooh... Stuck in the Rabbit's home.

The childhood story with a teddy bear, who ate too much and subsequently got stuck in the rabbit hole, comes to mind.

Unfortunately, there's nobody outside to yank the body out of the hole.

Unless I'm prepared to wait for Asmodeus' rescue service.

I slide to the ground by the wall against the entrance and I brace myself. My feet touch minion's head and I begin to stretch my legs, pushing at his head, pushing his body out.

At first, his body moves, but the harder I push, the more it folds within the bottleneck and in no time, it is stuck within the opening.

Somebody needs to push the body out, and it can't be me.

I come over to Mitish and yank him up to his feet. I pull the wad of fabric out of his mouth.

"Do you want to die here?"

His eyes grow wider and like a neurotic, he shakes his head at me.

"Not because, I'm going to kill you, idiot", I growl. "Although I should have. We're going to die if we don't get out. When Asmodeus comes he's not going to ask you questions. He'll kill you as a traitor. I know he will. Unless you are lucky enough to die of starvation before Asmodeus comes here."

He frantically nods his head and suddenly says: "Please, don't kill me, Beyelai Sar... *Mammí*."

"He speaks", I say. "Chill. I'm not planning to kill you, Mitish. If I wanted you dead, you'd be dead by now."

I point at the body.

"Push him out. We need to get out of here, and pronto."

Awkwardly and as much as the tiny space allows, Mitish drops to his front and begins to push.

It starts slowly, I've jammed the body pretty bad, but eventually, the dragging sound of the fabric over the pressed dirt fills the small room, and the body pops out, with Mitish climbing after it.

"Go", I tell Shana, nodding at the open hole.

I climb out last.

I half expect Mitish to pull the same stunt as earlier, but I climb out without any issues.

I stand up and begin to brush the dirt off my front, when I look down at myself.

What's the point?

The white tunic is no longer white. In fact the white is the last colour anyone would use to describe the colour of my tunic. It is stained and soaked with mine and Lis' blood, with the parasite's black blood, and caked in dirt.

I walk around both istana, marching down the quiet corridor, to the cell with the first angel I released.

The cell is quiet. The angel lies next to a wall and a large black puddle of blood grows on the floor under the creature.

I come closer, kneeling next to the angel.

Although his face is smeared with streaks of wiped, now drying blood, the ashen colour of his skin had dissipated, giving way to a soft and gorgeous caramel shade.

His chest rises with his even breathing. His eyes have stopped bleeding and his blue wings are starting to fill in, finding their earlier lustrous colour and shape.

His recovery fills me not only with joy, but also with hope. Maybe we can make it out of here in one piece.

I feel gazes on me, so I lift my head.

"Shana, can you please check on others, see how they're doing."

She nods and disappears, but I feel Mitish hovering behind me.

I want to apologise for the gag, threats, my manhandling of him, but it's not the godly job to ask for forgiveness, so instead I bark, without turning my head: "What do you want?"

I shuffle on my knees closer to the angel, lifting his head to my lap.

"I've heard of the prophecy only once", Mitish whispers behind my back.

Here we go again.

"Everyone was too afraid to speak of it."

He walks around me and kneels to the side of me.

"I've heard it from an old istanu, who served the corridor next to mine. He was very old and served the corridors of Wusuru Asar for three GA. He told me the prophecy and told me what it means before he died."

Mitish quietens and I raise my head to watch him scanning the pressed earth walls with his absent gaze.

"He died within the corridor he served all his life. He died on a muddy floor, alone. He had never cared for anyone. He said he never made any children, and when I asked him why, he told me that he didn't want to subject his children to the eternal slavery of his life."

Mitish sighs.

"I am grateful I met him. I'm grateful we spoke and I'm grateful he told me of the prophecy..."

I turn my attention to the angel, but I can feel Mitish's gaze on the side of my face.

"...Of the Goddess, who would come into these tunnels one day, to lead the Children of Ishtar to the freedom of skies", he recites.

"I never thought his story could be real. I never thought there was a chance it could happen. I thought he was a crazy old man, who lost his life and his mind in these tunnels, but now?.."

I can feel Mitish's hot gaze.

"Could it be true?" he whispers. "Could the prophecy be real? Shana seems to think it is. Could it be *you* that the prophecy is about? Could *you* be that Goddess?"

Holding the angel's head on my knees, stroking his hair and listening to his breathing, I sigh.

"I want to say: "decide for yourself, if you believe in prophecies, if you believe it's me", but you probably never decided anything for yourself", I say. "You were never allowed to make a decision, let alone to stand by it. I know it's not your fault. I get it. You were born in these corridors, in these shackles. It's all you've ever known, all your parents knew and their parents before them, so expecting you to make up your mind is a big ask."

I look up at him.

I want to tell him that I don't believe in prophecies. I don't believe in an intervention by heavenly powers, in their saving, guiding light. I don't believe that things get better, if you only wait, pray and believe. I don't believe that things come to those who wait.

I only believe in fighting. I believe that you have to fight, dirty and bloody, for everything you want from this life, fighting from your first and until your last breath.

I was unlucky all of my life. I'm aware of it.

Nothing came easy to me. Nothing was given to me freely, without asking for something in return. I had to fight for every slither of happiness and peace I've had, so it had damaged me, and I'm aware of that too. I'm biased to the magical prophecies realm, biased to stories of saving grace, biased to stories of saving Gods and Goddesses. Not only I know I'm not the one, but I resent to be called one. All in all, he is asking the wrong person, but as he asked, I'm going to answer.

"But what I will tell you, Mitish, is that at some point you need to ask for more. Goddess or no goddess, prophecies or not, at some point you need to *want* more, *demand* more, and not only from others, but from yourself too. It's just... One day you need to be brave enough to say "enough".

I shrug my shoulders, not sure how better to explain.

"One day, you will wake up to the realisation that nobody's coming to save you. Nobody will be there for you to hold your hand, to make things better. Nobody will give a shit if you live or die. In fact, on that day you will realise that you're surrounded by killers and parasites."

I gesture around us.

"And that day you'll realise, *and accept*, that death is not the scariest of outcomes, that often the lives we're living are much scarier. And you'll mark that day in your calendar and in your mind, because on that day, that happiest and the saddest day of your life, you'll learn a new way of living, you will learn to fight. And let me tell you something else. That decision, that understanding from that day, would make you free."

The angel on my lap suddenly draws in a sharp and deep breath. His chest rises with an intake of air, and his eyes fly open.

His eyes are distant and wild. The red is the colour of the outer edges of the whites of his eyes, but overall his eyes look well.

"Hi. Hi, can you hear me? Can you hear me?" I call to the angel, stroking his cheek. I want to call him by his name but I can't remember it.

"Hi. Hi", I'm calling, "Can you see me? Can you hear me? Sabrael's brother..."

At the name of his brother his dispersed gaze sharpens and he turns his head, narrowing his gaze on me.

The running rush of footsteps sounds down the corridor, stopping outside the cell.

"Mammí, they're waking up!" Shana gushes somewhere behind my back.

"Take care of them, help them", I answer, turning my head.

"Can you help her?" I ask Mitish.

He nods, rising to his feet.

"Come", he says to Shana, and the two sets of footsteps, one rushed and one slower, dissipate into the tunnel.

I turn my attention to the angel.

"Hey, can you hear me? Can you see me?"

While keeping his eyelids closed, his head moves to give me a small nod.

"Good", I exhale.

I stroke his soft black hair.

As his skin finds its colour, the scent around him grows stronger too. Whereas Sam smells of pine forest after the rain and Rafe smells of exotic fruits and ocean, this angel smells of flowers, a heady scent of spring lilacs.

I love lilacs. There was a lilac bush on the lawn across from my house, and every May I and my sister would play around it, lying on the grass underneath it, inhaling the sweet scent of lilacs above us.

A few times, I broke a few branches and brought the lilacs home with me, trying to bring with it a shard of happiness. But the lilac branches and the hope of happiness didn't last more than a few hours in the poisonous environment of my home.

"I'm sorry", I say as I'm stroking his hair. "I didn't think this would happen to you. Lis has betrayed me, *us*, but I made sure that she paid for it. I'm sorry that pledging yourself to me has brought you here, but we need to move if we want to survive."

The angel opens his eyes and looks at me.

"We need to leave the corridor and find a way out", I say. "I don't know who Lis bribed to get access to me, or how much time for the audience she was given, but Asmodeus runs a tight ship around here and it's only a matter of time before she'll be discovered. Besides, Asmodeus is expecting a report from his man, and there's no man to deliver that report..."

"...you?"

His voice is a weak rustle and I stop speaking.

"Sorry? What?"

I lean closer to him, holding my hair to the side, his lips touching my ear.

"Lis... His man... What did you do?"

I pull back. I hope he is not a pacifist or growing nostalgic on me. I don't have the patience to deal with an "every-life-matters" speech. Besides, I hope I didn't misjudge the brothers.

"I've killed them both", I clip.

The angel closes his eyes for a moment, accepting my words.

"*Gertüs Peluş?*" he asks.

As I frown, confused, he turns his head, raising his gaze to the dead parasite hanging off the ceiling.

"Oh, those things?" I say. "Yeah, the guy who serves this corridor has a broom, well, had a broom, now it's my weapon, and I stabbed them with it. Surprisingly, it worked out pretty well and straight forward. I have to say, I didn't think they'd be so easy to kill. Maybe in these tunnels, these things have no natural enemies?"

The frown grows over his forehead as he stares at me.

"But listen... mate", I say. I still don't know his name. "We have to go. Other prisoners are coming around, but we really need to move."

"Shana. Shana!" I call out into the corridor.

When she runs in, I lift the angel's head off my lap, placing it gently on the ground, and I get up.

"Look after him."

I walk out once she kneels next to him.

CHAPTER 9

I walk into the neighbouring cell.

The imprisoned angel lies on the dirt floor on his back. His long grey hair sprayed around him, his almost decomposed clothing barely covers his skin, failing to hide the whole of him and the shy pink touches my cheeks.

I shuffle closer.

He stares unseeingly into the ceiling above. I'm startled by his young eyes, framed by the gaunt and cadaverous face of his and old man's grey hair.

"Excuse me. Sir, can you hear me?"

I squat next to him and touch his shoulder.

The moment my fingers make contact with his skin he begins to scream with a one note howling of an animal or a crazed man, whilst glaring with his blank eyes into the space above him.

I pull my hand away and get up, taking a step back.

Shit, triple shit.

I don't know what to do. There's no way I can move him in this state when I can't even talk to him. I have one more corridor to visit, producing the same angel saving miracle over and over, and now I'm running out of time. Maybe my time is already up.

I jog out of the cell, running into the next and then the next.

Shana did a good job cleaning angels' faces and making them comfortable, comfortable as far as lying on the pressed dirt goes, but the angels are still out and only a few of them moan softly as they come around, all of them are the angels from my recruitment party.

It seems the less time one had spent bound by a parasite, the shorter the recovery and waking time.

The female angel with pink wings softly weeps, lying on the ground, her floral dress wrapped modestly around her, probably Shana's doing, her pink wings have grown fuller.

I find Mitish in the next cell.

He is on his knees next to an old angel, busy stripping the angel's rags off, turning the angel's lifeless form from side to side, and the Butcher minion's black trousers, boots and leather tunic lay in a heap on the floor next to him.

Mitish lifts his head to my footsteps, stopping his manipulations.

"So he is more comfortable when he wakes up", he says.

"Okay."

I nod.

How do I tell him that we may never leave this corridor if we don't leave it in the next few minutes, and even that might not save us as I have another corridor to visit.

I watch as Mitish struggles. The body of the angel is skin and bone, and fairly easy to manoeuvre, but Mitish is taking it slow, carefully turning the dried out angel.

I wonder if he knows the angel, if they've met before. I doubt they've met in a life outside these walls, as according to Shana, istana live and die in these corridors, but how long has this angel been locked in here? Was he already suspended off the ceiling when Mitish took over or did Mitish witness his arrival? Did they talk?

The grey paper thin skin of the angel is wrinkled, yet stretched over his bones, the pink hue of the relief from the parasite hasn't touched his skin yet.

But Mitish is not concerned, he is not worried. With tender care he turns the man, removing one rag at a time, ripping at a few, until the naked body of an old man, looking like a mummy, lies on the ground.

The body is shrivelled and weathered. It's the body of a dead bug left on a windowsill and found by a spider, who drunk its dead body dry, turning its shell into crumbling dust. Yet Mitish doesn't see a crumbling shell of a dead insect, he sees a person there, maybe someone he knows.

Watching Mitish crawling in the dirt, tugging trousers over skeleton legs, my earlier hesitation and fear become tenfold, mocking my decision, asking repeatedly, if I have the moral rights to risk the lives of twenty people for my need to save forty and if I should abandon my idea of going into the Sarin's corridor.

My resolve to execute the earlier plan of saving another twenty bound angels begins to dissipate.

If I can't move twenty unconscious bodies, what will I do with forty? Maybe even saving twenty was a mistake, and talking about saving forty is a pure suicide. Maybe now is the time for me to turn around and walk away from them all, satisfied with a small win of their chance for freedom and some dead parasites, including Lis.

Maybe I should abandon my plans and run away now, before it's too late.

If I stay here, saving them, I will probably never see Jess again... just like I will not see Sam, if I walk away now, leaving him behind, locked in one of the tunnels, hanging off the ceiling, feeding the snake.

I've made the decision to fight for mine and Jess' future and that decision has led me here. But it has backfired just as the choice to bring Jess to Uras had. The choice to keep her safe, allowing Rafe to share his essence with her.

In this world, I can't see further than two steps ahead and it frustrates me. My forecasting in this magic world, the world of essence transference, flesh-eating insects, ruthless leaders and shady coalitions sucks. At every turn the shockwave of my earlier decision sweeps me off my feet, catching up with me, pushing me forward without giving me a second to catch my breath, to think.

So far, I've manage to stand against it all, but how long do I have left?

Without knowing the rules of this game, the rules of this world, I'm like a blind puppy, everyone's pray and my own enemy. Stumbling, falling, yet pushing forward, I hurt myself, leading everyone following me off a cliff.

The muffled echo of stumbling footsteps pulls me out of my thoughts. I come out of the cell, turning my head in its direction.

Holding onto the wall of the pressed soil, one of the brothers, the one who smells of lilacs, shuffles down the corridor, pausing outside the cells, looking at the prisoners on the ground as if searching for someone or trying to convince himself that this is not a dream.

Shock is spilled over his drawn face. His lips move soundlessly, as he mumbles something to himself, while shaking his head.

I glance at him then look past him at Shana, who stands outside his cell, lost and unsure.

"He got up to find you", she calls to me and her voice quivers.

She probably expects to be flogged for this...

"It's alright, Shana", I call and walk to the stumbling angel.

It's a relief to see at least one of them on his feet.

Maybe the possibility of leading these twenty out of Hell is not that far-fetched.

My decisive strides and his weak shuffling brings us to another cell simultaneously, and when he turns his head to look into the cell, to see the prisoner on the floor, he lets go of the wall and stumbles towards the cell's opening, tripping then falling to his knees before it.

I rush over to him.

"Are you okay?"

But he shoves at my hand. His eyes don't leave the body on the ground.

On his knees, then dropping to all fours, he crawls towards the prisoner, his cornflower blue wings drag through the dirt behind him.

"Brother, *ahu mul*, brother."

His hot whispers grow to a call, morphing into a howl, the closer he gets to the body.

"*Em-nam kud Anshar, ahu mul... Isnarkabtu Shiimti ak essentu-uri*", he calls as his fingers dance over his brother's face, hair, shoulders.

The body on the ground is the one I spotted earlier, one of his brothers from my recruitment meeting, the one, who like him, had pledged himself to me.

If not for the different face, one would've thought that this is the same man on the floor. The identical black clothing, black hair and caramel skin, with cornflower blue wings behind his back.

I walk into the cell, coming closer to the angels on the ground, and at the sound of my footsteps the warrior snaps his gaze to me.

"Where are the rest of them? Where are my brothers?"

His hiss is hostile and although he doesn't say "it's because of you we're here", his loathing gaze relays it clearly enough.

"In another corridor, as far as I know."

"Let's go", the warrior barks, trying to rise.

But his rising is pathetic and clumsy. He brings one knee up, scans the area around him, looking for a support, but unable to find any, he brings his knee down, raising the other knee instead, and then after a few moments of gathering strength and breathing, he tries to get up, pushing at the ground.

His pitiful shuffling is painful to watch.

I come over and offer him my hand, but he pushes at it again, glaring at me from under his eyebrows. I withdraw my hand and my offer, taking step away.

"Where are we going?" I ask, watching him, my arms folded over my chest.

You're not going anywhere anytime soon, mate.

"Marsat manhu", he barks. Or so he wishes, but his weak voice is strained and out of breath. It's anything but scary.

"Where do you think, Uriel? To that corridor, to free my brothers."

The "Uriel" whips out of his mouth with a burning slap of an insult and his glare confirms that it was intended as one.

But I'm annoyed too.

Nobody wanted to end up in here, and as sure as hell, I didn't book my place in this mouldy and muddy retreat. I accept there was a lack of planning with some cowboy attitude on my part, but surely he didn't expect the process of defecting to the enemy side to be plain sailing? Surely he didn't expect Baza to open the Gates for him and pack him a lunch for the trip? Surely for someone like him, who was a pawn in the Celestial games before, fell out of favour and residency, living by Baza's, Butcher and Co. side, knowing their extracurricular activities and techniques this outcome should not be a surprise, so why the hell am I getting this pushback?

"How do you imagine it?" I ask. "Who is going? You? Me? Or maybe he is?"

I swing my hand to the body on the ground.

"most of them are still out", I say calmly, "and we don't know when, or if, they will wake up. To top it all off, you and I are not in a position to transport this many bodies. Unless you have a plan, in which case, of course, I'm all ears."

"You have led them here, Uriel", he hisses at me in his coarse voice. "It's your job to get them out. You said that you are the new leader, you said you can do it and we trusted you. We have followed you, we pledged ourselves to you. Now it's your turn to stand by your promise. It's up to you to lead them *out* of this place. Leave them here to die and there will never be another army for you. No one will ever follow you... and not only because there will be no one left."

The truth of his words steals the air from my lungs and anger from my heart. I feel deflated.

The anger can burn only for so long, I know it too well. It's a short term solution. Like a burst of adrenaline, it propels you further, giving that heady rush, that tunnel vision, zoomed on your target or goal, but it doesn't last long.

You have to make it to your destination under its blistering light. You need to score that goal while the blazing heat is raging, because once it withers, it leaves behind only the charred ruins of self-doubt and loathing.

The familiar guilt stirs inside. It knows its way around me. It had lived here for years, the tunnels of my heart are familiar to it.

But I can't let it grow. I can't let it spread.

I am no longer Ariel. I have nothing in common with the girl the guilt once knew. That girl died somewhere along the way, probably in the cell of the jail, under the threat of Scouser. But maybe she died as she watched the knife, drenched in my step-father's blood, had dropped from my sister's hand.

I am Uriel now. I am the one and only daughter of An, the archangel, ruling Heaven and controlling Hell. I am the unexpected leader, who rose from ashes of Hell and I will not be doubted by anyone.

I take a breath and square my shoulders.

"I am aware how we've ended up here. But may I remind you that you have sworn the oath to me of your own free will, of your own volition. The brother of yours has spoken for you and he knew the stakes, you all did. I never hid the danger from any of you, so this little predicament", I swing my arm, "should not come as a surprise, and damn sure, shouldn't all be put on me."

He glares at me and his jaw muscles roll under his skin.

"Damiq. It's fair", he says eventually. "But Uriel, *Beyelai Sar*, don't leave them behind. They swore themselves to you and have gifted their lives to your cause. You have obligations to them too, Beyelai. The actions on these obligations are what separate a leader, about whom the legend will be sung for many *GA*, from the short lived stories of a coward. Even if we never find the way out of Wusuru Asar's tunnels, the stories of your bravery will. It will be taught amongst our kind and passed among the others, seeding the hope, and when your essence will rebirth once again, the fight will be won."

He is pleading with me, and listening to him, I'm reminded why I am here.

"Please, find them, free them and I will do everything in my power to get us out of here. I will help you to get them all out. We will find a way, I swear to it, *Beyelai Sar*. With the last of my breath, I will fulfil my oath to you. The last of me I will give to you. If I leave, if my brothers leave, we will die in battles for you. For eternity, or until the last minutes of Udhad, you will have my life."

Time and time again, I have been told I don't know when to leave good enough alone, when to quit while on top. The last time I heard it was from Rafe, who begged me to stay in Uras, who warned me against my scouting mission in Hell.

I guess I don't know when to walk away, if I knew, I would've done it by now.

"What's your name?"

"Pronoia, my Beyelai."

"Damiq", I say and he eyes open wider and then he nods.

The more of the old me, Ariel, is lost, the more of new me, Uriel, comes forward. The change doesn't scare me. The loss of my old self is no longer daunting or frightening, maybe because I've crossed that line already or maybe because she is no longer the one I want to mourn.

The progression in metamorphosis...

"I will go and get your brothers. I leave you responsible for everyone in this corridor", I say, "and I'll leave Mitish behind too, but I think he isn't going to be much help, he seems to be having a moment over there."

I jerk my head toward the end of the tunnel, where I left Mitish.

"I will be back as soon as I can, although I still need to think how to move them."

I point at his brother on the ground, whose skin colour begins to find its earlier caramel shade.

"I've killed an Asmodeus' soldier earlier, to buy us some time", I muse to myself out loud, "but I don't know how much time that has bought. Asmodeus dispatched him himself, so he will come calling after that soldier eventually..."

I honestly don't know how much time we have left or if there is any.

The phone exchange in my head has gone duller somewhat. I still can hear the leisurely chatter of multiple conversations, but it has faded further into the background with no sign of Asmodeus' or Baza's voices, and I have to confess, that worries me the most. I don't know where they are or what they're planning.

"Did he say that Asmodeus had sent him?" Pronoia asks as he keeps his gaze is on his brother.

"Who? Asmodeus' soldier? No. I heard Asmodeus issuing the order, hence I know that this corridor will be checked soon enough, and we need to move. Lis came into these tunnels and never came out, now him. We're running out of time and saving a few extra angels could be the end of us."

The moment I shook my head, emphasising the word "I", Pronoia had turned his head to me, now openly staring, as a confused frown cuts though his forehead.

"What do you mean, *you* heard him? How? Was he next to you at that time?"

"No. It's just these conversations..."

I wave my hand next to my head.

"They're going non-stop in my head. Incessant chatter... It gives me a bloody headache, since Lis –"

I close my mouth. There's no need to describe to him in every animalistic detail what I've done to her.

"What's happened to Lis?"

"It's a lot of questions, Pronoia."

"My apologies, Beyelai Sar, but what has happened between you and Lis?" he presses on, his gaze on me.

I sigh.

"I've made a decision to survive and she had to die for that, and I do not want to talk about it."

I turn around and am about to walk away, when he calls after me, his words rushed: "Beyelai, did you have physical or mental contact with her when she died?"

"I'm done", I cut him off. "I've got a lot to do and so do you. You're responsible for every soul I leave behind in this corridor. I'll take Shana with me, she knows the way. We will be back soon..."

"Can you hear me, Beyelai Sar? Can you hear my voice?"

Pronoia's voice cuts into my mind, interrupting my speech.

I blink and shake my head, wanting his voice out.

"What was that for?" I turn to him. "Testing the radio?"

But my barbed comment is left unanswered as he stares at me.

"You're not supposed to have access to Arllu's kigru exchange", he mutters. "It shouldn't work for you just as the Sarukh's kigru would have been closed to us. Only the essence tied and pledged to Arllu would have access, depending on the access granted to the said essence."

Now it's my turn to frown at him.

"What are you saying? My essence has tied itself and pledged to Arllu? Uriel's essence?"

Although I huff at him, with everything that I've seen lately, I wouldn't be that surprised.

"I doubt Uriel's essence would ever pledge to the Lord of Arllu, but the other essence already had."

"God." I roll my eyes. "What other essence?"

He shuffles on his knees to the nearest wall then grabs at it, pulling himself up.

After my hand was pushed away twice, I let him do it himself, as I stand, pushing down on my impatience, which reminds me that this conversation is running away from us, and I'm running out of time.

"You can hear the Arllu's exchange", he says, taking a small step closer. "You have recovered faster than expected from gertüs peluş, Beyelai Sar. Your glow is by far too bright, taking into account your location and the loss of your energy, which all lead me to one conclusion that your essence has absorbed someone else's essence. What has happened to Lis?"

He stops speaking and his soft brown eyes, framed by long black eyelashes are on me. But as I say nothing, glaring at him, he adds: "Very well. It's irrelevant how you come to possess the essence, how it came to be, but the fact remains that somehow you have absorbed another essence, *someone* else's life energy, which has not only made you stronger, but has transferred the essence's pledges with it, which gives us the advantage we need."

He is a handsome man. Tall, taller than me, black curly locks brush his wide shoulders, stark and glorious on the backdrop of a pair of stunning, piercing blue wings behind his back.

But I ignore his looks, busy mulling on what he said.

I'm not surprised at his conclusion. Something felt off the moment I closed my teeth over Lis' neck and her blood began to pour into my throat. That light, the heat of the energy I felt, which travelled upwards, exploding the parasite above, then following it an assault of voices in my head, which I haven't had for a while...

I take this news calmer than I would have done earlier, at the beginning of my "becoming Uriel" journey. With every step further into the celestial cut throat jungle, with every miniscule transformation into Uriel, the world shifts and changes around me, and I change with it. The survival instinct takes on a ruthless streak of mindless elimination of obstacles.

"For argument sake, you are right. But what does it give me?"

"The powers that she had are yours now. Your essence has absorbed hers, expanding, becoming larger and stronger, making *you* stronger."

"Cool." I nod my head. "Now, if you still want me to save your brothers, I have to go."

I turn around to walk away.

"How did you do it, Beyelai?" he calls after me.

"That's just how infinite I am", I throw over my shoulder and I walk out of the cell.

CHAPTER 10

"Shana!" I yell towards the end of the corridor.

"Shana!" I turn and yell down at the other end.

Her small face pokes from a cell. She steps out, rushing towards me.

"Yes, Mammí Barragal."

"Come on. We're going to that other corridor, where they've taken the rest of my followers. You know the way, right?"

She nods.

"Of course, Mammí."

"Excellent. Wait here", I say to Shana.

I walk into the cell, where I left my crude weapons and scooping them up, I return to the cell where Pronoia sits next to his brother.

"Here."

I hand him the metal rod I've expropriated from Mitish's cubbyhole.

"Just in case."

I'm keeping both of the wooden stakes. I'll need them.

He nods, turning his attention back to his brother, but I won't have it.

"Listen, man, I do appreciate how hard it is to see a sibling in such a state, whilst being powerless to do anything about it, but you have promised. If I'm leaving all these people behind to find your brothers", I say, waving my hand towards the corridor behind me, "you need to keep your end of the deal. I need to know that these people would be safe and cared for. I need you to look after them, all of them. The female Ophanim is here, one of the girls in the floral dresses, I think the one who was providing "forgiveness", and there are others. You need to make sure they're all okay."

"Of course, my Beyelai, you are right. My apology."

He shuffles to rise and I offer him my hand. This time he takes it.

Once risen, he looks deeply at me for a few seconds, before he brings his four fingers to his forehead and bows low.

"May An guide you", he says when he straightens, "may she grant the infinite strength to her only daughter: The Harbinger of Chaos, The Keeper of the Gates, The Begetter of Life, The Dam of The Ends."

I nod, uncomfortable by his pompous farewell.

"Thanks."

I walk towards Shana, swinging stakes at my sides in time with my strides.

"Thank god they went for a "conveyer" execution style", I mumble. "Spreading this bunch over two corridors is bad enough, but can you imagine five or ten? And still I'm not sure if I'm making the right call."

"Are you talking to me, Mammí?"

"No, Shana, it's fine. I'm talking to myself. Let's go."

I shove the black ring into the metal bar, listening to the familiar sizzle.

We're through the metal door and I nudge it closed behind, leaving it ajar and not locking it.

Shana leads the way down another dark corridor.

I walk around and through dark puddles of stagnant water. Our breathing and footsteps are muffled by the hungry soil. The glow of my body disperses the sticky darkness, casting light to the walls, floor and ceiling, blinding small earth worms and the occasional rat.

A few more turns and crossroads later, Shana stops in front of a wall of thick metal rods, identical to the walls that separate every holding section.

I look at Shana.

She nods and then says, answering my unspoken question, "This is Sarin's corridor."

The soft moaning and cries resonate from the corridor's depth.

Knowing where to look now, I bring my ring to the bars and after the sizzle and glow of a seal, the door is formed and the seal clicks open.

I step through the door first. Shana is behind me.

"Call him", I whisper.

I don't have time to look for him.

"Sarin. Sarin. It's Shana", she calls. "Where are you?"

She takes a few steps towards the farthest side of the corridor and I follow her, glancing into the cubicles of Hell.

Every carved niche is occupied by a comatose angel. They are suspended off the ceiling in familiar fashion, bound by a familiar black slimy creature.

Every angel I see is a fresh, new addition. The colour of their wings is still vibrant, and although the wings behind their back have begun to shrivel, their skins still hold lively shades, hidden under the two bloody streams, running down their cheeks.

Every angel is familiar. Every angel is my newly pledged follower.

I gulp.

""*The Bringer of Doom" that should be my title*", I think bitterly.

A slim young man with a bent back and hunched shoulders rolls out of one of the cells with small shuffling steps.

"Shana, what are you..." the man begins, but stops at the sight of me.

His eyes bulge in fear and surprise. His gaze runs over my glowing face and my body, jumping to my folded wings, to the wooden stakes in my hands, painted black with parasites' blood.

At the last discovery, his eyes open wider and he takes a step back.

I push past Shana and in three wide strides I'm in front of him, shoving the sharp end of one of the stakes to his throat.

"Quiet, not a word."

I softly toss the stake from my other hand to the ground, and my free hand dives to my black corset, fishing out from behind it the dirty rag Shana was using to wipe blood off the angels' faces.

"Open your mouth."

He stares at me, ignoring my demand, opening his eyes wider instead.

"I said open your mouth!" I bark and I nudge the stake closer to his throat. The stake pulls and tugs at his skin, about to break it.

"I am not joking. Open! Wide!"

His mouth drops open.

I shove the wad of fabric into it.

"You need to be quiet and I'll let you go. I'm not here for you."

I grab his shoulder, turning him.

"Too much chance-taking lately, too much trust, too much of too generously given mercy", Rage hisses, shaking her head in disapproval.

"Turn", I bark and he shuffles his feet, facing away from me.

I fish out a leather belt that I pulled from the jeans of an angel, and after dropping my stake, I yank his hands behind him, looping the belt around his wrists, tying it with two knots.

I walk around to face him.

"I'm not going to hurt you. I'm not here for you. I don't need you. That", I nod my head to his gag, "is to make sure that you stay quiet and don't do anything stupid."

"Come."

I tug him by his arm, leading him towards the wall of metal bars.

"Sit."

I shove him to the ground, then I walk towards the seal, and after jamming the black ring into it, I close the door, locking us all in.

Pointing at Sarin's chest, I say: "Keep quiet."

I turn to Shana.

While I was threatening and binding Sarin, Shana stood nearby. Now, her large, concerned eyes bounce between Sarin's bound form on the ground and me, as her back pressed against the wall, and when her gaze meets mine, I see the beating fear of a small animal in her eyes. I see fear with which she sees me.

Unexpectedly, it hurts me, and suddenly, I'm pissed off.

I'm so sick of being judged. Judged because I'm too weak and too human, not an angel and not ruthless enough. Judged when I'm ruthless and ready to fulfil the prophecy at my cost. Judged by everyone at every turn.

"I'm not going to kill him", I bark. "He just needs to keep quiet and stay out of my way."

This corridor is the same as Mitish's but I haven't inspected every cell.

But it's irrelevant now. I have to save them all and I don't have time to faff about.

I scoop my sharp tools and stomp away from both of them, towards the closest end of the corridor.

I will start working the corridor, killing parasites, one at a time, and hopefully, along the way, I will think of a way to move my followers, who will begin to drop soon.

The first cell holds one of the female "pink" angels.

In the usual fashion, she is suspended off the ceiling, with her wrists pulled and bound above her head by a hungry monster.

Her long blonde hair has fallen forward, covering her face, as her head is slumped on her chest. Her two pink wings are shrivelled behind her back like raisins, and her pretty long floral dress is soaked in blood at the front.

I take a deep breath, coming towards her.

I lift her head.

Her earlier youthful face looks older now, riddled with wrinkles, with blood streaming out of her eyes and down her face.

"I'm sorry", I mumble.

I know she can't hear me but I can't help it.

I'm sorry for her being here, for the pain I'm about to cause and I'm sorry that I can't even promise that it will be the end of her suffering. I can't promise it yet. If I promised it, I would be lying.

We are far from done. The road we've started on is far from over. The war hasn't been won.

I take her chin in my hand, nudging her mouth open. I don't think I can prevent the snake from shrieking, but at least I can stop these angels from screaming, triggering another Asmodeus alert. If we stay quiet, we might have a chance.

Her mouth opens slightly and I shove a piece of fabric into her mouth. This rag was on the old angel's body only a few minutes ago, and it's all I have.

"I'm sorry," I whisper again.

I bend over and pick up my stake again. I cover her mouth with my hand as well, and once I know that her screams will be muffled, I jam the stake into the black, oily parasite.

They cry out simultaneously.

The shriek of the parasite and the muffled pained cries of the pretty girl echo in the cell for a moment, before she drops to the ground.

"Shana", I call towards the corridor. "Shana."

She runs in.

"Back to work, Shana. You know what to do."

I throw a spare cloth at her, take the gag out of the angel's mouth and walk out.

The rest of my followers are here.

In the next cells I find five of Pronoia's brothers, the bearded male, whom Rafe called a "friend and brother" and the husband of one of the Ophanims, a male Ophanim and three angels of love Lis had lured into the pledge.

In every cell I repeat the same process I used in the first one. I put the cloth into their mouths to quieten their cries, cover it with my hand to muffle it further, then stab at the creatures with my stake. I manage to catch some of the angels, before their bodies hit the ground, but some are too heavy for me or released by the parasite too fast, and then the body drops to the floor.

Every time an angel is freed, I walk out of the cell and call Shana, informing her of an extending list of patients.

Sarin is still on the floor where I left him, watching my manipulations with wide eyes as I methodically stroll into cell after cell, killing the snakes. My stake is dripping with their black blood.

I walk into another cell, stopping in my tracks the moment the glow of my body illuminates the prisoner within.

The body in the cell is small. It's a child and it's swinging a yard off the ground.

But as much as the sight of a tortured child is horrific, I fold over when my gaze travels over the familiar looking green chinos with millions of pockets, outdoorsy jacket, green Doc Martens and bright yellow ribbon in brown curly hair.

I straighten up, forcing myself to look at the tiny body.

I force my feet to shuffle forward, towards the small body of my friend, of a little innocent angel with a pair of grey wings, who called me her "sister".

Her head rests on her chest, and her chest is soaked in her blood.

Seeing her like this stirs up something new within, something, which with a final nail in the coffin of my naivety delivers a clear message about the world I am in and the stakes in the game I'm playing.

The brutality of this world is unparalleled.

Humanity doesn't exist here. This world is ruled by deceit and fear, and my honour and loyalty only gets people killed. My humanity, my forgiveness, my delay to execute is a handicap to survival in this world, in the world where I have agreed to live and where I have brought my sister.

My sister's new furry face rises in my mind, coming to the fore, before her face morphs onto the little body swinging in front of me.

I rush towards the body. The earlier plan forgotten, I grab her legs, lifting her body higher, trying to ease the parasite's hold.

Without the rag to muffle her voice, she cries out as I move her.

I release her and she whimpers again when her body is pulled down by gravity and her wrists are squeezed tighter by the creature.

"I'm sorry, Tabby. I'm so, so sorry", I mumble. "I didn't mean for this. I didn't mean for any of this", I blab and I cry, "I didn't want any of this, you know it. I wanted to get away. I never meant for anyone to get hurt, let alone you."

I lift her head. Her face is covered in blood.

"Please forgive me. I never meant for any of it. Please... please... please... Forgive me..."

I blab as I wipe her face.

"Please forgive me."

My vision is eroded by my tears, so before I do what I've done in every cell prior, I wipe my face with the back of my hand, smudging something warm and thick over my cheeks.

"Please forgive me."

I take the piece of fabric and shove it into her open mouth, closing my hand over it.

I stab at the oily neck of the creature, and after a short pained shriek it releases its hold on Tabby.

I catch the little angel before she falls and I gently lay her on the ground. I kneel next to her, moving her curly hair off her face. Her blood stains my fingers.

"Shana! Shana!!" I call.

The rushed paddle of the footsteps approaches from a few cubicles away.

"Yes, Mammí Barragal."

Shana is in the cell and next to me.

"Give me the cloth."

I reach above me, and when the damp cloth still hasn't touched my palm, I turn my head to Shana, glaring at her, yanking the cloth out of her hand.

"I'm sorry", I whisper to Tabby.

I wipe her blood stained face. Her blood smudges, coating her face in a red layer. I pull at a sleeve of my tunic and wipe Tabby's cheeks, which grow cleaner with each new stroke.

"I'm sorry. I'm sorry."

I mumble it over and over again, when the murmur of the radio in my head rushes forward and booms like a toll bell with Pronoia's voice.

"Uriel, Uriel!" he calls. "Where are you? What's going on? Can you hear me? Your voice took over the exchange. It is resonating on every wave. Everyone can hear you! Every angel and even an istana wardum. He is sitting here spinning his head and is about to lose his mind. Everyone can hear you, Uriel! What's going on?"

Stunned by the invasion of his voice, I'm about to answer him, when a few fresh drops of blood, like poppies, blossom over Tabby's face, betraying the bleeding of my own eyes.

"Where are you, Beyelai Sar? Have you found my brothers? Do they live? Answer me, salbat dalmu! Answer me!" he roars in my head.

Pronoia's thunderous voice wakes me, bringing with it a reminder, which rings in Shana's voice, about the energy loss through the bloody tears.

I dive into my mind, only to realise that the telephone exchange of the conversations has gone silent. The tense breathing of hundreds of people resonates over its waves, as angels and istana, as one, hold their breaths, listening.

Shit!

I fiddle in my mind, trying to follow the given instructions on angels' telepathy, and cut off the broadcast.

"Please answer me, beyelai", Pronoia pleads.

"I'm here", I answer in my head, fighting in my mind, looking to plug the leak. *"I'm here. I have found your brothers. Everyone is here."*

Pronoia's sighs with relief.

"Whatever you did earlier, opening all channels and transmitting, you have to stop it", he says. *"You have to curb it. Everyone has heard you here and I can only guess if you were heard across Arllu. But if you were, then they know that you are free and they are coming. They are coming for us all and they will be here soon."*

The urgency and panic ring in Pronoia's voice.

I want to ask him if I have managed to stop the leak, if he is the only one who can hear me, but the sudden barrage of voices, the explosion of multiple conversations answers me better than he ever could.

The crazy telephone exchange is back, hyped with dozens upon dozens of conversations between angels, who heatedly discuss what these cries and pleads for forgiveness were, from whom they came and who is the mysterious angel, strong enough to transmit across the entirety of Arllu.

But there are more important conversations laced within the exchange.

Baza, recognising my voice, roars at Asmodeus and the rest of his malakhims, demanding to know what in the name of Hell it was and how

Uriel broke into his network. The reprimands are followed by Asmodeus'
clipped instructions to his minions to go and check on me.

"Too late. They're coming", I tell Pronoia.

I lift my head, wiping my face with my sleeve. I cannot afford to fall
apart now. I can't afford to become weaker even by an ounce.

How many more chances will I get? How many more days do I have
left to live and fight?

"Is everyone awake?" I ask Pronoia.

"Everyone, apart from the two eldest prisoners."

"Everyone who's awake, can they move?"

"Yes."

"Then grab Mitish and tell him to bring you to Sarin's corridor."

"What if he leads us the wrong way? Can you send Shana?"

*"No, I need her here. She is helping me with your brothers. Ask Mitish to
lead you, but listen to my voice: I'll be singing to you. I'd imagine my voice would
grow stronger, the closer to me you get. Besides, it will show us where Mitish sits in
our little disagreement with Baza."*

"Yes, Beyelai Sar."

Once a soldier always a soldier. He doesn't muck about, ready to
execute the orders. After a moment of silence Pronoia asks: *"What do I do
with the two prisoners that are still asleep?"*

"You have to leave them behind."

Another pause rings with discomfort over our line.

"I need to save the ones I'm responsible for, the ones who pledged to me", I
say. *"We might need to carry the angels from this corridor, as none have come
around yet. We wouldn't be able to carry many. You decide whom you want to
save, your brothers or other prisoners."*

Pronoia is quiet for a moment before he answers: *"Yes, Beyelai Sar"*,
and I begin singing my little rhyme.

"Under the sky
Here I lie,
Under the sky
My sister and I
Trees above us and the bottomless sky
Here we'll live – my sister and I."

I sing the rhyme repeatedly, mindlessly churning the familiar words, thinking about new obstacles and new challenges, about new threats. But regardless of the length of my journey, I will make sure that today is not the day I die. I will make sure that I stand to fight another day.

I'm learning. I'm a good student. All of them have showed to me what their world is really about and now it's my time to use and implement everything that I've learnt.

I rise to my feet.

"Don't go anywhere, take care of her first", I say to Shana, pointing at Tabby's little body on the ground, and I walk out of the cell.

CHAPTER 11

But grief follows me into the next cell and my newfound conviction shatters when my glow illuminates Sam's body suspended off the ceiling, his white wings touching the muddy ground.

All emotions and feelings flee my mind, leaving behind a mumbling telephone exchange in my head, ringing like a radio in an empty room.

His soft comatose moans are interrupted by short bursts of hot unintelligible murmur.

I force my feet to move, bringing me closer to him.

"*Uriel, Uriel*", *Pronoia's voice screams into my mind.* "*I can't hear you anymore. Are you there?*"

"Yes, yes. I'm here", I stammer, unable to draw my gaze away from Sam.

"*We're about to set off.*"

"Okay, okay", I mumble. I have responsibilities.

"*Under the sky, here I lie...*"

Although, I have instructed Pronoia to leave the two old prisoners behind, warning him of the hardship of moving a body, I know I'm not leaving Sam.

"*Ariel. Ariel*", Jess' little voice suddenly breaks into my head, startling me.

"*Jess? Jess!*" I yell back. "*What's going on? How are you getting in? Where are you? Is everything okay? Are you okay?*"

My heart is about to jump out of my chest, expecting the worst.

"*Where are you?*"

"*I'm with Rafe and Dumah. We're still here.*"

She begins to cry.

"*I've heard you singing,*" she sobs, "*singing our song... I thought something was wrong. I thought... I thought...*"

She sobs harder, unable to finish her sentence.

"*Oh, baby. Jessie-boo, I'm here. I'm fine, and I'm coming to get you. I'm coming now. I'm coming to you.*"

My head is exploding with conversations and the demands placed on me, with games I'm forced to play, and my heart is breaking at the sight of damage and pain I have inflicted, at lives I've disturbed or ended.

I feel on the brink. I stand on the last inch of a cliff and the chalk is crumbling under my feet. I'm about to fall and I don't know how to hold on, as I cannot turn around and walk away.

I take step closer to Sam, leaning towards him, looking for the familiar and soothing scent of a pine forest.

But the rich scent of moss and undergrowth is gone, replaced with an iron tinge of blood.

"Under the sky here I lie..."

I keep singing, aware of angels listening, the ones I have led here and the ones who need to hear me to find their way out. I'm aware of my sister waiting for my return, waiting for me to come back and fix everything that I've done. I'm aware of the body of the little girl in the next cell, the girl who I promised to take with me, who's here because of me, just like everyone else, just like Sam.

The static of the telephone exchange is busy mumbling, distracting me.

The thin tendrils of their separate conversations are hard to find and even harder to hold.

The ephemeral voices dive in and out, muddling my mind, entangling me, and with it my grip on my mind begins to slip.

I lift Sam's head and kiss his blood stained lips. The taste of wild blackberries is gone too.

"*Under the sky*
Here I lie,
Under the sky
My sister and I

Trees above us and the bottomless sky
Here we'll live – my sister and I."

I've relinquished the hold, withdrawing the blocks I've put in place and held. I'm singing it into Baza's network, and the telephone exchange answers me with a shocked ringing silence.

I can hear every angel and istana in Arllu holding their breath listening to me, and I swear I can pick out Baza's calculating and Asmodeus loathing breathings, the shrewd and calm breathing of Nanael and her crew, and I can hear the soft humming of Jess' voice, answering my tune with hers.

I open Sam's mouth, shoving the wad of fabric into it. I kiss his lips again and place my hand over his mouth, then swinging my stick I jam it into the parasite above.

Released, Sam's body drops to the ground. The dying black creature shrieks, wriggling above, its screech crumbling the silence.

I gently tug the cloth out of Sam's mouth, using it to wipe his bloodied face.

"Under the sky
Here I lie,
Under the sky
My sister and I
Trees above us and the bottomless sky
Here we'll live – my sister and I."

The blessed silence of the broken and shocked telephone exchange in my head grants me some peace. It's white like clouds and open like the horizon of an ocean. It's light like a whisper and smooth as a surface of a mirror.

I don't think about anything but the song I've promised.

I don't talk in my head to anyone, not even Sam. I don't plead or ask for his forgiveness, concentrating only on my song, which is like a ray of light that will bring my people to me, people I'm now responsible for.

I sing it, over and over again, absent-mindedly stroking Sam's face and hair.

"Uriel, Beyelai Sar. We're here."

Pronoia's voice startles me, calling me from down the corridor.

I snap my head up.

"Beyelai Sar", he calls again.

I get up and plod towards the voice. I feel exhausted.

The weary angelic faces stare at me through the wall of metal bars, with Pronoia standing at the front. Every pledged angel from Mitish's corridor is here and so is Mitish, who stands to the side in the shadows, the body of the angel with grey hair that he was dressing so carefully, hanging over his shoulder. Against my instructions, Mitish had carried the unconscious angel with him.

"I said to leave them behind", I call, nodding at the angel over Mitish's shoulder and another one hanging between Pronoia and a female Ophanim.

"He wouldn't leave without that angel." Pronoia nods at Mitish and the angel over his shoulder. "He said it will be his weight and responsibility to carry. So what is an extra one?" Pronoia shrugs his shoulders.

I'm pleased to see how better Pronoia looks.

I reach out, pressing the black ring into a seal, opening the door.

"Irrelevant. He is now yours to carry", I step sideways, letting the angels in. "Good luck with your best of intentions, especially once you see how weak your brothers are."

Pronoia and the Ophanim walk sideways through the door, with the angel hanging between them. Pronoia touches his four fingers to his forehead, bowing to me as low as the body next to him allows. I nod in reply. The Ophanim touches her four fingers, bowing too.

Every angel bows at me as they cross the threshold and everyone is answered with my nod. Although, the angels are weary, shuffling through the door with heavy steps, they able to move.

With all of the angels through, Mitish is the only one left outside the gate. His unsure gaze dances over me and the open gate. He waits for an invitation or a punishment for insubordination.

"Come", I say.

He shuffles forward, struggling under the weight of the angel.

"You've disobeyed my order. It's the first and last time it happens. The next disobedience will be punished, do you understand me?"

Mitish drops his gaze and nods.

I step sideways, letting him in.

"He is your sole responsibility now, all yours. No other angel or istana will help you", I bark, but Mitish beams at me, nodding his head in agreement.

"Yes, Mammí Barragal."

Pronoia had laid the unconscious angel by the wall, next to Sarin, and now his bellows ring in the corridor as he runs from cell to cell, finding his brothers.

The rest of the angels are doing the same, plodding from cell to cell, looking for their loved ones, crying out at the horror of each cell. The corridor is filled with cries, exclamations and despair.

"Oh, no!"

A female voice gasps from the far end of the corridor, followed by tortured cries of someone, who is being tugged free from a parasite.

"No!" I roar towards the end of the corridor and begin to run. "Don't pull!"

In the cell, the female Ophanim tugs at a bound angel, the one who was responsible for the record keeping in Mik'hael's place and was cast out to give Mik'hael freedom to change Heaven's past to fit his own agenda.

"No! Don't touch him!" I roar.

I run at the female and push her away. Weak and no match for my strength, she flies into a wall.

"Do you want Asmodeus to come here? Don't touch him", I rumble.

She stares at me and I add, "I will do it myself. You can help me, but don't yank at him and wait a moment."

I walk out, looking for Pronoia.

I find him on the ground in a cell, rocking a body of one of his brothers.

"Pronoia."

He doesn't respond and I have to shake his shoulder.

"Pronoia."

He lifts his eyes to me, blinking through the haze.

"Yes, Beyelai Sar."

"You need to make sure that no one pulls the angels that are still attached", I say. "There are only a few left and I'm sorting it now."

"Of course, my Beyelai."

But before I walk away, I turn and add: "Please check on Sam for me."

Pronoia nods.

He moves the body carefully to the ground and gets up. Walking out, he glances over his shoulder at the body of his brother and a moment later, I can hear his deep voice talking to someone.

I return to the cell where I left the female.

She is up on her feet, spinning circles in front of the suspended body, clasping her hands.

I pull out the cloth, coming closer to the prisoner.

"Lift his head and open his mouth. We need to make sure he is quiet."

With a weak whimper she follows my instructions.

I do the familiar actions and once the body drops to the ground, I leave the sobbing female in the cell with her loved one, as I walk out to finish the job and freeing the rest of my followers.

I'm pleased to hear Pronoia's strong voice issuing instructions, arranging the help at the other end of the corridor. I can't be the only strong one.

I glance towards the wall, where Sarin sits, gagged, watching the chaos of the new arrival.

The bodies of the ancient angels on the ground are tended to by Mitish, who strokes their faces and hair. The angel's chests rise steadily with their even breathing.

I come closer.

In my glow their skins look fuller and younger. Their long grey haired frame young men's faces and the wings behind their backs begin to fill in too, finding its earlier shape, although covered in centuries old dust and dirt.

As I walk away from them, my heart calls for me to go into the cell where Tabby lies, where I left Sam. I want to kneel in front of them, drape myself over their chests and cry, letting the guilt to take over, but instead I call down the corridor, "Pronoia", and when he steps out of the one of the cells I add, "Help me to free the rest of them."

CHAPTER 12

Eventually, the cries and gasps settle over the corridor like disturbed dust, leaving behind a layer of hushed murmur.

The telephone exchange in my head had burst once more when Asmodeus discovered my empty cell with Lis' dead body on the ground. The short barking of commands run riot on the radio for a while, before the findings were reported to Baza, followed by the sudden buzz of the disconnected exchange.

I strain to hear into it, looking for a voice or a conversation, but I found only silence. I was cut out from their network. I was seeking peace from this crazy exchange, but now I realise the advantage I have lost.

The angels begin to come around and the occasional joyful exclamation pierces the grave of the corridor.

I've left Shana with Tabby, giving her strict instructions not to leave Tabby's side, calling me once she came around, while I took my post by Sam, watching the rising of his chest under a blood soaked jumper, waiting for him to wake up.

His wings are fuller and brighter beneath him, and it won't be long before he will wake up, but I know that we're running out of time. We have minutes before Asmodeus and his angels will be here, maybe they're on their way now, to inspect the tunnels with my followers. I know that what I'd be doing.

Sabrael's groggy voice mumbles something down the hall, followed by Pronoia's happy, tearful mumbling. I can make out only "brother".

"Mammí Barragal! Mammí Barragal!" Shana's voice rings in the hall, "she is waking up."

Tabby.

I scramble to my feet and with the last glance at Sam's still body, I run into Tabby's cell.

Tabby's child body looks feeble on the ground. Her once glossy hair is mottled and dull and covered in mud. Her skin is pale, but at least it has lost its ashen shade. Her open eyes stare at the dark ceiling of pressed earth.

I rush to her side and Shana gets up, and walks away, giving me space.

"Tabby. Tabby, can you hear me? It's Ariel. Do you remember me, Tabby?"

But my words left unheard, as Tabby stares into space.

"Tabby?"

I take her face into my hands, turning her to face me.

Her glassy gaze follows the arch drawn by her head.

"Tabby?"

But she doesn't answer me. She doesn't see me nor does she hear me.

What have they done to her?

The guilt punches once again, and tears tickle my nose. But I refuse their call. I cannot allow myself to unravel. Now is not the time or the place. Asmodeus is coming and if I don't do something, there will be no one left to mourn.

"Keep an eye on her", I bark to Shana as I walk out of Tabby's cell.

"Pronoia. Pronoia!" I yell down the corridor, and the angels begin to come out of the cells, in one's and two's, some walking strong, while some are shuffling with a help of their comrades.

Pronoia comes rushing out of a cell.

"Yes, Beyelai Sar."

"Asmodeus is coming. He's on his way and will be here soon, sooner than I thought. We have nowhere to hide and we can't move yet."

I sweep my gaze over the angels in front of me, tightly filled the narrow corridor.

"We have to fight them here", I say.

My announcement drains Pronoia's face of the colour. The shock of my proposal is evident.

"But, Beyelai", he stammers. "We don't have weapons. Not everyone is awake yet, and even the ones that are, are very weak..."

"We can't move so many bodies at once", I bark at him, swinging my arm at the dozens of bodies, standing in the doorframes, propped up by other angels. "Some are still unconscious. We won't manage to get away and we won't get far, so we have to fight. It's the only way. At least we have the element of surprise on our side and we have to use it."

I know I'm short with him, but I don't need to be told how stupid and suicidal this proposal is, I am well aware.

He thinks I'm crazy, and maybe he is right, but it's the only play open to us... apart from the one, where I abandon them all.

"Take all the unconscious ones into Sarin's cubbyhole", I bark. "It should be at the end of the corridor. Lay them there. You should find some tools in there too. Use them to make weapons. Where's the metal rod I gave you?"

"Here", he answers, nodding towards nearby cell.

"Use it."

The angels in the corridor are listening to me.

I raise my head, sweeping my gaze over their faces.

"I'm not asking everyone to fight. I know how weak some of you are", I call to them. "But if you think you can hold a weapon, then we need you. We all need you."

I scan the angels in front of me.

"Asmodeus is coming. I don't know how many soldiers he's bringing with him. I don't know how well equipped they will be, probably very, but I know one thing: whoever they won't kill, they will torture. They will make an example of you, an example of how Baza deals with a rebellion, and it will be bloody and ruthless. I'm sorry that I've brought you here. I truly am. But it is what it is. Now we need to survive one more time."

I have about twenty angels standing in front of me. Some are steady on their feet, while others swing wildly.

"If you want, and can, fight for your freedom and the freedom of your loved ones. Find yourself a weapon. The ones who can't fight will have to hide in the shadows at the other side of the corridor and the unconscious ones need to be hidden in the cubbyhole."

I know I'm asking for their trust, yet again gambling with their lives. I know that some of them are cursing me, cursing the day they pledged their Qal and loyalty to me. I know that some have changed their minds and want out, back to their measured, comfortable lives in Hell.

But I can't turn back time, and I'm not in a position to release them from their pledge. Even if I did so, Baza won't take them back, executing every traitor.

I've been here long enough to understand that.

The angels look at me.

"Let's start with them. Let's help the weak ones first", I say.

Pronoia and a few angels from the first corridor nod and walk away, beginning the process of moving the unconscious.

I turn to Mitish.

"Someone will help you move them", I say, nodding at the grey haired men and he bows in reply.

I walk past him, towards the furthest end of the corridor, looking for Sarin's cubbyhole.

His sleeping burrow opens with a low and small entrance like Mitish's, and just like Mitish's, Sarin's hole is small and dark, suitable for a small animal rather than a person.

A rake, a broom and a metal pole are propped against a wall, and two wooden shelves fitted into the opposite wall.

I toss the broom and the rake out of a cubbyhole, and armed with a metal pole, I swing it at the shelves in a tight space of the cubbyhole, banging at them from underneath, nudging the metal pole between the shelves and the earthy wall, and with a crack, the both shelves leave the fixtures of the wall, crashing to the ground.

I toss the shelves out of the cubbyhole, into the corridor, and crawl out after them.

Pronoia, a few of his brothers and two Ophanims stand outside of the cubbyhole. The bodies of two grey haired angels, Sam, Tabby and two more angels lie on the ground next to them, with Mitish nearby.

"The cubbyhole is very tight", I say to them, nodding my head behind me. "Fitting all of them will be tricky, but we have to make it work."

The angels nod.

"Mitish, you will go with them. Look after them."

He nods, drops to all fours and crawls into the burrow, ready to receive the bodies.

I scoop the tools and the shelves, feeling splinters from untreated wood drive into my skin.

"Pronoia", I call, nodding to a wall away from the group which has begun moving the unconscious angels into the small space.

I throw the tools and the shelves on the ground.

"Once we know how many are fighting, we'll make weapons out of this", I nod at the pile of wood.

"What are we going to do with him?" Pronoia asks, turning his gaze to Sarin, who sits on the ground, still bound and gagged, ogling the bustling activity of his corridor.

"I have a plan for him too, and it will be up to him if he is alive at the end of it."

CHAPTER 13

It was tricky to fit six unconscious bodies plus Mitish into the cubbyhole, but with careful negotiations within the tight space, it was done.

I wanted Shana to sit there as well, to keep an eye on Sam and Tabby, but there was no space left for her.

The cells were emptied and only the black oily snakes were left in them, suspended in every cell like an ugly light switch from the ceiling.

I picked the fourth cell for myself.

Positioned strategically across and slightly to the right from the metal door, which will open soon with a sizzle of the seal, my cell, filled with the glow from my body, should invite expected visitors to check on it first.

The ones who agreed to bear arms took their positions within the shadows of the corridor and within the three cells to both sides of mine.

Now, an angel stands in the middle of these cells, holding a dead parasite loosely wrapped around his or her wrists, so when Asmodeus comes, when he and his crew glance into the cells, all they would see is a bound angel in the thick shadows.

A few more angels took positions within the shadows of the cells. They stand with their backs pressed into the furthest corners and against the wall on the each side of a cell's entrance.

The ones who were too weak or refused to hold a weapon were sent into the cells at the far end of the corridor, to hide in the thick shadows there.

My stakes and the tools that I found in Sarin's cubbyhole have become our weapons.

I stepped on my long stakes, breaking each in two, doubling the number of weapons. The same was done with Sarin's tools. Under decisive kicks from Pronoia and his brother's boots, the wood from the shelves was split into sharp daggers, the bases of the shards were wrapped in rags, making handles.

I was pleased to see a few female angels stepping forward, demanding a weapon.

A beautiful and softly spoken angel in a floral dress had stepped forward, surprising me. She bowed to me, calling herself Sablo. Her long sleeved and floor length dress was shredded to create rags to clean the wounded, leaving behind a sleeveless mini dress. The female Ophanim asked for a weapon too.

Both females scattered in the shadows, peppering the male crowd of warriors.

Weakly swinging Sabrael had barked for a weapon, and no amount of pleas from Pronoia had stopped him from picking a shard of split wood, and shuffling into a nearby cell.

Now, we are ready and the stage is set.

I walk into the fourth cell.

With the fresh memory of the harm inflicted on me by the parasite, I stab its lifeless body a few times and once it doesn't respond with its usual screech, I grab its oily tail, and stamping down my revulsion, I wrap its dead body around my wrist.

My shortened and blackened stake shoved at the back of my corset.

Sarin's slim body is pressed to mine, his back to my front. He is bound and gagged and my free hand covers his mouth, as his thin dragonfly wings flutter in fright, tickling my neck.

"Don't be stupid", I whisper in his ear. "This has nothing to do with you. Don't make a sound and I won't hurt you."

I don't know how long we are set to wait. I don't know how far away Asmodeus is or how many coming with him. Locked out from the Baza's network, I'm deaf and blind again.

I was tempted to break into the network and try to connect with Jess, to hear her voice before it all begins, but I am afraid of drawing Asmodeus' attention to myself and I'm afraid my words to my sister would sound like a goodbye, wavering my determination for survival.

The silence of the dark devouring earthy corridor is deafening.

I can hear worms pushing their tubular bodies through the soil, beetles strumming their legs as they crawl in the corners of the cell, and water dripping from the ceiling into a puddle, somewhere past the metal wall.

The wait is pulling on my nerves, but it comes to a sudden end when rushed footsteps and a barking voice charge down the corridor and towards the metal wall.

It's time.

I draw in a rugged breath.

"Open. Come on! Faster!" Asmodeus barks.

The seal sizzles and the door screeches open.

The footsteps barge in.

There must be at least a dozen of them.

They fan out and I hear a few hushed voices whisper in the cells next to me. They're checking the first cells just as I thought.

But drawn by my glow, the most of the footsteps are coming my way. I hear their breathing and the shuffle of dirt under their heavy boots as they slow their pace, trotting carefully, and I could almost see a head nod of Asmodeus' instructions.

With eyes closed, I listen to a pair of footsteps walking into my cell, then another and then one more.

Three is not enough. I want more of them here, and I don't know if Asmodeus is inside with them.

Suddenly, Sarin begins to groan through his gag next to me, thrashing in my hold.

It's far too early, and not what I planned, but it will have to do.

My eyes fly open.

I push Sarin away from me. He drops to the floor, sliding over the mud and hitting the wall, but I don't care.

If I survive, he'll be sorry to be alive, but I need to survive first.

My left hand dives to my corset for my blackened stake, while my right hand yanks at the "light switch" of the parasite above, ripping it in two.

The most of its body comes away in my grip, showering me with the creature's black mucus.

In the glow of my body, I watch the faces of three Asmodeus' minions morph with disbelief as they watch my right hand drop to my side, holding the dead creature.

The few seconds of them frozen with shock is long enough for me to lunge at the nearest minion, sinking my stake upwards into his throat. I yank the stake out and the body drops to the floor with a thud and a gurgling noise.

The shadows next to the entrance come to life, throwing their rudimentary weapons at the remaining two.

But one shadow is not fast enough and a warning cry rings in my cell before another body drops.

This cry is like a call of a hunting horn and with its ring, the corridor and the neighbouring cells explode into a bedlam of noises.

Sabrael shuffles out of the cell into it and I follow him, his brother bringing up the rear.

The dark corridor is a crazy sequence of murky images of dancers in a nightclub. The sounds of rushing feet, mixed with startled exclamations, surprised or angry cries, clashes of angels' swords with the metal wall when my angels manage to duck, the pained cries of the wounded fill the corridor.

A few dead bodies of Asmodeus' crew litter the ground in the corridor and I know that I'll find a few more in the cells.

But a dozen of Asmodeus' soldiers are left standing.

Everyone is clustered in this end, fighting, and I'm pleased about that.

I need to draw the enemy away from the farthest end of the corridor.

My glow illuminates the area around me, and although I can see better with it, I am the brighter and larger target.

I scan the corridor and my gaze meets the gleeful and hungry gazes of Asmodeus' crew and worried glances from my angels.

Although, there are more of us than them, our crude weapons are not the match to their whips, knives and a few black swords of rippling fire, and my tired and exhausted followers are not a match to Asmodeus' rested soldiers. With the surprise of the first attack gone, we are now left to fight them with little we have.

Suddenly, a black sword whizzes in front of my face.

Startled, I jerk my head away just in time, stumbling backwards, narrowly avoiding the blade.

But I'm not frozen with shock for long.

Sensing Sabrael's essence behind me, I twist sideways, reaching out, snatching Sabrael's weapon out of his grip.

Straightening, I throw my hand out, towards the direction of where the sword came from.

Sabrael's jaggered wooden stake sinks into something soft, followed by a cry and a dull clonk of the dropped weapon.

One of Pronoia's brothers dives to the ground, scooping the sword. We haven't evened out the playing field yet, but I feel better for this little victory.

Asmodeus' crew rushes at me and so do my followers, the ones to kill me and the others to protect me.

More of my angels have upgraded their weapons, swapping their wooden shards and sticks for weapons of the fallen minions.

Surrounded by a tight circle of bodies, amidst the fighting and the commotion, I spin my head, searching for the one *I* need.

I spot Asmodeus by the open metal door, watching the squabble with a supervisory interest, a worried wrinkle has settled between his eyebrows.

His gaze meets mine and I smile.

I need him dead, and as much as destroying his squad will make a hole in Baza's army, it's not enough. It's not enough for me and it's personal.

I grab the arm of one of the brothers, who is fighting and slashing with a stolen black sword next to me.

"With me!" I yell, and when he looks at me, I nod towards the door. His gaze flies there and he nods.

He steps in front of me and begins to slash his way through the thinning crowd. He gurgles words at his brothers and a thicker wall of bodies comes around me, progressing forward, drawn by the angel's sword.

Suddenly, to my right, a body drops, creating a hole in my protective wall and exposing me.

With the stake in my hand, I spin towards the danger, coming face to face with one of Asmodeus' angels.

His face is young, clean and innocent. His eyes are wide open and scared.

I gawk at him for a moment, as my startled emotions play "tug of war" with my vulnerable humanity and ruthless angelic streak, confusing me further, before the thought of my sister slaps at me and I throw my stake at his face.

But I'm too late as a tip of a sword comes through the thin armour over his chest, and I watch Pronoia nodding at me from behind the young angel's back.

Giving him an answering nod, I turn away, listening as another body drops to the ground, churning something within me.

"Not now!" I command myself.

I bend over his body and tug a black knife out of his hold.

I straighten up, glancing towards the metal door, but Asmodeus is no longer there, the metal door is locked, making the wall complete again.

I spin on the spot, looking for him, but he is gone. Asmodeus is nowhere to be seen.

The brawl around me is dying down and only four of Asmodeus' minions are left standing, now pushed against the wall by Pronoia, Sabrael, his brothers and one Ophanim.

They don't need my help.

I rush towards the door, laying my hands on the cold metal bars, kicking the wall.

Asmodeus is gone. But I won't be going after him. I can't. It has to wait. My people need me.

I turn around and watch the frightened faces of Asmodeus' angels, confronted by the bloodthirsty circle of the warrior brothers.

I walk past and away from them. The brothers need their vengeance and I'm not going to stop them. I know it's mine to grant or take away, but it's not for me to command, not now.

I walk past and around fallen bodies, towards the farthest end of the corridor to check on Sam and Tabby.

CHAPTER 14

"We can't stay here any longer", I say to Sabrael and Pronoia, who have gathered around me, waiting for further instructions from their leader.

"Make sure everyone is ready to leave in five minutes."

Pronoia nods and walks away to instruct and supervise the preparations.

"Aye. Where are we going?" Sabrael asks me quietly after a few seconds of silence.

But it's not the questioning of someone who's ready to run away, but rather of someone who is ready to storm the enemy's building, clarifying which building it might be.

Sabrael stands strong next to me. His strength returns to him with every passing minute and I hope that the same recuperation is happening to the rest of my angels.

"I don't know yet. I have a few ideas but I need a minute to decide."

"If I may, Beyelai Sar", he says. "There's only one true decision and it's to fight. We must bring the Abyss of Udhad to Baza's door. We must deliver the vengeance for Tartys. The Qals of my brothers are crying for it. We need to avenge our fallen and we need to rip the weeds out before their roots take hold, before they have chance to grow stronger – "

"No!" I bark, interrupting him.

I've heard enough of his plan. I know what he wants, but it's not what we need.

"None of it is going to happen, at least not now. In case you hadn't noticed", I snap, raking my gaze over him and sweeping my hand around me, "we are still weak, outnumbered and inadequately armed. We have injured amongst us. We can't fight. We would get slaughtered."

I nudge my head towards the corridor with angels, as I continue quieter. "Some of them are barely standing and I wonder if they can move at all."

"Today, we will let the weeds grow", I add quietly, using his analogy. "*We* need time to grow stronger and that's all I'm concerned with. I need to buy us some time."

"Amongst other things", I mumble to myself.

I hold his gaze with mine.

"Baza will feel the force of our just retribution. I swear to you", I say. "The day will come and he will pay for everything he's done, but it's not going to be today. Today we won't strike. We won't march towards him. I'm not going to lead my people into slaughter, just because you need your revenge. Today, we are going to retreat and regroup. We are going to heal and grow stronger, but Baza will pay. I swear it to you."

His jaw muscles roll under his skin and thunder flashes in his eyes.

The need for vengeance rides high in him, clouding his judgement, and at this moment, I want to ask him if he thought that Baza would have let them go without a fight, if he really thought that no one would die at the end of this road.

But I say nothing. I'm learning to keep my mouth shut.

"We are going to avenge your brother and everyone else who has died at Baza's hand. But we are going to do it right. We'll have only one chance at it and we must to do it right, to rip the weeds out with their roots, once and for all."

Holding his gaze, I pull my lips into a smile.

I need to placate him. I need his obedience and his cooperation. I need him and his brothers with me. I need his warfare council and not the constant questioning and doubt.

"Besides", I add, "something tells me that it won't be long before this fight comes to us."

I place my hand on his arm.

"You will stand against Baza sooner than you think."

Sabrael nods.

"Please help to get everyone ready for the move", I say.

He nods again, bows lightly then turns on his heels and walks away.

During the fight with Asmodeus' crew, we lost one of the warrior brothers, Tartys. Pronoia found his body in one of the cells. A black sword had left a slim, long cut in the middle of Tartys' chest.

Three more of my followers were injured, pretty Sablo in her floral dress and Zaazenach and Iaoel, the last two are Sabrael's brothers.

All three have sustained shallow wounds to their upper bodies and, as much as they are in pain, are able to move.

As a result of our operation, we have acquired some weapons. Our group now has two long swords of the black fire, four black knives, a few whips and a few medieval-looking metal, spiky balls on the chains with handles.

It's more than we had before, but it's not an armoury. It's not enough to storm Baza's place or get into open combat with his troops.

I sigh and turn around too, plodding towards the cubbyhole, where Sam is.

I'm exhausted and fed up. I'm agitated and sick of it all.

I want to go somewhere, somewhere where nobody will find me and would not be able to put their demands and expectations on me, someplace where I can throw myself into a soft bed, switch on mindless daytime TV, eat chocolate and sleep.

I want a break. I'm tired of being hunted. I'm tired of every moment of my existence to be a fight for survival.

I'm tired of being alert at all times, making hard decisions for myself and others, tired of killing, to be on the run, tired of being the strong one, the fearless archangel Uriel...

I am tired.

Nobody even once had asked what *I* want. My wishes had never mattered in this world.

Since the moment it was sprung upon me, there was very little concern about what I want, and I know it's not going to change now.

I sigh and crawl into the cubbyhole, and the small burrow lights up with my glow. My purple wings drag over the dirt behind me.

I'm alone with Sam.

Tabby and the others were helped out of the cubbyhole after the fight. Mitish and Shana are tasked to keep an eye on them. I don't know where Sarin is, but quite frankly, I don't care.

Sam sits against the wall, conscious and alert, although his face is powdery grey when he lifts his head up.

I slide along the ground next to him.

The burrow's overbearing smell of mildew and mushrooms spores shrouds the Sam's scent of pine forest.

His gaze scans me for a few long moments before he says: "Every time I see you, you look progressively worse."

I smile.

He nods his head at me, covered in black creatures' mucus, which had crusted over my clothes and my hair. My clothes are stained with drying red blood of the angels too.

"But I have to say, you look magnificent, my Beyelai", he whispers.

I look at him. The usual cheeky twinkle bounces in his beautiful eyes but this time it's overshadowed by the open pull of respect and admiration.

It's the first time Sam called me "Beyelai", and I know that when saying this word, he meant it. His words and his tone... it feels like his acceptance of me as a leader, *his* leader.

I don't know what to say, so I keep quiet.

"Thank you for coming for me", he adds.

"I didn't come just for you", I reply, shrugging my shoulders.

I'm uncomfortable at the praise and I'm afraid of his emotions. I'm afraid to see his weakness or show him mine, although he had seen plenty of it already. I'm still mindful of the stupid words that slid from my tongue before.

"I know", he says, "thank you nevertheless, *Beyelai Sar*."

He is thanking me for not giving up on him, on the angels he has brought to me, whom he convinced to pledge to me. He is thanking me for not betraying him, like he betrayed *me* once.

I nod and drop my gaze to the dirt floor.

I came here to apologise to him, to apologise for my naivety, for unknowingly leading my angels into these corridors, to be locked up in here. To apologise for not being as strong as he told everyone I was.

I came expecting his wrath, his anger and blame, and now I'm speechless for not finding any. The conversation has not gone as I had expected.

"I'm pleased it is you", Sam says suddenly. "Who would've known that a small human girl would become one of the strongest archangels Sarukh and Arllu have ever seen?"

He smiles, shaking his head.

"If anyone could have predicted it, you would've been dead a long time ago. I bet Baza and Mik'hael are not happy bunnies right now, and I would have loved nothing more than to know what Mik'hael will do to Baza for losing you."

He begins to chuckle but stops abruptly when his laugh is interrupted by a fit of cough and his face pales with pain.

"What's our next move, Beyelai Sar?" he asks when his cough subsides.

I'm quiet for a moment. Although the decision is made, I'm not sure if it's the right one.

"We're going deeper into the tunnels", I say. "We need time to heal and I need time to think. Besides, I have an idea I want to try. So, if you're done sitting and resting, get your butt out of here and let's move."

I rise to stand up, but I have to bend my head down in this low burrow, so I drop to all fours before I turn around and begin to crawl through the opening.

"And don't call me "Beyelai Sar". It's just weird coming from you", I throw at him over my shoulder, as I crawl out.

"As you wish, háad Mermaid", he calls after me.

He says it as "hee-ad" and I want to turn around and ask him what it means, but I decide against it. Who cares what I'm called nowadays? All of my life I was called by different names by different people, and no matter what I'm called, I know that I only have one way forward.

CHAPTER 15

We don't set off for a bit longer.

Pronoia and his brothers have moved Tartys' body into one of the cells, starting the farewell service for him.

When I crawl out of the cubbyhole, I find the empty corridor, filled with hushed, repetitive chants, coming from one of the cells.

When I step inside that dark cell, for a moment I see nothing past tightly packed angelic bodies, but once my arrival is noticed, the wall of bodies opens, making a pathway to Tartys' body, which lies on the floor, in the middle.

In twos, his eight brothers have taken the four corners, standing around him. The seven of them are facing away from the body, looking outwards, while Sabrael, standing next to his fallen kin with his head bowed, repeats that sentence over and over again, and the rest of the angels in the tight cell mumbling are chanting the same words.

Although the hushed words are muted, they hold the weight of a meaning, which I don't know but can guess.

These words are like a prayer, sparking electricity in the dark cell. They brim with sorrow and regret, with tearful goodbye and promise of vengeance.

My gaze is on the body on the floor.

I think I can feel the burn of accusing glares of the brothers on me, the sting of doubtful gazes from the rest of the angels.

But maybe I'm wrong.

Maybe, driven by the guilt that I feel, I imagine denunciation that is not there. Maybe it's my own accusation I hear, maybe it's my own hate.

I want to walk away from the cell, to avoid the sight of the first body that had dropped in my name, to stop listening to his brothers' prayer, stop seeing the fearful gazes of the angels, wondering if they would be next, but I know I can't.

I am the leader that had led them here and I must stay.

Rage, from whom I haven't heard in a while, pops her head out, and rolling her eyes at the dead body, mouths a prophetic warning: *"There will be more."*

I want to tell her to shut up but I know that the bitch is right.

A hand comes over mine and I jump up.

Sam stands next to me, holding my hand, his fingers wrap around mine. I want to pull my hand away, but I change my mind, keeping it in his hold. His warm skin makes me feel less lonely.

While humming the words, Kafziel turns to face his brother's body, taking a step closer. Mouthing the chants, he lifts the black sword of fire above his head. He plunges the sword into his brother's body, drawing a line across his brother's neck and down his body, from neck to the stomach, opening him up.

I slam my eyes shut.

I feel the squeeze of Sam's hand over mine, but it takes me a few deep breaths before I manage to force my eyes open.

The prayer chants had stopped and in the silence of the small cell, Sabrael calls: *"Em-nam kud Anshar, lequ Tartys' Qal anur at margidda warki mummu."*

Sabrael drops to his knees next to his brother and dips his two fingers into his brother's open wound, painting the fingers red. Then he brings the bloody fingers to his own face, drawing two red lines across his own forehead.

Pulled by gravity, the blood runs down his forehead, filling the skin creases and dripping onto his nose.

Sabrael stands, taking a step back.

It's a sign, and one by one every angel in the cell does the same and soon, every forehead is marked with Tartys' blood.

The small cell is filled with a metallic stench of blood.

Sam lets go of my hand, strides to the Tartys' body and does the same.

I'm the only one, whose forehead remains clean.

With the chants gone, every blood painted face is directed to me, every set of expectant eyes waiting for my farewell wish to their fallen brother.

I kneel next to the body, and doing the same that everyone had done before me, I dip my fingers into Tartys' warm blood, bringing my fingers to my forehead.

Leaning in, I tell Tartys something from myself. Quietly, so no one can hear, I say: "I'm sorry."

Once I'm on my feet, with a last bow towards the body, the angels leave the cell, and the rushed conversations of preparation erupt in the corridor.

Sam and I are the only ones left in the cell with the body.

"Don't they need to bury him?" I ask, unable to draw my gaze away from the opened and abandoned body.

"No. We don't bury our dead in the ground as humans do. We believe that leaving them above the ground allows Qal easier progression into the next stage of rebirth."

We stand quiet for a moment. Sam doesn't rush me.

"I'd imagine one of them will come back for him", he adds. "We believe that the higher the body is left, the sooner its Qal will finish the cleansing process and the better chances it will have for rebirth in a higher level."

"So I guess cutting him open is part of it?" I ask.

"Yes, to allow Qal to float unobstructed. The less obstructions Qal finds, the better and easier its journey is."

I nod.

A fleeting question pops into my head, wondering where angels' souls are going, if it's Udhad or someplace else, but the thought is pushed out by the sobering determination of making sure that I don't visit any more of my people's funerals.

I walk out, looking for Shana, but one of the warrior brothers finds me first.

"If we can have a word, Beyelai Sar", he growls low as he bows.

"Sure. What is it?"

The brother in front of me is as tall and large as the rest of his brothers. His black glossy hair brushes his shoulders. His two bright blue wings are a stark backdrop to his black jumper and trousers.

His lips are a tight line and his brown eyes shine with steely purpose.

"The istana that served this corridor... he should die", the brother barks. "He must die and I would like the honour to carry the sentence."

I look at the angel. The hateful glow in his eyes confirms his intentions. The hate that swims there is raw and animalistic.

"What's your name?" I bark at him, matching his tone with mine.

"Kafziel."

"Then listen here, Kafziel. That istana is not going to be executed", I say, shaking my head.

"Not just yet", I add louder, looking up at him.

Kafziel's eyes open wider at the unexpected pushback. His large frame hangs above me and I notice the white knuckles over the hilt of the black fiery sword he still holds.

"Beyelai", he growls. "He had alerted Asmodeus' crew to our presence. Tartys is dead because of him. Sablo is injured..."

He leaves his brother's and his own injuries out of the list of damages.

"No. We're not going to kill him. Not just yet."

"We need to avenge my brother, my beyelai", he rumbles low in his throat and there's so much menace in his voice and gaze that I have to fight with my feet, which are itching to take a few steps away from him and agree to everything.

Instead, I take a step forward.

I crane my head at him, forcing my gaze away from the sword by his hip.

"I said "No", I clip, measuring each word.

I hold his gaze and I hold my ground. I stamp on the fear that dampens my back, whispering the warnings of the sword in his hand, and the fact that I'd be dead the moment I hit the ground if he decided to slice me with it.

His nostrils flare up, his eyes close into slits and I hear the grinding of his teeth.

We stand against each other, waiting for one to fold. I know that he is faster, stronger and more experienced than I. But only physically.

I take a breath and half step forward, then placing my hand onto his arm.

"We need him", I say softer. "We need him if we want to save everyone including your brothers. I need him and I need him alive. It's not the time to kill him. You have trusted me up until now and I need you to trust me again. Everything I do, I do for all of us."

His gaze penetrates me, but eventually, he nods and I exhale.

I take a step around him, confronted by the uncomfortable silence that only now I have realised swaddled the earthy corridor, as every pair of eyes is watching us.

But I ignore it all, returning to my task.

I find Shana at another end of the corridor, sitting on the floor next to Tabby, telling her something in a light voice, interrupting her own speech with laughter, as if telling an anecdote.

But Tabby doesn't participate or laugh. In fact, she doesn't appear to hear Shana, as her glazed eyes stare blankly into space.

"Shana, can I please speak with you?"

"Of course, Mammí Barragal."

She rises to her feet.

Sam shuffles past me, taking Shana's place next to Tabby.

He takes Tabby's hands into his, and while stroking them, he leans in, murmuring something to her.

I lead Shana to the nearest empty cell.

"Shana, you know these corridors, right?"

"Yes, Mammí", she answers and bows.

"You know which ones go to the surface and which go deeper?"

"Yes, Mammí, but, there's nothing below us. We are on the last level of the corridors."

"Okay." I nod.

Shana's answer has erased one of the paths for me and my followers, leaving me promptly with "Plan B", now known as the "only plan".

I brace myself for the question I'm about to ask.

"I need you to take us to your Elder", I say, watching her face, washed in my pearly glow.

I trust her enough. She has showed enough loyalty.

But all of it was a personal loyalty, it was her personal choice, at which no one else, apart from her would have died had it gone wrong.

Now I'm asking her to involve her kin and risk bringing Baza's wrath on the heads of her entire kind with some severe consequences if it goes wrong.

None of us here are stupid or naïve enough to think that Baza will forgive.

But I'm not planning to tell her the implications of her decision. That is for her to figure out and for me to veil.

"Why?" She starts but slams her mouth shut.

"I beg your forgiveness, Mammí Barragal. Please forgive me. I know it's not for me to question The Great Mother of All Gods on her plans."

She drops to her knees in front of me, swiftly falling forward, her face and front pressed into the dirt.

"Please forgive me. It's not my lowly place to doubt", she rumbles into the soil, which muffles her words, but I interrupt her: "Shana, get up."

"Get up, I said", I roar as her body remains on the ground.

Wearily, Shana rises, keeping her gaze to the floor.

I reach to her face, to touch her chin, but she flinches away, expecting to be hit.

I drop my hand and take two steps away from her.

"Look at me", I say softly.

I wait. I don't rush her. She needs to calm down and to understand that I'm not one of her masters. And slowly her head rises, her gaze meeting mine.

"Do you want to fly?" I ask. "To stand within the endless, open, blue sky and fly? Isn't that what your ikstaya told you? Isn't that what she promised? That I will bring you to the surface and open the skies for you? Isn't that what the prophecy said? For me to take you into the sky and give you wings?"

She nods.

"Would you deny your family the chance to fly too? Would you hide that chance from the ones who have heard the prophecy, like you and your ikstaya, and waiting for me? From someone like Mitish?"

Her neck is rigid when she shakes her head "no".

She's unsure but so am I.

I don't know if this move will pay off. It's another stab in the dark on my part, but it is the only way forward for me.

I need to hide my angels in these corridors for a bit longer. Baza would expect me to go up to the surface, and that's exactly why I won't.

But amongst other things, the number that I have now will not be enough. Even with Rafe, Domiel and Dumah, this number will crumble against Baza's troops.

I saw the parade of his army by the Gates of Uras. I remember that demonstration of his military force and I know that its entire volume would be thrown at us, to kill this rising, to execute this rebellion promptly, so no one else will ever dream of disobeying him again.

I know I would, and that's why I'm not kidding myself about our chances.

So when Shana had started to talk of her ikstaya's prophecy, I saw the weak, gleaming light of my opening. I saw my way forward.

I saw the gift that Uriel and istana's Old Gods have granted me. I saw the way to save myself.

"I want to remind your Elder of the prophecy. I want to show him that I have arrived. I want to offer him, and everyone else, the same that I am offering you. I will take everyone, who wishes with me. I'm willing to give the sky to everyone who wants to fly again. Wouldn't you want to see others fly too?"

With her eyes wide open, she nods. But the fleeting moment of excitement in her eyes is replaced with one tune, dull fear. I can feel it.

But I'm not going to let fear to take what's mine.

"Take me to your Elder, Shana. Take me to him. Let me gift the sky and safe refuge to others, to your brothers and sisters, to your friends. Let me show them the way out of these corridors, the way to the sun and the blue sky. Let me save them from their daily beatings, from forceful copulation, from starvation and slavery. Let me save the children, placing them back into the arms of their mothers. They need to be given the same chance that I am giving you."

Shana nods animatedly now.

Good.

Sam appears by the entrance to the cell, behind Shana's back, and I wave him to come in.

"You will lead us, Shana", I call, "and when your kin take to the sky, when new generations are born under the freedom of the endless sky, with bigger wings", I nod behind her back, where her see through, small and veiny dragonfly wings flutter, "they will remember *your* name. Your name will be passed from generation to generation. The children will be taught that it was *you* who led them to the light."

Shana's large eyes are ablaze with possibility and duty.

"The new chapter for your kind starts today, with *you*. Are you ready to lead? Are you ready to offer them freedom?"

"Yes, Mammí Barragal", she answers, breathily. She drops to her knees and I know that another splat on the ground is coming, so I place my hand on her shoulder, keeping her in place.

"Go and get ready, Shana."

She lifts her gaze to me and I nod. After an answering nod, she walks out of the cell, on her way out bowing to Sam.

Sam and I are alone in the cell now.

The voices ring in the corridor, Sabrael is the loudest. With a mixture of angelic and some modern languages he barks orders to others.

I look at Sam, waiting to hear what he wanted, but he just stares at me. He shakes his head.

"Who is the angel I'm looking at? Although she looks like someone I knew, she has nothing in common with the girl I met in your town only a few months ago, and I'm not talking about the wings."

I raise my hand, interrupting him.

"I don't know where you're going with it, but if you think I will be apologising..." I begin rumbling low, but before I can continue, he interrupts me.

"No, no", he rushes in. "Absolutely not, Mermaid. I'm not asking for an apology. For An's sake, I wouldn't dare."

He laughs.

"And what for?" he says, shrugging his shoulders.

"Why are you here?" I ask but he ignores me.

"You are glorious, Ariel", he says, continuing his earlier thought, looking somewhere in the distance, past my shoulder. "You are the leader they were waiting for. You are what their prophecy had promised. You will sculpt their future, I can see it clearly."

Sam brings his gaze to me.

"And not only theirs, Dingir – Ki will never be the same. Rafe was right; you are more than they saw."

He shakes his head. His stupefied gaze is on me.

I want to ask him when he spoke to Rafe and how he knows about the prophecy, and if the prophecy is the truth, when Pronoia strides into the cell, announcing: "We're ready to leave, Beyelai Sar."

With a glance at Sam, I nod to Pronoia and walk out of the cell, leaving Sam behind.

CHAPTER 16

The corridor is packed with angels and istana.

Everyone is on their feet, ready to march forward, following my command and my lead.

As a weathered and experienced commander, Sabrael stands at the forefront of our group. Shana stands next to him as she will be leading the way, with Sam on Sabrael's other side. Sam holds Tabby's small body is his arms.

Tabby still hasn't come around and although awake, she looks dazed, lost and weak. I'm pleased that Sam took responsibility for her. I feel much better, calmer somehow, knowing that he is the one looking after her.

The next row is a row of four.

Two warrior brothers and between them are the two beautiful female angels of love and forgiveness, the injured Sablo and her friend. With their floral dresses gone, ripped for bandages, the both blonde girls wear black trousers and dark jumpers, which I could swear, I saw on Pronoia and his brothers earlier.

Both girls are swimming in the large clothing. The sleeves of their jumpers and bottom of their wide-legged trousers are rolled up in fat rolls, and belts encircle their petite waists, gathering extra fabric.

Sablo's pale face is drizzled with sweat, betraying the pain she is in.

The brothers on either side of the girls are strong and alert, ready to fight off any danger, protecting the girls. Their torsos are sealed in the black leather tunics of Asmodeus' "little helpers". Laced at the sides, the tunics expose the brothers' biffy arms and dips of their hairy chests.

Sablo and her friend bow their heads to me, while the brothers meet my gaze and only fleetingly close their eyes, acknowledging me.

But it's fine. Either I will earn their respect by saving them or will be killed for leading us into death, then none of this hostility will matter.

The three weary-looking Ophanims, the record-keeper Pravuil and the bearded Yofiel form the next row. The female leader of the Ophanims and her bearded husband bow at me as I walk past, her pretty slim Asian face still ashen.

I give an answering nod.

Behind them stands Mitish next to an old angel, for whom he cared so tenderly.

"The old angel" is awake now. He stands up, looking at me with young, bright blue eyes of a twenty something year old man, although his face is pallid and wrinkled. The angel follows the other angels with his eyes but doesn't say a word, quietly surveying the ready to march platoon.

The angel's arm is draped over Mitish's shoulder as he leans in, struggling to stand, but Mitish doesn't mind. In fact, Mitish seems rather pleased, beaming with a smile.

The three angels of love that Lis had coaxed into the pledge cluster into a small, scared flock a few steps further away. They still wear their flamboyant clothing from the party, although now it looks muddy and sad, as if they are royalties in exile, left to survive on the streets.

Lis was wrong. They didn't get an "explosion" of their social calendars for attending that meeting and playing a part in annihilating of Uriel. They were not embraced by Baza. They didn't get any perks at all. Instead, they have found themselves locked in Baza's tunnels of Hell with the rest of my pledged.

They don't speak to anyone and when the gaze of one of them meets mine, he drops his gaze as if I've burnt him.

Sarin, surrounded by a tight circle of brothers, closes our joyful penal platoon of the condemned, bringing up the rear.

He leans against a wall. His face is marred with fresh cuts and bruises, his left eye swelling up.

When I move my gaze from Sarin's face, it collides with a steely glare of Kafzael, challenging me to say something.

But I don't.

I understand his need for revenge more than he knows. I understand him. I understand the hole that the death of a loved one leaves inside, and after everything that Sarin has done, he should be happy to be alive.

The experienced warriors lead the expedition and the battle weathered soldiers bring up the rear, keeping the weak and injured in the middle. This formation reminds me of a pack of wolves, but as it has turned out, it's the way of military expeditions too.

Returning to the front, I glance into the cells.

The naked bodies of Asmodeus' soldiers lie on their fronts on the floor in some cells. Their backs are bloodied and naked, bare of wings, which were cut off their backs and thrown to the ground.

I'm torn between shock at the cruelty of my angels and the understanding of their rightful anger. The soft, human side of me wants to demand and call on their civility, while the pragmatic and wiser part of me understands that these are the ancient rules of their "life and death" games, and most importantly, lately I am the last one to preach.

I walk past the angels and istana, to whom I've promised the saviour's land, and take my place next to Sabrael, Shana and Sam.

"Ready?" I ask and as the three nod, I command, "Let's go, then."

We march towards the wall of metal bars and after the familiar sizzle, the door forms within the bars and I push it open.

* * *

"Istana's Great Hall is the next level up. I checked with Shana", Sabrael says as our group plods through the tight corridor, filled with sounds of dripping water, the rustle of earth worms and smells of mushrooms and mould.

As much as he was one of Baza's angels, the desire to find out the location of the istana headquarters had never crossed his mind.

Shana is a few steps ahead, leading our weary group.

At the approach of every turn, she picks up pace, jogs forward, scanning the crossroads in every direction, then standing by the chosen path, directs us.

I walk between Sam and Sabrael.

"We have quite a long maze of corridors to navigate before we get there", Sabrael adds, "but at least it's only one level change."

"Uriel", he says again after a pause, lowering his voice. "Are you sure we can trust her?"

He nudges his head towards Shana's lithe body.

"You have commanded your brothers, led the battles, right?" I ask and Sabrael nods in agreement. "What would you have me do in this position?" I sweep my hand around me. "Would you go up, to the surface?"

He thinks for a moment.

"No. Baza will be there", he answers. "Our numbers are by far too small. We're tired, unarmed and we have injured among us. We can't meet him in open battle right now."

"You see..."

I shrug my shoulders.

But do I trust her?

To a degree. I don't trust anyone anymore, and haven't for a long time. Life taught me well what blind trust can do, the amount of damage and havoc it can cause, and I'm not willing to try it again. For every little bit of trust I grant, I have a plan "B" stored away, and I can only pray that my back up plans would never wake up to their use.

Since I laid my eyes on Baza's glorious Arllu, I began to wonder if I'm ready to kill anyone to survive, to get back to Jess, to save her at the cost of someone else's life?

The earlier unsure, scared answer is replaced by unyielding "yes" of today.

I stop and turn to Sabrael.

I scan his soft caramel skin, darker inside this corridor, his steely eyes and the bright blue wings.

"Just be ready for anything", I say to him, "and you can trust me in one thing, Sabrael I need to survive and I'll do whatever it takes to survive. I need you, *all of you*, to survive, and if I live, you will live with me. My freedom will be your freedom. I'm not in the business of gathering slaves."

I return to my walking and catch up with Sam with Tabby in his arms in a few long strides. The rows behind us resume their marching too.

As we walk through the tunnels, we walk past the walls of metal bars, separating the prisoners' holdings.

I stop by the barred walls for a moment, looking into the locked sections.

Some istana come towards the walls to gawk at my troops and glowing old me, while some hide in their cubbyholes, not to be seen or heard, but I know that they're there.

The braver istana shuffle towards the metal walls and begin talking to Shana, who in their tongue chirps something, animatedly waving her hands, and I can hear "Mammí Barragal" a few times. Sabrael stands next to her, arms crossed, listening, the embodiment of doom and gloom.

I'm not worried about istana seeing us, reporting our movements to Asmodeus or Baza. They don't have an access to Arllu's network, just as service dogs are not issued with a radio. Istana are slaves and treated as such.

We've been walking for hours now.

I called a few stops but they were brief.

During them, some angels stood under dripping from the ceiling water and either washed their faces with these pitiful drops, or lifting their faces upwards, let the water slide into their throats, drinking it.

None of my angels rush me when I stop outside the prisoners' corridors. A few gasps of recognition and a low mutter from my crew rustle behind my back, when the cries of one of the prisoners are recognise as of the angels they knew. Outside of some sections, the cries and whimpering of prisoners rings louder.

I press my face between the metal bars, straining my eyes, looking into the locked sections, trying to make out the carved cells and the bodies within. And sometimes I manage to see a glimpse of a wing, lighter shade clothing or a pale face.

But most sections remain quiet and dark, and seeing the occupied cells, I wonder if the prisoners of these corridors are dead.

Baza's prison is full. Every section has someone in there.

Some sections hold more prisoners than the others. Baza's punitive juridical machine mills the bones and bodies of disagreeable with tireless efficiency, but now I know where to come for more followers, if I survive this.

When I leave the barred section, my angels follow me, more morose with every sight of every new torture chamber.

But I stop at every one of them. I need to see the angels inside and as much as they can't see me, weirdly, I feel the need to show them that they're not forgotten to rot and die in these corridors, that someone remembers that they are in here and that someone will be coming for them.

We walk past another section and although I've stopped counting them by now, I still come towards each metal wall.

It stokes up my fire. It shows me what will happen to me if I fail. It reminds me of who Baza really is, reminds me of the game I'm in, hardening my resolve and steel.

I come towards the metal bars of a new section and my platoon stops behind me. A few angels slide down against a wall and onto the floor.

This section is quiet, void of the cries. Only a shuffle of a single set of steps rustles past the metal bars.

My glow creates a pool of a light, spilling on the floor past the bars and filling the air.

The shuffling steps stop for a moment and then with a sudden rush, run towards me.

"You", a weak voice breathes out in disbelief.

CHAPTER 17

There's something familiar in this voice, something from a long time ago, as if a memory of a dream.

I raise my eyes towards the voice.

My gaze glides up the dark trousers to the sullied by dirt and blood shirt, until it arrives at the face, and a second of confusion is replaced with a virulent slap of recognition, followed by draining fear and then scorching wave of hate.

My eyes fly open and my breath leaves my lungs. I grab hold of the bars to keep myself from falling.

His feet shuffle closer and I'm face to face with the one I never thought I would see, the one, who Baza had sworn is long dead.

I hold on to the metal bars as if they are a lifeline.

I can't move my body. My tongue is not mine to command and nor are my feet. The poisonous feelings of exposure and shame numb my muscles like novocaine.

Again like years ago, my body and my mind don't belong to me, and I can't breathe.

His face is in front of me now.

It had healed since the last time I saw him. The bloodied cuts that my whip had left behind have turned into ugly white scars, which cross his face in every direction, distorting the right side.

His gaze travels over me, dropping behind my back, towards my wings, returning to my face.

The earlier disbelief is replaced with loathing.

"You are one of them", he comments in a quiet lisper. The corner of his mouth lifts and I can see missing teeth.

An inch and a few metal bars is all that separates us.

I feel his warm breath on my face. I smell its stench, and suddenly, the images of my past and present fuse in my mind.

I feel alone and bound again, yet sensing the presence of angelic essences behind me. I see my Jess as a monster, chewing on the bones of a lizard, with her human, scared face on the steps of my mother's trailer. I hear the dull clunk of the knife, falling down the steps, and at the same time I hear a dull, absorbing silence of this earthy corridor and... his old basement.

The earlier knowledge and powers are gone, replaced by fear and panic. I feel young, human and weak again as if time has turned back, as if the last few months of my life had never happened.

"I should've killed you when I had the chance", he hisses at me. "You're one of them, a monster like all of them. I should have done more and worse things to you. Monsters like you deserve to be tortured and die in agony, pleading for their lives just like you force us. I should have protected the world from you. If only I had known then..."

He brings his face closer to mine and a side of the chain on his neck catches the light, winking through the opening of his shirt.

The gleam of his chain crushes my throat, stopping me from drawing a breath, forcing the retching.

My hands crush the metal bars and my joints scream in pain.

"I wish I'd killed you when I had a chance", he repeats and spits at me. His spittle lands on my dirty tunic.

In a daze, I turn around from him and walk towards my angels, my lower wings trail behind me.

In a hushed voice, Sam talks to Sabrael, and Pronoia and Kafziel stand nearby, listening to him.

I walk to Kafziel and outstretch my hand with my open palm to him. "Give."

Sam stops midsentence and all four turn to me, looking, trying to catch up with me, to understand what I'm saying.

Kafziel's gaze dances between my open hand and my gaze, glued to the black sword in his hand.

"Sword?" he asks, baffled.

"Give it!" I roar and the hushed chatter in the corridor dies.

I feel confused gazes on me. I feel the prickling of gathering tears at the back of my eyes and I'm afraid to cry.

"Aye. As you command, my Beyelai."

The warm and heavy hilt lays into my palm.

I close my hand over it, turn around and walk to the metal bars.

The sword is too long and too heavy, so I let the sword drop to the ground, trailing after me, its tip cutting a shallow trench in the pressed soil.

"Uriel. Uriel!" Sam's confused voice calls after me. "Ariel, what is it?"

But I don't turn around, don't look back.

"Uriel! Mammí Barragal! Mermaid!!" he calls.

I ignore him.

The heavy black ring on my thumb slides into the opening and *he* takes a few cautious steps back, away from the metal wall. The formed door swings open under my hand.

"Ariel! Ariel!"

Sam's voice and his rushed steps are behind me.

I step through the door, pushing it shut behind me.

"Ariel! Ariel, what's going on?"

Confused, panicked, Sam screams past the closed metal door, pleading with me.

"Ariel!"

With the door shut, I turn and glance at him, at his beautiful yet distraught face.

I turn away.

"I will be back soon", I say. "I won't be long."

I answer Sam, but my gaze is on the one in the corridor with me.

I take a step closer to *him*, dragging my sword of black rippling fire, and suddenly, a few heartbeats later, I hear Sam's sharp exhale of recognition and understanding.

"Ariel. No! You don't have to do it. There's nothing to do for you here. He's not going anywhere. He will never leave these corridors. His miserable life will end in them. He will die here."

I take a step forward and *he* takes a step back, his gaze bounces between my face, the sword and Sam. His loathing is palpable, although now diluted with fear.

"You don't need to kill him", Sam roars behind me. "There's no need for it. It's done. He's done. He is where he supposed to be. He will never harm anyone ever again. He will never come out of here."

"I have to do it", I say, keeping my gaze on *him*.

"No you don't", Sam roars. "You didn't kill him when you had chance. You didn't put it on yourself. You knew what it would do to you. You saved yourself. You haven't protected him, you have protected yourself. And you need to do the same now. He is not worth it. He isn't worth the pain he causes you, the guilt you'll put on yourself."

It can't keep coming back to me, mocking me. He is mocking me. What the leader will I be if I leave this behind? Unfinished, unresolved? The shame that can be used against me and return to taunt me forever? If not by Baza then by someone else...

I think this but I don't say it to Sam.

I don't think he would understand, and I'm busy.

"I must do it", I say simply.

"Then let me do it. Please, Ariel. Let me do this for you. Please! Please, don't put it on yourself. It no longer matters to me. My Qal is damned and already rotting in Arllu together with me. But you can stay clean, pure, above the dirt of it all, of Arllu, of your past... You can stay clean, virgin and virtuous like the sky of Sarukh, The Archangel of Sarukh that you are, The Mammí Barragal, The Begetter of Life..."

"And The Dame of all Ends", I answer, without turning my head.

Tired of our squabble, *he* butts in: "Can you even swing it?" and he barks out in a short laugh.

"Ariel, open the door! Open the door immediately! Let me in!"

But I'm done talking to Sam.

There's nothing more to say and nothing more to add.

My mistakes are mine to fix and my sin is mine to carry.

I lift the sword, grabbing the thick hilt with both hands.

The sword is heavier, longer and clunkier than my little swords were, but even this is irrelevant.

I raise the sword in front of me, pointing at *him* and the smile weathers on *his* lips, as *he* takes another step backwards, deeper into the corridor.

Behind me, the heavy metal bars vibrate under Sam's hands.

"Where are your friends? Here?" I ask.

"What?" he chuckles with a wheezy high pitch of a hyena. "Want more?"

I thrust both arms forward and the tongue of the sword licks his chest, ripping his shirt, drawing blood underneath. But he jumps away in time.

The red mist had descended over my vision, bringing with it pure hate, which vibrates in my ears with a buzz of a released string. I'm blind and deaf with my hate, but I blink through it, suspended in my cocoon.

I ignore its call.

I ignore Sam calling my name.

I ignore the gazes of the angels on my back.

I push distractions away, concentrating on the task at hand.

He and his mates need to die.

I need a clean slate and freedom from my past.

"Where?" I repeat again, taking a step forward, perfectly matching his backwards.

"You, stupid bitch", he screeches, "look what you've done."

His hand presses over his cut at his solar plexus, but the blood still pools through.

I'm not telling him that it's only the beginning. I'm not telling him that this scratch is the least of his worries. I don't tell him of my plans for him.

"Where. Are. They", I repeat, carving each word.

I dive forward, sweeping my sword from left to right.

Another clean cut opens on his shirt and a thin trickle of blood begins there.

He raises his gaze at me and after a moment of loathing glare, he answers: "Long dead, probably. At least they are not here. What is it to you?"

"Good", I mumble, "one kill will clean all."

"What?" he asks but I ignore him.

"Why are you here?" I ask, but I think I can connect the dots myself.

Baza had kept him alive as leverage against me, available day and night and at a moments notice, whilst using his ruthlessness and self-preservation in these overflowing corridors, the self-preservation will mean that *he* will do anything to stay alive and the ruthlessness that *he* will do it extra well.

The hate and loathing are rising within me again.

The smile pulls at his lips, showing the gap in his teeth.

"Waiting for you", he answers.

I want to rise on my wings above him. I want to show him what I am now. I want to drink his fear. I want to feed on it like he once fed on mine. I want him to beg for forgiveness, crawl in the dirt like a worm that he is.

But there's no space in this tight corridor, I can't fly up and gloat, looking down at him, letting him admire my glory the moments before The Mother of Gods will bestow her vengeance upon him.

So he will be executed, slaughtered like an animal, with no frills or emotions.

My every step forward is met with his backward, and in this manner we've walked through most of the corridor.

His gaze darts from side to side, scanning the walls, finally realising that I'm not going away.

He looks for a way out. He looks for the miracle of a saving grace.

We are outside of another carved alcove and a string of weak moaning comes from there.

I turn my head, glancing into a dark cell, noticing an outline of a male body suspended off the ceiling and the broken shadows of dark wings behind him.

Suddenly, I feel a hand on my leg, a heavy punch sinks into my stomach and I'm airborne.

My wings flash open, but they don't come to life in time and there's no space for them.

The sword in my hands draws a trajectory with my fall.

I crash onto my back, jamming a side of my wing under myself, and I scream in pain, dropping my weapon.

The sword clanks by my side, but not before its tip nips my shoulder and I scream again.

With my peripheral vision I see a meaty and hairy arm diving for the sword's hilt.

I swoop for the sword too. I roll to my side and through the pain in my back, wing and the shoulder, I reach towards the sword.

"Ariel!" Sam's voice roars.

A heavy punch rams at the side of my face and my head hits the ground, my fingers brush over the hilt.

A boot steps on my wrist and I cry out, feeling the carved metal of the hilt escaping my fingers.

No! I'm not losing my weapon.

Still on my side, I raise my free arm and with all hate that courses through me, I drive my fist into the back of his knee.

He howls and his knee gives in, bringing him down.

I feel the wind above my head as the sword wizzes, slicing the air.

He roars and the sword changing its dance.

Now its tip flies towards me time and time again as he tries to skew me like a kebab.

I roll away. I roll to my back and then to my side, away from him, and with his another advance of another step, his boot frees my wrist, freeing me.

"Ariel!" Sam roars but I wish he'd shut up.

I roll to my front and I am about to get up, when a sudden pain explodes in my top wing.

"Little bitch. Dirty angelic whore", he roars above me. "You will all die, and I will start with you. Everyone will see what Mitch can do. Maybe I will even get out of here, if I trade you off."

I need to make a decision.

He thrusts the sword above my head again, aiming at my wings.

His feet in the worn-out black boots are not far from me, but the sword is even closer.

Will my arms be longer or the sword?

I'm about to find out.

With one short but violent lunge, I propel my body forward, and closing my hands over his ankles, I yank at them with all my might.

He falls backwards and screams, hitting the ground like a chopped down tree in a forest, sending a vibration through the ground.

The sword, released from his grip, skids over the ground, towards the middle of the corridor and the metal door.

I scramble to my feet.

I'm up, jumping over and around his sprawled body, diving towards the black vibrating sword, exhaling when my hand closes over its black hilt.

I'm on my front, and as I rise onto all fours, my gaze travels up, noticing the layer of red blood bubbling on the sword's blade.

It's my blood.

My gaze travels up the wall of the metal bars, catching a glimpse of Sam's distorted face, behind the bars he desperately shakes, and the tight line of angels past him.

Holding onto nearby wall, I rise to my knees.

"Ariel, open the door immediately. Let me in", Sam hisses at me through the bars. His face is low down as he crouches, keeping his face level with mine.

I'm up and so is Sam.

"He will kill you. Let me in", Sam pleads. "I will kill him for you if you can't leave it be."

I don't answer him.

I turn away, but not before my gaze skates over the faces of the angels, a few concerned and the rest expectant.

They are eager to see the leader they are following in action. All of them want to see what they "bought for their money", who they agreed to follow.

I spin away from them, facing the one in the corridor with me.

He crawls up, and at the moment *he* stands on all fours, swaying, his chavvy necklace falls out of the opening of his shirt, swinging back and forth with him.

And I can't take it anymore.

Too many memories and too much pain... It engulfs me. It rips from within.

The swing of his chain... Back and forth, back and forth...

I take a step forward. I grab hold of the hilt with both hands and I raise the sword up.

His eyes fly open, first in surprise and then in fear, pure undiluted fear of someone who knows that he is about to die.

He shuffles backward on all fours, trying to scatter away from me, but there's nowhere left to go.

I take another measured step forward.

"No, please, no", he stammers. "Please, no. Please. No, no –"

His tearful pleas and his mumbling cries are cut with one swing of my sword.

CHAPTER 18

I force myself to stay in the corridor for a bit longer.

I can't run away from what I've done. I need to own it.

I glance at the faces of the angels past the metal bars.

My gaze slides over approvingly smiling Sabrael, over the nodding brothers, over the wide-eyed faces of istana and the sorrowful frown of Sam.

I don't rush to unlock the door and let anyone in.

Without looking at the body on the floor, I walk over to the nearest cell. One by one, I inspect every cell, absent-mindedly glancing at the already expected continuous pictures of dying angelic bodies suspended off the ceiling, again musing at the scope of Baza's punitive facility, yet noting the vastness of a pool of potential supporters I can gain.

I wonder what Rafe would say when I tell him about these corridors and the amount of angels in them. He never thought that the number would be so large, but neither did Sam.

If I knew about this vastness before I'd set off, I would have hit the corridors only, bypassing bitches like Lis altogether.

When I come out, Sam again holds Tabby's little body, taken from Sabrael's care.

He looks at me. His gaze is long and lingering as if he wants to say something, but unsure how to start. He looks at me but doesn't say a word.

I walk to Kafziel.

"Here."

I hand him the sword.

Kafziel bows as he takes the sword. A smile tugs at his lips and a little glimmer of approval dances in his eyes.

I come to Shana.

"How much further?" I ask.

"Not far, Mammí Barragal", she rushes, bowing deeply and keeping her head down, but not before I see fear flickering in her eyes.

"How far is "not far"?" I press.

"About the same as we have walked", she adds.

"It had better be there, and as soon as you've said."

Scared Shana nods.

She's afraid of me. So be it!

The studious gazes of the rest of the angels and istana follow me, as I take my place at the head of the group.

I stop next to Sam, but I don't look at him. I don't want to see these gazes anymore whether scared, approving, surprised, disapproving or sad. His judgment is the last thing I need.

"Shall we?" I call to Shana, who's somewhere by the middle of the group and she hurries towards me.

Our avant garde spends the rest of the walk in silence.

I hear the soft hushed conversations behind us, but I can't make out a word nor do I try. I don't care what they say. Although even if I may be losing the followers, they have nowhere else to go and neither do I. Only one way is left for us all, forward and upwards.

At the next stop Sam doesn't rush to find me. The distance between us is tangible.

He walks away from the main group of angels, gently lays Tabby on the ground and sits next to her.

Sabrael comes to him and they speak for a while in hushed voices, but Sam's heavy and broody gaze, which is directed into the distance, gets to Sabrael and eventually Sabrael walks away, leaving Sam alone with his thoughts.

But I need to speak to Sam.

I walk to Tabby. Her gaze remains empty, directed to the dark earthy ceiling, and for the first time since I found her, I truly fear if this might be the end of her and she will not come back.

"That could be the end for some", Rage whispers. *"Remember yourself?"*

She thinks she is helping.

I kneel next to Tabby, stroking her face and her curly hair.

I want to apologise to her again, but I bite my tongue, conscious of too many eyes on me.

I walk over to Sam, sliding on the cold and damp ground next to him. His wings behind him are no longer pure white, they are covered in dirt, but I don't think Sam cares.

"How is she?" I ask when he raises his gaze to me. I nod at Tabby.

"Same."

"Why hasn't she come around?"

He sighs.

"She is the youngest of angels created. *You* created her", he answers and sighs.

"Pardon?"

He lifts his gaze to me.

"Uriel had created her as the angel of free will and self-determination for humans, to inspire the ability to see and choose alternatives. But her essence is the youngest, therefore the weakest. Gertüs peluş must have really done a number on her."

He sighs again and we fall silent.

We sit for a while before I approach the reason I came to talk to him.

"You think I made a mistake, back in the cell. You think I should not have killed him. Maybe you think I overreacted", I say quietly into the spore filled air.

I don't need to ask him this. I know.

But I need him to understand me too. I wish someone had understood me for once, for the first time in my life.

I want to say that I didn't have a choice, but I know that's a load of bull.

This phrase is just a pretty excuse, used too many times by too many people, to remove responsibility, and I don't want to remove mine. This responsibility that I've placed on myself is what will separate me from "them". It's something tangible I can hold on too.

Everyone has a choice.

Every action taken is a choice that one has made, and I will own mine. I will own every decision of mine. I will stand up, claiming it as my own, as I'm sick of living on my knees, living in the gutter, pleading for understanding and mercy.

Even now, I don't want his forgiveness. I'm trying not to lose another friend, but I'm prepared for that outcome too.

"It was my call because it was my past I was correcting. You may think it was cruel, harsh. Maybe it was the wrong thing to do in front of other angels –"

"I couldn't care less about them", Sam barks, interrupting me. "I didn't want you to do that to *yourself*."

He glares at me for a moment, before turning his head away.

"I didn't want you to dirty yourself with lowlife like him. He wasn't worth the heavy weight of guilt you'd put on yourself."

"I don't feel any guilt", I snap. I'm not about to tell him what this journey does to me, how much it changes me.

He looks up at me.

"Maybe... maybe not now. But that day will come. One day, when you are least expecting it, all your past dues will catch up with you..."

"It didn't catch up with him", I bristle.

"But you are not him", he cuts me off.

Then he adds calmer: "You are not him and you are not us. You were not born into the ruthless cruelty of our world. You didn't suckle it with your mother's milk and you didn't fall asleep every night to stories of vengeance and bloodshed. You're different and it's the best thing about you. You are...*you*, and your humanity makes you who you are, and it's the reason why I know you will save us. You will *forgive* us, all of us, even the least worthy. Look what you're doing for them."

He looks at the angels away from us and I follow his gaze.

A few angels are watching us.

"You bring salvation to those who never thought to find any, to those who thought they will die, rotting for their sins, who never hoped to see their home again, to see the skies of Sarukh. You are bringing salvation to stained, dirty souls...like me.

"You are not like us, and it's the most precious gift you have. Your humanity and forgiveness is what was missing from Sarukh for many GA, and even we didn't know how much of it was missing and how much we needed it. Your soft soul is what has brought you here and what leads us from these depths. You are clean...You are a clean and forgiving soul..."

I can't, nor do I want to, listen to his regrets and disappointment in me.

My life was full of regrets, my regrets and regrets of others, and I can't do it again. I can't allow this new life to be swollen by regrets too.

"You know what they did", I cut him off. "You know who they are and what they've done. I thought out of all them, you might understand", I hiss. "You were there when Baza brought them. You saw the entertainment it has become. *I* was the spectacle! *I* was the show! For everyone to see."

My voice is rising and I fight hard to keep it low. I take a breath, swallowing past the lump in my throat.

"I cannot do it again", I say, shaking my head. "I will not relive it again. Never. It is time to leave my past behind. It was the only way I could make sure it would stay there, after Baza brought it back, resurrected it twice."

The sad smile pulls at his lips.

"Mermaid, there will be another past. There's always a past, for us all. Now this, what you have done, became the past you might fear, the past that could come and haunt you, even if not by the others, then by yourself."

I'm done listening. I don't need his baggage being placed on me too. As he said: "what's done is done".

"I will find a way to live with it. People live with worse."

"But will *you*? You are always comparing yourself to others, but you're not them. You're not merciless like them."

"Maybe not yet, but I'm learning", I say, smiling at him, but the smile doesn't touch my eyes. "I'm the new leader of the new Sarukh. If you hadn't heard, I'm the prophesised Mother of All Gods. I bring the change to your whole world and I will see it through. But what is Mother of All Gods not going to be? She is not going to be a weak human, a human who doesn't stand up for others, including herself. In fact, Mother of All Gods is not human and neither am I."

I get up.

"And tell me", I ask Sam, "how much of the forgiveness is just cowardliness, fear to confront and take what's yours?"

I walk away.

CHAPTER 19

We stop a few times, and my penal platoon takes these breaks with a different degree of enthusiasm, proportionate to the speed of their recovery.

Some of the angels, the ones who were weaker when we have set off, look progressively worse now, their faces paler and their eyes closed as they sit on the dirt floor, their heads resting against the wall, while some, who miraculously recovered during the march, start conversations in the tunnel and occasional bursts of laughter echo in its dark underbelly.

Shana and Mitish sit away from the rest of the angels, quietly chatting to each other. The angel who Mitish was tending to, sits on the ground next to them with his back against the wall, while Mitish tenderly, like a mother, wipes the angel's face with a cloth he had wetted in a dirty puddle.

The angel's face has found more colour since the last time I looked at him. The colour of his dark mahogany skin has turned warmer and richer, spilling a slight golden shimmer underneath the skin like a cognac in a glass under sun. His black hair is darker and glossier. His eyes are lighter, replacing the earlier milky white with the palest yet brightest blue colour I've ever seen, the colour of sea foam of an ocean in the tropics.

With all these changes, his face looks younger, making him even younger than me.

As much as his wings have filled in over the course of our trip, at the same time, they have *lost* that milky colour, becoming the see through, veiny affair of istana.

It's the weirdest of things.

The four feathered wings, roughly the same size as mine, yet see through like glass or crystal, and when caught by the occasional glimmer of my light, his wings would shimmer, breaking the light like a prism into shards of rainbows, exposing the blue veins running through.

No bones, no muscles, just a crystal with a network of blue veins within.

I look at him and he looks at me, without dropping his gaze. There's an arrogance or self-assurance in his gaze.

Who is this stray dog I've picked up along the way?

I need to figure this one out but not right now.

I turn to Mitish and Shana who are on their feet now, waiting to be addressed.

"Do any of you know where I can find the small swords I came with?"

I still carry the crude spikes I have created in the corridors.

The brothers and Ophanims have shared the trophy weapons of Butcher's crew, but I can't bring myself to touch those weapons. The swords are too long and too heavy for me, while the whips bring back too many memories, and I can't guarantee that I won't injure someone, or myself, if I begin swinging a metal spiky ball on a chain.

Shana and Mitish exchange glances.

"There are some weapons in the armoury next to the istana headquarters, Mammí Barragal", Mitish stammers unsure, shrugging his shoulders.

"Istana has access only to the weapons of ibnatums and wardums, who serve the corridors, Asmodeus and Abzu quarters", a soft young voice interrupts from the ground. "No angelic weapons are placed in istana care, neither of malakhims nor of angels."

I turn my gaze to the angel with the crystal wings.

"Heavenly weapons would be solely in Abzu's care", the angel adds, keeping my gaze.

"And who are you?"

I should have asked this before offering him a place in my marching platoon of the demised. But better late than never, I suppose.

"My name is Dšarael", the young angel says. He pronounces his name as "Shaarael" and there's a lull of Arabic accent in his voice and words.

He looks at me from the ground, not rushing to get up, glaring as only the one with a high status accustomed to be.

"I'm the eldest son of Ishtar", he starts, lifting his chin up, "the rightful ruler of Arllu and the commander and father of all istana."

Shana and Mitish gasp and drop to their knees in front of the angel, promptly following it with a full flop on their stomachs into the dirt.

I want to roll my eyes at this sycophantic spectacle of obedience, but I need to deal with a self-proclaimed god first.

"Sure, mate, and I'm Batman. No", I interrupt myself. "Wonder Woman! I always wanted to be her. Some kids wanted to be doctors or teachers, and then there was me "one Wonder Woman, please!""

Ishtar is the Goddess Shana has mentioned before, the Goddess who has left them behind, but not before prophesising that Mother of all Gods – *me*, according to Shana – will come to rescue them. But that's neither here nor there.

Not only do I question the prophecy itself, but even if I to believe it to be true, how anyone can tell if he's the one who he claims to be? It's not like there's a heavenly Passport service. Can you imagine, a little booklet, issued to every angel and there's a picture of that angel inside next to their name, allegiance and brief summary of powers.

I bring my wandering thoughts back to the issue at hand.

"Isn't it convenient how easily one can spur a lie, claim to be... well, whatever he wants to be, really", I say, "and there is no one to validate that story or to argue? Very convenient. I can proclaim myself literally anyone right now. Who would argue?"

I take a step closer, careful not to step on the two bodies sprawled on the ground, and leaning towards him, I whisper, as if sharing a secret: "The key is to tell the lie with self-assurance and aplomb, and then the crowds will follow you into Hell, right?"

"I am who I say I am", he insists after a moment of silence.

"Okay, let's go with it, mate". I nod, straightening up, "let's roll with it. Let's say I believe you. I love hearing crazy-ass stories, if for nothing else than the entertainment value. There have been a lot of them lately, but I'm always open to more. Hell, look where I am?" I spread my arms wide. "If I didn't believe any of them I'd go crazy."

"Ooh", I adapt a musing tone, "that actually could be another possibility, a more plausible one. Maybe you got confused? You know, overwhelmed?"

The angel stares at me, not proclaiming his regal birth right any longer, but not taking my bait either.

"Get up!" I call to the bodies on the ground. "Mitish, Shana, get up and stop dropping to the ground every five minutes."

I nudge Mitish with a toe of my shoe, and as they lift their heads, unsure scanning me and the angel, I yell "Now!"

Both rush to stand up. The fronts of their clothing, the side of their faces and hands are covered in mud.

"No more dropping to the ground!" I bark. "As your Mammí Barragal, I forbid it. Understood?"

They both nod.

"Good. Now, did you know about this?" I turn to Mitish.

"No, Mammí Barragal", Mitish stammers.

"You want me to believe that you didn't know who was in your corridor and who you dragged with us? I might be naïve and gullible, but not to that extent."

"Kafziel", I yell down the corridor.

The warrior brother turns to my call and so do the rest of the angels.

"Kafziel, bring your sword."

"Please, Mammí Barragal. I swear I didn't know", Mitish mumbles. "He was a prisoner in the corridor when I started. He was there way before me. He was there many *GA* ago, under the previous caretaker. I was never told. I never knew."

Mitish drops to his knees in front of me, while Shana takes a step away from him, putting distance between herself and the sentenced man.

Kafziel comes to stand next to me as do the most of the angels, with Sam and Sabrael pushing through the crowd.

For the second time today, I take the sword from Kafziel hand. Kafziels' and Pronoia's swords are the only weapons we have, that would kill an angel.

I ignore Mitish on his knees and bring the tip of the sword to the angel's throat.

"Who are you?"

"I told you. My name is Dšarael", he answers unfazed. "I'm the eldest son of Ishtar. I am the rightful ruler of Arllu and the commander and father of all istana. Killing me would be your biggest mistake, Uriel. Or should I say, *Nintinugga*."

He holds an ominous pause before he adds: "Nintinugga, or Uriel if you'd like, is my aunt, and it means *you*."

"Of course", I say, smiling, "and now we're related. Blood related and I will never harm my blood. Is that what you are banking on?"

But as he doesn't say a word, I ask: "Are you sure we're not married?"

My sarcasm is on point but I don't know how well an ancient angel, no matter what the descent, is equipped to understand it, but it doesn't stop another session of my eye rolling.

"Who do you think you are" the celebrity edition. The dumbest soap opera has nothing on this inbreeding bunch and this place. Aunties, brothers, sisters, mothers... Like a sick experiment.

"And you", Rage giggles from the side line, barely containing herself.

I want to demand the little bitch remember her place, but I mentally wave my hand at her.

I turn to Sam, then to Sabrael, while keeping the sword next to the angel's throat.

"Any thoughts? Have any of you heard of anything?" I ask them.

But instead of answering me, both stare at the angel. Sam's gaze dances over angel's face, searching for something.

"I suppose it is possible", Sam eventually answers, stretching *"it is"*. "I'm not saying that he is who he claims to be, but it's completely plausible for Arllu to have a foregoing ruler, and it's completely believable for Baza unseating him, or her. But I don't know who was here before Baza, but even if we knew, there'd be very little chance to verify if it is him."

"Oh, god", I roll my eyes upwards.

To say that I'm sick of them all would be the understatement of the century.

"Okay, let's roll with it", I say and nudge the blade of fire towards angel's throat. With another millimetre I would break his skin and draw blood.

"For argument sake, let's say it's the truth. My first question would be "so what?" Why would I care? But the second and most interesting one, if you are who you say you are, why did Baza keep you alive? Killing you would make more sense. From what I know of his methods, I would have thought he wouldn't keep his competition alive."

"Because only Ishtar and her children can rule over istana", he says, "and with the death of last of us, the tie will be severed and istana released from servitude."

Shana and Mitish exhale.

I laugh. I begin to laugh and can't nor do I want to stop.

"You should not have said that in front of them, mate. Now you're a dead man", I say through the giggles.

That has cheered me up.

"Would anyone like to open a betting pool on the chances of this one", I nudge my head at the angel, "surviving until the next rest?"

I giggle, scanning the crowd.

"No? Wise. I wouldn't bet on him either."

"It's not that simple, Nintinugga", the angel says, his measured gaze on me. "The release from servitude in that instance will not mean freedom for istana. It will mean death."

Shana and Mitish gasp again.

"Would you two, please?!"

I turn my head to them.

"Like retired Shakespearian actors", I huff under my breath.

"Istana are my *ngissu*, shadows", he continues, "when I'm alive, they live, remaining with me, but once I'm no more, they will vanish too."

Shana is about to gasp but I glare at her and she slams her mouth shut.

"What, all of them?" I ask the angel.

"Every single one", he nods.

"Thoughts on this disclosure?" I ask Sam and Sabrael, but as they remain quiet, I look at the crowd of the angels behind them.

"Okay", I sigh, "We'll deal with that when, or if, we have to. Right now, Sabrael, can you please assign one of your brothers, the fitter one, to keep an eye on this Sumerian god and Arllu's rightful ruler?"

I can't keep the acid from my voice when I say the last words. Everybody here is a ruler or a god, yet no one "ploughs the fields".

Sabrael nods.

"Pronoia", he says, "keep an eye on the numpty."

"Thank you", I say to Pronoia and he nods, acknowledging my gratitude.

"Bring him towards the head of the column, so I can speak to him later as we walk", I add and Pronoia nods again, tugging the angel by his shoulder.

"Get up", he roars.

I drop my arm, bringing down the sword, and a second later Kafziel's hand comes over mine, and I release the sword's hilt to him.

Dšarael gets up and plods away, Mitish shuffling after him.

The other angels return to their conversations and places too, as curtains fall on the show, leaving me and Shana alone at this side of the tunnel.

"Don't worry too much about him or what he has said", I say to her, coming closer, gently touching her arm. "We're all dependant on somebody at times, more often than not."

As she says nothing, I continue, "You know, there are stories, books, about princes and princesses, kings and queens; about their lives, conquests and wars, their victories and defeats, their love stories, love for other royalty who lives in a shiny, white castle. There are plenty of stories about them. But I always thought: "Why there are no stories of their servants?"

"Why are there no stories of a queen's scullery maid or of a king's butler? Why don't we know their names, even when they've dedicated their lives to serve others? Why don't we care about them? Why are there no stories about a foot soldier, who has died in a war initiated by a king.

Everybody knows the name of the king, no matter how evil he has been, but nobody knows that soldier's name, nobody knows of his parents or his children, nobody thinks to tell a story of his hard and short life.

"That always confused me and bothered me. Even when I was little and I would read a story of a princess, rescued by a handsome prince, I would imagine another story, the story of her maid, meeting a handsome boy too, imagining what that maid might be up to, where she'd live or where she'd go dancing. Would she meet other maids for coffee or would she go dancing with stable boys?

"But as I got older, I realised that this scullery maid would have no time for dancing, coffee, or idle chatter in which their masters would indulge daily and probably would die at the young age from constant exposure to toxic cleaning products."

That was a joke and a laugh comes out of me, but it sounds nothing like laugh should. It's too bitter, sad and raggedy.

"Nobody cares about servants", I sigh. "No one spares a second thought for them. Nobody is interested in these people or their lives. They live and die unknown. They serve their purpose, serve their masters, create glory for a king and die, their bones turning to dust and their children taking their places. These people are there to do a job, like a clock or a cooker, and once they no longer work, once they're broken, they are chucked to the side, replaced with new, shiny, more energetic equipment."

Shana stares at me and I smile back at her.

"I was like these people, so I know. I was them my whole life", I explain to her. "I was you, only by some freak of a coincidence, I am Mammí Barragal now." I wave my arms, saying the title she'd given me with a mock.

"But I was you. So what I'm trying to say, Shana, is that no matter what he says, what he expects or demands of you, from any of you, I will be on your side. I have promised to give you your freedom, I have promised you sanctuary and I intend to keep my promises."

CHAPTER 20

We're almost here.

Shana said that the place where istana are housed will be at the end of this corridor.

But she doesn't rush to cover the last few yards of the corridor. She's not running forward to be reunited with her kin, and as if infected by her suspicion, my angels are not eager to move forward either.

My platoon huddles tighter. The shuffling feet scraping the ground, as my soldiers wait for my lead.

"Okay. Everyone, remain in the same formation", I call to my angels. "Anybody who's weak or unable to fight, there's no shame, stay within the centre of the group. I'd rather know that everyone's alive. Anyone who has weapons and feels strong enough, take your places on the outer circle and remember, should anything happen, you're protecting the centre."

"Agreed?" I ask, turning to Sabrael and Sam.

Both nod.

The three of us have already discussed how we're going to approach our arrival.

The ideas were ranging from sending a scout, to splitting the platoon in two, or maybe three groups, to coming in as one, and after a lot of "back and forth" we decided to keep the group together and the platoon sealed, coming in at once, bringing with us the weak, the Sumerian god and istana.

Sabrael had voiced his suspicions that the istana is leading us into a trap where we all will get slaughtered, while Sam was more concerned with the reception we might receive, bringing the treacherous istana and the unknown, ousted god of Hell into istana's residence, and how the Elder will receive this news.

These were their arguments for dividing the group and sending out a scout, but I was against splitting my platoon.

The idea of leaving the injured behind in the corridors seemed too cruel. Sabrael's compromise of leaving two of his stronger warriors with them didn't suit me either. I didn't want to make my already pathetic squad any weaker and smaller. If we're about to die, we are going to die together. I'm still nursing the hope of coming out of these corridors in one piece and maybe, with more supporters.

I've stayed clear of the Sumerian god, unsure what to do with him or how to play that newfound advantage. I haven't decided if that was an advantage yet.

I have another god on my hands and with it another unknown power, another claim over Hell, and probably dreams of Heaven. The game I'm playing complicates with every turn. The chess board is more crowded than ever.

Marching into istana's residence, I don't know what to expect and don't know how we will be greeted. Apart from the istana, none of the angels have been there. We don't know if we're marching as conquerors or liberators. I don't even know if they'll be armed.

During the reshuffle, Sabrael and his brothers, Sam, two Ophanims and the bearded husband of the one push forward.

There's a small scuffle as one of the "floral" girls tries to come forward too, but she is nudged towards the centre by Kafziel, who whispers something in her ear.

To my disappointment, all Lis' friends remain in the centre, even though, their faces are tinted with a healthy pink glow and they haven't broken sweat once during our trek.

Mitish with the Sumerian god and Sarin are sealed inside the circle too.

Sam and I discussed the issue of the Sumerian god and Sarin, and after another quick "pow wow", we agreed that gagging Sarin would not achieve much, nor would the hiding of the god.

For better or worse, I am dragging all of my angels, istana and self-proclaimed gods into this unknown, tying all of us to the same fate.

"Ready?" I ask Sam and Sabrael, and both nod again.

"Redum Usi", Sabrael calls into the platoon. "Get ready. Take your positions."

His brothers, experienced and seasoned warriors, straighten their backs while clinking their heels, the folds of their bright blue wings rise higher above their shoulders.

Following their military training, they raise their weapons, but the two lonely swords look pathetic and non-threatening, whilst the whips hung lifelessly in their hands like flags on a windless day.

"*Du ngir!* Move!" Sabrael calls again.

The first row, formed of me, Sabrael, Sam and Shana, take small steps forward, with Sabrael setting the pace. The platoon moves with us, keeping its tight formation.

Rachiel, the leader of the Ophanims, took Tabby out of Sam's hands before we set out. Now, positioned in the centre of the platoon, she hugs the little body close to her chest as she walks, her lips moving, and when I think that she might be saying a prayer, a soft tune like a lullaby floats to me over the shallow breathing of the scared angels and the shuffling of their feet.

The corridor turns, ending abruptly into the vast darkness that lies ahead.

The draft of stale air strokes my face, moving my hair, indicating an opening ahead, probably with more corridors.

I can't see anything, and apart from that draft, I can't feel any presence either.

My heart pushes at my chest and my mouth dries up. I glance at Sabrael, then turning my head to Sam, who reads me well.

"We don't have to do it", he mouths. His hand finds my fingers, squeezing them.

But he is wrong.

I have to do it. I have to do all of it if I want to survive.

I pull my fingers out of his hold and step forward, into the darkness.

My glow disperses the viscous blackness in a small pool of light, revealing the floor of soil I'm walking on, but my light is not enough to illuminate the room I am in. I feel the open space around me and I can hear the echo of my breathing returning to me with a few seconds delay.

I am in a cave. The damp air slides into my lungs and somewhere deep in the darkness a thin trickle of water runs down a wall.

I shuffle forward and my platoon steps through the opening, coming behind me.

The glow is mine and only mine. Their bodies, no matter how recovered, don't produce a glow in Arllu, Sam had explained to me the bounds were placed on them once they were cast down, especially once the oily parasite had its fill.

I am the oddity here. But it's nothing new to me. I am used to feeling like an odd ball.

I'm straining my eyes but I can't see anything.

"What now?" Sabrael's raspy whisper asks next to me.

"Shana", I whisper and a dark shadow darts to my side, stepping into a pool of light, emerging as her.

"Yes, Mammí?"

"Where are we? Is this it?"

"This should be the Grand Hall, but I've never seen it so dark. Every time I have been here, it was lit up. If it's the right room, more tunnels should be coming off it, and those tunnels will lead to the istana quarters."

"Where are the tunnels? How far? Do we go across and the tunnels will be there?" I ask her.

I can't see shit in here. I'm blind in this cave, yet I'm supposed to lead.

I feel that this room is large, but I don't know how large. I know it's tall, but I'm unable to see its ceiling. I can't see anything apart from the immediate area around us.

Following Shana's very vague directions, I need to find the tunnels and then decide which one to take, choosing the one which will lead me to their elder or at least to more istana.

"Why is it so dark in here?" I mumble to myself.

Then to Shana, "Is there a light switch?"

"Mammí, please forgive me, I don't know what the "light switch" is", she mumbles.

"Can we make it lighter somehow?" I bark.

"I beg your forgiveness, Mammí Barragal. I don't know how to make it lighter."

The glow of my angelic body is all that we have.

I take a breath and turn to my platoon.

"Right", I call in a loud whisper, "this is the place. We've made it to here, we're almost done. There's not far to go. Now we need to find a network of corridors that would lead us to the one we need. The corridors are here and there are many of them. We need to find them. As much as I didn't want us to split, I see no other choice.

"Sabrael and Pronoia will come with me, while the rest of you stay here, by the exit. We will come for you once we find the next tunnel. There's no need for all of us to circle around this room. Kafziel, you're staying with them."

Against my better judgement, I'm splitting the platoon and the weapons. I'm taking one sword with me and some experience, leaving the large group with one sword and plenty of fighting power from the brothers. But I'm leaving non-fighters with them too, taking away their mobility.

Kafziel nods.

"Keep an eye on him", I say, nodding at the god.

Kafziel's gaze follows mine. He looks at me, nodding again. He understood me.

Earlier I spoke to Sabrael, Sam, Pronoia and Kafziel, instructing all four to kill the god if he runs. I wanted to add "or if he tries anything funny", but this instruction would've been so vague, giving them too much cart blanche, that I wouldn't put past them to skew the god just because he sneezed three times in a row. So I've left instruction it as it is.

I pull the two black stakes from the back of my corset. Pronoia lifts his sword, while Sam finds the handle of his whip, wrapping its tail over his wrist. Sabrael doesn't do much as he is already swinging the metal spiked balls by his sides. He walked, swinging them at the ready, since the moment he accrued them.

"We won't be long", I say to the group I'm leaving behind. Once I step away from them, they will be submerged in a complete darkness.

"Shana", I call. She is coming with us and she knows it.

I look at my platoon before we set off.

As my gaze scans the collection of the fearless and scared faces. A weird and unsettling feeling moves at the back of my mind, questioning my call, as if foreboding trouble.

I dash and take a step forward, before I change my mind.

CHAPTER 21

We walk along the wall. My glow illuminates the wall of the soil pregnant with moisture. At every yard a wide wooden plank is nailed to the wall, facing upwards. Another plank joins it, leading higher, joined by another until the line of rotting wood disappears towards the dark ceiling.

I don't know how tall this room is, which had not naturally occurred like a cave, but was made.

Our deep breathing and the heavy footsteps shuffling the dirt is all I can hear for a while, until Sam unexpectedly stops and I bump into his back.

"What? Can you see a tunnel?" I whisper.

Although walking for the last fifteen minutes, we haven't come across a tunnel nor have we completed the circle around the room yet.

He doesn't answer me. Instead, he remains quiet, frowning, glancing around and straining to hear something.

"What?" I repeat.

"Can you hear it?" he whispers.

A few steps away from us, Sabrael and Pronoia, noticing our absence, turn around and walk back.

"Hear what?" I ask.

"Listen... This..."

Sam lifts his finger up and he tilts his head. He is barely breathing.

Sabrael, Pronoia and Shana listen too, while turning on the spot, Pronoia in a slow fighting stance and Shana in a panicked twirl.

I lift my head too and I listen, but I can't hear anything new, nothing out of ordinary.

I hear water glide along the walls, sliding into puddles on the ground, dripping onto the floor in the distance.

But these noises were here before. These noises are nothing new.

"What are –"

My demand dies in my mouth when I hear *it*.

I don't know what it is. Who or what is making this noise. I don't know what it means or why Sam is so interested in it, but the fact that he is unsettles me. It means that this sound shouldn't be here, or that it's not good news.

Sabrael and Pronoia hear it too. I can see it on their baffled faces.

Next to me, Shana lifts her head, scanning the pitch black air above her.

The noise is low and faint, vibrating somewhere in the distance, hidden, yet promising and menacing, and it's getting closer. It's getting louder. It is growing with the approach of *something*.

Sam turns to Shana, grabs her by her shoulder, spinning to face him.

"What lives here? Where have you brought us?" he roars in her face, shaking her.

"What? I don't know. I don't know what it is. I swear to you. I don't know what it is", she cries. "We are in the halls. I'm pretty sure of that. We must be. Please, master! You're hurting me. I swear I don't know."

Her tearful pleas ring in the air, rising with the noise.

"Sam! Stop it!" I hiss at Sam. "Quiet!"

"Stop it!" I call louder. "Both of you!"

They fall silent, raising their heads upwards.

The five of us stand in the wet emptiness of the cave, looking up into the darkness, hoping to see something, to understand what's going on, what's coming for us.

Our shallow breathing is a pitiful accompaniment to the rising, vibrating noise.

In the newly-settled silence, the noise is clearer and it's closer.

I can hear individual strings woven into the noise's pulsating song. Like waves at the shore, it grows louder, crashing over us only for the next second to retreat, to grow duller and fainter.

But with its next wave, I hear many thin noises, forming this one. I hear its every individual screech.

It's the high-pitched buzz of crickets, the pulsating vibration of locusts' knees, a rhythmic, crying hum of living creatures, and there are many of them.

The millions of voices cry and screech in unison. The voices have a living pulse and they are coming closer.

"What is it?"

I turn to Sam, but he doesn't hear me.

"Sam!" I cry out. "What is that noise?"

"I don't know", he mumbles, looking up, around. "I don't know. But I don't like it. It can't be good. I don't like it at all."

He snaps his gaze to me.

"We have to go back, now!"

"But what about the tunnel?" I cry.

"Pagru di mursu sadhu", he screams, "tunnel is the least of our worries right now."

He turns and takes two steps but I catch his arm.

"We don't know what it is", I call to him over the growing noise. "Maybe it's nothing. We can't go back. Where are we going back to? Back into the tunnels, to run? Are you sure we'll manage to outrun this? We have nowhere to go! We are stuck!"

The vibration is growing.

I spin, looking around, *feeling* and hearing the noise but still seeing nothing. It scares me more than I can say, but I won't admit it.

We need to move forward. We need to find a way out of these tunnels. I want to live. I want to see my sister and the blue sky again, and I don't want to die here.

The noise is here. The creatures that make it are here.

I can feel it.

The miles I've walked, the panic I've pushed, the things I've done can't end here. This can't be the end. All that I have done can't end with this. This damp cave can't be my grave.

I am about to plead with Sam, when with a sudden push the pulsating and screeching wave comes over, and I can *feel it* next to me.

I slam my mouth shut and drop my hand, releasing Sam's. My gaze slides over the cave's wall.

I take a frightened step backwards and almost trip.

The soil in the wall ripples under my gaze. It moves in waves, vibrating, coming alive with small dips and hills over its surface. The countless circular waves grow over the surface of the wall as if the wall if made of water.

The soil caves in places, suddenly erupting with millions of miniatures volcanoes, spitting little fountains of soil upwards. The soil moves and vibrates in time with the noise.

I take another step away from the wall as do my companions.

"Uriel! Beyelai Sar!"

Yofiel's voice comes through the screech and vibration.

The large angel roars my name, but his voice is drowned under the waves of the buzzing.

I can't pull my gaze away from the wall.

I watch its breathing life. I listen to its buzz and I can't command my feet to move. I want to see what is making this noise, to see what is coming.

The next moment the wall in front of my eyes explodes with insect heads and I scream.

The insects' heads push through the soil. Their antennae, folded behind their heads, suddenly flop forward when their heads fully emerge.

The insects are fairly small. Their heads are no bigger than the half of my thumb, but there's millions upon millions on them. The soil is alive and crawling with them. As far as my glow lets me see, there's no empty space left, the wall is covered with a live blanket of moving bodies.

The insects in front of me push forward. More of their bodies emerge.

I shuffle backwards and so do the angels next to me.

The insects' bodies are sealed within a hard shell of a beetle, but their shells are colourless and clear, revealing brown bodies beneath their "glass" shells.

The brown bodies work hard. The beetles' legs are moving, pushing the soil, their feelers spinning, scanning the air.

"Uriel!" Yofiel roars.

"I'm here. I'm here", I mumble, unable to draw my gaze away from the living wall.

All the while the beetles push through the soil, the pulsating noise continues, sustaining the same buzz, but one by one the beetles fully emerge, coming forward, sitting on the top of the soil and one by one their screams are dying, until the silence hangs over the cave.

The silence cocoons the air.

It rings after the earlier buzz, and its ring is unsettling.

It vibrates with unnerving, brooding promise. It rings with a warning, and just before I turn to the angels next to me, about to tell them to get the hell out, the beetles as one raise their heads and jump.

The millions of brown bodies under the glass shells are airborne.

With a dull clunk, one by one and in clusters, they land on me, on my hair, my face, my back, my shoulders, and before long my entire body is covered in a layer of busy insects.

The buzz and the pulsating have returned, only this time, their pitch is higher. It's impatient and urgent.

The screams of the two dozen of angels toll in the distance. I scream too.

I wave my arms, trying to shake off the beetles, when the buzz of the insects changes once again, rising to a high, ear-bleeding pitch and millions of teeth sink into my flesh.

I scream, in pain this time.

I shake my arms and my legs, jumping, dancing in agony on the spot.

When my shoes step on the fallen beetles, I hear the crunch of their shells under my feet.

I bring my hands to my face, shaking the beetles off, while countless numbers of hungry teeth sink deeper into my body, through my clothes, into my head, crawling into my shoes.

The beetles are all over me.

They cover my body in a solid layer, and for every few I manage to shake off, many more land on me, taking their place.

Their buzz is impatient and hungry. Their legs and antennae are busy, feeling me, anchoring themselves onto me, while their mouths tear at my skin.

I scream. I bawl.

I feel Sam's essence next to me. I feel his body above mine. His wings are open wide around me. His hands travel over my body, shaking the beetles off me, but insects are still here, crawling, biting and tearing.

I throw my head up and I roar. I roar in agony, and many more voices in pain join mine.

Suddenly, through the closed eyelids, I'm blinded by a bright light. The feeling of a new vibration moves the air. The light and vibration are new and don't belong to the insects.

The beetles on me screech, falling off in clumps like dried dirt. The panicked beetles scatter off my body, but not for long before they drop to the ground too.

The light is around me. I can feel it. It engulfs me, blinding me, and I squeeze my eyes tighter.

The light grows, answering the new vibration, bringing with it a deep and low beat.

The insects screech louder.

A few of them, in a desperate attempt to hold on, sink their teeth deeper into my skin and I roar again.

The light and the vibration suddenly spike.

The beetles' voices scream as they cry in unison.

Their cry rings on one note, rising to the pitch of a glass shattering wave, until it suddenly explodes and silence coats the cave once again.

CHAPTER 22

I nudge my eyes open past the piercing light.

I scan the area around me. The blistering light is mine. It's me, who is glowing, again.

The earlier, softer glow is cranked up to the white light that illuminates the entire cave. It fills the cave, catching on the glass elytras of the beetles sprinkled over the floor, breaking into shards of rainbows and light over their shells.

My gaze drops to the ground, concealed under a layer of dead beetles.

A few beetles screech, trying to turn, to run away from the light that is killing them. But with every passing second, their shrieks grow quieter, until the upper silence swaddles the cave.

I step on the beetles, listening with a satisfaction to the crunch of their shells under my trainers.

I look up at the wall in front of me.

The wall is back to being a boring, earthy wall, although marred now by millions of tiny holes like a sponge.

My gaze travels up the wall and up to the ceiling. The cave is a gigantic, man-made dome, with the planks of wood that I saw earlier, which are fitted into the walls to support the structure. They rise up from the base of the dome, meeting at the top, at the centre.

The dome's circumstance is a size of half of a football field, and the same in height.

The walls and the ceiling of the dome are adorned by decorative sets of wings, and I'm about to look closer at the nearest one, when a weak cry and pained grunts bring my attention to the ground.

I turn my head and cry out at the sight of Sabrael and Pronoia, who are getting up from their knees.

Their clothing is shredded, showing the blooded wounds underneath and their faces are marred with bloody tracks of scratches, bites and chunks of missing skin. Their wings are shredded too. The cornflower blue feathers litter the ground.

The angels' hands are shading their eyes from my light.

I turn to my left, where I last saw Sam.

He is still there, standing, while swinging on his feet, the ground around him littered with his white feathers.

I rush to him and touch his arm.

He turns his face to me and I gasp.

His beautiful face is mangled, with the chunks of skin and muscle missing all over. His piercing blue eyes are glazed with shock, stark against the mutilated face.

He looks at me but I don't know if he sees me.

"Sam", I call him. I want to stroke his face, but I don't risk touching this mess for fear of hurting him more. I scan his shredded clothing with bloodied gaps through it.

"Sam."

His eyes move and he looks at me. His mouth with missing lips moves.

I see muscles and teeth through it. I see the movement of his cheeks. I can see the side of his tongue through the gaping hole in his cheek and I can't help it any longer, I fold over.

I want to throw up, but nothing comes. I keep forgetting that I'm no longer human and human responses don't work for me.

I drop to my knees, then to all fours, crunching the shells of the beetles with my knees and hands.

That crunch pisses me off. It makes me livid and I stamp my fist on the dead shells over and over again.

I breathe, grinding my teeth, holding down the sobs and screams.

I know that I have more angels with me in the dome, and I know they would be injured, how could they not be when Sam looks like that?

I need to get up and walk to them. I need to see their damaged bodies, see the blame in their eyes and stand against it, swallowing the blame, hate, fear and my self-loathing, pushing it down, while whipping myself forward.

"*Get up! You bloody get up! Right now! You get up and see them, see them all and take what's yours! Take everything they'll give you! You've brought them here. All of it is your fault.*"

I sit back on my heels.

I'm afraid to get up, to lift my head, to look at Sam, to meet his gaze, to hear the blame that will come for me, but I must do it. It's my payment for what I've done and where I've lead him.

I slam my fist on the ground once again, and grinding my teeth, I begin to rise.

The footsteps come over, crunching beetles' shells.

"Nintinugga, it's over."

I don't need the sound of the young voice to tell me who is above me. Only one person has called me that.

I rub my face with my hands, hiding the fact that I'm wiping the tears.

I push myself up and rise.

"I know it's done. I'm aware", I bark at the angel.

I turn to face him, about to add more, but my acidic words stop in my throat at the sight of his glowing body.

His light is like mine, identical and just as bright.

His skin is spotless, unsoiled by the bites or gruesome mutilation. My gaze travels over his body, taking in the torn clothing with smooth skin underneath.

I raise my arm to inspect my skin. I remember the bites tearing at my skin. I remember them all over, but my gaze slides over clean, glowing skin.

We look at each other. His gaze is calm and expectant, and mine is confused and dumbfounded.

I speak first.

"What is this?"

I wave my arm over his glowing form.

"That is what rulers of Arllu do. This is who we are."

Glowing torch lights. Of course.

I note his "we are" remark, but I don't ask him any questions. There will be time for that later. That's it if we live.

I turn to the brothers.

Sabrael and Pronoia are up, stamping their heavy black boots on the beetles, as they murmur hateful profanities, spitting on the ground, releasing their rage.

I come over to Sam.

I touch his hand, taking it into mine. His hand is a raw and the skin is missing, exposing muscles and tendons. His hand looks weird and unnatural, like a mock human hand in an anatomy class.

I gently lay my lips on his hand.

"Thank you", I breathe.

I lift my head, meeting Sam's checked out gaze.

"Come", I say, and holding his hand in mine, I gently tug him, leading him towards the wall.

He shuffles his feet like an old man. The fog of confusion is tight around his head.

When next to the wall, I gently push on his shoulder and he slides along the wall to the ground.

I kneel next to him, stroking his soft hair, looking into his frozen eyes.

I lean towards him, pressing my lips to the mimed flesh of his, kissing the space where his lips once were.

I pull away. My lips are wet and I lick them.

The iron taste of his blood slaps me, stealing my breath and blurring my vision.

"God", I whisper.

But I'm not asking for guidance or forgiveness.

I turn my head, looking for another person, searching for another face. I have a taste for blood but it's not for Sam's.

I march to the spot where Shana sits and without warning, I grab her by her shoulder, scooping her on to her feet.

"You knew it! You, little shit!" I roar. "You knew it all along! Who told you to bring us here? Baza? Butcher? What did they promise you? A better corridor to die in? An extra slice of your pathetic slaves' dinner? A mattress? Following the masters 'til the end, are we? Want to die in these tunnels and for your children to die in them too? Chains are too familiar, better than freedom of which you have never heard of?" I scream, shaking her small body.

"Mammí Barragal", she cries, her eyes closed against my light. "Mammí, please. I swear I didn't know. I swear. Please."

Her face and arms are marked with beetles' bites and scratches too, but she doesn't look anywhere as bad as Sam.

I grab a wad of her shirt by her neck and drag her with me, across the brightly lit dome to where I left the rest of my angels.

"Pronoia! Sam", I bark over my shoulder, nodding at the mimed angel next to the wall.

Pronoia looks at me from under his hand and nods.

"Yes, Beyelai."

"And him", I add, nodding at the shining god.

Pronoia squints, nodding again.

I stroll across the bug sprinkled floor. Their shells pop and burst under my trainers.

CHAPTER 23

The angels ahead are weeping.

I walk over crunching shells, dragging Shana behind. Her legs run after me, struggling to keep up. I need to find Mitish too, to demand to know why the god is strolling around like he owns the place, and how long he has been glowing.

My gaze travels up the curved wall of the dome and I stop.

In the bright light of my shine I realise that the sets of the wings on the walls that I took as decorations earlier, are *real* feathery wings of angels.

I slow down until I stop, frozen in front of one heavily decorated wall.

I stare at the wings. My gaze jumps from one to the next.

They are hung on the wall in busy clusters. Some of them smaller are as if they had belonged to a child, whilst some are larger. Some are as big as mine, like Rafe's or Sam's. The tips of the feathers on the wings move with draft in the dome, giving them even more disturbing feel of living wings.

I shuffle closer to the wall.

The wings all are nailed to the wall with thick rusty nails, in the same gruesome fashion, and finally it clicks...

It's a trophy wall.

I turn on the spot.

The wings cover the entire circle wall of the dome. There are thousands upon thousands of them.

It's a trophy room of slaughtered angels... and now I am here.

Shit!

The wings were chopped off bodies with blunt and sharp cuts. Some look as if they were torn off, and I can see the sharp edges of broken bones.

My gaze darts to Sam, to Sabrael and Pronoia. Sam is still on the ground, while the brothers walk next to the wall, gawking at the nailed wings above their heads.

The god stares back at me, unperturbed by the gore surrounding him.

I hold his gaze for a moment, before turning away and look at the crowd of angels ahead, those that I've left to fend for themselves.

Did he know where we were going? Is this room his handy work? He sure is not surprised by it all... And I've brought him here, with us. Shit!

I force my gaze away from the wall and command my feet to move.

The crowd of angels ahead is in muddled disarray.

Most of them with shocked expressions gape at the morbid trophies on the wall, while most cluster within a circle, murmuring to each other.

I come closer.

Sabrael's brothers turn their faces away from me, when I pass them, and I see bites and chunks of missing skin, marring their faces.

The angels in front of me shield their eyes against my glow, shuffling out of my away and opening the circle.

Sablo and Hasdiel kneel inside the circle. Both girls lift their faces to me, their eyes closed, and I have to close my mouth against a gasp at the sight of their once pretty, and now damaged faces.

But they are not the ones who are in the centre. Two bodies lie on the ground past the girls.

Sablo and Hasdiel are helped to their feet by a brother.

"Thank you..." I start saying to him.

"Tagas", the warrior brother helps, giving me his name.

"Tagas", I repeat.

I must learn their names. I must memorise the names of the angels who put their lives on line for me.

The girls step to the side, giving me way.

There are three bodies on the ground: two bodies on the ground are the angels from Lis' crew and one "ancient" angel, rescued with the god. I can tell by their clothing, but the clothing is all that is left to identify them.

Their faces are eaten away and their bodies are the bloody mess of a butcher's disposal bin underneath their torn clothing.

The silver disco ball of a blazer of a male is dull, now washed by blood. The girl's sparkling and glittery mini dress and a few shreds of long blonde hair is all that is left to tell who the victim is.

And I've never learnt their names.

"Tagas."

I turn, looking for the warrior angel.

"Yes, beyelai."

I notice that *"Sar"* has been dropped.

"The beetles did it?" I ask, pointing at the bodies of the angels on the ground.

"Yes", he nods.

"But why them?"

He shrugs his shoulders.

"These things just pounced on them. When the swarm came, at first it settled over us all, but as we begun to move, trying to shake it off, these things turned and dived for these two."

He stops for a moment.

"I can only think it's their clothing", Tagas adds. "As we started dancing around, waving our arms, their clothes begun reflecting light from the beetles' shells, and once they started to descend and settle, the more that came, the more that followed. We were not able to do much then."

"And that angel?" I nod at the body under the rags.

"He was unlucky by being too close to these two and didn't manage to run."

Three more are dead, killed, following me.

I scan my troops. The cluster of angels is pathetic and weathered.

Their number drops with every step we take forward. My soldiers are dropping like flies and if I don't take them to the surface soon, there might be no one left to bring there, to face Baza and Mik'hael.

I've taken them into these corridors to recuperate, to heal, to find us some time and space to breathe, but instead I've injured them, killing two.

I look at the wounded faces of my angels, as some sit against the wall, as they watch exhausted shuffling of a few who meander, lost and confused.

Rachiel sits under the wall, hugging Tabby's face close to her chest, rocking the young body, humming something.

The gazes of the angels dart to the two bodies on the ground, and their faces are grim and sullen.

I turn and look at Sam. His beautiful eyes stare into nothingness.

I have done it. I have killed the ones who agreed to follow me. I promised them the freedom of skies of Uras and instead delivered them into the lethal corridors of Hell, in which we will all rot very soon, dying one by one.

I turn to Shana, sinking my fingers deeper into her shoulder.

"Happy now? Accomplished what your masters have asked you? You've brought us here and more of us are dead. But I hope you asked for payment in advance because you are not going to live long to collect your pitiful reward."

My wings burst open around me, following my emotions.

"Your masters are not here. They can't protect you now, in the tunnels with us. In fact, I know they don't give a shit about you. I'll tell you a little secret, Shana. No matter what the masters ever tell you, no matter the lie they spin, they never give a shit about the slaves. Never have and never will."

My wings flap heavily around me, lifting me off the ground, and I pull Shana with me, my hand refuses to let go of her shoulder.

"You're an animal to them", I roar. "No! Not an animal. Worse! They look after their animals, their pets and their belongings. They care about those. Their pets are rewarded with treats. Masters care about anything that brings them joy, everything but you! You are dirt under their feet, a nuisance, something they have to tolerate to keep their lives going the way they are used to, to the way they are accustomed."

My wings lift us higher. The angels on the ground turn their heads to us, as Shana's screams ring within the dome.

"No, Mammí Barragal. No, please! I haven't... I would never... Please!"

But I don't listen to her.

"You are despised by the masters", I roar, bringing her higher with me, "you're loathed and hated by them. They will use and abuse you. They will abuse your children should their fancy take them. To them, your life counts for less than the life of their beloved pet, and it always will. They'll use you, drain you, squeezing you dry until you can't give any more of yourself, and then, they will let you rot. They'll let you die. Once they're done with you, once you've stopped serving purpose, once you're useless to them. You are nothing to them, and you thought to serve them? You thought to bet on them, wishing to get back into the master's good books? That was the wrong choice, girl! Wrong choice", I bellow.

With every new word, with every fresh wave of hate, my wings lift us higher.

Her hands grab hold of my arm as she screams, as she looks down, her feet dangling above the ground.

I will let her go. In a moment I will open my hand and will let her fall, but before that, I will have some of my questions answered.

"Who told you to bring us here? Who?! Baza? *Him?*"

I point to the god below.

Shana screams louder.

"What is this place? What were those things?" I yell at Shana.

"I don't know, Mammí Barragal! I don't know! I swear to all gods, I don't know!"

Shana cries, screaming under my hold.

"She wouldn't know what the *furgaahtu* are."

A weak, rustling male's voice suddenly calls next to me, under the ceiling of the dome.

If I had been religious, I might have dropped to my knees, certain that a god is speaking to me, but I know better now. I've seen their angels. I've seen their gods. I have one with me and, apparently, we're related.

So instead of dropping to the ground, I turn my gaze towards the voice.

An old man stands in an alcove, cut in the wall of the dome, high off the ground almost under the ceiling.

The man is frail. His hair is grey and long, thinning on the top of his head, running down and spilling over his shoulders in thin spider webs. His slim body is covered in dirty rags.

Two small clear wings move behind his back, the blue veins running underneath the glassy surface.

The man on the balcony could have looked like a leader, if not for his bent back, indifferent gaze under his hand shielding his eyes, and his lethargic voice. He doesn't look or sound like a leader. Instead, he is a parody to Juliet in the famous balcony scene.

"And who are you?" I demand, calling to the aged "Juliet of the underground".

I keep my hold on Shana, while quickly turning my head, scanning the ground, noting the bright light of mine and the god's bodies, the locations of all of my angels, istana and the god himself. My gaze slides along the walls and ceiling, looking for more beetled surprises, but I doubt this particular lightening will strike us twice.

But I expect Butcher's mates. I expect trouble. I expect more trickery and death. Death hasn't stepped far from me since the moment I was born.

"My name is Gil'Amesh", the old man rustles, blinking against the bright light. "I am the Elder of istana and they are my children."

"Ha", I huff a short puff of laughter.

"Isn't it funny how these poor children have two fathers and each as useless as the next. Father here, father there yet your children are dying in packs. But I was looking for you."

"Oi, you! God", I call down, and when the god and a new "father of istana" lift theirs heads, I add: "Here's another father after your flock. Care to check?"

I nudge my head at the male on the balcony.

Following my call, Dšarael opens his four wings and soars up, towards us.

It's the first time I've seen the god using his wings and I'm troubled to see the confidence and ease with which he is flying, beating a solid rhythm with his glass veiny wings.

The god is next to me in no time.

"I am Dšarael", the god announces to the old man. "I'm the eldest son of Ishtar, the rightful ruler of Arllu and the commander and father of all istana."

The god hangs level with the balcony, while I cruise not far from him.

Paying attention to ongoing conversation and eager to see which "father" will claim dominion over the flock, I scoop my arm around Shana's waist and instantly she clings to me, wrapping her legs and arms around me like a vine, bringing with it a punching memory of my sister, hanging on to me just like this in the woods, refusing to let go, wanting my protection, scared of the world around her and... me.

I need to take Shana down but this standoff is not something I am willing to miss.

The frail old man shuffles towards the rail free edge of the balcony.

His eyes are shielded, as he squints, turning his head sideways trying to see past the blinding light of the god in front of him, and the silent moment of studying is replaced with a gasp of recognition, and his milky eyes open wider and his mouth drops.

"My Lord... Belum Irkalli... It is *you*", the old man gasps. "I can't believe it. May Ishtar and her path be bright and her children live long", he recites the long forgotten greeting, as he stumbles a few times delivering it.

"I was a very young boy, my Lord, when I saw you last. Countless *GA* have passed and washed away since then. I have changed but you... you, Belum Irkalli, you remain the same."

The old man bows, and keeping his head down, tries to kneel in front of his god.

But after a few long minutes of granting and shuffling, moaning and mumbling, tired of the unending performance, I step in, interrupting the old man's efforts.

"Gamesh, enough. There's no need to kneel", I call to the old man. "We get it. You are impressed meeting him."

"We all are", I add, mumbling to myself.

"Gil'Amesh, my beyelai", the old man corrects me with another bow.

"Apologies. Gil'Amesh." I repeat his name, pronouncing it just the way the man did and once I finish, the old man turns his gaze to his god.

"It has been GA, Belum Irkalli. You left us. The new Lord was seated, commanding istana, taking the leading from you..."

"None of these were my wishes, Gil'Amesh. But we can speak about all of that later. Right now my aunt, The Great Nintinugga", he nods at me and a cheeky smile pulls at his lips as he says "aunt", "and her *redums* would like a place to rest, and I have promised them the hospitality of istana."

"Of course, Belum Irkalli."

The old man nods.

CHAPTER 24

We are in the place I wanted to be in.

I wanted to meet the Elder, and now he is here.

"What were those things? Back there, the beetles", I ask the old man as we take steep steps carved out of compressed soil upwards.

The tight staircase rises, leading us into the istana headquarters. My exhausted angels shuffle behind me, the dead left in the dome, their stomachs slashed open by a sword the same way the brothers did to Tartys in the corridors.

The injured are carried with us, with Sam swinging between Sabrael and Zabkiel. I still find hard to remember the brothers' names and the identical colours of their wings and clothing, their very similar faces don't make it any easier, but I push myself to use their names more often.

After I brought her to the ground, Shana sprinted away from me, darting scared gazes at me over her shoulder, and after mumbling something to the old man, she disappeared through one of the crude doorways.

I still don't know if I am safe here, or if my angels and I are living the last minutes of our lives. I'm trudging deeper into the corridors of this world, running away from Baza and Butcher, but finding unfamiliar danger. Rafe is not here to steer me away from a cliff edge or to educate me on new creatures I meet, and it's quite possible that my crazy and erratic running, leads me straight into Baza's open arms.

"Isatum Palahu or some call them *furgaahtu*", the old man answers, glancing at me within tight darkness of the staircase. "The new master had infested the soil around the istana's living quarters with these creatures."

I want to ask why, but after seeing what these beetles can do to a flesh, I think I can guess the reason. The new master has put up an electric fence around his slaves either to keep slaves in or the rest of the world out, quite possibly both.

"How do you leave your..." I start and wave my hand around the tiny staircase, looking for a word that wouldn't offend the Elder. But the squalor, underground, bunker or cave is all that comes to my mind. I don't know what to call their living arrangements and not to offend them.

"Area", I say eventually.

"We don't have any need to leave the living quarters, my beyelai. Istana cross the doors of the Grand Hall only under two circumstances: when istana start their duty in an assigned tunnel and when they are called upon into this room for briefing."

"But what about the bugs? How do you move then without being bitten or killed?" I ask.

"The light that the masters bring with them disperses the isatum palahu, allowing our safe passage."

The staircase ends with another curved doorway, and I follow the god and the old man through it.

The walls of the small room are weeping with moisture. The moment the glow of the god bursts into the room, many voices squeal and feet run as I catch a glimpse of dark bodies darting into holes, burrows and tunnels off the room.

Confused by the manic dispersement of the shadows, I spin on the spot.

"I beg your forgiveness, my beyelai", the old man says, raising his milky eyes to me, "istana eyes are not adapted to the bright and glorious light of deities like yourself and Istana's father. I have been almost blind for the last two GA and even I can still see it."

One by one, my angels cross the threshold, filling the burrow.

Some shuffle forward

Some walk in, inspecting the new room, whilst some, exhausted, shuffle in and slide down along the wet wall.

The last to come through are Sabrael and Zabkiel with Sam. Sam's eyes are closed and his breathing is raspy. The wounds on his skin are as raw as they were earlier.

I rush towards them, but both brothers wave me out of the way as they walk towards a wall, laying Sam gently on the wet ground.

"My angels had a very long journey, Gil'Amesh", I say after a deep breath, as I turn to the old man. "As you can see some of them are injured. Can I please bother you for more hospitality? It was very kind of you opening your home to us, but can you please find us some clean water to drink and clean the wounds? And maybe you have somewhere comfortable where they can rest? If you have a medic, who can take a look at the injured, that would've been great too."

"Of course, my beyelai. Istana will see it as a great honour to assist the father of istana and his auntie. We are honoured to have both of you with us. I will send for clean water, but we don't have a healer here, my beyelai. All that our kind is ever required is a midwife who's versed in istana birth giving. We were never required for anything else."

"Don't any of you get sick?" I ask.

"The sick ones die, my beyelai", he replies, nonchalant. "Only the strong children survive past birth, and once they reach ten GA, they leave the Hall for their assigned corridors, never to return. It's their duty to remain in the corridor until their last breath for the glory of our master, who gave us the refuge when Ishtar had abandoned us."

"I'm sorry, Belum Irkalli", he adds, turning to the god.

"We don't have a need for a healer", the old istana continues. "The masters have strict guidance, beyelai. Only the strong should live, living for as long as they earn their keep", he recites.

"Look."

He points to the stone slabs, suspended on thick rusty chains from the ceiling, following the perimeter of the room.

The slabs are of a grey porous stone, marred by deep scars, carved over time by the constantly running streams of water, and each slab holds a unique symbol, a sign.

I spin on the spot, scanning the slabs, counting them. There are fourteen slabs around the room.

As I complete my turn, my gaze slides over the god's face.

A lethal look took over his face, the look I didn't think he was capable of. I thought his entitlement hadn't developed this kind of emotion in him.

He scans the slabs too, rumbling something through his closed teeth.

"Okay, if you don't have any healers just send over a midwife", I say, and answering confused gazes of my angels and the god, I add, shrugging my shoulders, "maybe she'd be able to help. You never know."

"As you wish, beyelai."

The old istana bows and keeping his bent back folded, he plods through a low archway and out of the room.

Once he leaves, the room is quiet.

The shallow breathing of my angels is the only sound left.

I come over to Sam, kneeling on the wet dirt next to him. I listen to his laborious breathing for a moment, before I shuffle on my knees towards the wall, and sitting against it, I lift Sam's head onto my lap.

I stroke his hair caked in mud, watching his mangled face.

The earlier shock at the damage done to his face has worn off.

I begin to realise that I'm shocked less at the brutality of this world, and even when it arises, it doesn't last long, prompting shallow rippling emotions on the surface, settled soon by another shockwave of a new brutality.

This murderous and cruel world is changing me, but I don't know what to do with it. I don't know if I should mourn the loss of my humanity or rejoice in the chance of surviving in this world, maybe even winning against it.

The god still stands in the middle of the room, head up, reading the slabs, his lips moving with the words and his hisses.

"Don't like it, huh?" I call to him. "Don't approve of a Hell's new management? Not how you left it? Don't worry, you always can fill in a comment card, point out areas for improvement. Who knows, maybe one day Baza will introduce free education and healthcare for your children", I tease him.

"There are many words that I don't understand in what you're saying, but I can understand when I'm being ridiculed", he answers.

I lift my gaze to him and shrug my shoulders.

"Maybe a bit. But honestly, mate, what did you expect? What did you think would happen once you were gone?"

"I haven't had a chance to think or object to anything, being bound to a snake", he bristles.

"Suppose, that's fair."

I stay quiet for a moment, scanning my angels around me. None of them is looking at me. When their gazes clash with mine, they turn their heads away.

Their regret is clear.

The god is about to add something, when the old istana shuffles into the room, his hand shielding his eyes.

Two shadows dart behind him.

The shadows are small, folded on themselves and after a moment watching their erratic movements, I realise that they are young istana, two children dressed in rags with see-through veiny wings behind their bent backs.

The children are scared and confused. Their small hands cover their eyes, protecting them from my and god's light.

"Tarkan and Halish have brought some water", the old man announces.

My gaze slides over the small bodies only now noticing large sacks hanging on their fronts, like back to front backpacks.

"And midwife?" I ask, stroking Sam's hair and darting my gaze over damaged faces of Sablo, Hasdiel, Sabrael and others.

"She will arrive here once the birthing ritual is over. The mother shouldn't be much longer..."

But he doesn't finish the sentence as the god marches forward.

"What have you done to yourself?" the god barks at the Elder. "What have you done with my gift? What is this place? Why did you come here? How could you?"

The god's voice grows louder and angrier.

"How could you submit yourself to him? Is this the way I taught you? Is this what you were created for: to hide under the ground and die like menkurrum?"

The god's voice booms in the tight room.

My angels gape at him, while the old istana takes a few steps away, towards the hole he came from, his back bending lower, his little helpers disappeared through the hole already.

"Oi", I call to the god, but he doesn't hear me, striding closer to the old man.

"Oi!" I yell louder, lifting Sam's head off my lap and getting up.

I come between the god and the old man, facing the god.

"Lay off of him!"

And as the god takes another step forward, I take step forward too and place my hand on his chest.

"Back off, now."

I feel the godly muscles roll under my hand. He is definitely recovering fast, and very soon I would need to think about eliminating this threat too.

"Not now and not here", I say, and dropping my voice, I add, "you will not change the past with your screaming, but we need him. *I* need him and all of them."

I nudge at his chest, before turning around to the old istana.

"My *nephew* didn't mean it. We are grateful for your hospitality, but as soon as you've arranged everything for us, can I please have a word with you?"

Gil'Amesh glances at me and after a moment of delay, after his gaze scans the god's face, he bows at me and answers: "As you wish, beyelai."

CHAPTER 25

The old istana have offered to us the use of his cubbyhole, but after seeing where Shana and Mitish used to sleep, I politely declined his offer. Instead I asked him if we could return into the room where we met, into the Grand Hall.

Taking a step onto the room's floor and under the accompaniment of a morbid crunch of beetles' glass shells, I walk towards the centre of the large hall.

The tip of a long black fiery sword I borrowed from Kafziel drags along the ground behind me.

I lift my head up towards the dome ceiling, listening to the footsteps of two men behind me: the large strides of the god and shuffling tired scuffles of old Gil'Amesh.

Earlier, while coming down here, I've noticed an angel feather tucked in at the rope that encircles Gil'Amesh's waist. The long feather was glowing with a weak pearly light.

I've spent so many days underground in these tunnels now, that I barely notice the smells of air: of mildew, earth and stagnant water.

I close my eyes for a moment, trying to remember the smells of my town, of my previous life: the smell of sea salt at the pier, the smell of fish and chips on the Friday night, the smells of my home and the soft smell of my sister. I try to pull the memory of Rafe's smell of tropical fruits.

But I struggle to bring any of them forward. The smells of the underground had weaved into my memories and me.

I haven't seen Shana since she disappeared through one of the arched pathways. Mitish stayed in the room with us and so did the tied up Sarin.

I saved Sarin's life, by promising the brothers that we need him as leverage, promising that he will help us secure safe passage, but now, after speaking to the old istana, I doubt that the old man would do anything to preserve Sarin's life should I threaten it. I doubt any of his kind will jump to his defence if I had brought a knife to his throat.

The masters made sure to indoctrinate into istana's heads that their lives hold no value, and it seems that the message took hold, being drummed so often into the servants' heads.

My leverage appears to be useless now, and I see that the brothers are clocking it too, and it's only a matter of time before they will demand their vengeance.

"What's with the feather?"

I turn and ask Gil'Amesh, once I hear the old man's raspy breathing, pointing at the feather tucked in behind his belt.

"This was given to me, my beyelai", he answers, bowing, darting his gaze to me and then to the god.

"By whom?"

"By the masters, beyelai."

Another darted gaze towards the god, before he corrects himself: "By our current, unlawful masters that took us away from the leadership of yours, Belum Irkalli."

He bows to the god.

"Why would you be given this?" I ask, ignoring his sycophancy.

"To give us some light as we move, my beyelai."

I nod. I raise my head toward the ceiling, and after standing like this for a moment, I walk to the place where Sam and I stood, where he protected me from the beetles, covering my body with his.

The ground is sprinkled with shards of broken insects. The shards are tiny, almost powder in places, as if gone through a peppermill.

I lift my gaze to the trophies on the wall, towards the angel's wings cut root and stem out of someone's body.

"And what about these?"

I point to the wings on the wall.

The trophy wall is strangling and encircling me, taunting me and my mortality, as an absolute reminder that no one is immortal in this world, not even immortal angels.

"I don't know, my beyelai", the old man rustles. "They have appeared over time, a few at a time. When the m –", he breaks off.

"When the unlawful masters", he corrects himself, "who nefariously have seized Belum Irkalli dominion, when they would call us into this hall for new instructions or for parade flogging, there will be more wings nailed to the walls. I do not know where or from whom they were acquired."

But after seeing Baza's punitive system, I can guess it very well.

Baza's tunnels are bursting at the seams with imprisoned angels, and surely, this old istana would know it too, if he cared to know or think.

I take a breath, ready to start the conversation I brought him here for.

"As your *real master*, the father of all istana have returned", I start, "it is the time for istana to leave these tunnels, this life and the rule of *unlawful* masters and to come with us."

I emphasise the "real master" and "unlawful" as I face the old man.

"Your father is here now. The great son of Ishtar has returned, and I have brought him to you", I continue. "I saved his life and I saved him from his eternal imprisonment. He owes me his life and eternal gratitude."

This old man needs to know who is in charge here. He needs to understand who holds reigns, so he relays it correctly to his flock. There will be no mistake as to who is in charge.

I am not going to hand over the advantage I've gained.

I am calling the shots right here and right now. I will be the hand that moves them on the chess board, irrelevant of the names they give themselves and each other. I will lead and make decisions. They will follow my call. They will answer my needs.

I am in charge and I'll take down every single one of them if I have to.

I don't look at the god. I don't need to. I don't care how he feels about my proclamations. I don't care if he agrees or if he has a problem with this statement.

I intend to use him as long as he serves a purpose or for as long as he stays in line. I hope he knows it, and if he doesn't, he will soon find out.

"I saved your god and he is not the first person I've saved. But there are more whom I killed", I say, watching the old man's face, holding a pause.

"Your god chose to align with me. He follows me now and you are following him. Istana have pledged to follow their father, him", I point to the god, "and if you follow him, you are following me."

The old istana darts his gaze from me to the god, his panicked gaze looks for assurances.

To some degree, I feel sorry for him.

Trodden down, he is no longer his own person, just like his people. Pushed from one master to the next, handed over like belongings, he has no say over his life or the lives of his people. He and his people are abused and enslaved. Their lives cost nothing to any of the masters.

But that's where the "feeling sorry" ends.

For generations they've submitted themselves to the masters, to the one next to me and then to the one, who took over. Generation after generation, they gave birth, releasing their precious children into the abusive hold of Butcher and his mates.

The istana haven't fought. They haven't jumped at the master's throats, demanding lives and freedom for their children.

The memory of Shana's screams in the tunnel, when Butcher's soldier was beating her, comes to my mind. "The scheduled beating" she said.

They sold themselves and they have sold their children with it.

They have chosen a longer life, instead of a free life.

"But that is what a master would say. That's what a master would demand. But I am not your master and I don't wish to be one. Although your father is here, I'm not asking you to submit to him. I don't even ask you to follow him. I *invite* you to follow me."

The old man gawks at me, not saying a word.

I try to say it differently.

"Aren't you sick of living like this, Gil'Amesh? Living in these tunnels, never seeing a day light? Selling every newborn of your people to the masters, to work in tunnels, to be submitted to a scheduled beating, starving, to be punished, tortured? Do you want continue watching the wings of istana whither into nothing, until you are no more than a bunch of worms?"

The god has told me that once istana had wings like his, the see through and veiny, but strong and large enough to lift their bodies off the ground, to hold them in the air. The synthetic blue sky of Arllu, that spreads around Baza's place, used to be theirs. The charred and burnt out land, now filled with industrial buildings, was once populated with istana. There were no lizards there. The istana ruled Arllu.

"I am offering you what is yours by birth. I am offering you something that should belong to everyone, it is their freedom. I can't give you your Arllu back, but I'm offering you a new home. I am *inviting* you to come with me. Not to follow into more slavery or submitting your lives and the lives of your children to another master, but come with me, freely, come with me into Uras. I am inviting you to come with me as free people, to live next to me, in my place as equals.

"There's plenty of space for everyone. I have plenty of room for us all. There will be no more masters, no more flogging. Relinquish your masters, leave them behind and come with me. I offer you safe sanctuary, equality and... freedom."

I glance at Dšarael, but he doesn't interrupt and he doesn't object.

"You will be free in Uras, all of you", I say to the old istana.

The old man either doesn't understand my offer or he doesn't believe it as his head turns from the god to me, then back to the god. His stunned gaze jumps from my face to Dšarael's as he doesn't say a word.

But I don't rush the old istana. He needs time. He needs to think and I need to keep quiet. I can't sound desperate or needy. This decision should be his and he must want it.

Eventually Gil'Amesh speaks.

"But, my beyelai..." he mutters. "Nintinugga Sar..."

"Belum Irkalli..." he turns his head, pleading with the god.

Gil'Amesh turns his head to me.

"H-how is this possible? I don't understand... How this can be done?" he stammers. "Have you spoken to the masters already? Have they agreed to this?"

But as I stay quiet, glaring at him with my lips pressed tight, he drops his voice and whispers: "Do they know about this?"

I don't say a word, watching him, waiting for a penny to drop, and finally his strangled gasp relays his understanding.

"What are you proposing?" he whispers. "If they hear of this... If they ever find out... They will kill us all. They will put you back into the tunnels, Nintinugga, and then they will kill many of us! That's right. Shana told me where she found you, and you must know there will be punishment! You have experienced it first hand, and there will be more, a lot more! There will be so much pain that you will beg to be returned into the tunnels! Your wings will be on this wall!"

He takes a step away from me and my crazy ideas.

"The masters will never release us. They will never grant us freedom. We will be dead before we cross this room. They will never let us leave. They will kill us all."

The old man rambles, as he takes another step back.

"You have to leave now! All of you! Take the istana that you have brought with you too. I want nothing to do with you. I don't need any of this. You will get us killed. Just get everyone and go! I will not tell them that you've been here, but if they come looking, I will not risk a lie. I will have to tell them everything you have told me, but you can leave now. You still have time. Please. Leave."

He is scared. The beetles crunch under his feet as he keeps progressing backwards. But I take a few long strides forward, crossing the distance between us.

"We are not going anywhere, Gil'Amesh", I cut off his pleading. "We have nowhere to go."

I shrug my shoulders.

"We will stay here, with you, and when your masters come, looking for us, I will tell them that it was *you* who helped me to escape", I say, smiling at the old istana.

"I will tell them it was you who saved your "father" and has brought us here. I will tell Baza that you planned it all along. I will tell him that you're planning to overthrow him and that you're plotting against him and his glorious rule."

I smile at the old man, and the longer I talk, the paler grows his face, as my heavy promise sinks in.

"But that's not true", he heaves. "They will never believe you. I will tell them. I will explain. They will believe me. They trust me", he rushes. "I have never betrayed my master. I've served him well. He will believe me, I know he will. If I explain it to him... If I only explain, he will believe me..."

The old man rumbles and his heated words begin to leave him in a confused jumble, which I struggle to understand. He has begun begging for his life with the masters already.

"Believe enough to keep you alive?" I interrupt his hysterical preaching, "enough not to decorate this wall with your pathetic wings? You are the one who is responsible for all istana if I'm not mistaken. You are in charge. Everything that happens here is your responsibility. Your head will be the first to roll."

The smile on my lips grows wider as Gil'Amesh's frightened gaze collides with the steel of mine.

I am not bluffing.

"Baza knows me", I say. "We've met. Not only does he like me, but he *needs* me."

I wave my hand.

"I will cry, telling him in glorious detail how you've freed me, bringing me here against my will and how scared I was, as I didn't want to come. I'll tell him how you were looking for your old "Father", how much you wanted him to grant you your freedom, how desperate you were to find the Ishtar's son. I will tell Baza about your plans that you shared with me to unseat him, to kill him, to kill all of them, and I will tell him how shocked I was to learn of it. I can make you dead, Gil-Amesh, every one of you."

My smile is promising, whilst my voice is soft.

"But…" the istana stammers, looking for a rebuttal. "If you were bound by Baza then you are not favoured by him anymore. He will kill you."

"He might", I agree, tilting my head to the side, "but he might not, especially if I convince him it wasn't my fault. Or he might kill me straight after he pulls *your* head off of your shoulders."

I take a step closer with a crispy crunch of beetles' shells.

My face is close to the istana's face now. I can smell mildew on his clothing and I can see the skin through his thinning hair over his scalp.

"But we can leave now", I say, dropping my voice, "pack up and leave. Right now. Before he even gets here. No one needs to die, but only if you come with me, bringing all istana. Think about it for a moment, Gil'Amesh. What am I really offering you? A better life, freedom, no masters, a new home. There are much worse offers that could be given to you, so if you really think about it, you are getting a very good deal."

The old istana glares at me and his thought is splashed over his face: *"I should've sent you away when I had the chance."*

"Even if you would have sent us away", I say, "you and I would still have been in the same position we are now. We would still have been here."

"Look at it from this angle, Gil'Amesh. Sometimes things happen, happen to you and not all of them are good. Sometimes they are so bad that all you can do is scream, asking "why me". Most of the time you get no answer, you get no help from anyone. You're left to fight through it on your own.

"But no matter how hard and burning the suffering is, there's one good thing that comes out of all pain: that pain makes you stronger. Sometimes it teaches you a lesson, but more often than not, it teaches you how to survive. Pain and suffering are great teachers. The corners you are forced into sometimes can protect your back better than people. When you fight on your knees, sometimes you can hit them where they are not expecting, you can reach deeper. When you fight on your own, you learn to fight dirty and fight with all you've got. But it's only if you fight…

"That pain only helps if you fight, with everything you've got, but *fight*! Once you stop, once you lay down, the pain and suffering will take over and that will be the end…

"Gil'Amesh", I say, "I promise you one thing, I will fight. I was always fighting and I always will be, and this little situation is no exception. If Shana has told you where she found me then ask her how I freed myself. Ask her how I freed every angel in the two corridors, how I haven't abandoned my followers. And while you're at it, ask her about your Father of Istana's little disclosure. Ask her how istana lives are tied to his, and then, with all information available to you, ask yourself if you should risk pushing someone like me, if you would stand a chance against me."

I wrap my other hand over the sword's handle, lifting the sword off the ground.

I point the tip of the fiery sword at Gil'Amesh for a moment, watching his scared face, before I turn to my right.

The sword draws its trajectory with me, stopping in front of the god's chest.

I gaze at the old istana, giving him a moment to process my threat.

Then after a few heartbeats of silence, I bring the sword down, listening as it sears the ground full of insects.

"I want every single istana in this hall within two days", I call to the old man over my shoulder. "You will contact them, telling them to come here, but you do not tell them why."

I turn to the god.

"Come on, dear nephew. We need to rest. We have a long journey ahead of us."

As I walk out of the room, I begin to hum a song, as I'm listening to the crunch of the beetles under my feet and the short pulls of the tip of the sword through their dead bodies behind me.

CHAPTER 26

I left the old istana behind, in his hall.

He needs to think on my propositions, promises and threats. I hope he is smart enough to see the benefits of the offer presented to him, but if he can't, then I will handle him another way.

I need the entirety of the istana numbers behind me, and if I don't get them to submit to me and follow me, I will die in these god forsaken tunnels, but only with him dying first.

"Nintinugga, with all due respect, but what you've said there, earlier to Gil'Amesh...They are *my* children to command, not yours. You should have spoken to me first", the god hisses behind my back as we are climbing the tight staircase.

"Finally", I say, turning my head and glancing at the god. "I thought you'd never speak up. I could feel you were brewing since we left the hall."

I wait until we're in the open space of another corridor, before I talk to him.

"This offer is not exclusive to them. You are very welcome to come to Uras with me, nephew."

Dšarael is a young god, but only in appearance.

I know that all of them have existed millennia upon millennia before my ancestors were born. They were born long before myths were written. Some myths and stories within sacred books are written *about* them. They are the ancients of many worlds, creatures so old that many have forgotten of their existence.

His young face with a healthy glow under his caramel skin stares at me when he says: "Maybe I don't want to come to Uras, auntie. Maybe I want my people and my land back. Maybe I want to stay here. Have you thought of that?"

I have to remind myself that it's not a young man that stands in front of me, and that it's not a teenager whinging I hear, even if it's uttered in a young voice.

I need to remember that I am dealing with ancient and wise creatures who ruled Heaven and Hell, possibly Earth, way before the first people learnt about fire.

I nod at him with acceptance and understanding.

"I apologise if you think I should have spoken to you, but that was one of the decisions I had to make to keep us alive, including you. We are facing a real threat, Dšarael. Baza is on our trail, and I don't know how long we'll manage to outrun him. Honestly? I don't think for much longer. But what's worse is that Baza and Mik'hael are talking to each other now. The need to eliminate me has united them."

I pause, watching his reaction.

"You're very welcome to stay here once we've dealt with Baza", I say, "but I don't see how you can stay here currently, if you want to live. I need your people to stand against Baza, to get rid of him once and for all."

The god glares at me in the darkness of the tunnel for a minute, before he utters: "The Istana are mine. If you needed them, you should have spoken to me."

Here we go again. Stubborn much, little god?

The smile pulls at my lips.

"When I found you, Dšarael, you were not particularly ruling the roost. In fact, if I remember correctly, you were swinging off that thingy, covered in a thick layer of dust. So I would be safe to assume that you had been there for a while, which illustrates my point exactly, that you were there for god knows how many years before I showed up and rescued you, and if I hadn't have, who knows how many more years you would have swung there. So if it's all the same to you, you need to pipe down and get on with the programme. I am not interested in your istana. I'm not interested in Hell. I'm not interested in being another master, but after seeing what I've seen, you'd be major asshole if you don't let them leave when and how they want."

I shake my head.

"I know you're a god, son of what's her face, ruler of Arllu and so on and so forth, but so am I, if you'd forgotten. While you were swinging off the ceiling, I was living life out there. While you were resting, I was trekking through *your* Hell. Trust me, it's no longer the place you left and remember. It has changed. It's no longer your domain. It was taken from you by force, so if you want it back, you'll have to apply the same force in obtaining it. Baza is not going to give you your land. Surely you accept that?"

I glare at him. He needs to understand that the numbers are not in his favour.

"I don't want Arllu. I have no need for it", I say. "Once I'm done with Baza, and Mik'hael, if you wish to retire to the scorched landscapes of this hell hole then be my guest. But for now, dear nephew, a little advice, don't piss off your angry aunt, who is angrier and stronger than you are. It will not end well for you. So I suggest, mate, you think twice before opening your mouth again with all of the hysterics and demands. I will cut you out of my inheritance and will let you rot here. Remember, I need your people but I don't need you. I only keep you alive because you're attached to them, or them to you, so for now, butt out if you want to survive past the next few days."

I turn to walk away from him.

So much for being diplomatic. Shit.

I stop, then turn around and walk to him.

"And, Dšarael, another bit of advice, take it or leave it, of course. But drop that crap with "my people". Seriously, not only do you not own them anymore, but they would love you more, hell, they'd *worship* you, if you gave them their freedom. Can you imagine? "The god, who freed all his children". They will write stories about you, maybe songs too..."

I stop for a moment, letting this new idea to brush over him.

"You don't have to own them. All you need to do is care for them. That's just a thought."

And trying to lift up the mood and to take the sting out of everything I've said, I add with a lopsided smile: "The free advice from your aunt, from the height of her life experience."

I don't tell him that once they are out of here, the istana will be free. Free from him and from Baza. I don't tell him that they will stay with me in Uras, as I plan to fulfil my promise. I need them far more than he does. I need an army and they need a place to stay, it will be a perfect arrangement for everyone. And once they've made Uras their home, they will fight until their last breathe to defend it against anyone and anything, who would threaten it. Free people who have something to lose fight far better than slaves under a master.

And if needed, I will duplicate the god's residential arrangements during the Baza's rule. I'm not above it.

But I've said plenty already, so I keep these plans to myself.

I need to learn how to play dumb better.

"Shall we?" I chirp, threading my arm through his and pulling him towards a small room where we've left my angels.

* * *

The angels are in the room where we've left them.

As soon as we arrived, the two istana that were called into the room by Gil'Amesh to assist, squeal, slamming their eyes shut, dropping the bowls of water, and blindly scatter out of the room, bumping into the walls and bodies of my angels on their way out.

I scan the lit up room, noticing Mitish and Sarin, sitting under a wall, but away from each other. And whereas Mitish jumps to his feet and blossoms at Dšarael's arrival, Sarin grows gloomier at the sight of us.

Sabrael and Pronoia rise from the floor, coming to us. Kafziel rises too, probably coming to collect his sword.

When the heavy hilt of the sword lays into Kafziel's palm, a long breath of relief leaves him and the wrinkles smooth over his face.

Mitish shuffles, drawing circles around us, looking into Dšarael's face, a content smile plastered over his face as he's waiting to be acknowledged by the god.

"Do you want to start the ground work?" I ask Dšarael, nudging my head towards a smiling Mitish. "You can start preparing your istana for departure. Maybe test drive the idea of freedom, to see how it will be received, although you have a very friendly audience here."

Back in the tunnels I noticed the dedication with which Mitish cared for the forgotten god, how obsessed I heard he was, looking after Dšarael without knowing him, seeing only an exhausted blood-stained face and the grey hair of an old man. During the trek, it became apparent how smitten Mitish is with the god, but now every new step and passing minute it becomes clearer, and I begin to wonder if Mitish is in love.

Mitish couldn't get close enough to the god, consuming every word coming out of the god's mouth, whilst using every opportunity to touch the god's body, even if only to rub shoulders in the tight turn of a tunnel, so eager to assist, to please.

I think I'm witnessing the blossoming of new love.

"Mitish, is it?" The god asks, and Mitish's face beams brighter with a light of shared love. All Mitish can manage is to rapidly nod his head in response, unable to speak or to believe his luck.

"I would like to talk with you, if you're not pre-occupied with anything pressing", Dšarael says, receiving in return a frantic shaking of the head, Mitish's face is pure elation.

This guy absolutely adores the god.

Once both leave the small room, I turn my gaze to the mingled faces and bodies of the angels around me.

Sablo's and Hasdiel's beautiful faces are not as mauled as the others. The bodies and faces of the male angels are riddled with deeper injuries.

A few males, the bearded husband of Ophanim, the angel of the record-keeping and a couple of brothers carry the most damage to their backs and wings, with some wings shredded almost to the bone just like Sam's, and with the pattern of that damage, I wonder if they were covering others with their bodies too.

Sabrael follows my gaze.

"The injuries are not healing, Beyelai", the brother booms.

"Do you know what these beetles were? Have you seen them before?"

The first step in treating a wound is to understand the animal which inflicted it.

"Nay, my beyelai. In all my time in Arllu, I have never come into contact with these, and I have never heard of them."

"Gil'Amesh said that Baza had infected the hall with those, to keep the istana in and uninvited guests out", I share information.

"Why their essences are not healing them?" I ask after another sweeping gaze over the room.

"A dinnae ken", Sabrael says, shrugging his shoulders. "As I said, I've never came across these thingmie before."

Another trip down shit creek without a paddle.

I sigh. I don't know what to do now or how else to heal my angels if Sabrael doesn't know. I can't contact Baza, asking for help, looking for an antidote.

Suddenly I feel very home sick, although not for the home I left on Earth, but for the safety of Uras.

"I wonder if these thingmie have attacked their Qals", Sabrael says, musing to himself. "It must have damaged the Qal somehow if the essence doesn't heal..."

With the talk of the Qal, Amy's pissy voice comes to mind with her lectures on the Qals and of her healing equipment of choice, the black healing orb that healed the Rafe's Qal.

"Sabrael, listen, do you know this thing..."

I click my fingers, trying to remember the word.

"You know... It's an orb, black orb, but sometimes it lights up, and when you put it to the universe above, it gets energy from there, sending it then to your Qal..."

My rushed words are muffled and confused under Sabrael's gaze.

"Beyelai?" he asks, his gaze searches mine.

But I wave him off.

"Listen, I'm not going crazy, I promise. Have you ever seen a black orb, anywhere? It heals angels. Have you seen any?"

Silently, with eyes wide, he shakes his head "no".

"Okay, if you haven't seen it then it's really pointless asking you if it will work here", I mumble, waving my hand at the big man.

I turn my back to him, taking a step forward then another.

"I would need to ask someone who knows, Amy for example, but she's not here", I mumble, talking to myself. "But this orb might work. It might. Of course there's the question of how much of this energy thingy all of them would need, and if there's any of it left in the orb at all or if Rafe had used it..."

I keep speaking as I walk, my gaze sweeps the ground.

"Let's hope he hasn't and there's still some, at least enough for a few of them or for the stronger fighters, 'cause once we're through the Gate and into Uras, I will get them shed loads of this energy. Of course if it works... But even if it doesn't, when I get them into Uras, Amy will think of something, one way or another. There's a reason why Uriel kept her. Amy was probably the best in her class, hence the attitude, but I like her... Domiel is funny tho, and Dumah is adorable too in his silent way... I hope they're keeping Jess safe, even if Rafe hasn't made it back to her... But the sphere might just work..."

Suddenly aware of the silence, I close my mouth and lift up my head. I turn around and my absent minded gaze collides with worried and quizzical gazes of the angels and istana in the room. Everyone is listening to my mumbling.

I clear my throat.

"I think I might have a solution for the injuries, but first, we need to get out of here, which we can't do until I've seen and spoken to all of the istana. I'm sorry, but we need to wait a bit longer. I am very sorry", I say.

"But once we're out of here, we'll get straight to the Gate and from there it is only one second jump to Uras. We're almost home."

I don't tell them that it wouldn't be that easy. I don't think Baza will let us leave without a fight.

CHAPTER 27

The next two days were tedious and long.

A few times Gil'Amesh came in, playing the good host, asking if we needed anything. But his gaze was avoiding mine and his lips were sourly pressed.

But his istana kept on coming at regular intervals, bringing fresh water and clean, to a degree, gauzes, each time opening their eyes a bit wider to the bright light in the room.

My body was continuing to glow, but after a few attempts at dimming it, I gave up on it, deciding instead to concentrate my energy on helping the wounded angels and rehearsing my speech for the upcoming istana gathering.

Once, a fat woman plodded into our room, announcing with a bow that she is a midwife and is here to inspect the wounded. But when after the "inspection" I asked her if she could help them or if she knows what would heal them, she just shrugged her shoulders, confirming what I had suspected all along, that she doesn't know much about angels.

Shana hasn't come once, but Mitish hasn't left the side of his god even for a moment. A few times I spotted them sitting at the farthest side of the room, talking in hushed voices, Dšarael waving his hand above their heads, gazing dreamily upwards at the black ceiling of dark soil, and Mitish, following the hand of the god with his eyes, smiling.

I spent all my time in that room with my angels.

In a tight dark room and constantly confronted by my mistakes, failed responsibilities and broken promises, the guilt had very nourishing soil to grow in. Every second and at every turn of my head, I was reminded of the dangers of the road I've chosen, of the danger and damage I was inflicting on others.

One day, I called a meeting with Sabrael and Pronoia. Rachiel came over to represent the Ophanims and to hear what I had to say. When I asked Sablo if she wanted to be present, she shook her head, declining the invitation without further word.

I briefed the three angels on my plans concerning istana, explaining why we are still here and what we're waiting for. I explained that waiting for istana was the last step in my plan to build an army, and after that, we would be able to get to Uras, fingers crossed, in one piece.

I told them about the god, about Rafe, Domiel and Dumah, who are waiting for me, and of a few loyal angels in Uras.

But I've kept a few things from them.

I haven't mentioned to them the size of Baza's army I witnessed in Uras, or of the little pact that he and Mik'hael have made to annihilate me. I might tell them about it later, but I might not tell them at all.

The three angels listened to me and haven't interrupted once. They stood there, their faces thoughtful and broody, while they were taking all of the information in. There was no emotion, not during my little speech nor after. Once I had finished, the three bowed to me and, without a word, walked away, probably to deliver to their kin of how deeply screwed we are in juicy detail.

Now I sit on the ground with my back against a damp wall. My bottom wings are underneath me and the top wings are wrapped around mine and Sam's bodies.

Sam's head rests on my lap as I stroke his soft hair, playing with its silky waves. The mauled side with a gashing gap in his cheek is away from me, and looking at his face from this side, I can pretend that he is sleeping.

But my thoughts, prompted by my guilt, keep drifting to the path of destruction I left behind.

The quest for safety and owning one's place under the sun had turned into a bloodier path than I'd expected. Rafe, Jess, Chamuel, Lis, two of her angels, the grey soldier, who died in my hands, many of Butcher's minions, the list of the victims to my desire to be free is growing, and I'm pretty sure that many more will follow them.

I'm making a great start, covering plenty of the ground to be worthy of "The Harbinger of Doom". No one is as bloody as me. No one makes blood rivers run faster. Even my followers are not safe with me.

But I don't know what else to do or how else to fight. I don't know how else I can stay alive.

"Maybe you shouldn't?" my mother's voice whispers in my head for umpteenth time, mocking me.

"I need to look after Jess. I need to keep her safe."

"So you said. And how is that working out for you? Or for her?"

I'm about to begin arguing, when a voice calls: "Beyelai Sar... Uriel."

I lift my gaze up to Sabrael who stands above me.

"Can we have a word?" he barks and I nod.

"Sure. Slide down next to me", I say, and then add, "Unless you want privacy?"

"Nay, Beyelai Sar. We can speak here."

He sits down on the ground next to me. His gaze darts to Sam's hair, wrapped around my fingers but he makes no comment.

The brothers are very tactful. Maybe Uriel is excused for any behaviour, or maybe only to a point.

"We need weapons, Uriel", Sabrael says. "We can't fight like this."

He waves his hand around the room, calling on me to witness the sorry state of my platoon.

"I know, Sabrael, but like this", I say as I glance behind him at the exhausted angels on the ground, "is the only way left for us to fight. Although, I agree with you about the weapons, we need them, but at this point, these angels are not going to manage another detour. They are barely walking."

I nudge my head at the body of comatose Sam on my lap, to the angels sprinkled in the room, clustered in small groups and by one, sitting, waiting.

Sabrael is quiet.

"The idea to find weapons and get ready to fight was floating before most of us got mauled", I continue. "This attack has changed everything. Now we need to get out of Arllu as fast as we can, and I need to find the way to heal them, then take them to safety and pray that when Mik'hael comes, we are ready and able to fight."

"Beyelai, I am not proposing a "de-to-ur"", he answer, churning the last word in his mouth, "for everyone. Isnae my plan. I know it won't be possible, but we need weapons nonetheless. I propose going into Baza's armoury and recover as many weapons as I can find and carry."

"On your own?"

I study his face.

"I will take Sabaoth. He knows the place better than anyone. He was commanding one of Baza's battalion of malakhims. He knows where the armoury is, how it's guarded and the best way getting there undetected."

I sigh, keeping my eyes on him, although they are desperate to roll at his ridiculous proposal.

"Sabrael, you do realise that since I arrived and you've jumped ship, there will be tighter security? I was told that Baza already has brought his troops back. Arllu is crawling with every angel under his command. Now, as they are looking for us, the exits will be closed, more security posted at all major turns and junctions. Baza is not stupid. He would double the security, including the one for the armoury. I'm already expecting bloodshed just trying to get through the Gate... He knows where we're going and what our destination is. He will be waiting for us. There will be more of them at the Gate, waiting for us..."

"Aye, and that's exactly why we need weapons!" Sabrael barks, interrupting me.

The heads of the angels in the room turn to us.

"Sabrael, I have a plan", I say, dropping my voice. "I have a plan to distract them, to get extra cover so we can pass through the Gate..."

"Is it the same, as the plan you carried out earlier?"

He swings his hand, implying the angels in the room.

It feels like a slap and stings like one.

My cheeks grow pink under his gaze.

"I didn't plan on these beetles", I say, pushing words past my gritted teeth. "I didn't know they'd be here. *You* didn't even know what were. You didn't even know that they exist."

I close my mouth and sigh, gathering my calm.

"The bottom line is, Sabrael, we're still alive. Who knows, maybe alive *because* of this detour..."

Although, I say these words, deep down I know that he is right. I wanted to give my angels time to recover but instead I damaged them further. If we had gone straight to the surface, we might have end up fighting, but the number of Baza's warriors would have been less than what I'm sure is waiting for us know.

Baza is waiting for us by the Gate. He's expecting us to leave via the Gate and he's right, it's the only way out, Baza and I both know it. As I told Sabrael, Baza is not stupid.

There will be an army waiting for us at the Gate, and twenty odd exhausted and injured angels will do little to fight it. It will be a slaughter, massacre, and that's why I'm not leaving without the istana. I need them. Now I need them more than before. Now their numbers are the difference between victory and defeat.

I sigh.

"I think it will be suicide mission and I think you'll die for nothing, without achieving anything. We have weapons in Uras..."

"But we have nothing here", he interrupts me.

"Uriel", he adds quietly, "I believe we need to try. We need to be ready. Yes, you're right, we don't have many able who can fight, but we need to make sure that those who can have weapons."

He stops for a moment.

"You forbade the rescue of the imprisoned angels of the corridors, and there were dozens upon dozens of them in each. Aye, you were right, we didn't have capacity to save them all", he continues. "As we're now, injured and on the run, we wouldn't be able to rescue and save more, and I understood and respected that call. But this is different. We need weapons to survive. However many of us left, we need to survive. I need my brothers cross the threshold of Uras, otherwise my pledge, my decision was for nothing and I've led them to their deaths, and I wouldn't be able to live with myself after that. Can you understand that, Uriel?"

I understand. I can understand it better than anyone, being responsible for the one I love whole of my life.

"I will take only one brother with me, the rest will be left with you, instructed to follow your every order. I need to save my brothers. I need to make sure that I've done everything I could to save them. I hoped that *you* would be the one who'd understand and respect that need."

Our gazes link as we stare at each other.

He is talking about my sister. Maybe Sam told him, but maybe someone else. It's irrelevant now. He wants to save his brothers, he wants to do everything he can, and even if he'll die trying, it would make him feel better, knowing that he tried.

"Of course I understand."

I sigh.

"Fine, leave now. It will give you head start", I say. "Outside of Baza's tower, if walking towards the Gates, Rafael and two more followers from Uras are waiting for me. We'll head to meet them first then will progress to the Gates. Please, make sure you're there before us. I don't know how long I would be able to wait for you there."

"Thank you, Beyelai Sar. We will be there."

Sabrael smiles and bows to me.

I watch Sabrael walking over to the group of his brothers, speaking to them. Throughout his speech, a few glances dart towards me and a few minutes later, I watch them saying their restricted manly goodbyes, as they exchange a few brisk hugs and short thumping on the shoulders.

Sabrael and Sabaoth bow to me and I rise to my feet, answering their bows with my own, before they walk out, through the archway, and out of the room.

CHAPTER 28

N ow and again I take the tight staircase down into the big hall.

The Istana have begun gathering. Their numbers increase with my every visit.

Every time I set a foot on the beetle covered floor, the light from my body blinds the nearest istana, prompting the same response of shrieking and covering of their eyes, followed by darting away.

But with each visit, I begin to spot the istana that have been here the longest. They no longer cry out and are not trying to run. Instead, they shield their eyes, gazing at me from underneath their hands, studying me, following my every move.

I spot Gil'Amesh amongst the crowd during one of those visits.

"How many left? How much longer do I have to wait?" I ask him in a way of a greeting as I approach him.

He jumps up at the sound of my voice and turns to me.

"Beyelai", he mumbles, bowing, his back at a right angle to his legs. "Most of the istana are here. We are waiting on a few from the distant gilar-dhu but they shouldn't be long."

"I will be addressing the istana that are here tomorrow, first thing in the morning. We need to leave", I bark, turning and starting away from him. But his confused glance darts at me when I utter "tomorrow" and "first thing in the morning", as he straightens his perpetually bent back.

I don't know if time is measured here, underground, but I have to move on.

The time to dilly dally came and went. The countdown began the moment I bit into Lis' throat, and it sped up when I broke into their transmission.

But now? Every second I spend here, I do more damage to my followers. I need to go. I need to leave, and I need to take the istana with me, but with a speeding up countdown and injuries to my angels, the objective of my visit here has changed from "I want them all" to "I'll take what I can".

The door on the trap began closing a while back, but the spring is about to burst now, threatening to slam the door shut in front of my nose, trapping me in.

The istana numbers are growing. Istana meander within the dome of amphitheatre, chatting in hushed voice, while a few of them are sitting by the walls or in the centre.

But there are many of them here, probably a few hundred, and more are coming.

When I climb up the stairs, I am confronted with a solid wall of bodies, gathered together around something on the floor, towards the far wall.

"What's going on?" I call to the backs of a collection of mauled wings.

A few faces turn to me and eventually someone says: "Tabbris is awake."

Tabby.

I rush towards the centre of the circle, pushing bodies out of my way, shoving, nudging, until I am in front of her, sitting against the wall, and I stop.

I look at her and she looks at me, and for a moment I don't know what to say, until I take the last two steps and I fall to my knees in front of her, hugging her tight, whispering in her ear, through the wall of her tight curls: "I am sorry."

I whisper it again.

Her curls tickle my nose, but she doesn't say a thing, she doesn't respond, and I'm about to pull away, swallowing my tears, when the two small arms come around my back, and suddenly I burst.

The tears well up in my eyes as I hug her tighter, squeezing her body against mine, murmuring over and over again: "I'm sorry. I'm so sorry, Tabby. I'm sorry."

I rock her body with mine, and I feel the angels in the room moving away from us, giving us privacy.

We sit like that for a while, while I cry into her hair, in my pathetic attempt to hide my tears and my weakness from the angels.

Eventually, I pull away, wiping my eyes and my nose.

Her hold has given me the bravery to look her in her eyes, to take the blame she has to give, knowing that even after it's all received, I'll be forgiven.

"I'm truly sorry, Tabby. I didn't mean for any of it to happen. I would not have wanted anything like this to happen to anyone, let alone you."

She looks at me for a second. She doesn't say a word, but her old and tired eyes tell me that it will be a long road to forgiveness.

"Did you find your sister?" Tabby asks suddenly.

"I have", I answer, not sure how to tell her that I didn't manage to save my sister either, just the way I have failed to protect her.

"I hope she's alright", Tabby breathes out and closes her eyes, resting her head against the wall.

My audience with her is over. She's done talking to me.

I get up and walk away.

Another person I have failed. Another promise was broken, damaging another life.

The list of the lives I've broken grows longer, but I don't feel like perusing that list today. I can't do it now. Right now is not the time. I have to take all of them out of here, making sure that my list doesn't get any longer, before I can then sob over my uselessness and wallow in self-pity.

CHAPTER 29

"Come on. It's time", I say to the god, nudging my head towards the archway.

Dšarael pulls his hand out of Mitish's hold and rises to his feet.

He nods to me. He is ready.

I am about to play the role of a fearless deity, with a supporting act of the self-proclaimed god, all while the scenery of the stage and the settings are anything but regal.

My tunic and trousers were white only once, when I left Uras.

They haven't been that colour since. Caked in the blood of different creatures, covered in dirt, my tunic lost its colour long ago, becoming a patchwork of a rigid smelly mess.

But my wings remain bright purple, dusted with a bright golden shimmer. My wings are as glorious as they were and they are my weapon that will help me tonight.

I've told Mitish to clean and polish god's see-through wings, to make their glass surface sparkle.

The god that now walks down the stairs behind me, has been given a black leather tunic and trousers of one of the Butcher minion's that the brothers had appropriated in the corridors.

After a short debate and a choice between a black tunic of the masters' enforcer or a casual black jumper and trousers of the brothers, I instructed the god to pull on the black leather tunic, to send a message.

I've prepared him to play the role, the role that I assigned to him. I've dressed up my puppet and I've arrange my stage.

It's time for the grand show.

I step down from the last step and stop by the doorway. The light off my body spills onto the floor of the amphitheatre of Great Hall beyond, and the sudden silence of the expectant audience rings through it.

"Ready?" I mouth to the god.

Dšarael nods.

I turn away from him, taking the final step forward, listening to the gruesome crunch of beetles under my trainers.

The door swings shut behind me. A thick wooden bar slides against it, locked under my instructions by Tagas.

I stride forward.

Mine and the god's light flood the large hall.

I march under the accompaniment of frightened gasps and squeals, as the wall of istana parts in front of us.

The istana are like a spooked colony of ants under my feet. At my arrival they dart sideways, running away with crunchy sounds of the beetles' popping shells under their feet. Blinded by the light they've never seen and giving way to their panic, istana crowd begin to spin erratic circles around the room, bumping into the walls and each other, blindly looking for an escape.

The earlier stunned silence is swallowed by their cries.

The Hall is abuzz with blind fear.

That's enough!

The burst of my wings is met by the shrieks of the nearest istana. I flap my wings, rising towards the carved ceiling.

The panic and screeching of the istana multiplies with my rising.

The ground is busy, rippling with their erratic movements. A few istana have stopped, and draw their heads upwards, they gawk at me. But some istana have remembered about the multiple exits in this room, and now begin banging on the locked doors, crying for help, as more and more of them rush forward, crushing those by the doors.

There are a few hundred istana in here. It's a tightly packed crowd of a small concert.

"Enough!" I roar down to the sea of the bodies below.

"Enough of this, Children of Ishtar! Stop and listen, istana! Stop and listen to what I have to say and I swear no harm will come to you."

More of them stop, lifting their heads towards me. But it's only a few.

The banging of hundreds of fists on the barricaded doors multiplies at the exits. Their panic and cries spike. A few istana drop to their knees, and closing their eyes and raising their arms, they begin singing chants.

"The doors are locked and there's no way out", I roar over the chaos below. "You're all going to stay here until you hear me out. I have something very important to say and you need to listen."

But my voice is drowned by the hysterical cries of hundreds of scared people, by their monotonous chant, which grows stronger as more of them join in, by the banging of their fists on the wood of the closed door and their pleas for mercy.

My voice is weak against their blind panic and I'm not being heard.

"Under the sky

Here I lie," I begin to sing.

My voice is rising with every new word, desperate to drown the hysterics of the people below.

"Under the sky

My sister and I".

I close my eyes, lifting my head upwards, singing the song I've sung so many times to my sister, and the words, amplified by the dome ceiling above me are bouncing off, echoing, as my song grows louder.

"Tre-e-es above us and the bo-o-ottomless sky

Here we'll li-ive – my sister and I."

I take a lungful of damp underground air to repeat the words again, to sing the song again, when I'm confronted by a sudden ringing silence.

With the weak sound of a deflated balloon, the air escapes past my lips as I turn my gaze downwards.

Every head of every istana is turned to me. Every pair of their eyes is on me.

The chants have stopped and so has the banging on the door. The cries have withered, leaving behind the ringing of my voice, which dies too when the echo of the last word of my song dies.

The ones on their knees clasp their hands, gazing at me. The ones standing, as if in a haze, turn to me, falling to their knees too, and soon the entirety of istana kneel on the ground in front of me.

There is a complete silence in the room.

But this silence is not dangerous, threatening or brooding. Oh, no. This silence is pregnant with ecstasy and content. It's full of wonder and hope for a miracle. It's full of willing submission.

Their faces are expectant. The soft smiles blossom over their lips.

I take a shaky breath and tentatively start again:

"Under the sky

Here I lie..."

A few voices begin to hum, following my tune, and more new voices join in.

"Under the sky

My sister and I..."

The hundreds of voices moan and croon the tune with me.

"Trees above us and the bottomless sky

Here we'll live – my sister and I."

A forest of hundreds of arms is thrust upwards towards me, as hundreds of voices sing, hum and cry my tune, the words unknown to them, turning it into something else on their tongues.

I look down and see the confused face of the god.

I smile at him.

He doesn't understand this connection. Maybe he hasn't heard my song.

But the istana have heard me before. Their humming of my tune is the proof.

They heard me when I've broken into Baza's network, ripping it open, filling it with my voice, making their masters look weak and inferior to me. With my one song I showed the strength that is me. I've shown what I can do and how much weaker their masters are in comparison.

If I said that I can turn water into wine, they would believe me. They would believe anything I say and do now, because they've seen one miracle and that miracle was enough. That show of strength was enough for them.

At the end of the song, in the silence of the amphitheatre, a single voice suddenly calls, "Mammí Barragal".

I look down, looking for a person, who had said it, when the same voice calls again, louder this time: "Mammí Barragal!" And I spot the person, I see the face.

It's Shana.

"Mammí Barragal!" she calls, looking at me, and a few tentative voices follow her, whispering these two words with her.

Quiet at first, barely a murmur, these words grow louder, escalating with every new wave, turning into a chant, which is eventually roared by the hundreds of the voices below.

"Mammí Barragal!

"Mammí Barragal!"

"Dakha-las!"

"Mammí Barragal!"

"Dakha-las!"

I smile at Shana, listening to the growing chants, which vibrate the air and the walls, as hundreds of hands reach upwards, towards me.

They are calling me "The Mother of Gods", which means only one thing: Shana has told them about the prophecy.

I spot the stunned face of Gil'Amesh amongst the crowd. He is shocked to find out that it's me, who has broken into the Baza's network, making his masters look weak, that it's me, who is stronger than his master or the istana's fear. He is shocked to realise that I am the *Mammí Barragal*.

I smile at him.

My smile is the acceptance of his fear and the confirmation of my power over his people. My smile is a warning to him not to piss with me.

"Children of Ishtar", I call into the crowd and the crowd falls silent, listening to me.

"Istana!" I call again. "You have lived under the ground in these tunnels forever. You have lived in darkness all of your lives, for generations. You were born into it. You were born into the shackles of slavery, your parents and parents of your parents were born into it too. You haven't known anything else.

"You have lived underground for so long that you no longer remember what the sky and the sun look like. How warm the sun feels on the skin. How the wind feels when it moves your hair or of the scream of the trees under the power of storm. You have lived here so long that your beautiful, glorious wings shrivelled into nothingness and your eyes can't look at the light without a pain."

I pause and hundreds of istana hold their breaths, taking in my every word.

"The great, beautiful people of istana have been imprisoned for centuries. You have been bonded into servitude. You've been held here against your will, chained to these tunnels, forced to live your lives for masters' profit, for their pleasure and for their lifestyle. You were sold and given into slavery and you live in it now.

"You have lived in slavery for far too long", I call. "Since his mother," I point to the god below, "left you behind, abandoning you, selling you to the masters."

Every istana turns their head towards the god and I can see him shuffle and squirm under their gazes.

"But what mother would do that to her children, I ask you? What mother would abandon her children, leaving them to fend for themselves? What mother would willingly walk away from her flesh and blood? What mother would sell her children into slavery?"

I fall quiet, shaking my head.

"Not a good mother", I say.

"I wouldn't call her a mother at all!" I cry out.

I scan the crowd and when my gaze falls onto the god's face, I see anger in his eyes.

He knows where I am going with it. I'm undermining his power and his claim over these people. He gets it now but it's too late. In a couple of minutes, the istana will be mine.

A smile plays on my lips as I spread my arms wide.

"A good mother would never abandon her children! A good mother would lay her life on the line for them. She would do everything in her power to save her children from the dark slavery of masters like Abzu, or Baza as he calls himself.

"You have been abandoned and forgotten. You were forsaken when you finished serving her needs. You have been left here to rot and to die. She has abandoned her children to the mercy of cruel masters, masters who cast you aside like used rags after you finished working for them, after you had served your purpose, masters who care about nothing but themselves.

"Baza's empire is growing because of you! It's growing on your bodies, on the bones of your parents and bones of your children. You are worked into the ground, used and abused, dying hungry without ever seeing the fruit of your labour! You don't reap the benefit of your work. You are treated like animals, bred, used, punished and then killed. Your children are beaten on a regular basis, just because masters are bored. This cycle is unending. Your children are living your miserable lives, and the children of their children are going to live the same nightmare."

The mass of the faces below me take in my every word.

"But there is a way to break this cycle", I roar. "There is a way to change your path. There is a way to get freedom for you and for your children!"

"You are a great nation. You are the great, brave istana, yet you have forgotten your glory. You have forgotten where you came from, forgotten that you are the children of gods, that you are godly! You have forgotten your history and your roots. You have even forgotten how to fly!

"There is a god in every one of you! There is a universe in each one, a universe which cries to be set free and I want to remind you of that! I want to show it to you!"

I pause, readying them for my proposal.

"I want to take you to my home. I'm inviting all of you to come to Uras with me. I am opening my arms and my home to you, a home of gods, the castle of gods, suspended in the sky with only bright blue sky around it. I'm inviting every istana to share my home with me!" I cry out.

But the stupefied silence is all that I get in return. These people wait for, yet still can't see, the catch. Taught well by Baza, they are waiting for the terms of their new slavery.

They don't trust anyone, and I'm no exception.

"I am not interested in acquiring slaves", I continue. "I have no need for slaves. But I do want free the istana! I want to take the free istana to where the children of gods were born, where they belong. I want to be your mother, the mother who showed her children the way to their freedom, the mother, who gave her children a happy future."

I fall quiet but they still listen.

"I know you've been told about the prophecy, the prophecy about Mother of Gods, who would be sent to free you", I say.

"But the truth is I can't give you your freedom. In fact, nobody can and nobody ever will. Nobody is going to give you your freedom", I call. "Ever! No one will grant you that gift!"

I pause again for a moment, before I roar: "I can't give you your freedom, but I can lead you to it! I can give you the refuge. I can give you safety and a future."

"Your freedom is not mine to gift and it was most certainly not Baza's to take", I roar. "Your freedom is yours and only you can take it for yourself. *You* have to take it back. *You* need to stand up and demand your freedom, demand everything that is yours! You need to fight for it and if it comes to it, be prepared to die for it, die for your own freedom and the freedom of your children!"

I stop speaking, gathering my breath.

"I will show you the way out. I will lead you. I promise you the refuge of my home, but it's up to you to take that first step. I know it's scary and I know that the first step is the hardest, but nobody will take it for you!"

I take a deep breath to issue a warning that may lose me followers, possibly many of them, but I have to be honest with them. If I am honest with them, then they'll trust me, and when there's trust, there will be commitment and loyalty.

Besides, I need strong followers. It's not a nursery outing I am planning.

"The road to freedom is never straight. It's never easy. It's paved with loss, heartache and blood... plenty of blood", I roar. "Every step down that road is a fight. Everything will be thrown at you to stop you from getting where you want to be, from getting your freedom, and this one is not going to be different. Baza loves this little arrangement and he won't release you without a fight.

"But everyone who makes it through to the end of this tough road, will see the open blue skies again, will learn how to fly and will discover the forgotten feeling of growing children for the children's future, not for the master's needs. The rewards will be yours to reap, but only for those who are brave enough to take the first step..."

I pause.

"And lucky to survive", I add quietly. "I need you to know it, before you make your decision. I must be honest with you."

I scan confused faces.

"But I am here to teach you! I am here to lead!" I roar. "I am here to fight with you, alongside you! Your fight for the freedom will be my fight too! Your desire to be free is my desire. I understand it only too well. But if you make that decision, if you take that step, you will be the first generation who will die as free men. Your children will be the first free generation. I swear on my undying Qal, I swear it to An. I swear on my life and on everything that I hold sacred. I will grant you your freedom if you come with me!"

Well, that's it. There's nothing more to add and there's nothing more to say.

I hope I've said enough and I hope I was heard. I hope there are brave istana amongst them, and not all of them are as spineless as Gil'Amesh as I have no need for the spineless slugs.

Baza won't be the last one who'll come at me and at everyone who is with me. Once we make it through the Gates, anyone who operates their worlds in Baza's style, will come for us, desperate to crush us, to make an example of us to any dreamers. And of course, Mik'hael will come knocking too.

Maybe death of Lis' friends was inevitable. It had demonstrated the fight I have started.

I haven't involved Dšarael in my little speech. I don't trust him.

As much as I know that his loyalty doesn't lie with Baza, it doesn't mean that he's my fan either. His goals could differ from mine, but again, it's just a side note for me to fix. I will take him to Uras with me, even if I have to gag and bind him, and I will keep him safe for the sake of the istana, who coming with me.

I'm prepared to imprison one to free hundreds, maybe thousands.

"I have only one question to ask you, and unfortunately, I can't give you time to think as I need to leave now", I call to the grey mass of expectant people. "Who of you want to leave Arllu and Baza's service behind? Who wants to be free and is prepared to fight for that? Who wants to come into the blue skies of Uras with me? Who wants to raise their children free? Raise your hand."

A soft murmur rustles over the ground, as many voices whisper, asking each other for advice, as istana afraid to take the first, and possibly the final, step.

My heart sinks at the sight of the petrified crowd of slaves, with not one hand raised. Even Shana keeps her hand down, talking to istana next to her.

I feel defeated. I've dragged the angels who believed in me here for nothing. I've killed them for nothing and have injured many more.

Tartys and Lis' friends are dead and there will be many more, as now everyone knows where we are and where we're going. I've overplayed my hand, handing the advantage over to Baza and time to prepare, to block my routes for escape. He is the hunter now, suited and booted and ready for the chase, ready with his army to meet my platoon.

My chances of survival are beyond pathetic now.

I sweep my gaze over the circular wall with angels' wings nailed to it.

My wings will be there soon. Unless Baza would like to nail mine in his dining hall and look at them every time he has a dinner. How often does one bring mighty Uriel down?

I close my eyes for a moment, steadying myself, readying myself to return to the angels who have trusted in me and tell them that this plan was a bust, and we're now on our own.

The bitterness burns in my throat.

I open my eyes, ready to say something jabbing, as we part our ways, when my gaze collides with a thin grove of raised hands.

But the thin grove is growing, filling up, thickening, turning into a familiar dense forest of raised hands, like the one I saw before, when they reached out to me, calling me the "Mother of Gods".

I exhale a surprise.

A small smile forms and blossoms on my lips, and I can't stop it. I know that the battle is far from won and we have a long way to go before we reach the safety of Uras, and even then, Baza and Mik'hael will come knocking, but I feel an incredible wave of the sweet relief washing over me.

CHAPTER 30

"You are going to get them killed. They are not soldiers. They don't know how to fight."

Gil'Amesh utters in his old raspy voice in a way of a greeting, before crossing a threshold of the room he gave to me and my angels.

"Hello to you too", I answer.

It's only me, the injured, the god and two istana that are left in the room. Everyone else, who is physically well, had left, following mine and Pronoia's orders for preparation.

I left Pronoia in charge of the military organisation of our new army, and now he and his brothers, led by a few istana, were on their way to the repair tunnel, where istana repair and service the Asmodeus' crew weapons, bringing to us as many weapons as they could find there, ideally enough to arm every istana.

Rachiel and Sidqiel, the two female Ophanims, went down into the Grand Hall to speak to the istana, to reassure them, telling them stories of Uras and Dingir-Ki, in a bid to improve and raise the morale and suppress any last minute jitters.

Dšarael went upstairs after my speech.

He tried to speak to me, but once I had landed to the ground, I was swept off my feet by the hundreds of hands, which had lifted me above their heads, chanting: "Mammí Barragal! Mammí Barragal! Mammí Barragal!"

He tried to talk to me again, once I came upstairs into the room where the angels were waiting for me to hear the news, but I was busy then, delivering the good news, receiving a few pats on the back and discussing the strategy for the departure, sharing tasks and giving out orders.

"You are going to get them killed", Gil'Amesh repeats.

"Hopefully not. If we leave pronto and we have plenty weapons with us. If we move fast, we should be alright."

"And what happens if you don't "move fast"? If Baza and his malakhims catch up with you before you get through the Gate?"

"Then we'll have to fight. I've told them that, Gil'Amesh. I've warned them. I didn't lie to them... unlike you."

I glare at the old istana as I pause for a moment before turning away from him, continuing with my round of checking on the wounded.

"They will die", he repeats, telling it to my bent back, as I wipe the healthy side of Sam's face.

This parrot is seriously getting on my nerves.

I straighten up and spin to face the old man.

"They will die here just as well. Millions have died under your watch whilst you were busy bending backwards for your masters and licking their boots. I hope it worked out well for you. Your people are dying, Gil-Amesh, dying every day, by the dozen, whilst serving the masters, so you are the last one to lecture me on their deaths."

"You're using them just like the master", he begins, "leading them to their death –"

"How dare you? How dare you?! You, little old slug", I hiss.

I feel stunned and slapped. I feel hot and livid. I want to tear this old man's head off his shoulders.

"Once spineless, always spineless!" I spit at him. "What would you know of freedom? What do you know of a free life?" I roar.

"You don't know the smell of fresh air, you have probably forgotten or maybe never experienced it, and you have the audacity to block your people's quest to find their happiness?"

"Their happiness or yours?" Gil-Amesh quietly asks, and I need to take a few breaths to disperse the red veil in front of my eyes and unclench my fists.

I'm not going to explain myself to this man. We are not going to braid each other's hair, and I'm not going to share my past. I'm not going to share my memories with him, the taste, the smell and the feeling of being powerless and trapped.

"Yes, they might die, but so could I!" I bark once I can breathe. "I put my life on the line next to theirs. I don't hide behind them, I will fight *with* them! Unlike Baza I don't send them forward to do my dirty work. I don't find myself a cosy little corner to hide in, like *some*", I narrow my eyes at him. "While the people who I am responsible for are beaten, starving, whilst pleasing my masters."

I glare at the old man, but he glares back at me, his head tilted to the side.

"*You* need them to get out of Arllu, to stand a chance against Baza", he rustles at me, pointing his finger at my chest.

"I swear to god, Gil-Amesh, my patience is running out", I hiss a warning at him. "You're crossing the line."

I'm livid now, but I am above it, I'm irritated at this old asshole and at the fact that he got under my skin.

I take a breath, anchoring myself, looking for regal indifference which will be a more appropriate response from the Mother of Gods to my current outburst.

"I am responsible for them", he says.

"You should have thought of that earlier, before sending millions of generations into the tunnels to die."

"I've helped them to survive, the only way I could!"

I come closer to the old istana.

"That's what you tell yourself", I whisper, leaning in to him.

"Maybe now it's the time to look past survival?" I ask, straightening up. "Maybe it's time for a change?"

I am calmer now.

"Yes, I need them to survive", I admit, "but they need me too if they want their freedom. They need me just as much as I need them. If they want to see the sky again, if they ever want to be free, they need *me*. Me!"

I jab my finger into my chest.

"Nobody else is swooping in, offering them their freedom on a silver platter. Where are those heroes? How many of them came here before me? Huh? How many offers of freedom have the istana declined?"

The old man says nothing, because there's nothing to say and there's very little way to argue with truth.

"The decision is not yours to make, Gil-Amesh", I say. "I have made an offer, a genuine offer, and it's up to each and every one of them to decide. It's the istana's choice, not yours."

Suddenly another thought hits me.

"I bet you've already shared your fears and predictions with the istana", I say, holding my gaze to the man, and he doesn't protest.

"I thought you might", I sigh. "I don't force anyone to come with me, never have and never will, unlike your masters", I say.

I come closer to the man, his bent head is an inch from me.

"But as I've given the istana a choice, I'm giving you a choice too, Gil-Amesh, a personal choice, especially for you. You either stay here, sit next to Sarin and keep your mouth shut until we leave or I will *make you* stay here and to be quiet. I don't need you to mingle with my people, spreading your poison."

His eyes fly open at my threat.

"Take a seat", I rumble low.

"Now!" I roar, yanking the shard of my weapon from my corset and pointing it at the old man.

"You will kill them", he repeats, once he sits on the pressed ground.

"Your problem is that you never asked them what they want from their lives", I say, turning away from the man, returning to my earlier task of wiping Sam's face.

"If they would rather live free, even for a moment, than survive as slaves for eternity. You have never given them a choice, no one has. Leave them alone, Gil-Amesh, and let them make up their own minds, for once in their lives."

"*Why the hell are you still talking to him?*" Rage mouths at me, rolling her eyes and picking dirt from under her nails with a narrow dagger. "*What are you trying to explain to him? Some people simply never get it.*"

It's clear what she'd have me do.

"Only dreams of freedom can keep one going", I say, "can help one to survive the daily torture. And as I promised, anyone who doesn't want to take this risk, is *free*", I make the emphasis on the word, "to stay here and continue with their lives full of servitude and scheduled flogging."

Now, I have nothing more to add.

I can't and would never be able to explain it to this man, to someone who doesn't see what is happening to his people, who doesn't see anything wrong with his current life, who would rather live on his knees all of his life than to stand and fight, even if it means dying.

We are completely different. He will never understand me, never will get my need for freedom to be myself and choose for myself, no matter how fleeting that freedom might be. And I will never understand him.

"It is better to die on your feet, than to live on your knees." A quote that I read many years ago couldn't be truer for me, and maybe he sees it as me forcing my ideas on the istana, while I see it as giving them a choice.

Zabkiel bursts into the room.

"Beyelai, we have weapons!"

He is out of breath from running up the stairs but he is smiling. It must be good.

He leads the way and I follow him, coming with him into the large hall.

Istana stand in a tight circle around a dark pile on the floor, as more istana come through the side door, carrying heavy loads of weapons, dropping them into a heap in the middle.

The black weapons meet each other with deep metal clanks.

The pile of weapons is growing and so is the crowd around me.

Zabkiel stands next to it, proudly beaming at me.

"We should have plenty for the armament of everyone. We didn't find any of the malakhims weapons, only of Asmodeus servicemen but this should suffice to arm every istana and boost our needs."

I look at the pile.

It's a heap of black metal, with sprinkles of black leather glossing in places. The heap is made up of short and narrow black daggers, wide and curved knives, black double sided axes on long black handles, leathery snakes of whips, metal spiky balls on thick chains attached to the black handles, short and long metal poles with stars or with axes atop, thick black spiked clubs and war hammers.

This selection is impressively menacing, and it's growing.

Following my gaze to the open door through which the istana come, balancing weapons in their arms, Zabkiel adds: "None of it is going to be lethal against an angel, but it's most certainly a start."

He comes over, and leaning closer, he adds in a whisper so only I can hear him: "Unarmed civilians are going to flee, whereas the armed ones are going to fight."

I lift my gaze at him, wondering if I need to protest here, remind him of my promise to take *all* istana to Uras, but I keep quiet, as I know he's right. I have omitted a significant number of the dangers of Arllu and Baza in particular from my new recruits.

"Pronoia is finishing raiding the armoury. Once he's done, we'll be able to leave."

"Let every istana pick a weapon", I say, looking at the growing pile. "The ones who refuse, yet are coming with us, don't force them, they can help with injured. Once the istana have chosen their weapons, teach them a few techniques, show them how to use their new weapons, so they don't injure themselves."

I'm proposing a training camp although we barely have enough time to pack our belongings.

"It's not going take much of our time, but might save their lives", I add.

I sigh.

"Let them hold the weapons at least."

I'm thinking of Domiel and the training he gave me on our way here. Zabkiel nods.

I bend towards the pile, and fishing out two black slim daggers from its metal core, I stash them into the sheaths at my corset.

"Listen up", Zabkiel roars. "Everyone, choose your weapon! Come on! Come closer, don't be shy! There's plenty to choose from, every weapon, every size and every shape. The colour is only black, but I'm sure we'll make it do, Anshaan Kataaru."

I step back, giving way to the istana, who approach the metal pile with a different degree of enthusiasm and fear.

"Beyelai. Beyelai Sar!"

Above the roar of the angelic guttural calls of the brothers, exclamations of approval and the uncertainty of istana, it takes me a while to hear that someone is calling me.

I scan the room and spot Sidqiel, one of Ophanims, waving frantically at me, her slim frame sealed in black trousers tunic and trousers, barely visible within the istana crowd.

I walk over to her.

"Yes? What is it?"

A cluster of istana stands to the side of her.

Some of them are old and some young, but all keep their heads down, looking at the dirt floor under their feet, avoiding my gaze.

"Beyelai Sar", Sidqiel says, "they said, they won't come with us."

Sidqiel's beautiful slim face is concerned as she looks at me. A few deep wrinkles have settled over her forehead and her dark beautiful almond shape eyes open wide. She doesn't know what to do.

"Why?" I ask.

She shrugs her shoulders.

"They say they will not go."

I come closer to the cluster of men, women and a few children with subservient postures. I don't know if I'll get an answer from them, let alone if I will hear a real reason, but I need to try. I want to know.

"Why won't you come?" I ask the small crowd, keeping my voice as soft as I can. "Didn't you hear me earlier? You are all invited. You are invited into my house, into glorious Uras with bottomless blue sky, where you can grow your wings and fly again. I'm inviting you into my house as my equals."

Not a single head is lifted to look at me.

"I swear to you, it's not a trick. I gave you the sacred An's oath. I don't know if you know it, but once this oath is given, it has to be fulfilled."

I look at the bent heads, waiting for a response, an acknowledgement of any sort, but I'm met with a silent submission.

My gaze darts to Sidqiel, who shrugs her shoulders, the folds of her dark red wings moving with her shrug.

I shake my head.

"Fine", I sigh. "So be it." I spread my arms.

"It's your choice and I'm not going to force you into it, if you want to stay, stay", and I'm about to turn away, when with a corner of my eye, I notice a movement to the side of the cluster.

As a reflex, my hand jumps to my corset, closing over the hilt of a dagger, tugging it free, as my body completes the turn towards the people.

A pair of grey eyes looks at me, before their gaze darts to the half-naked dagger, the eyes opening wider.

"Mammí", a soft voice stammers.

A woman stands in front of me. I can't tell how old she is. Although her long, plaited hair is grey, her posture is perfect and her eyes are young.

Cautiously, she shuffles towards me, a few steps closer to me and further away from the cluster of the submissive people.

My gaze drops to her hands but I can't see any weapon.

"Mammí Barragal", the woman says in that soft voice, keeping her gaze on me.

"I can't leave, Mammí", she whispers. "My children are still in Arllu, all of them. The youngest two are in the nursery tunnel, and others are... Well, I don't know where they are, but I know that they are alive and serve in Arllu..."

She drops her gaze to her clasped hands, sighs and utters: "Mammí, I can't leave my children. As you said, "What mother would I be?"

The sadness in her voice is tangible and it tugs at my heart.

"You can bring your youngest with you, if that's what you're worried about", I say, coming closer, placing my hand on her shoulder.

She jumps up at my contact.

"It's most kind and gracious of Mammí to allow this", she stammers and lifts her eyes to me, "but... I beg Mammí to grant me permission to stay. I can't leave even one of my children behind."

With the last word she suddenly falls to her knees, then spreading on the ground like a cross, with her arms spread wide and her legs together. It's not the first time I've seen this pose from an istana.

"Please get up, get up", I mumble.

I kneel, and when I tug at her shoulder, her body jumps as if electrocuted. She is expecting to be hit.

I sigh.

"Please, get up", I repeat, rising myself and after a turn of her head and a long gaze at me from the ground, she begins her slow rise.

"What's your name?" I ask.

"Rizim, Mammí."

"Rizim", I repeat.

"Of course I understand and if you need to stay, stay", I say, shrugging my shoulders again.

"Who else can't leave because they have relatives here?" I call, turning to the small cluster of istana.

Half of them shuffle forward.

"If you need to stay behind, stay", I call. "You will be free to move and return to your..." I stop for a moment, looking for a word, "*jobs*, as soon as we leave. For now, can you please sit against the wall over there?"

I wave my hand towards the furthest side of the Hall, and as they move, shuffling to take their places at the shown corner, Sidqiel comes to stand next to me.

"Forgive me, Beyelai, but I don't think all of them have kinfolk in Arllu. I think some have used this woman's reason as an excuse for their cowardice."

The old and young, women and men slide down the wall and sit on the ground, pulling their knees to their chests, dropping their gazes, hiding their faces, desperate to take as little space as possible, hoping to disappear, as they close their eyes and pray for this upheaval in their lives go away.

"And you might be right", I say, keeping my gaze on them. "Quite possibly you're right, but whatever the reason, they're not coming and I've promised to respect that."

"By the way, Beyelai", Sidqiel softly says, "Pronoia has advised the istana that no children will be taken with us. It's just so you know, in case you promise another parent their child."

A sudden burst of laughter explodes at the other side of the hall.

I turn my head.

Pronoia towers above the now grown to a substantial size pile of weapons, saying something to Zabkiel and Tagas, who bursts out laughing once he utters the final word. The cornflower blue large wings of the brothers are easy to spot.

"Thank you, Sidqiel", I say before I march through the crowd and towards the jolly brothers.

As I walk, some istana stop and bow at me, while some dart out of my way as if I'm a leper.

"Pronoia, can we please have a word?"

I'm not going to reprimand him in front of the others, especially in front of the istana. I need them, *all* of them, and I can't afford to have a spat over a bruised ego.

"Yes, Beyelai Sar."

The smile on his beautiful face is bright and his brown eyes twinkle. He is a gorgeous angel, but mind you, I could say that about any of them. So far I haven't met an unattractive one apart from me.

His brothers bow out, walking away from us.

Looking into his unguarded eyes, smelling the spring scent of lilacs, I see that he expects praise for the excellently conducted scouting operation for weapons, and I want to give him that praise, but I need to say my piece first.

"Pronoia, I thought we agreed to bring the children with us", I say.

Confusion mars his face for a moment, until the understanding washes his smile off, sobering him.

"Forgive me, Beyelai", he begins, narrowing his eyes at me, "but it will stifle our manoeuvring. It will slow us down. I have issues with this order, because some of the children are babies –"

"Are you arguing with me?" I interrupt him, raising my eyebrow at him.

He closes his mouth, without saying a further word, glaring at me.

"We can't leave them behind", I say.

"I would never dream to argue with Beyelai Sar", he pushes past his teeth, "I'm merely advising Mammi Barragal on our inability to bring the youngsters with us."

He bows.

When he straightens, he holds my gaze before he drops his voice and adds, "Beyelai Sar and I are both aware that we might not make it to the Gates. There's a treacherous road between here and Uras, and if something happens along the way, do you want more bodies on the ground? Do you want them being children and babies?"

He is right. Damn him, he is right at every point, but leaving the children behind? Leaving the most vulnerable at Baza's mercy? That doesn't sit well with me.

"I can't leave them", I repeat but the heat of the conviction is gone from my words.

He comes closer and his scent and the warmth swaddle me.

"If we all die before reaching the Gates, at least these children will live", he whispers.

"And if we make it through, Baza will take it out on them", I say, looking up at him. "Baza will take it out on everyone who will be left behind, and I hope you're not naïve enough to think that he'll spare babies."

Pronoia places his hand on my arm, giving it a little squeeze.

"I am not", he shakes his head. "I've run a few campaigns under his directives. I know. But we can't bring children with us."

Although he is right, so am I.

We are leaving the most vulnerable behind. We are leaving behind the istana's future, and I know what fate will come to every istana left behind in Arllu if our mission is successful.

But no matter his reasons, it's me who will have the final word here. It's my name attached to this jolly little trip. It's me who will be blamed should anything go wrong. And as I am the Mother of Gods, The Harbinger of Chaos, The Keeper of the Gates, The Begetter of Life, The Dam of The Ends, I am Uriel and this is *my* fight. The responsibilities are also mine.

"If we make through the Gate", I say, keeping my gaze on his, "if we make it to Uras, I task you and your brothers, every living one of you who makes it to Uras, to return back into Arllu and free every last istana that is left behind."

I look into his dark eyes and he looks at me.

His face is closed off. I can't read it. He doesn't answer me, doesn't say a word.

"You have sworn an oath to me", I remind him softly.

I step closer to the tall man, lifting my gaze up at him. I take his large, warm hand in mine, while holding his gaze.

"Pronoia, will you help me save the children? Will you be that brave warrior and the first angel who shows them mercy? Will you be the one, who rescues the last istana? Will you do it with me?"

I ask him, and although I plead with my eyes, I am holding the steel in my gaze too. He swore his oath to me.

It's a difficult task to encourage cooperation, to inspire, to turn an opinion and someone's will, to make them see your side and above all, trust and follow you. But I am learning. And as I hold his gaze, his eyes blink then soften, and he gives me a small nod.

"Yes, my Beyelai. I swear it to you. I will do it."

I smile at him.

"*Look at you, not bad*", Rage gives a few slow claps, "*you're learning, acquiring not just armies and followers, but worshipers. Not bad.*"

I know. I am pleased with myself too. Finally, I feel in control of my destiny and my world. I've turned the tide and have begun bending this hellish world to my will.

"Thank you", I say to Pronoia, squeezing his hand.

And before turning and walking away, I add: "It was an excellently done job, by the way, Pronoia. The weapons... Very well done. I am happy that you are with me, guys. Thank you."

CHAPTER 31

Following my instructions, Rachiel and Sidqiel, moved the "refusers" to the farthest side of the large hall, away from the ones who will be coming with us and giving space for the brothers to train the istana.

Although "training" sounded far better than what actually took place for the next couple of hours. There was a lot of aimless shuffling and faffing about, throwing of arms with weapons held tight, and near misses during which I was convinced we'd lose a quarter of the istana through accidents or self-inflicted injuries.

The little group armed with metal spiky balls on chains have proven to be the most lethal to themselves and others, and I would hold my breath each time one of these istana would swing a heavy ball, narrowly missing their own head or a the head of a nearby comrade.

After five minutes of watching them, Kafziel took over the command of this unfortunate troop himself, ordering wider gaps between them, barking orders and counting, whilst demonstrating the moves himself. A lethal ballet class of sorts.

The istana became accustomed to the constant bright light that I exuded, as less of them were shading their eyes or squinting.

The istana, who refused to pick up a weapon yet agreed to come with us, were led away by Mitish to the room with the injured angels where he would show them how to look after the injured and where Dšarael was sulking.

I'll need to keep an eye on him. I can't afford his ego or appetite for power to undermine my campaign.

Now, I stay in the large dome, providing the light to the training istana and to my angels, leading the preparations, but my heart wants to be in the room where Sam lies, where Tabby sits against the wall, avoiding me. My love pulls at me, fogging my head and knotting my insides.

But it's irrelevant what I want. I know that I need to be here, inspiring and supporting.

The elegant Sablo and Hasdiel, the angels of grace and benevolence, came down once to rummage in the black metal pile, and walked upstairs with extra weapons tucked behind the belts around their oversized trousers.

A few times I tried to reach Rafe or Jess with my mind, poking into Baza's network, but I was truly blocked out of it, as each time, my mind would run into an absorbing dull wall of silence.

Pronoia strides through the istana's troops, his large body with folded blue wings rises high above istana heads.

He comes over and stands next to me, watching with me the training attempts of our new army. His exposed biffy arms are folded over his chest sealed in the black leather tunic.

"We need to go", he says, keeping his gaze on the nearest group of the istana, and his words sound like an apology.

I sigh.

"I know. We must."

I turn and look up at him.

"I was thinking about the best way to get out", I say. "Rafe is waiting for us a couple of miles outside of the Baza's building, east, towards the processing factories, so that's where we need to get to first. Speak to the istana and find out which way would be faster through the tunnels, and ask a couple of them to lead us but verify the route with the other istana as well. I don't want any sabotage."

Pronoia stays quiet for a moment.

"I think you might be right, Beyelai Sar", he eventually utters. "I would expect kyriotes or malakhims to block a few corridors, although I don't think they will close off all of them. It's far too many corridors to cover, and then Baza would lose the advantage of his entire army by the Gates. Besides, it's not easy to fight in a tight space, therefore I don't think there will be many of Baza's soldiers there, if any. Whoever will be there, we should be able to handle them. I think right now, our safety is in numbers, and we need to keep them, and the tunnels are not what I am worried about."

He stops speaking as he turns his head to me.

He looks at me for a few long seconds before he adds: "I've led a few of Baza's campaigns. I've sat in a few of his war councils, and..."

He stops again.

"What?"

"I think he will be waiting for us by the Gates", Pronoia says. "In fact, I can guarantee you that. It would make the most strategic sense, less movement, accumulating forces in one place and it's the only way out. And even with these new numbers", he turns and looks at the clumsy istana, "as much as I admire your move, it won't be enough to withstand his force. He will bring everything he has at you. I hope you understand that."

I do. That is one point on which I am completely clear and agree with him.

We stand quiet for a second, watching the tired, malnourished istana in rags, swinging the dark heavy weapons. It's a pretty sad show to watch and I know it too.

"We should have gone straight to the Gates from the tunnels", he says quietly next to me, without looking at me.

He said it again. He said it twice already.

None of them understands that I am playing the long game and I'm not here to save him or his brothers. I'm here to save myself, long after we leave Arllu.

But I don't say it. A soldier doesn't need to know the plans of a general.

"Coulda-woulda-shoulda", I say instead. "We're here now, so we'll have to work with it."

I turn to him.

"I suggest splitting the istana into four maybe five groups", I say, "So it's easier to organise them. I want you and your brothers to lead and command them, the twelve of you have more military experience than anyone else here. Each group will be responsible for a few unconscious angels and the istana assisting them. Agree with that? Any suggestions?"

I look at him and suddenly an unexpected thought pushed in: *"I need more weapons. One dagger is not enough."*

I don't know what I'm suspecting or why I need to armour myself looking at him, but I came this far trusting my gut and I'm not going to stop now.

"I think this is very wise plan, my Beyelai", Pronoia answers and bows.

"Start preparing the departure then", I say and with the last nod of my head, I leave him.

* * *

Within minutes the amphitheatre bursts with craziness of hundreds of the istana running from side to side and in circles, confused, trying to figure out where they are supposed to go or what they are supposed to do, whilst Pronoia and his brothers roar and swear at them from different sides of the hall, cursing a few individuals and the entire istana kind along the way.

At the first eruption of chaos, I step aside, resting my shoulder on the wall, watching it, but after a while, the chaos surrounds me tighter before it engulfs the entire hall.

So I open my wings, and frightening the nearby istana, with a couple of powerful beats, I take myself up, towards the ceiling.

Untrained and unorganised, the istana are like a flock of freshly hatched spring chicks.

They scatter around, aimlessly following each other, walking, then suddenly bursting into a jog, chasing one another, jumping up at the sounds of the brothers' tuba voices, while the brothers, like dark hawks, hung above the scared crowd, roaring and barking orders.

It would have been hilarious to watch, if not for the fact that I've placed my faith in this group in my war against Baza and Mik'hael, laying my future into their hands.

I float above, watching the preparations.

But even mercury can be contained, and eventually this scattered crowd is organised into four squadrons ready to march.

The weaponised istana were placed at the forefront and at the sides of the formations, whilst the istana, responsible for the care of injured angels were pushed towards the back and the ones carrying the injured, sealed in the centre. Within the centre of each squadron, four istana hold the four corners of a long rag, which serves as an improvised stretcher, on which an unconscious and mauled angel lays.

The brothers tower at the front of the each squadron, ready to lead.

The injured angels are divided amongst the four squadrons. The Ophanims stand next to their fallen males, while Sablo and Hasdiel, angels of forgiveness and benevolence, stand next to the last angel from Lis' crew, a scared female, who has finally swapped her glitzy party dress for dark and comfortable clothing.

Tabby shuffles amongst the istana of Pronoia's squadron, next to the stretcher with Sam on it. When she hears the beating of my wings, she lifts her head upwards and our gazes meet for a moment, but without a word or a smile, she turns her head away.

Although it hurts, I force my gaze to another squadron of istana, forcing my mind away from her anger.

"Beyelai Sar!" Pronoia's voice booms, as he calls to me, his hands cupping his mouth.

I drop to the ground and walk to him.

"We're ready", he reports.

Pronoia's body is still sealed in the "a-la Butcher" black leather tunic. A glowing feather of an angel is tucked behind the belt.

I glance at his troops, then turning my gaze to the troops of his brothers.

Every istana and every angel of every squadron has a glowing feather pinned or tucked into their clothing: the feathers of an angel, who was like me and the god, glowing even in the depth of Arllu's tunnels.

How many glowing angels were slaughtered and who were they?

"Good", I answer Pronoia, pushing the dark thoughts of premonition out of my head.

Kafziel, Tagas and Zabkiel stand at the ready at the head of their squadrons, looking at me, waiting for my instructions.

I nod my head at them and then, turning to Pronoia, I say: "Take care of yourself and the others, and do your best to bring everyone to the surface."

"Of course, my Beyelai." Pronoia touches his four fingers to his forehead and bows. "You have my word."

"READY! FORWARD!" he roars to his squadron of istana. "Fold by three and GO!"

And the istana shuffle, picking up pace, beginning disappear through the doorway and into a tunnel.

"READY! FORWARD! Fold by three and GO!"

"... FORWARD! Fold by three and GO!"

"... Fold by three and GO!"

One by one the brothers call to their troops. Their calls overlap, drowning each other's out, but one by one the squadrons vanish into the tunnels, until I'm left alone to stand in the large amphitheatre full of my light and the morbid wings.

I walk upstairs into the room where my angels were resting earlier.

Now, only the god, Mitish, Shana and Gil'Amesh are left in the room. The istana who wanted to stay, were sent away at the time of the departure of the first squadron, leaving the amphitheatre through the side door.

"Where's Sarin?" I ask the room.

"Your angels took him", Gil'Amesh answers, raising his gaze to me, the old man sitting on the floor, resting against the wall.

I don't need to ask him what for or where they've taken Sarin, I can figure that one out. But irrelevant to my opinion on their vengeance or how much I disagree with it, I have promised them their payback. I have promised Sarin to them.

"Ready to go?" I address Dšarael and the two istana and the god rises off the ground, whilst Gil'Amesh glares at me without adding another word.

CHAPTER 32

The narrow and wet tunnel snakes forward into the darkness, and slaves to its will, we follow it, trudging into the unknown, into the promised freedom, allowing the tunnel to lead us.

The light of mine and god's bodies disperses the darkness, scaring away any lost worm.

Dšarael and Mitish are walking ahead of me and Shana, discussing something in hushed voices. Even from ten steps away, I can see the adoring twinkle in Mitish's eyes, as he hangs on the god's every word, smiling, laughing at the god's jokes, peppering the conversation with an occasional question or a remark.

I hope Dšarael sees what I see and I hope he will let Mitish off gently if he is not interested. But whatever the outcome, it's not my place to butt in.

Shana walks next to me, keeping quiet.

"I am sorry, Shana", I say, keeping my pace and without looking at her, I add, "for earlier, in the hall... thinking that you'd betrayed me. I scared you. I jumped to a conclusion and I'm sorry."

It's hard to apologise when a title of "Mother of Gods" has been assigned to you. I don't know how to do it.

The word "sorry" has always been a hard word to say, but now, I'm afraid to show any of them my weaknesses. I'm afraid not to look godly enough for these people, who have placed their lives and trust in me. I'm afraid to look weak. But above all, I'm afraid to be found out for the fraud that I am.

The pace next to me falters, stumbling for a few seconds, before finding her footing again.

I push a strand of hair that fell out of my loose plait behind my ear and glance at the girl next to me.

My gaze collides with her petrified gaze.

"Mammí", Shana says in quiet rustling breath, "please don't be cross with me, I beg for your forgiveness, but I don't understand what you're saying. I understand the words but they don't make sense."

Her eyes are wide as she moves her lips slowly.

"Please don't be angry with me, Mammí, but I don't understand."

I stop, turning to her, and she stops with me.

"What do you mean?" I shrug my shoulders. "What don't you understand? I said I'm sorry."

I repeat the words, watching her face, which crumbles under my gaze in slow motion.

"Please forgive me, Mammí. I don't understand".

Suddenly, she drops to her knees.

"Please don't be angry, Mammí. I don't understand. I don't know what I have done to anger you but I beg for your forgiveness."

She closes her eyes and tucks her head in between her shoulders.

She expects to be hurt. She braces herself for my outburst, expecting to be punished, and now *I'm* confused. I'm apologising to her, pushing the ungodly apology out of my throat, yet I'm scaring her.

Maybe I'm saying it wrong? But how could I? Amy had reassured me that my mind is tied with the essence now, having full command of the old Sumerian. How can she not understand me?

Shana is on her knees in front of me and she's crying.

She wraps her arms over her head, protecting it, while she's sobbing, begging for forgiveness and bracing for the punch. I'm staring at her, lost at her reaction.

The god is next to me now.

"What's going on, Nintinugga?"

"I don't know", I mumble, waiving my hand at Shana's folded form. "I apologised to her, said "I'm sorry", but she started apologising to *me*, saying that she doesn't understand what I want from her then she dropped to her knees..."

Suddenly, I feel at fault. I don't know what I've done, but whatever it is, it must be of my doing.

"She was never apologised to before", Nintinugga", Dšarael says. "Not by someone with a higher status. "Sorry" is not the word used with istana, especially never directed *at* them. The word with the meaning such as the one you're trying to relay, does not exist in their lexicon. Nobody has ever asked for an istana's forgiveness."

I turn to him, staring at him, looking for a twinkle of a joke behind his eyes, but I can't find any.

I stare at the god's solemn face and I can't comprehend his words. I can't wrap my mind around the possibility of a language in which one does not hear an apology, the language which has been passed down to the children, in which children don't hear an apology from others, a language which is filled with commands and demands only, a language which serves to kick one into a corner, bringing one down, to be yelled at and broken down.

I turn to the sobbing girl in front of me, and the earlier embarrassment at my rush anger is replaced with heavy guilt and shock.

I drop to my knees in front of her, pulling her close, hugging her, rocking as I used to rock my sweet Jess, who just like her hadn't heard "sorry" from her mother once.

I stroke Shana's back, murmuring soft words in her ear, suddenly realising the depth of abuse her people have suffered.

"I will not be that kind of "mother" to these people", I decide suddenly. *"Maybe I don't have to survive by sacrificing them."*

"Come on, Shana. It's alright. I'm not angry, not at all, my child, not at all", I say, rocking her. "You are the best child any mother could hope for. You are a wonderful and kind girl, and I love you. I would never hurt you. Never again will I frighten you. Let's go, Shana. Please. Let's get up and go. We have far to go."

She nods into my shoulder, wiping her eyes, and I turn, gazing at the god above me.

You did it to them too. You are responsible too. The blood of their abuse is on your hands too.

I get up and pull Shana to her feet. I wipe her eyes with my thumbs, determined to give her a different future, not following the god's path, not to hurt or sacrifice these people for my gain, but to love and care for them instead.

"Let's go", I murmur, stroking her dark dirty hair. "We need to meet everyone by the Gates. Can you imagine if we're the last ones to our own ba —"

I begin a light-hearted joke, but before I can finish the last word, the screech of a badly tuned radio pierces the silence of the tunnel.

I slam my mouth shut and yank the two black daggers from my corset, spinning on the spot, looking for the danger and the source of this noise, but I can't see anything.

Suddenly, the screech is cut with Baza's voice.

"Ariel, darling girl. How are you?"

Shit!

I spin on the spot but even in my light I can't see or feel anything or anyone, apart from the two istana and the god, who are spinning their heads too.

"You hear it?" I whisper and the god and Shana both nod.

Thank god. I'm not losing my mind.

"I hear you're still running, hoping to find a way out?"

Baza's voice echoes in the tunnel. His soft baritone is as deep and velvety as the last time I heard it, but occasionally, his voice fades out for a brief second before coming back with earlier clarity.

"Let's move", I whisper, sliding the daggers into my corset and turning Shana towards the direction we were going, nudging her down the corridor.

"Let's go", I hiss at Dšarael and Mitish. "Move it!"

"You have surprised me, I have to confess", Baza's voice continues. "And that's not an easy thing to do, Ariel. I hope it will give you a sense of achievement when you die, which is not going to be much longer now."

I nudge Shana to move faster, and slowly, her pace next to me gathers.

"You've surprised me time and time again", Baza announces. "I hadn't anticipated your arrival into Arllu. Clearly, I should have stayed behind and oversaw the campaign in Apkallu myself, but mind you, I should have brought more malakhims with me too. Who would have thought that you and the mingled lapdog of yours would manage to cut your way out. But after that, I was sure you'd go to Uras and hide behind its walls for a few GA. I have begun planning how to extract you from your fortress and here you are, surprising me, again. Wow, wow, wow."

The four of us are running now, our heavy panting is absorbed by the earth around us.

"You do have a knack of surprising me, Ariel, and trust me when I say it, I'm not easily surprised."

As we run along the corridor, Baza's voice grows louder then fades away as if the tunnel is outfitted with speakers at every meter or so.

"So when Lis ran to me, informing me that you are in *Arllu*, recruiting the fallen to bring them into your fold into Uras?.."

His soft grandfatherly laugh echoes down the tunnel and I can imagine the wrinkles folding around his eyes and his tummy move with his laughs.

"Surprise, after surprise, darling girl. The cunning brain and bravery? Brilliant and ballzy play, girl! I was so proud of you. I still am."

We are running at full speed now, Mitish ahead, leading the way, behind him the god and after him me and Shana. I don't know where we're running to. I don't know what the plan is. Our running is a primitive "fight" response to the situation where there's no one to fight.

Baza keeps on talking.

"And then, when I was about to see my brave visitor, to issue my personal admirations before the big execution, I hear that you had escaped! Can you imagine my surprise? The girl had *absorbed* another's Qal, exploded the gertüs peluş and whoosh, left. The surprise of it!"

He falls quiet for a moment.

"The little, stupid *badhu* Lis should not have been there, but it's too late asking it from her, I suppose."

He laughs.

"You've made sure of it. The little girl is far more resourceful and unexpected than anyone ever thought, and I have to confess, I didn't expect any of these moves either, which is an extreme rarity for me."

"Mitish, Mitish!" I hiss ahead into the corridor, and when the istana slows down and turns his head, I ask: "How far? How far to the surface?"

"A while, Mammí", he answers, slowing down to a jog.

"Then let's increase the speed, guys", I call and he turns around sprinting into the darkness, followed by the god.

"But your running is coming to an end", Baza's voice announces via his hellish tannoy. "Gil'Amesh, like a good slave should, has told me about your little istana recruitment drive. On one hand, another surprise and another unexpected move on your behalf, and I applaud your boldness, but on other hand, that was a naïve move, my dearest child. If you thought for a moment that istana will fight for you, fight and, especially, *win* against my malakhims, you're sorely mistaken. Istana are weak little rats, useless worms, who are afraid of their own shadows. Giving a farmer a weapon will not make him a soldier. And you'll learn very soon, that placing weapons into the istana's hands won't make them an army. You'll learn that lesson a hard way."

I run down the tight corridor, the bottom tips of my wings dragging behind me, as the folds of my top wings brushing the round dirt ceiling.

"Irrespective of what I've told you before, Ariel, I will give you the truth now", Baza continues with his godly speech and announcement. "I admire you, girl. I swear to Ki Founding Gods, I do. To come into Dingir-Ki, holding your own against the gods and not to fold, to keep on fighting? That is brave and resourceful. The new schemes of yours, new moves, one bolder than the next? Damn! Kirzin Dakuu! That is worth every bit of admiration."

He stops speaking, but I don't stop running.

"I truly wish you had agreed to share my Council, when I offered it to you", Baza sighs over the tunnel. "It would have saved me killing you and besides, it would have been nice to have someone at my table who I respect. But you declined and had made the decision for both of us. Your resourcefulness and valour has changed my position too, Ariel. It is clear that I should have killed you earlier, that I should have tied that loose end up when I had a chance. Now, as I clearly see what you are capable of, I won't allow you escape again and I will not take you prisoner. There will be no more agreements, no gifts, no clever plans.

"Now, I need you dead and I am coming for you. I know where you're heading and I will be there, greeting you. You can't outrun me. There's no place for you to hide and there's only one way out. I'm coming for you. With the entirety of my mighty army, I am coming for you.

"And here's another, and the last piece of truth I'll give you. You will be dead soon. The glorious Uriel, young Ariel, both of you will die shortly. You will die under the Gates you command, only this time the Gates won't open for you. The Gates will stay sealed and your blood will run underneath their closed doors, and no little smart plans of yours will save you. The fallen you've convinced to pledge with you, the istana you've lured to your side, all of them will die under the doors of the Great Gates. All of you will die there, and when your blood mixes with theirs, soaking the grounds of my kingdom, you should know that *you* have sentenced every single one of them to death, Ariel. Everyone will be dead because of you. I'll make sure to kill everyone who chose you."

Baza's propaganda tannoy falls silent, but I feel a strange vibration through my feet, every time my foot touches the ground.

"Every one of them will die because of you, Ariel. They will die *with* you. The Arllu's soil will be your grave, absorbing your Qal, leading it into Udhad."

The vibration is more noticeable now. I feel it through the air in the tunnel too. It comes off the walls and it is rising.

Mitish stumbles and stops. The god stops next to him, scanning the tight tunnel, lifting his head up to the ceiling.

A few steps away from them, I stop too.

"Remember, Ariel, *you have* made that choice", Baza's voice repeats.

The vibration shakes the ground and the walls. It shakes the tunnel. The soil rolls off the walls in clumps and drops from the ceiling, landing with heavy wet thuds on the ground around me. The sprinkling of the dirt coats my head, my wings and my body.

The tunnel shakes harder now, crumbling around us. It's an earthquake and we're locked within an earthy grave.

A large chunk of dirt drops from the roof, landing in front of Shana, while another chunk flops between Mitish and Dšarael, spraying both with sticky mud. The god and Mitish carry on running, disappearing in the distance.

"Go!" I roar, when Shana's scared gaze meets mine. "Run!"

Unsettled and disturbed by the vibration, the heavy black soil keeps on falling.

Shana sprints after them, and as I am about to follow, another heavy load of black soils lands on the ground in front of me, cutting off my path.

Suddenly, with heavy thuds, the round ceiling crumbles.

"Arllu's soil will be your grave."

And with a fresh wave of quake, the roof of the earthy tunnel collapses on top of me.

CHAPTER 33

An unbearable weight crushes me, pressing on my lungs, crumbling my ribcage.

I can't breathe.

In a peaceful moment of denial, I think it's the end of my usual nightmare, that I am in my bed, about to wake up, but when I try to move, my body doesn't respond to my command.

I can't draw in a breath and I can't open my eyes.

The last minutes of my life rush forward, reminding me of my running down the earthy tunnel under the accompaniment of Baza's threats, the fall of dark earth ahead, which hides the bodies, and then the sudden weight on me.

The weight bears down on every bone in my body. It's on top of me, on top of my stomach, on my legs, on my face and even on my eyelids and it's breaking me.

The pressure is everywhere and I can't shift it.

I try to thrash, but my body doesn't move.

I try to breathe, but my lungs don't open to draw in the air and my chest doesn't rise.

I open my mouth to scream and the wet dirt falls into it, sliding down my throat, choking me.

My ghostly moves are futile and my silent screams are never to be heard.

My face is smothered under a blanket of soil. It's wet, black and silent. It's dark and crushing. It's alone, final and empty.

I thrash. I scream, soundlessly, swallowing more dirt.

A distant rustle breaks the absorbing silence, interrupting my panic.

The sound is weak and obscure, trickling into my consciousness through the layer of isolation.

The rustle is feeble yet it grows stronger.

It's pulsating through the coffin of soil.

It's approaching.

It's coming at me.

I open my mouth, swallowing the dirt again, pushing it out of my mouth with my tongue. I try to raise my arms, to move my body, trying to get away, but the soil is pressing too hard, stealing my freedom and my life.

The rustle is now next to me.

It's no longer feeble. It's the sound of a body making its way through the wall of soil and I feel the moving soil crumbling and shifting around me.

I try to move again but my attempts are useless.

Now, the body is next to me. It's next to my head.

I can hear grains of sand and dirt move around it, falling and rising. The grains of sand rub small stones, and suddenly, through the wall of wet soil, something cool and slimy touches my cheek.

I open my mouth to scream but the black soil shuffles my cries back into my throat with its weight. My screams don't come. My throat is now clogged with the soil.

I kick.

My coveted moves to freedom don't materialise, as the soft and cool body keeps moving along my face, coating my skin in its mucous.

It's large and fat. I can feel it around me, as it presses its body against me. It's long. I hear the movement of soil far in the distance. I'm coated in cool slime and I am cold. I am shivering now.

The chilling body above is tubular. I can feel the movements of its segments as it's making its way across, pushing its body along mine.

I don't know what it is. I can't see anything.

The body turns, changing direction, and slowly it begins wrapping itself around my shoulders and my face, suffocating me further.

Suddenly, a face of a handsome man rises in my mind. The man is smiling as he runs across the green, chasing a ball, and a young boy runs next to him, laughing, as he is trying to tackle the man down.

The slimy body makes its way across my face and the image in my mind changes.

It's the same man, only now he holds a beautiful bride in his arms, who is smiling brightly at him.

The vision changes again, this time bringing an image of a dark body on the ground, shrouded in the shadows of dusk. The body lies on a pavement, as the man stands above it, holding a knife and pulling a wallet from the victim's pocket.

The shivers rake my body as the strange images progress.

The slimy body is around me now. It's on top of me and it's below me.

I am wrapped in its pulsating hold. It's heavier than the tonnes of soil above and it's colder than the wet earth.

The image in my mind changes once more, as I watch the handsome man shaking hands with another man, a man dressed in an impeccable suit, with finely trimmed beard above a slightly opened collar of an elegant shirt, which shows a glimpse of a... golden button in the middle of his throat.

The tubular body lies on top of me. Like a vine or a snake, it has wrapped itself around me, cocooning and smothering me.

Another image bursts in. This time, the same man, now naked, walks with an empty, checked out gaze across the barren landscape of Arllu, as lizards with gold collar crack their whips and tongues at him and at the naked humans around him.

The tubular body on top of me grows colder. It's now colder than ice.

It suffocates me, taking the last of the air out of my lungs, sucking it out with something else, something that is far more precious than the air itself.

I don't know what it is, but as it is being pulled out of my body, it hurts harsher than anything that I've experienced before, as "that" refuses to leave me, clutching itself to me...protecting me, saving me and keeping me alive.

I throw my eyes open into the black emptiness and the mucous of the tubular body, mixed with the soil, covers my open eyes, bringing with it another image of the man, naked as before, now stepping into a black room.

The image is interrupted by a violent rip, surrounded by an agonising cry of a dying body and disintegrated soul, whilst the brilliant white thin tendrils illuminate the dark room, escaping through the shaft above.

The rupture of the man's soul in the image is answered by the breaking of something of mine. The pain in me grows, exploding in my head, tearing the veins through my body, whilst growing into a mind blinding agony.

The sound of an explosion deafens me, while it rips at my body.

I must have exploded and died, because suddenly, I don't feel anything. I don't feel any part of my body.

I don't feel anything on top or around me.

The cold slimy weight of the tubular body has gone too and so is the wet heaviness of the soil. The rustle of the body through the soil has disappeared too, giving way to a softly ringing noise of a nail striking a crystal glass.

I can't see anything. I can't smell a thing and that high ringing is the only feeling that is left in me.

A complete lightness has taken over my body, filling it with a tingling buzz of tranquillity, and, forgetting the law of gravity, my body floats.

But I don't feel it as a body. I don't feel it as one or as a whole.

I feel dispersed and scattered like rain or fog.

The small particles of me dance in the air like dust in a ray of sunshine, and I feel at peace, floating through the air for a long moment of infinity, before the dispersed bits of me are suddenly yanked back and violently amalgamated, fusing my strained muscles and wrung out veins with my crumbled bones and my exhausted mind.

A yellowish light seeps through my closed eyelids.

The stench-burdened air moves my hair, scratching my skin with its dust, bringing with it a memory of a familiar cacophony of dust brushing over metal and banging of loose metal sheets on the outer buildings.

I move, rolling to the side, feeling the solidity of the pressed earth underneath me.

I lift my eyelids, blinking against the light. I lift my hands and rub my face, and the thick layer of dirt rolls and crumbles under my touch. I twist and turn, pushing at the ground with my hands, bringing myself to my knees.

I open my eyes and look around.

I am sitting in a centre of a wide and deep crater. The wall of the crater is twenty, thirty yards away from me, surrounding me in a perfect circle. The rim of the crater rises a good few yards above my head.

Pushing through giddiness and pain, I rise to my feet, swinging unsteadily.

I cannot see from the bottom of the crater, but the air holds the familiar stench of the surface of Arllu, and the earlier banging of dust on the metal sheets of the buildings, sounds clearer as the fog in my head evaporates.

I trudge towards the wall, stumbling at the harsh and steep rising of the bowl of the crater, tripping over, falling and rising again, crawling up the tall wall, sinking my fingers and nails into the pressed red soil.

I lose my grip a few times, tumbling and sliding to the bottom of the bowl, before eventually I manage to climb to the top of the wall, throwing my leg over the edge, then hurling myself over.

CHAPTER 34

I lie for a few minutes, listening to the sounds of Hell. The distant brushing of sand on the metal sheets of the buildings, a faint banging of loose sheets and to the wind, singing over the ground.

I feel the dim yellow light through my closed eye lids and its warmth on my skin.

I don't know what that tubular slimy thing was. I don't know its name or how it ended up there, but I know that back there, in the tunnel it wanted me dead.

I knew it wanted more than just to kill me. It wanted my soul. Buried deep under the layers of soil, it was starving for it.

The images of the man in my mind were confusing though.

I'm afraid to assign a reason for them, give them a name, to think what it could've been or what it could mean. But I know that a moment ago I came very close to my death, and not just a death, but to a total annihilation that would have left nothing of me.

The air is hot and rancid. The mud began to crust over my clothes, my hair and my body, stifling my movements, binding and restricting like the grave of soil was only moments ago, and surprising myself, I roll over and begin to cry.

I don't want any of this. I don't want to do it anymore.

I am tired. I haven't had the easy life of a normal childhood or loving parents, and now I am here, adding insult to injury, swept away from my normal world, the world I knew, fighting for survival every second of my life, in a world I don't understand.

This world is waiting for its chance to chew me up and spit me out. It wants to break me the way it has broken so many before me.

I know that my road is far from over. I know that I am miles away from home, but... All I want is a moment of peace, a slither of love and trust. I want to rest.

But I know that there's no more home for me in this huge world. There's no safety. If I stop and rest, it will be the end of me. To take a break from fighting in this world means to stop living.

I never asked for any of it. I never asked for that essence with its past lives baggage. I never asked to be chased or hunted, worshiped and idolized. My prayers for loving and caring parents never came true just as my wishes for this torture to end will never come bearing fruit.

I curse this world, myself and my weakness as I pull myself up.

The mud crunches, falling off in clumps.

I haul myself up, first to my knees, then to my feet.

I need to get to my sister, to the child who would be the worst off if I am dead and who is a monster because of me. I need to fix that mistake along with many others that I've made along the way, and countless others that I'm sure I am making.

I wipe my eyes and my nose with the inside of my tunic. I am the grubbiest I've ever been, covered in dirt, mud and the dried blood of every creature populating this world.

I bring my hand to shield my eyes against the dust and scan the horizon.

The Baza's glass skyscraper twinkles in the yellow light a few miles away.

I turn.

There are a few hazy buildings in the distance in the opposite direction. I can barely make them out, but every time the dusty veil lifts, I can see the flashing white lights of the chimneys.

If my orientation as good as I hope it is, I should find Rafe with Jess, Domiel and Dumah if I walk, keeping these lights to my right.

Bending my back against the raging wind, I trudge for hours through the red landscape, seeing nothing and meeting no one but the omnipresent dust, red dirt and wind.

Suddenly, the long shriek of an animal rings in the sky. I hear it before I can see anything. The red sand had turned the sky low and hazy, yet through the whistle of the wind, another shriek rings closer, and a moment later, a dark cloud descends above me, blocking the light.

The measured beating of large wings reverberates through the sky above me. I raise my head, shielding my eyes against the dust.

A large shadow hangs above. The wingspan of a creature that is seven, maybe eight yards long with a large stout body suspended in between.

The thought of running briefly crosses my mind, but confronted by exhaustion, the thought doesn't morph into a coherent request and doesn't result in any action. So I stand on the ground, narrowing my gaze at the large creature above.

As the creature descends further, my gaze travels over its black leathery wings and the dark fur covering its body, and as I squint, the creature bends its head towards me, flashing a wet pink snout and the floppy ears, releasing another screech.

Jess!

It's Jess, but she is bigger than the last time I saw her.

After releasing another cry, she draws a circle above, banking on her wings, before descending to the ground in front of me, folding her large wings behind her back.

Jess has grown.

Her body is the size of a large elephant, but holding the body shape of hyena. As usual, her front legs are longer than the back ones, but this time, when she plods towards me, she doesn't wobble. Instead, her moves are confident and lithe and a moment later, I feel the soft head ram at my chest and she begins to purr.

"Jessie, Jessie-boo", I coo as I stroke her furry head. "How have you been, sweetie? I told you I'd come back to you. I promised. Did you think I would leave you behind? Not a chance, baby girl, not a chance."

Jess shuffles closer, leaning her big furry body against mine and I have to widen my stance to keep my balance under her weight.

"How you been without me? Behaving, I hope", I murmur. "I hope you weren't giving Rafe hard time."

I stroke her head and her neck. She lifts her head, inviting me to rub her under her chin, and I do what I'm asked. Her eyes are closed and her purr is steady.

"You've been eating well I see", I say, rubbing and roughing her neck, which had thickened out too. "And you're flying better."

I talk to her, hoping that she understands me.

Since we crossed the Gates and stepped on the red soil of Arllu, our minds' connection was severed. Only once her mind had connected with mine, when I broke into Baza's network, but it's now gone too. Again, she isn't able to speak to me and I can only pray that she understands me when I speak to her.

We have both changed. We are both not what we used to be. We're miles from our home, from our old lives, from what we were, and I can think of only one way to finish this nightmare.

"Let's go and see Rafe, shall we?"

I lift Jess' furry face, and looking into her brown wet eyes, I kiss her pink snout.

"I will fix this too", I say to her.

And it's irrelevant if she hears or understands me. I'm making this promise for myself. It's a reminder of what I have to do after this battle is won. It's a reminder that I need to stay alive and *win* this battle. This promise will keep my resolve against the inevitable and against my weak human morals of right and wrong.

After one last hug, I release her head, stepping around her, taking a few steps towards the camp of Rafe and brothers.

Behind my back, the heavy wings slap the ground a few times, and then her body takes to the sky, flying above me, rising higher, leading the way. And looking at her, I open my wings too, and after kicking at the ground, I rise with the beating of my wings, following my animal sister.

Jess' wings are bigger than mine and a couple of times I lose her within the curtain of moving dust, but I manage to catch up with her every time, as she slows her pace and waits for me.

But we don't fly for long, and after ten minutes of Jess leading the way, she screeches, disturbing the air, and points her head towards the small dark crowd on the ground below.

She descends suddenly, dropping down like a stone, and my heart jumps into my throat as I watch her, ready to yell a warning or swoop down. But Jess is confident on her wings and before my mind remembers how to form sentences, the crowd below scatters and Jess lands her heavy body, raising with it a large dust cloud.

A few brave bodies that are left on the ground possess angelic wings, and amongst them I spy the glittery purple wings of Rafe.

I descend too, although with less speed and agility than Jess, landing to the side of the meandering crowd.

The crowd is my istana, one squadron, which has already made its way out of tunnels and have found Rafe.

Once my wings are folded, the istana rush towards me, smiling and waving their hands, and a surprising new chant begins: "Mammí! Mammí! Képar-taa. Képar-taa, képar-taa."

The hands reach towards me, touching my clothing, the feathers on my wings, and with it the chant grows stronger.

I don't know what they are saying, what these words mean, but the adoration is clear and I am relieved to see some of my istana alive.

The god's words about his life tied to theirs has rung in my head on my flight back. I was prepared to find lifeless istana bodies littering the ground or not find any, knowing that they had died under ground. I was prepared for another wave of blame for another mistake.

So, the god must be alive. That's good. Maybe Shana is alive too...

I smile, nodding my head at my people, as I walk through the crowd, around Jess and towards the group of angels, who are waiting for me.

The istana don't follow me past Jess. They stop before reaching her, crowding and pushing on each other like a swarm of insects pressed on a glass window.

Rafe, Domiel and Dumah stand next to Tagas.

My earliest companions look as fearless as they did the last time I saw them, especially next to trodden down Tagas. The pockets of their tactical gear and sheaths are full of weapons and ammunition.

"Were you here long?" I ask Tagas.

"No, Beyelai Sar. We arrived not long ago."

Answering me Tagas bows, his gaze travels over the muddy look I carry, his eyebrows furrow with confusion. But Rafe asks the unspoken question for him as he steps forward, eyeing me with open shock.

"What has happened to you?"

My hair is dishevelled. It and my face are caked in mud and my clothes are beyond dirty.

I feel Domiel' and Dumah's gazes on me too. It's been a while since the three of them saw me, and I bet my transformation is as shocking and phenomenal to them, as the pictures of "before" and "after".

Saying goodbye to three of them and Jess feels like a life time ago, while my human life feels like a forgotten dream.

I want to ask Rafe where he wants me to begin, but instead I say: "You all know each other so we can skip the formalities."

"Were you the first to leave?" I ask, turning to Tagas.

"Yes, my beyelai." He nods.

"Okay, so the other groups should be joining us soon", I say.

"Fingers crossed", I add quietly to myself.

Rafe comes closer, leaning in.

"Ariel, can I please have a word?"

"Sure", I sigh.

I know Rafe well enough to expect a "flight debriefing", followed by a lecture.

We take a few steps away from the angels.

"Ariel, what is the meaning of this?" Rafe asks, nudging his head towards the flock of istana, and following his gaze, I look at the exhausted and dirty people, congregating in a tight scared flock.

"I expected to see Tagas and the other *angels* with you", he continues, "and sooner than this, but instead Tagas arrives, without you, with hundreds of the istana in tow. He began explaining why he has the istana with him, but maybe now you can fill me in? Why are the istana here? It's not what we have agreed. It's not what we have planned."

I sigh and turn to face him.

"No. It's not what we planned and I'm aware it's not what we have agreed, but things have changed and I had to make a decision. Now we have the istana with us. They will be fighting with us when Baza comes."

Rafe's eyes fly open and he stares at me.

He thinks I've lost my mind.

"The istana are not fighters", he mumbles after a while. "They don't know how to hold or swing a weapon, and back up a bit, "fighting with us when Baza comes"? What does that mean? What's happened to "a quick get in, get out and nobody would know we were there"?"

He is screaming now.

"That was before Baza cracked on our secret meeting", I say and sigh, "before I was locked up, waiting for my ceremonial execution in the presence of the leaders of all parties, including *Mik'hael*, before I had to run and build an army on the go like a freaking take away burger."

I take a breath.

"Yes, Baza knows we are here, at least he knows that I am here. He is coming for me and he has announced that much. He will be waiting for us by the Gates with all of his malakhims. That was announced too. Apparently he is sick of chasing me."

"Irtu Etu Dalkhu!" Rafe hisses through his teeth.

"Yep. Something like that." I sigh. "So, the whole plan of ours kinda went out of the window, Rafe. Now we have a new plan: fight, with everything and everyone we've got until we're either out of here or dead."

Rafe narrows his gaze at me and stares for a few seconds, before he pushes out: "I hope you know that it's more likely to be the latter."

There's nothing I can say to his remark that won't be bullshit or a lie, so I shrug my shoulders, turn around and walk away.

CHAPTER 35

I walk over to Jess, who lies half a mile away.

It's surreal to look at the creature from a crazy mythological experiment and call it my sister. But what painful is the knowledge that I am responsible for this. Every time I look at her furry face with a pink pig snout, I know that I brought her here, refusing to accept her fate and leave her behind in the human world.

My decision has made her a monster. I might as well have done the deed myself.

"How have you been, sweetie?"

I lean against her soft fur, hugging her neck and stroking her face.

"You've grown. I don't think I need to ask you if you've been eating well", I laugh. "You look nice and clean. Did Rafe take a good care of you? I hope he did."

She doesn't answer me, because she no longer can.

I sigh.

"We'll be leaving this place soon, Jessie-boo. And once we're out of here, I will fix it, baby. I promise. I will fix it all."

As I stand, talking into her fur, I feel the presence of a group behind me, I hear the rattle of their hushed voices and their number is growing.

I lift and turn my head.

The circle of the istana gathers and grows around us. One by one they shuffle closer, mystified by the creature, as their mouths hang open and interest twinkles their eyes.

In their eyes, the friendship of their "mother" with the monster is a confirmation of the creature's kind intentions and a seal of approval issued by the "mother", and soon, in the corner of my eye, I notice a slim body and a hand, reaching out towards Jess' furry side.

With the "touch permit" not signed by my monster, Jess spins, throwing me off with a push of her muscles, as she bares her teeth at the face of the young istana, her saliva dripping from the corner of her mouth. The push of her muscles makes me fly, before landing on my arse.

From the ground I watch her, as she is about to launch, and I yell: "No! Jess, no! No, girl!"

She stops an inch from the slim body and the petrified istana freezes.

Both stare at each other as Jess continues to growl.

"Jess, no!" I call again. "Absolutely not! Don't you dare!"

I get up and rush closer.

"No", I say calmer, squeezing myself between the two. "We don't eat them. We don't eat the istana. They are our friends and we don't eat friends", I murmur.

Standing next to the young istana, I listen to the panicked beating of his heart and I can smell his fear.

I turn my head to the boy.

"They are our friends", I repeat, and when he turns his head to me and his gaze meets mine, I take his hand in mine, reaching with it towards my sister. But the scared young man tugs his hand out of my grip, pushing his feet at the ground, refusing to come closer.

"It's okay", I say, turning to him. "It's okay, I promise. She's not going to hurt you. I am with you."

His gaze studies my face for a few seconds and when I tug at his hand again, he lets me bring his hand forward until it makes contact with Jess's fur.

The moment his hand connects with the Jess' fur, giving it a first stroke, Jess growls louder and the young man gives a little squeak. Both are rigid, ready to run, Jess to chase a new food source and the istana away from the monster.

The Istana crowd grows tighter around us, in spite of Jess's growls.

I ignore Jess's threats. Instead, I lead the istana's hand with mine over Jess's fur, brushing it, stroking.

"You see?" I murmur. "Nice, isn't it? They are nice. They are our friends." I tell it to my sister, while guiding the istana's hand down the side of her neck.

"They are our friends and we are theirs. We need to know who our friends are and we need to trust them. We will need them very soon", I coo to my sister, moving the istana's hand up and down my sister's fur.

I look at the boy's face frozen in shock, and once his gaze meets mine, I lift my hand off his, freeing it. Keeping his stunned gaze on me, on autopilot he gives Jess's fur one stroke, then another.

The animal in my sister has stopped growling and when I take a step around her, I see her eyelids hang heavily as she releases her fear, finally relishing the attention.

"Beyelai Sar! Uriel!"

I snap my head towards Tagas' voice.

He points somewhere at the distance, and when I turn my head towards the shown direction, I see a small squadron of the istana emerging from the cloud of dust that they are raising with their feet.

Kafziel marches ahead of his tribe.

Behind him, are the three angels, the two female Ophanims and the angel of the record keeping, and after them plods a tight crowd of the istana, which has lost its earlier formation, looking like a mob rather than an army.

Rafe and I reach the group at the same time from the opposite directions.

I glance at Rafe, for a moment watching his gaze dance over the group, scanning the faces and bent backs, darting to the bodies of angels, carried on the make shift stretchers.

He rushes towards the stretcher carrying his friend, but not before his confused gaze collides with mine.

"What's happened to Yofiel?" Rafe asks Rachiel, who stands near her husband.

"Samu tonur Ilkhu", she answers and Rafe's back snaps straight.

"How? I haven't heard of them for three GA. Where did you find them?"

Rachiel turns her head to me and Rafe turns too, following her gaze.

The floor is mine and I'm expected to explain and defend myself.

"Some sort of beetles with the clear shells that Baza infected the soil around the istana's headquarters", I say.

I don't like the way I sound. I don't like the weakness I can hear in my voice. I don't like the position I am placed in, forced onto a stand, being demanded to explain myself.

I clear my throat.

"We were ambushed", I say, carving each word, sounding stronger, "more angels were injured and they should be here soon with the rest of the istana."

Rafe glares at me without a word. The accusation is crystal clear in his eyes.

But I steel myself against it as I gaze at him, keeping my back straight.

I made the decision. I chose to lead the pledged angels that way and I'm going to own it, and what's more, without me and Sam, there wouldn't be any pledged angels. If I'd followed Rafe's advice, I would've been hiding behind the walls of Uras, waiting for Baza to come, jumping at every noise, expecting to die every minute.

I clear my throat.

"Rafe", I say, moving the conversation from a plane of accusation into one of a solution. "The orb, the one I filled for you and left for you, do you still have it? Is it full?"

Rafe turns his head, looking at the angels on the stretchers.

"For Yofiel and Ophaniel?"

I nod.

"Yes. I have it and it's still full. I haven't used it."

He looks at me.

It feels as if he is about to tell me that it's my fault, but instead he says: "I think it should work. How many more are injured?"

"Two more in the next group and Sam in the last", I answer, searching Rafe's face for reaction at Sam's name.

But Rafe doesn't give me any. Instead, he steps closer to Rachiel, and taking her hand in his, he says: "We'll fix my brother. He will stand next to you in no time. I swear it to you, as An be my witness."

Rafe turns around, starting briskly away.

I sprint after him, and catching his arm, I spin him towards me.

"Rafe. Please, don't. Not just yet. Can we please wait? Can we please wait for everyone to arrive? Can we wait for Sam?"

"Why..." he starts, but falls silent looking at my face.

My motives are not a secret to him.

"That is my brother lies there", he hisses at me, throwing his arm and pointing behind me. "A brother, who pledged himself to you and followed you. We owe him that. *You* owe him that. Do you want to go to his wife, to the woman who saved Uriel's essence, who was faced with Mik'hael's wrath because of it, was exiled because of it, and tell her that her husband will be left like this indefinitely? Or until your boyfriend arrives or maybe until your fancy strikes?"

Rafe's voice rises with every new word.

"Watch yourself!" I bark. "Don't you dare imply that I don't care. Don't you dare! I asked you to wait and that's all. Or have you forgotten why you are still here and who you should be grateful to for such a gift? Isn't it the selfish girl, the one who thinks only of herself that brought you to life?"

I glare at Rafe, who's glaring at me in return, and past the hammering of my heart I can hear the ringing silence around us.

I turn my head and spin to find that every angel is watching and listening to us, and even the istana have stopped petting my furry sister, batting the eyelashes of their wide opened eyes, like innocent children watching a parental argument. Now I understand why the god has called them his "children".

I clear my throat and take a breath, before announcing: "All I'm saying is that we should wait for arrival of *all* of the injured, to make sure that there is enough energy in the orb to heal everyone. We need to heal everyone, if not to fight with us, then at least so they can move unassisted."

I turn my head, scanning the crowd, as I raise my voice.

"We need to give everyone a chance and their fair share", I call to the attentive crowd. "We are going to leave this place as one, all of us, just as promised and we're not going to leave a man behind."

Another rousing speech from me. I have to say, I'm tired of them.

"Everybody will get their fair share, agreed?" I call to Rachiel, and she gives me a small nod.

I have an incredible itch to add that it's my essence in the orb, so if push comes to shove, the decision would be mine, but I don't say it. I am learning diplomacy. I learn how to push my agenda behind their backs, and the earlier outburst would be the last...or at least, one of the last.

I don't think my earlier disclosure has won me any votes, but what I know is that we need to move fast and stay united. As soon as the last two groups arrive, we need to progress further. I need to move my army towards the Gates, for our last push.

The longer I am stuck here, arguing with Rafe over my decisions, the weaker my leadership becomes, and the weak leadership is not something I can afford right now. I'm far from home, and my battles are far from won. I have invested far too much time and blood into bringing myself and others here.

But Rafe is here too, with them, and that's the danger.

Rafe, who would look the part in their Heavenly Games, who fought many battles with many of them, who shares their bloodlines and their history. Rafe, who is their own, through and through, born and bred in the Celestial Halls, who knows and understands their world, the one who didn't lead old angels and Ophanims into tunnels of Hell, injuring and killing many.

He would be the perfect leader for them. The leader they would yearn to have, who has the perfect name with all required regalia and pedigree, and I need to move fast, to prevent these thoughts from rising, as once they bloom, they would take hold, and then I will be left to fight another battle, looking over my shoulder, expecting a knife in my back.

I scan the faces of the angels and narrow my gaze.

Maybe I am already late.

Maybe the thought has crossed their minds already, the idea of a familiar leader, appealing to them as they charge into the unknown.

And over time, as we wait, the divide grows in my army ranks, splitting my followers into the two clear cut groups: the angels and the istana. The small cluster of angels had gathered around Rafe and Domiel, talking in hushed voices, while a much larger crowd of the istana have congregated around Jess, who is now happily receiving the petting from them.

Dumah is next to Jess though, and his vigilant stance reads as him standing guard, while he is watching over her. But he is smiling, as he watches furry Jess roll around on the red soil, as the istana are petting her belly.

CHAPTER 36

Zabkiel arrives promptly after Kafziel. The unconscious bodies of his brothers swing on the pieces of long fabric, between the istana.

Pronoia with his squadron of the istana comes last.

In preparation for Sam's arrival, I've scooped the black orb from the small orange tent in which Domiel, Dumah and Rafe were waiting for me, and not trusting Rafe, I walked around with it, hugging its bloated form tightly to my hip.

The swarm of twinkling lights woke up the moment I brought the orb to my chest, pulling on my glow, making it brighter, creating the fine threads of energy between the orb and my chest.

It must be one thing to be told of the orb, but another to see it, as angels' stupefied and scared gazes follow my movements, taking steps away from me and my black "bomb" when I come near, their hushed voices rising with my departure.

But I became accustomed to scared expressions around me. Since the moment the essence woke inside me, it's the only expression I see.

Now, watching Pronoia's tired group coming through the dusty horizon, I scan the crowd, desperately looking for a gap in its formation, where I know the body of Sam will be swinging.

Finally, I spot that narrow gap, Tabby's slim body walking next to it, and my heart drops. She is the first disillusioned follower of mine, and there might be many more if I don't handle it well.

Once the squadron arrives, it unambiguously splits into angels and istana. The division is too stark for me to ignore, adding another issue to my ever growing "to do" list. The unified army is the only army which can stand against Mik'hael and Baza, and this cast or race division, whatever it's called, won't do.

I sigh and drop my gaze to the orb.

It's full of millions of golden swimming, giggling specks of light. It's full of my energy. It's full of me.

Adjusting my hold on the orb, I waddle to the small group of angels gathered around the new arrivals.

"Pronoia, Domiel, Dumah", I address them. "Can you please bring all of the injured together?"

Although most of the injured are already clustered in one place, Sam was placed away from the group, laid on the red soil and left there, away from everyone, and seeing him like that, abandoned and rejected, something punches at my chest. They are taking their dissatisfaction in me out on him, waking my anger and hate towards the rest of the angels, those he thought as his friends.

The angels walk over to him, picking up the corners of the tarp. I rush to them, grabbing the fourth corner, and carry Sam next to the rest of the injured, bringing him into the fold.

I will not allow them to isolate him, to take it out on him. If they have a problem, they had better grow a pair and come and speak to me.

"It might be sooner than you think", Rage huffs, lifting her eyebrows at me. The girl fancies herself a prophesier.

All of the injured are here now. The bodies are lying side by side, five bodies, all males.

I pray that the orb would have enough energy for them all. I pray that it'll have enough to bring everyone to their feet and no one will be left out. I don't expect much. I don't expect them to walk out and fight, although it would be great, but I need them, at the very least, be able to stumble away and hide if we were to lose.

The hush of voices dies and the circle of angels parts in front of me, as I come through, carrying my orb. The angels wearily take steps away, their gazes glued to the live orb.

I waddle with the orb to the nearest body, kneeling next to Rachiel's husband.

In the expectant silence, the sounds of moving dust and shuffles of hundreds of the istana's feet are prominent. The wind is billowing and screeching above the plateau. The screen of dust is as thick as before. The air is hot and smelly.

I rest the heavy orb on my knees.

The orb is brighter now. The light that had started as a few weak tendrils, connecting my chest and the orb is now a thick and steady beam and my chest is aglow with a golden light.

I don't risk placing the heavy orb on Yofiel's chest or hold it in my outstretched arms above him for the fear of losing grip and crushing him with it, so I lift Yofiel's hands, placing them on top of the sphere.

The moment his hands make contact with the orb's smooth surface, the orb grows brighter, calling the swimming specks towards the top, where his hands are resting.

Suddenly his chest lights up with a weak, interrupted golden glow, and the first thin tendril of golden light connects his chest and the globe and the dozens of voices around me exhale and gasp in surprise.

The stream of light between his chest and the orb grows brighter and stronger. The opening of the brimming light in his chest widens. The chatter of the golden and silver specks in the globe rises, and suddenly, a few specks begin to fly from the orb into the light in his chest, through the bridge of the light connection.

The first specks swim into his chest, giggling and chasing each other.

Another gasp, louder this time, rumbles around me, birthing an urgent and hushed chatter.

But I don't tell them to keep quiet. I don't need to concentrate. I know the process well enough by now and I leave the orb to do its job.

One by one and in clusters, the golden and silver specks disappear inside Yofiel's chest.

I shift my gaze, scanning the body on the ground in front of me, and sure enough, his skin begins to illuminate with light, as the luminescence of the specks begin to gather under his skin.

The mixture of gold and silver rises to the top of his mauled face and to his arms with chunks of missing flesh. It covers his wounds in a living mercurial layer and tiny voices of laughter ring louder in my head. The sparkling layer covers his mangled wings and with it his body lights up, extracting another unified gasp from the audience.

I glance at his growing muscles and his skin, but my gaze is glued to the living orb as I am more concerned with the amount of the living specks left in the globe: I have five mauled bodies on the ground. I need to make sure that what I have inside of this globe is enough for everyone.

Rachiel shuffles from the circle of angels, closer to the body of her husband.

She drops to her knees next to him, and is about to touch him, when I cut her: "No! Don't touch!"

She raises her gaze to me and nods, dropping her hand onto her lap.

This has to be enough.

I lift his hands off the orb and the connection, the light bridge between the orb and his chest dissolves, leaving a few last specks to swim under his skin, doing their job, finishing off their healing, before they disappear too, absorbed by him.

I rise to my feet.

The orb is as heavy as it was before, only now the glittery fish tank is darker.

Balancing the orb next to my stomach, I waddle around the bodies, to the body resting on the opposite side.

I kneel next to the body of Sam. I reach out, placing his hands on the glowing orb.

I raise my gaze and it collides with dozens of gazes. I see awe, approval, concern, love and... the studious gaze of Rafe, who watches me carefully, before giving me a short nod.

He thinks he gives me permission. He thinks I need it. He thinks he is in charge. He thinks I'm the same naïve girl he met in the school cafeteria. But I am not and I don't need his blessing to do what I want or need.

Keeping my face closed off, I give him a short answering nod and turn my attention to Sam.

The connection between his chest and the orb is bright and strong. The silver and golden specks are swimming through the golden bridge and then spreading, covering in a thin, shiny mercury layer his once gorgeous, but now salvaged, face.

The layer spreads over his entire body, coating his skin and his wings. The feathers straighten with the soft cracks of set bones, restoring their normal look and positions. The muscles knit and the skin grows.

The rising hush of voices pulls my attention away from Sam, and I lift my head.

On opposite side of the circle, Yofiel has opened his eyes, and Rachiel begins to cry, mumbling some relieved graces as she drapes herself over his chest, while the rest of the angels begin to murmur amongst themselves.

Rafe pushes past the angels, coming closer to Yofiel, kneeling next to him. He says something quietly to his friend, and I see Yofiel nodding. Rafe brings his forehead to the forehead of his friend, clasping the friend's neck.

I return my attention to the body in front of me.

Sam's face is full again. The muscles and skin are weaved over the gaping holes.

The giggling and twinkling specks are happy. They don't mind where they swim. They don't care whom they heal.

But as much as I want to hold the healing orb next to Sam forever, desperate to give him all of it, I pull his hands off the smooth and glossy surface, heavily rising up. There are three more bodies waiting for my help.

As I leave Sam's side, Tabby slides over and kneels on the red ground next to him, taking his large hand into hers.

Yofiel is helped to his feet by Rafe and Rachiel, and being led away from the centre of the circle, which parts for them to give way.

I kneel on the ground next to the one of the warrior brothers, on the ground where Yofiel's body laid only a moment ago. Resting the orb on my knees, I place his hands over it, beginning the process all over again.

The crowd is closer now. The circle is tighter around me. I can feel them with my wings and my back.

The hush of excited voices is busier. The brothers are looking forward to have their kin back, whilst the istana behind them are eager to witness another miracle produced by the "Mother of Gods".

Over the busy murmur of voices I hear a sharp intake of air by Sam. I hear his gasp, his heavy breathing after that. I can imagine his eyes fly open to his new surroundings, to the perpetual veil of the red dust and orange sky, and I want to be there, with him. I want to see him and I want to be the first one he sees.

But instead, I watch Tabby lean towards Sam, giving him a small hug, and I watch his arm rise, hugging her close, while I hold the hands of one of the brothers on the sparkling orb.

A gasp of the body in front of me brings me to my job and my responsibilities.

I pull the angel's hands off the orb. I let him have too much energy. He is the first one who opened his eyes under my touch.

"*But maybe he wasn't injured as much*", I tell myself.

The angel on the ground moves his lips and the soft "thank you" in Sumerian pops into my head, as his soft brown eyes gaze at me.

I nod, rising to my feet, and my place is taken by his brothers, who help him to his feet, leading him away.

I shuffle closer to the next body. Only two bodies are now left on the ground, a male Ophanim with dark burgundy wings and one of the warrior brothers.

The crowd behind me is ecstatic.

The earlier murmur is replaced by cheering and excited exclamations of anticipation. The istana are stretching their necks, pushing closer, the back rows climbing over the front, hungry to witness the miracle of resurrection.

Sam unsteadily rises to his feet and Tabby is the only one who helps him up.

I want to drop the orb, leave it here and be there for him, *with him*, holding his body as he moves. I want to touch his face and his wings, to check that he is alright, that he is fixed, that he doesn't hurt anymore, but the orb won't work without me.

Without my light to ignite it, it won't wake the specks, won't push them forward. Apart from me, Rafe is the only one who can access and induce the orb but I won't give him the satisfaction of asking him for a favour, of him watching me running to Sam, choosing Sam over the bodies on the ground, confirming his doubts in my leadership and in my strength.

I will not let him use my weakness against me.

So I let my duties override my wishes, as I watch Sam stumble past and through the crowd, with only the help of tiny Tabby.

CHAPTER 37

I place the empty orb on the ground.

Finally, it's lifeless and quiet.

There's nothing left in it. The luminescent shine and giggling of silver and golden specks is gone. The specks have left their temporary home, finding a new purpose and new bodies.

The tight crowd of the istana cheered me on as I shared the specks with the last body on the ground. With every new body that had walked away, the istana's excitement grew and it wasn't long before they begun another chant, calling my name.

The miracle that I have performed in front of their eyes has ignited them. It had fuelled their purpose and their belief in me, raising me higher on their pedestal.

Whatever doubters I had within the istana, they were eliminated with this little resurrection trick when healed bodies walked away with the help of the loved ones.

The adoration of the istana became palpable, their belief in me complete. The followers have become worshipers, and I can build on it. I can lead the army of hundreds who trust in me, an army that believes in me and my promises, in my ability, and in what I can deliver.

Rafe will never swing them away from me. The istana are mine. Their adoration is mine to keep.

I walk through our camp, which is formed of small clusters of istana, answering with a wave or a smile to their waving and cheers.

"Mammí" is the only word on everyone's lips. This word is said, whispered or called.

The group of angels is one small, solid mass within the camp. Their large and colourful wings stand out through the sandy veil. The angels, like frightened rich girls caught in a bad neighbourhood, cluster and huddle together, talking to each other in hushed voices.

The newly brought to life angels swing on their feet, propped up by a friend or two. The last angel didn't get as much energy from the orb as the others, and now he stands next to his brothers, with his eyes closed, leaning heavily on them, his forehead is damp with sweat.

What's his name? Za... Za-something.

And for the third time, I remind myself to memorise their names.

Sam stands at the edge of the group. It is a subtle, yet noticeable message, and I don't like it one single bit.

Although, I notice it, I don't say a word. There will be more time for that later.

Tabby stands next to him, hugging him tight, and I am pleased to see that there is someone for him.

I come to the cluster of angels and the group opens up, allowing me in, as a few angels shuffle to one side.

"How do you feel?" I address the bearded Yofiel next to Rafe.

"Well. Thank you, beyelai."

He nods. His wife next to him nods too, but nobody else does.

Fair enough.

"If everyone can move, we need to progress towards the Gates", I say. "Rafe must have filled you in already on the latest development that Baza has announced that he will be waiting for us by the Gates. It's quite possible that it's just a ploy and he plans something else, but either way we need to move to the Gates, if we want to get out."

"What about Sabrael and Sabaoth?" Kafziel calls. "We are not leaving without them. When are they coming?"

I turn to him.

"I have agreed with Sabrael that he will meet us by the Gates. That's another reason why we need to move."

"Wouldn't it be more prudent to wait?" A female's voice calls from the group and I need to scan the face to find the one who spoke.

Sablo is looking at me, before adding: "Shouldn't we gather our strength, find weapons, maybe think of a better plan before we attempt to pass through the Gates?"

I scan the faces of the angels in front of me.

"No." I shake my head as I answer, turning to her, "I don't think so. Every minute we're not crossing the Gates is another minute for Baza to plan and regroup. Right now, it's only his army and his malakhims, and as much as it's more than plenty, it's only him. But Mik'hael is coming. He was invited to the execution. And if he comes, if he brings any soldiers, any fighter into Arllu with him, to help Baza while we're here..."

I stop and pause, letting their imagination and common sense finish the sentence for me, but for the ones with a weaker logical thinking, I add: "We are done in."

"Like we are not done in now", Tagas mumbles under his breath, his blue wings flash open behind him.

"We have the istana with us", I rebuff, glaring at his bent head. "We have weapons."

My gaze slides towards Rafe for support, but he holds my gaze, saying nothing, letting me fight this one on my own.

Fine!

"The istana, who are not soldiers or fighters", Tagas says as he rises his head, glaring at me, "and the weapons of ibnatums."

He nudges his head towards a nearby young istana man with a black whip tucked behind his belt.

"What are they supposed to do with these against malakhims? Tickle them to death?" Tagas huffs.

"It's all we have at the moment", I cut. "Rafe, Domiel and Dumah will share their weapons. Hopefully Sabrael would come through with his plan, and if he doesn't – "

I stop and scan the angels' faces.

"Then it's all we have."

I pause, looking at the exhausted faces of my followers, meeting their sceptical and accusatory gazes with the heavy glare of mine.

"Do any of you want to stay behind?" I ask. "Have any of you changed their minds and don't want to come with me to Uras? To follow me?"

I scan the faces, inviting anyone to come forward or to answer, but nobody says a word.

"I am not dragging anyone with me against their will", I say. "I never said it would be easy. Never have I promised that, to any of you. Never! And now we're at the final push, the final push towards the Gates and through them, after which we're home. The Gates are the only way out. You know it. I know it, and so does Baza. So when he said he will be there, waiting for us, I believe him. That's where I'd be. It's the only door out of this Hell. But if any of you don't believe in the cause anymore, *in me*, if any of you want to stay behind and save your lives, you are welcome to go back to Baza. It's not a long walk from here."

I wave my hand towards the direction of the Baza's skyscraper with the green of a golf course around it.

"I've promised a home to every single one of you in Uras, and I will deliver it", I say, keeping my voice low, as I battle with a hiss, which is scratches at my chest, wanting to come out. "There's a home in Uras for every one of you. I promised it before and I swear by it now. However, what I haven't promised is that everyone will make it. I never promised that I will keep every one of you alive."

I shake my head.

I watch their faces, and I don't know what the angels see in my gaze, but many drop their gazes, maybe ashamed or maybe submitting to me, but at this point I don't care.

"I've given you a choice. I have offered you future and I will stand by my promise. But that's about it. I'm not going to carry you on my back across the finishing line. I'm not going to fight your battles for you, as for damn sure no one has ever fought my battles for me", I bark.

I am sick of it. I am sick of being constantly questioned and doubted, double crossed, betrayed, belittled, used.

I am the Harbinger. I am the Beginning and I am the End. I am the powerful archangel, even if I still look like a weak mortal girl. I won't be doubted and played anymore.

What did I promise to Rafe in the woods? That I am here to fight and survive, to take this world for my own and to bend it to my will, and I wasn't kidding. I'll do whatever is needed.

"Maybe you had it too easy", I hiss through my teeth, my civility finally lost. "Maybe that's the problem. You've never suffered, any of you. Sitting high in your skies, in your holy towers, or roaming Hell, none of you had to die. None of you starved. None of you watched loved ones die, watched abuse or have been abused themselves, or lived in fear. Your angelic existence was easy and blissful: pick an owner, serve him well, slaughter or enslave a few humans for him, and even when cast down, keep the same lifestyle with the same perks. You have swapped one party for another, one DJ for the next. You don't know what it means to die. A few of you have died in the tunnels and suddenly you're rallying together, shocked at the unfairness of it, wondering how this could have happened to *you*, the godly, untouchable you, and who is to blame at this unfairness? And then you have found me...

"Me! Because with my arrival your world has turned upside down, with my arrival, you've tasted death for the first time, so naturally, I am at fault. But I'm not to blame, and it's not me, refusing to take responsibility, no! It's the universal laws, the laws that govern all of us, apply to all of us, mortals and istana, and shock of all shocks, you have found out that these rules apply to you too, and you don't like it", I roar. "You don't like it one single bit."

My gaze collides with a few stunned gazes, but at large, it slides over the bent heads.

"But you know what, dear angels? Tough shit", I push past my clenched teeth. "Death is here and it eventually comes for us all. Life is unfair and then we die, but it's up to you is *how* you die."

I take in a breath, adding calmer, "More death will come and you need to accept it. You need to accept that you can die at any moment, and you need to accept that any second of your life could be your last, and you need to learn how to live with it, because once you do, you'll find an incredible, stunning bravery in you, a bravery that will shine through, a bravery that you didn't even know you had. You will find a whole world of possibilities and future around you, and you will be demanding it all. Once you find the bravery to live, you will find the bravery to dream!"

Not a single angel interrupts me. Even the istana stopped their rumbling chatter in the distance.

"It's something you can learn from humans", I say. "Not those who live their entire life under the thumb of a master, on their knees, afraid and submissive, following strict rules, afraid to raise their head, to ask questions, but those who believed in a better, brighter future for their children. Those who are not afraid of death, those who stand up for themselves and others, stand up and fight, dreaming of a better..."I trail off.

I stop speaking and rub my face with my hands.

"You know what? I'm sick of rallying you, motivating you. You, them."

I wave my hand towards the istana.

"I feel like a perpetual cheerleader for the angelic kind. I'm so tired of explaining myself, all my life. So extremely tired and fed up, fed up with proving myself, every second of my life."

I rub my eyes with my thumbs, pleased to find them dry.

"I want you with me", I say, rising my head, scanning their faces, "I do, and I will keep my promise in offering you a home in Uras, but I am not going to be begging anymore. I am not going to be explaining myself and I'm done being questioned. If you have an issue with my plans, come and speak to me, offer me an alternative and let's talk. But complaining for the sake of complaining? It's done, and this will be the last of it. I came looking for strong fearless fighters and dreamers, instead I've found submissive doubters. With fear ruling us, we'll never achieve what we're dreaming of, that much I can promise you. I am here with you, every step of the way. I swear to fight and die for you, with you, for every single one of you, but I won't be able to eliminate the danger for you."

There's still not a peep from my "army", although most of the heads are raised and the gazes on me.

"Hell! I'm not Baza", I say. "Why would I want weak ones in the new Heaven we're building? Do you think it will be the last test of your loyalty, to me, to each other? Do you think others won't come to break, submit and enslave you? Do you think Baza or Mik'hael will let us live in peace? Do you think they won't be coming at us? You're naïve if you think so. By surviving and leaving them, choosing our own way, we are breaking their way of life. We're breaking the status quo and for that they would want to punish us, making us a cautionary tale to anyone else who ever would dream of freedom. And you should be ready for that. When Baza or Mik'hael, or anyone else comes, do you want the weak around you or do you want those who will have your back? Do you want the strong and decisive to stand next to you?"

I let my questions hung there for a moment before I turn around, and I am about to walk away, but I spin back and add: "If any of you want to jump ship, now is your chance. Baza's place is that way."

I wave my hand in the direction of his home once again.

I don't tell any of them that I've lost the god, the god's whose life is attached to the lives of the istana, and as much as istana are alive and kicking at the moment, it doesn't mean that they won't drop dead where they stand any moment now, and that every second of delay makes the possibility of losing the istana army more real.

I take a few steps away, but then turn around and walk back.

The circle of angels that had begun to close opens again and they look expectantly at me.

"Decide who is staying and then find me. We need to organise the istana for the march."

CHAPTER 38

I walk over to Jess. She is easy to spot: a brown hill amongst an otherwise flat landscape. A few dozen of the istana are around her, rubbing her belly, stroking her fur, petting behind her ears, and she rolls on the dusty ground, accepting the attention.

I walk towards her, and with greetings and bows, the istana giving way, and sensing my arrival, Jess turns her head to me.

My last few steps are a mad dash.

I jump up and wrap my hands around Jess' furry neck, and I begin to cry.

"I'm sorry, Jessie-boo. I'm so sorry. I will take you back. I will take you through the Gates and I will take you back. I will make you whole."

Jess' fur under my face is dusty and smells of an animal, but her body is warm. It rises with her breathing and I can hear the beating of her animal heart.

"I will fix it, I swear. I will die, but I won't let you die in here. Please forgive me, Jessie-boo. I thought I was helping. I thought I was protecting you. But I should have left you behind. I should have walked away."

With her head, Jess pushes me closer to her shoulder blades, to her body, as if she's hugging me.

The crowd of istana had dispersed, giving privacy to their Mother of Gods. They are wonderful like that.

Heavy steps come towards us, churning the grains of dirt on the ground, and at the sound of them, I shuffle, adjusting myself.

Discreetly, I wipe my face on Jess' fur then turn my face sideways, as if resting on her body. Jess lifts her head towards the newcomer, and begins to growl, quiet at first, vibrating her chest, but the growl grows stronger the closer come the footsteps.

I know it's not Rafe, Domiel or Dumah. Jess knows them. It's someone else.

I lift and turn my head.

Sam stands in front of me.

"Hey", he breathes and pulls his lips for a smile. But his smile is so weak, that his dimple winks and disappears.

"Hey", I answer.

I get up off the ground and Jess pushes onto her feet with me, shuffling closer.

She is by my side now, growling. Her body towers above mine and I barely reach her chest.

"Shush, Jess. It's okay. It's Sam. It's okay."

I reach out and stroke her muscly shoulder and with another low growl, she falls silent, yet remaining by my side.

I wait for Sam to say what he came here for.

"So this is your sister?" he asks eventually. "An Adar?"

"This is Jess", I say, glaring at him.

"Jess, this is Sam."

I turn to my sister, finishing the introductions.

"Nice to meet you, Jess", Sam says.

He takes a step closer and stretches his hand towards Jess, maybe out of habit or maybe for a stroke, but she growls at him and he drops his hand.

"Okay", he says and gives a small smile.

"Can we please talk?" he turns and asks me.

"Okay", I nod.

"Here?"

"Yeah, why not? I shrug my shoulders. "As good a place as any."

"Fine."

He shuffles closer.

"Ariel", he begins, "I know that not everyone is happy, least not with my involvement and the part I've played in convincing them to pledge to you, in luring them to your side."

He rolls his eyes at the word "luring", clearly repeating someone's bitching.

"But I want you to know that I don't share their doubts. I don't doubt any of the decisions that you've made, and I don't blame you for what happened in the tunnels and I am not complaining."

He gazes at me and I don't rush him.

"I know the tough choices in front of you, Ariel, I see them. I can see them all and quite honestly, I don't know if I could have done better, if any of them could've managed better than you're doing now. Irrespective of what they say, I think you've made the right decision by looking for an army, even if it's the istana. As much as they are not soldiers and fighters as Tagas had pointed out, there's no taking away from the importance of numbers. Of course it's better to have hundreds of assassins and not hundreds of farmers, but farmers, who are fighting for their freedom might surprise you."

I listen to him, not rushing. It's him who wanted to talk.

"What I am trying to say, Ariel, is that I'm with you, all the way, háad Mermaid. Always. But you know that, or at least I sincerely hope that you do."

He comes closer and takes my hand into his.

"I'm here for you, no matter what you need from me. No matter what you ask of me I will do it for you. Maybe it's stupid of me, and a little misguided, silly at my age after so many GA of my life to fall for it", he mumbles, almost to himself.

But then he snaps his head up, gazing at me, as he says: "But I will always be near you, whenever you need me, whatever you might need from me, I will give it to you. I will be there for you. I will happily give my life for you. I hope you know that."

He slides down to one knee in front of me, whilst holding my gaze.

"I swear to An's eternal guiding light that I will always be there for you, that I will come to your aid the moment you call, that you will always have my counsel and it will always be issued with your wellbeing in mind."

He is pledging to me. He is saying the pledge that the other angels have already uttered, and I'm surprised to suddenly realise, that he hasn't given me that pledge.

"I will slay your enemies for you should you direct me to. To do your every bidding", Sam continues. "I pledge my Qal to you. I swear that only the death of my Qal will preclude me from fulfilling my duty to you, Mermaid, to the Great Ariel, the Uriel incarnate, the first of her bloodline, The Harbinger of Doom, The Begetter of Life and The Dame of All Ends."

He covers my hand with his.

"I am prepared to die for you, with you, if needed. I pledge my eternal life and my eternal service to you, for as long as I shall live, An be my witness."

He falls silent for another moment and drops his gaze to the ground, but he doesn't get up to his feet. He hasn't finished.

I don't rush him.

There's something else he needs to say and it seems more difficult for him than the sworn allegiance. I don't rush him. He needs to say everything he needs, because this might be the last chance for both of us.

I am smothered with his scent of pines and moss. I know that something big is coming as since he has started speaking his scent was growing stronger, illustrating his rising emotions.

"It would sound so stupid", Sam mumbles, "and many would laugh at me, and they would be right by doing so, but I'm unable to do anything about it. I have tried. An is my witness, I have tried."

Sam is tripping over his own words as if he's unable to catch them or find the right ones. The eloquent and self-assured Sam that I know had disappeared, replaced with a mumbling, confused man, who is lost for words.

He brings his gaze to me and his beautiful blue eyes shine with a light I haven't seen before, in anyone's eyes directed at me, ever.

There's no sign of his usual teasing or sarcasm in his gaze. His eyes are wide, wet and earnest.

"Baza thought I was playing the role very well", he starts quietly. "I thought I was invested in it because of the task. I thought that what was happening, around me, to me, was happening because I was telling myself it was how I felt. But when you ran, I was devastated. I was lost. I've never felt so alone. And it's an absurd thing to say, as I was always alone, forever, for as long as I remember. But after you left... It was different somehow. It was new. That was a different kind of loss and loneliness. It was as if finding something that you never knew you needed and then suddenly losing it, which is very funny to find so late into life, and funnier still to find it in a human. It's laughable really, those feelings..."

I open my mouth to say something, but he interrupts me, shaking his head: "No! I am not asking anything of you. I never will. It's my issue to handle. I don't want to make it uncomfortable for you, or force you to say something you don't feel, something that's not there. I don't want to make you feel guilty or, worse, sorry for me. I didn't tell you for that. It's not here for that."

He stops suddenly.

"I don't know why I am saying it now", he mumbles to himself.

"No, I do know", he says suddenly and looks up at me. "Because I am afraid to die without telling you how I feel. I don't want to die without you knowing what you are to me, and we might die, I know that. I have been ready to die for a while now. Sometimes I wish for death to come but it avoids me. And flying to the lakes of Hinnom feels weak somehow..."

I drop to my knees in front of him, pressing my lips to his. The taste of wild blackberries is back and I want to lick their lips-staining juice.

I don't promise anything. I don't say anything.

Right now I am afraid to die, just like he is, only he is afraid to die without telling me how he feels and I am just afraid to die. Period.

I am petrified and I keep my lips on his, afraid to let go, to pull back, having to explain myself and this crazy sudden outburst, or tell him how I feel, or maybe how I don't, but I don't want to say any of that either. That's not the conversation I want to have and it wasn't the conversation I was expecting. I might be dead soon, finally and for sure, dead as I was meant to be so many times before, and I am afraid. I am scared.

I want to crawl somewhere and hide, close my eyes and wake up the next second. But of course, it won't achieve anything.

Uriel's essence might survive, but I never will. My death will be the end of me, I feel it. I know it. There will be no "bringing back a human". One mistake is enough for their angelic lifetime. Their history books will note that time when the essence was born and stuck within a human by mistake, and they had to tolerate the unsullied animal within their

Heavens, taking the dumb animal's commands and orders. It will be the one and only mentioning of me, a little paragraph, for a short life full of misery.

There will be no more resurrection, not for me or the others. The orb now is empty, but even the orb would be useless against a beheading in Hell by a weapon of fire.

I keep my lips on his. I keep my eyes closed, and I feel his lips nudge at mine, and his arms come around me, closing around me, pressing my body to his, squeezing me tight.

His hold is desperate. It's strangling me, as if he is afraid to let go. It's like Jess used to squeeze me at night, when she would listen to the fights of our parents.

It's an embrace of a scared and lost person and my head swims.

CHAPTER 39

"Beyelai."

The wedge of a voice nudges through the fog in my head. It pushes through, calling to me.

"Beyelai."

It grows louder and I rise to the surface, towards it, pulling my lips away from Sam's.

I lift my head. Sam and I are surrounded by a circle of angels standing around us, with Rafe, Pronoia and Yofiel towering at the forefront.

As I scan the faces above, I notice the shock written on most of them. Most, but not all. Rafe's face is frozen in a stoic mask of carefully-cultivated indifference.

Judging by the appalled faces of the angels, I have committed another indiscretion. But I shrug this off, just as I've done with so many prior.

"Yes?" I ask them, unfazed.

I push with one leg onto the ground and Sam offers me his arm, and leaning on it, I rise.

I am now face to face with them. Their tight expectant circle has the formation of a mob, and the uninvited memory of the lizards' mob outside of my mother's caravan park comes into my mind.

But I raise my chin up, taking a step closer to the three males ahead.

"Yes?" I repeat.

Sam rises to his feet, his body brushes over the tip of my wings sending a shiver down my spine.

"None of us want to return to Baza", Yofiel booms in his deep voice, "none of us is able to return. That path is closed to us. We can move only forward, and we should move forward together."

"Uriel", he adds, addressing me by the name of one's essence inside me. I noticed it before, but I am not yet sure what to make of it. "You need to understand, that the path is far more difficult than many of us had anticipated. I don't want to use it as an excuse, because you were right earlier, we need to move forward, together, and we need to be braver in our advance. We would like to finish the journey with you. We have pledged and committed ourselves to you and we need to keep our promise, and we shouldn't be swayed by the difficulties in our path. We are here, to stand with you and to move forward with you, under your command."

When he finishes speaking, he bows his head to me, touching his four fingers to his forehead, and the rest of the angels copying him, bowing to me.

Although I've quashed another rebellion, it doesn't feel like a victory. I am not happy or pleased about it. I know that I threw a blanket on that fire, but the embers will remain there and will fester, for me to handle later.

"Okay." I nod at Yofiel, accepting his plight. "I am glad you are coming with me. Have you decided how we are going to organise the istana?"

"Yes, Beyelai", Pronoia answers, stepping forward. "We march in the same squadron formations and under the same commanders as when we left the tunnels. We march now, that way we should reach the Gates soon. If you think that Baza is busy, pulling his troops, we're unlikely to find them along our way, and as you've pointed out, if we leave earlier, we might be lucky enough to meet only a fraction of his army by the Gates."

"Damiq", I say, nodding at him, noticing a few surprised glances after my use of their old Sumerian. "Get the istana ready and let's move it."

"Domiel", I call, stretching my neck, addressing the angel at the back. "We need a scout. Can I count on you?"

"Of course, Beyelai. What am I scouting for?"

"Baza", I answer. "I can't afford to march us into a trap. His troops must be by the Gates now, hopefully not all but I would imagine some. I need to know where they are. I need to know of their locations so we can prepare. Obviously, you need to find out Baza's positions without being spotted. I have very little room for surprises and manoeuvres left. I must utilise whatever I can. If we know his positions and numbers, we might manage to survive."

He nods in agreement with my words.

"Good luck. We'll set off after you", I say, and after bowing to him, I walk away from them all, from the angels and Rafe, and from Sam.

* * *

The wind pushes the red dust with relentless speed, throwing the abrasive haze over the faces of lined up istana.

Finally, we are ready to march.

Domiel left straight after we spoke, promising to be back as soon as he can.

The four squadrons were lined up under the same commanders as before, only this time the angels had formed a small group ahead of the istana. Two dozens of the angels had arranged themselves into three ready to march rows, following mine and Rafe's lead.

I have insisted on Sam taking his place at my left, after which Yofiel took his place to Rafe's right. This shuffle game would have been childish and pathetic, if not for the destinations and the stakes of our march.

Rolling my eyes at that power play, I rise on my wings above my army.

"Ready?" I yell, calling to the four brothers, readying them for our march.

My call is caught and repeated by every of the four commanding brothers, their voices echo above the wind and plateau.

"Let's do it then", I say, after dropping to the ground, turning my head to Rafe, then to Sam, and I take a first step towards on what could be the last day of my life.

A few suggestions to fly came from some of the angels, but I rebuffed them, adamant to cover the distance by foot.

"We'll walk across Hell", I've told them, "just like the istana behind us will. We will keep a united army. We'll suffer the hardship together, angels with their new brothers, istana."

But that's not the only reason.

I want my angels to walk past Baza's processing plants. I want every angel to admire the handy work of their leader and commander. I want them to see what has been done to the people under their unspoken agreement.

I won't let them skate around the issue they've created, to fly above it, pretending that it's toys on the ground beneath them and not real people. I will make them plod through every yard of burnt soil, seeing all of the torture and hearing every pain, and if that won't make them brave and determined, then nothing will.

The march is tedious and boring, at least for me. I've been here before, twice, I've seen it all and I've swallowed more dust than anyone of my marching party.

The moment we took the first step, Jess took to the sky, heading in the direction of the Gates, her gigantic wings slapping the wind.

After a few miles, the constant sound of the billowing wind became choppy, cut by the low metal buildings of the expansion to Baza's empire.

I know that after a while, we'll come across the first herds of naked humans, and after that, we will enter the district of the processing plants.

I wonder what will be angels' and istana' reactions, what emotions will play on their faces when the first herd would come our way. I wonder what their reactions will be to the brutality of lizards, to the knowledge of what would happen to the humans next.

The morbid need in me demands to scare them the way I was scared, to shock them, to make their hearts bleed as mine bled once. That need wants to see if there is any compassion left in my followers after their long and docile service to Baza's reign.

The wind brushes the dust over the metal on the low buildings as it did before. It whistles through the gaps between the metal sheets.

"Hold!" Zabkiel roars over his shoulder at his squadron, lifting his arm up.

"Hold!" Kafziel roars, echoing Zabkiel's call and gesture.

"Forward!" Pronoia booms, urging his squadron to move.

"Forward!" repeats Tagas, and following the brothers' calls, the widespread formation of my army folds in two, extending lengthwise.

The longer snake of istana troops shuffles forward, manoeuvring between the buildings, breaking and stretching around their metal bodies.

With a few flaps of my wings, I take to the sky, inspecting the horizon and the slim, grey stream of my army, which bends around the metal buildings.

The sound of a beating of another pair of wings rises upwards, bringing Rafe with it.

"Everything's okay?" he asks.

"Yeah", I nod. "Just checking the area. I don't want to be proven wrong that early into my reign and go into your heavenly history as the one who underestimated Baza."

"Now it's your history too", Rafe corrects me.

But I am not interested in starting an ethological debate with him, so after a quick glare at him and with another spin above my followers, I'm about to descend to the ground, when Rafe dives, blocking me.

"What?" I call to him, straightening up and bringing myself higher.

He rises with me.

"I don't think it's prudent to get involved with Sam", Rafe says, the beating of our wings and the wind drowning some parts of his words but he is loud enough for me to understand him.

"Not only because of the reasons I've highlighted earlier", he continues, glaring at me, "but more so now, because of the confusing message it sends to everyone around you."

"And what the message that might be?" I call to Rafe above the wind.

"You and I share the essence", he replies. "We are the Great Arcanum and we need to remain whole. We shouldn't be broken in two, shouldn't be separated by anything or anyone. It would be confusing for the angels that have pledged to you or will pledge in the future. They've chose Uriel. They've pledged to Uriel, to her essence in every form."

I stare at him in disbelief for a few long seconds before laughter begins to rise in my throat. Soon, my laugh rings in the busy air and I feel confused gazes of the passing istana below.

Although his remark is not particular funny, his demand is ludicrous and absurd.

"We are not sharing anything, Rafe", I say, sobering. "Not anymore. It's *my* essence in you."

I narrow my eyes at him.

"The piece that *I* gave you was mine. There's no more of *your* essence left. It's all gone. Poof!" I wave my hand.

"It would be a very interesting question to put to *my* army", I say, "to whom did they think they pledged, Uriel or Ariel? Who they'd like to follow? I think you'd find that most will say my name. Uriel is not the one, whom istana call "Mother of Gods". Uriel didn't come into Hell to free them, but Ariel did. Uriel didn't offer them sanctuary, I did! The essence inside might have been important at some point, but not anymore. But of course, we won't ask those lovely people these questions, it will be far too much in bad taste."

I narrow my gaze at him and smile.

"Rafe, it's me and *my* essence. It's me and *my* life, and you have no say in either. You are very welcome to live *your* life however and wherever you want, pinky promise, I won't butt in." I lift and wiggle my small finger.

"But you won't dictate to me what to do with mine", I add. "That time came and went. Did you think I would be stupid and needy forever? Rely on you and your wisdom, led by your agendas? I hope your answer is going to be "no", because I'd hate to think that you are that arrogant and obnoxious."

I look at my army marching below.

"Things are changing, Rafe. Everything is changing and I have to say, changing faster than I had anticipated myself. But that's okay too. I am ready to play ball, and soon the entire Heaven and Hell will learn one thing about me, I do things my way, only and always my way. That could be my weakness, but I'd like to think it will give me an advantage and a big advantage at that. No one anticipates or predicts my moves, because I don't think like you.

"And regarding Sam: it's not something for you to get involved in. You have shared your opinion before, remember? And I listened, and now, keeping this information in mind, I will do what I want or need to do. This will be the last time we speak of Sam. I am grateful to you for everything that you've done for me, how far you've helped me to come, for the life you've given for my sister, but it will be our last conversation on this topic."

I fold my wings around my body and dive towards the ground, without waiting for Rafe's reply.

During my next scouting flight, I spot the first herd.

It's small, no more than a dozen of humans surrounded by three lizards, and no further than a mile away.

Jess spots them too and with a high pitched screech, she propels herself towards the group, chasing her dinner.

At the sound of her screech, I beat my wings faster too, flying after her, needing to catch up with my sister and restrain her appetite.

But her wings are wider and stronger than mine, and by the time I reach her and drop to the ground, one of the lizards is already missing a head.

"Jessie-boo", I coo as I come closer to her. She sits on the top of the lizard's body, loudly chewing the head. Her soft brown fur around her face and her pink snout are covered in lizard's gooey blood.

"Sweetie, how about you take this one and go, huh? Go and sit there." I wave my arm to the right.

"Take your dinner and go."

I shuffle closer and once I am an arm's length away from Jess's dinner, she lifts her head and hisses at me, sinking her claws deeper into the body underneath her.

"Go, baby, go. There", I murmur, waving my hand again, shooing her.

And finally following my order, she loudly swallows the last bit of the head, her throat gulps, and then she sinks her fangs into the body, dragging it away, looking at me and growling low. Even she's not happy with my orders, seems like I'm pissing everyone off right now.

The remaining two lizards stand behind my back, hissing, as their blind heads spin, looking for the danger, they can only feel but not see.

"Haal-dih, pulhu-nasu. Haal-dih", I turn, saying to the lizards.

"Go back to your work."

And with a last low hiss, the lizards turn their attention to the humans, returning to their duties.

I turn away too, taking the first step away to meet my foot soldiers, when behind me a sound of a wet clap of the lizard's tongue connecting with a human flesh rings, followed instantly with a human cry.

It yanks at me like a leash, but I push against it, closing my mind and my heart to it, keeping my stride firm and my gaze forward.

The sight of the naked humans surrounded by the lizard guards had produced the result I was seeking, but only in the angels.

Unperturbed, the istana march steadily past the little group, following my lead, while the angels, keeping their horrified gazes on the maimed naked bodies, trip over their own feet and small stones on the uneven ground, slowing down to a stop to watch the unexpected horror show, their eyes are as open as their mouths.

Half a mile past that herd, I had to call a halt on our advancement as most of my angels were left behind, gawking at the gruesome show like I once was.

"You see? That is Baza's business model", I say, approaching the cluster of angels.

"This is what he does in his spare time and judging by your reaction", I add, waving my hand at their faces, "none of you knew."

I walk behind the angels. I don't want to obstruct their view of the show that was raging under their noses for centuries. I want them to drink it in. I want them to feel ashamed, horrified and embarrassed. I want them to be unable to look me in the eyes after this.

"Do you know where they are being taken now?" I ask the angels, raising my voice above the wheezing of the wind, weeping of the humans and loud chewing of my sister.

"Probably not, and not because you've never heard of it, I bet you had. I bet at some point, during one of your fancy dinners, you've heard something about "harvesting", "extracting" or "procurement", but you never paid any attention to it. You never stopped to think what these words meant and what is happening around you, because it has never affected you. If you don't see it, then it doesn't exist, right?"

I stroll back and forth behind my angelic group.

"These humans are being taken into one of many of Baza's processing plants. The one where the essence is ripped in a most violent way from the body, separated, later to become a source which will nourish Baza and his court, and it means..."

I lean into Sablo.

"*You*", I murmur and she jumps.

I straighten up.

"All of you", I roar.

"Maybe once you were fearless angels, keepers of Gates, Oaths and Peace, maybe once you were fearless fighters", I say, strolling behind brothers' backs, "defenders of the balance", I say behind Sablo, "but not anymore. Now you are scroungers, users, consumers just like Baza. You've become like the others in that tower. You became compliant and complicit. All of you are responsible for what's happening in those factories. The blood was on your hands for a while, only now you've seen it. We will see many more factories before we reach the Gates. We'll see many of these herds. You will hear the screams of humans who are losing their souls in there, their screams ring for miles and miles, and maybe it will ring finally into your hearts too."

"Gildikh, pulhu-nasu. Move", I call to the nearby lizard, and whipping his tongue out, he slaps at a nearby human, ushering the naked bodies forward.

"The show is over", I yell against the wind to the stupefied angels. "Let's move. We can't stay here forever."

But before walking away, I murmur to another lizard: "Keetah."

I return to the forefront of my army and Rafe gives me a sharp glare, displeased with my methods, but he doesn't say a word and I can't be asked starting another fight.

"I'm not their wet nurse to be concerned with their wellbeing", I mumble under my nose.

CHAPTER 40

After the show, the angels became quieter and morose, the earlier chatter gone, replaced by a brooding silence, with only the brothers' calls to the istana ringing across the landscape, as they steer my army.

As I promised, the red terrain became busier. The shorter one storey sheds were replaced with three and four storey factory buildings and the first of the lighthouses came into view, its white light piercing the red haze, shining bright above the chimney.

The Gates are getting closer but there's still no sign of Baza.

I don't think he is trustworthy, but rather arrogant enough to think that he can take me and my pathetic army down, and the warning that he issued had only added excitement to his chase.

For a moment, the thought that maybe it's not the arrogance spoke in him but rather a calculated military knowledge comes into my mind, but I push it out, pressing forward, as forward is the only way left.

We are closer to the first chimney now. The wind brings the first human screams of the white light, causing a stumbling havoc in my army.

The measured march of the istana falters, while the angels behind me stop completely, spinning their heads, distraught looks washed over their faces.

"Let's go!" I turn and yell at my angels. "No stopping!"

The beautiful angelic faces are wrung with emotions when they turn their heads to me. Fear, pain, confusion and discord are ruling them.

My glorious followers, who haven't seen or experienced Baza's processing facilities but were happy to utilise the final product of it, are shocked by the agony of the singing death. Suddenly, they are confronted by death on their doorstep, the death that was here all along but unseen to them, death by a brutal end, put in motion by their beloved and kind "Father Christmas".

I see that their world is turning and tilting. It's like a final drop, absolute proof of who, or what, they've been serving for millennia.

Their own imprisonment they could have shrugged off as a part of the game their kind plays, the rules of a ruthless world they live in, where no deed should go unpunished. Where's this, here... This is farming, and farming of something that looks scarily like them.

I glance at Rafe, who turns back and yells: "Move! Push through and move. We can't stop!"

The group begins to shuffle forward.

I take to the sky, flying above the mass of the istana.

"There's nothing to worry about. This", I call to them over the singing of the wind and human cries, "is nothing to do with you. You will not be disturbed or affected, and you won't be seen. Keep your heads down and march. We are not far from the Gates. Save your energy for the Gates!" I call as I circle above the istana.

"Forward march!" Rafe roars on the ground, and Pronoia and Kafziel repeat after him, Tagas and Zabkiel following suit.

I leave my army to soothe themselves, as I take off after Jess, who's now circling above the factory's fenced area, eyeing the selection of juicy lizards.

On the ground behind me, hundreds of feet resume their shuffling, eventually finding the rhythm, bringing my army closer to their final battle for their freedom.

And hopefully not to a slaughter.

* * *

A few times during our trek I had to block Jess from snatching lizards.

My sister's enormous shadow would move over the ground, covering groups and buildings, reducing in size, when called by her appetite and hunting instinct, she would fold her wings, diving towards a chosen lizard, and I would fall with her, blocking her every attempt at picking a quick snack.

These lizards are mine. I need them. I have a plan for everyone in here. Everyone has a part to play in the upcoming battle and I'm not going to let Jess to reduce our numbers, I have Baza for that.

Below, on the ground, the army moves forward, around the fenced yards of the factories, past the increasing number of naked humans groups, and it's not long before my angels, one by one, take to the sky and when they fly past me, I see the tear stained faces of Sablo and her friends, the angry face of Yofiel, the stressed face of his wife who flies above me with her ears covered with her hands.

My angels have proven to be weaker than I thought.

Not only the number of them wasn't great to begin with, but with this escapism, this inability to deal with something that upsets them...that has confirmed that I made the right call by attracting more and different kinds of supporters to my cause.

I dive down, worried that my marching army of istana is left unsupervised, but as I circle the area, I see the bright blue dots of brothers' wings at the forefront of each of my squadrons.

I am torn between babysitting greedy Jess, keeping up morale and appearances for my istana and herding the scattered angels.

To hell with them!

I wave my hand at the angelic bodies flying above me, instead speeding after Jess who had disappeared in the distance.

As I fly, finally I spot the brown furry hill on the ground and when I land, I see the bottom half of a lizard dangling out of her mouth.

"Stop it! Jess! No! Spit it out! Spit it out, now! Immediately", I say. Spit it!"

I land on the ground, and running to the lizard, I grab hold of his scaly and webbed feet and begin to pull.

Jess's brown eyes gape at me over the body.

"No, Jess! Spit it out, immediately! Spit! Who I'm talking to? Spit!"

Her wet eyes hold my gaze for a moment before her chin and mouth begin to quiver, rattling the lizard's body within.

Holding my gaze, she gives a little burp and opens her mouth. The body of lizard slides out.

The lizard on the ground is covered in Jess' saliva like a newborn calf freshly out of its mummy's womb, but it's intact.

"Good girl", I say, coming to her and pressing my finger to her covered in black goo snout. "But no more. Not yet. I'll tell you when you can have more, not just yet."

But Jess is not interested in being disciplined.

She looks at the slimy lizard for a moment then turns her head to me, before she throws her head upwards and begins to wail.

She howls and wails like a child refused chocolate on Christmas morning. Her blaring voice travels with the wind.

"Oh for god sake!" I mumble, dropping my head. "God sake, girl."

Jess wails on one unending note.

"Oh, just have it!" I turn and yell to Jess. "Stop screaming. Just have it."

She slaps her large jaw shut, her teeth clack.

"Have it! But it's the last one until I said so. Is that clear? The last one. No more!"

Jess drops to the ground and, carrying her body low, she crawls to the lizard, who began coming around, and after whipping her large purple tongue, she scoops its scale body back into her mouth.

Resigned, I wave my hand at her too, taking to the sky, as the chewing and crunching of the bones resonate behind me.

"Pronoia, Tagas", I call to the brothers at the forehead of their squadrons, landing in front of the row of the remaining on the ground angels.

"Stop."

"Stop."

The brothers call to the istana and the army grinds to a halt.

"Pronoia", I say. "I need you to round up the angels and bring them to the ground. We're giving away our location when they scatter like bloody mad pigeons. They need to remain on the ground."

Pronoia nods, and without a further word opens his wings, taking off up into the air.

I turn my head to his brother.

"Tagas, we need to call a stop. Domiel is not here yet and I can't risk pushing forward. We're not far from the Gates. Besides, there's still no sign of Sabrael. Please prepare the troops for a stop."

He nods and then turns to yell instructions to the squadrons of istana behind him.

The god is missing, although must be alive if the istana are standing. Where could he have gone? Maybe back to Baza, to get a deal? Unlikely, but who knows...

"Why are we stopping?" Rafe calls, marching over, but the noise of the beating of dozens of wings in the air and guttural exclamations of multiple voices interrupts him.

I lift my head, watching the shadow of an angel above grow darker, before morphing through the dusty haze into Domiel's body.

"Beyelai!" he calls, dropping to the ground and running to me. "Beyelai!"

The flock of the unsettled angels drops to the ground behind him, brought down by the new arrival carrying news, and Pronoia's instructions to suck up and drop to the ground.

"Beyelai", Domiel gushes, out of breath. "Abzu is not far from here. His army is in position and they are waiting for us. They have blocked the access to the Gates."

As he warned and he planned.

I nod.

"How far from here?" I ask.

"Past the last building with the chimney and about a hundred paces towards the direction of the Gates."

"How many solders could you see? How many did he bring?"

"I'd say a few hundred malakhims, but I can't say for certain. Following your instruction, I didn't risk coming closer. They're already in formation."

"Malakhims. It's his angels, right?"

Domiel nods.

"Was anyone else there, apart from his angels?"

"No, Beyelai Sar, just Baza's malakhims. Who should I have found there?"

"Nobody, nobody", I answer, waving my hand, busy with my thoughts. "If they were there, you would have seen them."

I lift my gaze to him.

"Thank you very much, Domiel", I say, and raising my four fingers to my forehead, I bow to him, provoking a stifled gasp from the angels.

"Thank you", I repeat.

I turn, taking a few steps away from the angels.

"So, Baza brought just angels", I say to myself, musing out loud as I kick up the red soil. "But it doesn't mean that there's nothing else going on, or somebody else isn't there, who we can't see. But on the other hand, he might also think that these hundreds will be enough against two dozens of sparsely armed angels and a couple of hundreds of istana. He doesn't know how many istana I've taken. Hopefully they haven't carried istana census as of late, so the number I've taken would remain a mystery to him. So potentially, it could be only malakhims... I thought he'd call on the rest of his army. But it doesn't mean that the rest won't meet him later, and if that's the case, I need to beat him to the punch..."

"Right", I call, spinning towards my angels.

I am confronted by a wall of the attentive angels. Every pair of angelic eyes is on me. Not expecting it, I stumble a bit.

"Good. Everyone's here", I say and clearing my throat, I add louder, "Baza is here and he is not far. He is waiting for us just as he promised and just as I thought he would."

I turn to the army of istana behind me, and to make sure that my next words are heard, I open my wings and take into the sky, rising a couple of meters above the ground.

"If we want to get out of here", I call, "if we want to make it past the Gates and into Uras, we'll have to fight our way through, past your old Lord and his army."

"But we don't have the numbers for a full frontal attack. We don't even have enough weapons. So..." I pause. "We are going to fight smart. We are going to use the landscape to our advantage. We're going to utilise whatever element of surprise we can. Although our numbers are not great, they are not pathetic either. We are going to surprise them, seeding discord into their ranks. We are going to split them, killing them one by one. They are expecting a small and unarmed herd of scared people, but they are going to find an army", I roar, "an army of fearless warriors, who know what they are fighting for and prepared to fight until death."

I scan the faces drawn to me. Every set of eyes is on me. Their attention is mine.

"His soldiers are fighting for their master, for his rotting and dying empire", I cry towards my army, "but we will fight for something more precious, something extremely valuable, in fact, priceless! We will fight for our freedom, for the freedom of the children we had to leave behind", I raise my hand, pointing towards the direction we came from, "still locked in the darkness of the tunnels. We will fight for our future and for theirs, and because of that, we will win!"

I roar the last words and my army cries out with me, as every istana raises their arms towards me, as bliss takes over their faces.

CHAPTER 41

The plan is in play. The stage is set and my army is in position.

Everyone knows what is expected of them and what they have to do.

We have covered the last few miles on foot, pressing ourselves to the buildings, using their cover and the cover of dust to disguise our approach.

We have used the increased number of the human herds and lizards to our advantage too.

So close to the epicentre of Baza's food production empire, the number of processing facilities was greater and so was the number of herds milling around. The herds were larger, with more humans and more lizards, and the dust cloud raised by their feet stood in a constant thick drape, hiding the area.

Following the hushed command of the brothers, the istana squadrons would surround a moving herd and mimicking their slow and stumbling shuffle, my army would progress further, closer to the Gates, to the place where Baza was waiting for us.

My angels have found it extremely hard to walk next to the farmed humans, whose essences they used to consume with Baza. The females would begin to whimper, whilst males would break into a short run. But I have warned all of them that whoever takes to the sky, and by doing this gives away our location, will be sentenced to death with the punishment carried out immediately by yours truly.

No one was allowed to threaten our progression and our cover. Under no circumstances was I prepared to reveal to Baza our true numbers, location and the make up of my army.

We were swapping the herds, making some shrink and some grow larger, but at every shuffling step we were pressing forward.

Domiel and Dumah have shared their weapons amongst the angels, with Dumah kindly giving me the short dagger of his, the dagger of white rippling fire.

I lost my small swords a while ago, and without any sign of Sabrael, I have resigned myself to fighting with the dark blunt weapons that we had. Even if we couldn't kill Baza's angels with those, we could create enough damage displacing them, pushing them out of our way and, hopefully, making it through the Gates.

Killing Lis back in the tunnels has taught me what the basic, animalistic need for survival can achieve, and how much damage I can do with my teeth, so the lack of weapons hasn't bothered me much. I had more surprises in store, but as there was no sign of Sabrael, I began to wonder if his brothers will ever see him again, at least alive and in this lifetime.

Rafe has given one of his long swords of white fire with purple and gold encrusted handle to Yofiel. Yofiel had bowed deeply to his friend, accepting it as a sign of trust and gift for survival. Rafe shared the rest of his weapons amongst the Ophanims and some brothers, keeping only one of the long swords of his for himself.

But there weren't enough heavenly weapons of fire for every angel, let alone for the istana.

I knew that I was leaving them exposed, narrowing their chances for survival, but fighting smart and outplaying Baza was the only weapon I could gift them now.

The large, shining new buildings of metal move to the both sides of our column as we trod past them. The buildings stand empty, their doors wide open – ready for the upcoming livestock.

Moving further away from the last processing plant, with its piercing white light shining behind our backs, my army and I march openly through the red terrain.

Now, we have nowhere to hide.

The Gates are ahead of us.

If Baza is coming, he will be here. This is the last plateau before the Gates.

The angels and istana raise plenty of dust with their feet, and I have instructed every soldier to raise their weapons as we march through, while Pronoia calls out the rhythm, keeping the count going, "Left, right; left, right...Three, four, forward; three, four, march..."

Pronoia's voice rings above the red terrain, when suddenly, through the veil of dust, the formation of the large army ahead arises.

The grey wall of bodies ahead spreads to a couple of miles in width. The marching footsteps behind me falter, losing their rhythm, and feeling fear behind me, I turn around and roar: "Forward march! Keep up the pace!"

I can't afford fear in my camp. I can't afford show it to Baza. Right now, we can only go forward. If we turn around or run, we'll be finished.

My call is picked up and carried by the brothers, urging my troops forward, until only a few hundred meters divide our armies and I can see the stout body sealed in black, at the head of the opposing army, with the raven black wings open wide behind his back.

"You are finally here", Baza calls. "I'd begun to worry that maybe you had changed your mind and decided to live out your life in the tunnels with the rat friends of yours."

"Change my mind and not to see you again, Baza?" I answer, raising my voice, and the wind carries my words with the ease. "Not a chance. I would not have missed it for the world. How about you let us through, peacefully, and I'll leave you alone, doing the dirty deeds of yours in peace and quiet as you've done for so many years. Huh, Baza? *I'll* grant *you* your life. What do you say?"

His deep baritone laughter is my answer.

"I see your youthful optimism doesn't leave you even when faced with such a glaring warning. It's admirable but misguided. Why would I do as you asked, dear child? If you hadn't noticed, you're in no position for demands. Look at my glorious army", he spreads his arms. "And now look at yours."

He points behind me.

"I will get absolutely nothing out of the proposal of yours, whereas I will get everything I've desired if I capture or kill you, dear Ariel."

"Out of that deal, dear Baza", I call, accentuating "dear Baza", mimicking his pet names for me, "you will get your life. You and your angels will survive. I promise to leave Arllu and you in one piece, whereas I'm not going to guarantee the same outcome to any of you if you decline my offer."

Baza laughs again.

"Your spirit is bright, dear child. I'll give you that. Making such a bold statement when *that* is your numbers and your chances?"

He nudges his head at my army.

"You make me laugh like no one else and the bravery of yours is truly refreshing. The moxy and self-assurance with which you take on every challenge of yours is admirable and I wish more of my angels showed that much bravery and determination."

He spreads his arms, turning to his army.

"But those are my personal feelings and they have nothing to do with my needs as a leader to my malakhims and Arllu. There are certain things that need to be done", he calls to me. "How much I do wish you had listened to me and taken *my* offer."

He tuts and shakes his head.

"Instead *I* will be killing you, child, and it saddens me, but not enough to stop what is about to happen."

"So, is that a "no" then?" I call to him.

But instead of an answer, he raises his arm up, as he keeps his gaze on me.

"*Guh-shtar!*" he roars and throws his arm down, and following his call, the ranks of the grey angels behind him explode into action, running at us with a guttural roar that vibrates the air.

With one word and a wave of his hand Baza had started the war.

So be it!

It will be the war in which one of us will die.

"Now!" I roar.

And following my call, two dozen of my angels open their wings, taking to the sky, and I rise with them.

The confusion on the ground lasts only a moment, before Baza calls again and a group of the grey angels separates from his army. They open their wings and flies towards us.

"Lift!" Pronoia calls and his command leads to a wall of metal sheets rise in front of the squadrons of istana on the ground like a shield wall.

Protected by it, the istana from the depths of the squadron, pull their black long poles with metal daggers, stars or sickles at the ends, and balancing them at the ready, they aim those poles up, towards the sky.

"Throw!" I roar, rising higher, and my angels follow.

The sharp black poles fly through the air and into the group of the "greys". Baza's angels are showered with the heavy poles.

The weapons make connections and with cries and roars as the bodies of the greys begin to fall, thudding onto the ground, the black poles lodged in them.

Baza calls again and another group of the "greys" separates, taking to the sky.

The ground below is littered with the grey bodies. Some are impaled, some pinned to the ground with a heavy pole like butterflies to paper, although some of the "greys" are on their feet, trying to yank the poles out of their wings and bodies.

The grey army on the ground wasn't sleeping either while we were flying.

Thunder crashes above the ground as their bodies collide with the metal shield wall of the istana, swallowing the fallen comrades of theirs on the ground.

"Hold!" Pronoia, left on the ground to command the fused squadron of istana, roars. But the istana are barely holding their shields against the pressure of the hundreds of the grey bodies.

"Throw!" I call and another swarm of long black poles whizz through the air and more "greys" fall.

The ground below is now the two solid masses of tightly pressed bodies, divided by a thin metal wall.

The third, larger this time, group of the grey angels takes to the sky after us, and this is my cue.

"Jess!" I roar.

"Jessie! Je-e-ess! Now, girl! NOW!"

The nearby hangar explodes with the bent and wrecked metal sheets as the monster of mine, my little sister, takes off running along the red soil, her heavy paws pounding the earth. With the flaps of her powerful wings, she takes to the sky.

Her appearance shocks the grey army, as the roar of the attack falters and dies when they see her. Hundreds and hundreds of gazes follow my sister's flight, their weapons down; the fire of the strike is no longer burning.

That second of confusion is what I've been banking on.

"Open!" Pronoia roars and the pockets open within the shield wall.

Istana step forward into the sea of the "grey", hitting, smashing, piercing the bodies, dragging as many as they can into the istana's crowd, freeing them of their angelic weapons.

Jess crashes into the group of the flying grey angels like a ball into pins.

The screams of fear, confusion and pain ring through the air, echoing the crying above the plateau, heightened by the rushed and petrified beating of wings, as my monster chases, bites and tears, ripping apart the bodies she has caught.

The blood and body parts of her handy work shower the armies below.

"Down!" I call to my angels, and as one, they fold their wings behind their backs, diving to the ground into the depth of istana ranks.

"Release!" Pronoia's voice booms with another command, and the spikes of the long black poles grow through the gaps between the metal sheets, stabbing at the avant-garde of the "greys".

With a side glance, I watch more "greys" take to the sky, after my sister.

I am amongst the istana now, pushing through, pushing forward to where the scramble between the istana and the "greys" rings the hottest.

I need their angelic weapons. I need all I can get.

Some istana has already outfitted themselves with angelic swords of black rippling fire, utilising and testing those by sinking them into the flesh of Baza's angels on the ground.

My sister's roar booms in the air above, answered by the cries of petrified and hurt "greys".

But suddenly my monster roars in pain, and as I turn my head up, I watch my sister spinning, as a long sword of one of the "greys" is plunged into her side.

"No!" I roar.

My elbow makes a connection with someone's face. My fist sinks into a face and a body.

I scoop a dropped long fiery sword off the ground.

I push at the bodies around me, climbing and crawling on top of them, before opening my wings above their heads, I take to the sky where my sister is.

My sister is surrounded by grey bodies.

Although she has made a dent in their number, she is still outnumbered, and now, as the element of surprise has worn off, she has to fight them at their full strength.

As I approach the outer circle, I swing the heavy sword and without slowing down, I land it onto the body of a grey soldier in front of me.

The body cuts in two, the two parts drop to the ground.

He didn't see me coming, but his mate turns in time and our swords crash with a heavy ring, which sends the vibration down my spine.

I withdraw my sword. Swinging it, I throw it forward again.

But my sword is blocked once again, and with a heavy push I'm sent tumbling backwards, gliding on my wings.

I am not a match for these angels in strength and expertise. The only way I can outfight them is by playing with them, making them chase me, surprising them.

I bank and turn on my wings, gliding under my sister, under her furry belly, my belly touching hers.

I glide on my wings around my large monster, as my sister screeches, busy fighting the angels around her, and listening to her cries, my sword and I are ready to drink their blood, and it doesn't have to be the blood of the one I fought before.

I fly from underneath her, appearing between the two "greys".

"Surprise", I call.

I throw my right arm with the sword.

I spin and throw the arm with the sword out again. The two slashed bodies fall to the ground below.

I turn and dive. I appear and I hide.

During one of my diving trajectories, I throw out my sword which collides with another weapon, and I am about to turn, pushing at the new sword, when I notice the familiar pastel yellow wings behind the body.

I am recognised too.

Dumah's hand pushes me out of the way, as he reaches with his sword behind my back and an angel cries in pain behind me.

"Thank you", I say and he nods silently, true to his way of never speaking a word.

Dumah is fighting the "greys" around my sister, protecting her. But my brave little girl doesn't need much help. She is doing a great job by herself, chasing the grey bodies, ripping them with her claws and uneven sharp teeth.

As it turned out, all she ever needed was someone watching her back.

CHAPTER 42

The fighting rages on the ground too.

"Brothers! Ahu-uunum!"

Pronoia's voice roars over the red plane, issuing another instruction for another tactical surprise.

"Istana! Come! Stand for your Mammí!"

"Istana! Don't fear! Your Mother is with you!"

The voices of Tagas and Kafziel are ringing from opposite directions of the plateau, as they call to their two squadrons.

As I glance, two thick red clouds grow, raised by the hundreds of feet which run past the metal buildings at Baza's malakhims from both sides.

The two squadrons were hidden amongst the landscape just as my sister was earlier. They hid inside and behind the metal buildings, amongst the nearby roaming human herds. They were waiting for the brothers' command.

Running at Baza's malakhims, their purpose is to cut the grey army in two, dividing them, pushing the broken pockets of malakhims further and further apart, in preparation for my next surprise.

The white wings of Sam, the blue wings of the brothers, the pastel yellow wings of Domiel and the burgundy wings of Ophanims bob within the ocean of dark bodies. I even spot a pair of pink wings of one of the floral girls. My angels are still standing.

By now, most of the force of the Baza's army had managed to push through the metal shield, now wreaking the havoc amongst the istana.

I watch the brave yet weak hands of istana swing the spiky metal balls on the chains, throwing black daggers and whips at the army of the grey angels, and when I scan the plateau, past the raging fights, my gaze stops at the short figure, sealed in black with four black wings behind, as he floats a meter above the ground, surrounded by a tight ring of the grey bodies of his soldiers.

Our gazes meet and a pleased smile pulls at Baza's lips.

With another quick glance at my sister and Dumah, I dive into the depth of the battle where my "children" fight for their freedom and their "mother".

The two new squadrons have divided the grey army, pulling its force away from the original squadron.

But my malnourished and untrained "children" are not a match for Baza's malakhims, whose sole job for centuries was killing living creatures.

Although, encircled, the malakhims fight with angelic weapons, dropping my istana at every second.

That is my cue for the next step of my plan, for the release of more support, another injection of the fresh, dispensable forces, and with another furious stab at the nearby "grey" and under the accompaniment of his dying cries, I rise up.

"Pulhu-nasu!" I roar.

"Pulhu-nasu-u-u!!" I call down the wind.

"Haal-dih, pulhu-nasu. Haal-dih!" I roar.

"Uleen, pulhu-nasu! Hurry, my children! Come to me. Remember who has created you, remember to whom you owe your lives. Return to your rightful owner, pulhu-nasu. Come to your mother! Come to me!"

I call the forgotten words in Old Sumerian, the words that I discovered not so long ago. I've tried these words already. I saw how they work. I've tasted their power.

I call the *lizards* back into my fold, under my governance and my control. I'm bringing them under my command, taking them away from Baza, restating my hold on them.

I'm relieving them of their obligations to the Lord of Arllu. By speaking these Old Sumerian words, these creatures are mine again, and they will fight for their creator and their ruler until their death. They will protect me, and what is mine, with their lives.

"Come to me! Uleen, pulhu-nasu!" I cry.

And following my calls, the low vibration of shuffling of thousands of heavy feet rises from the ground and into the air, radiating from the horizon.

The dark cloud of an upcoming animal herd covers the sky. As I spin, I see the endless crowds of lizards coming toward us.

With a relieved smile on my face, I glance at Baza, whose stunned face betrays his shock at the turn of the events. This possibility had never occurred to him, it had never crossed his mind. He hadn't planned for it.

I hold my gaze on his face and, eventually, when his gaze meets mine. I read the loathing and detest in his glare, as his nostrils flare, his lips baring his teeth.

"Do you think it will save you, wardum?" he growls, as he is calling to me. "Nothing will save you, not these mindless animals nor your weak slaves. You are going to die here, one way or another you all are going to die! And I will make sure that you die the longest and most painful death I can create. You will be begging me for a quick death, but I swear, I will grant you none", he roars.

The hate on his face is tangible.

"Do you think you are equal to me? *You?* An animal is equal to the oldest Lord of Arllu? Never will I tolerate or allow that."

The thousands of lizards' feet march on the ground, drowning his words.

The lizards are getting closer, and from this vantage point I can see the incredible number of the approaching herd, their gold necklaces twinkle in the red sunshine.

"It's not up to you anymore, Baza", I call to him over the rising noise. "You're not going to be the Lord of Arllu for much longer."

The two large lizard herds crash into the battling crowd from south and east.

They trudge their blind bodies into the heat of the battle, swinging their whips, opening their mouths and clapping their tongues at the nearby bodies.

The screams begin to ring as the chunks of flesh begin to leave bodies.

But my istana are crying too.

The dumb lizards can't see or differentiate within the crowd or between the armies. They don't know or don't care who is on their side.

"Istana! Watch out!" I call.

I never thought of lizards as intelligent creatures, and they haven't proven me wrong.

My angels, all armed with angelic weapons are fighting better, especially and not surprisingly, the brothers. The cornflower blue dots of the brothers' wings sprinkle the dark sea of the bodies. The areas grow clearer around them, as number of the grey bodies littering the ground around them rises.

With istana and lizards we finally begin to push our advantage.

The little pockets of malakhims are struggling to break the encirclement of the fighting lizards and istana, and when my angel or an istana with an angelic weapon reaches them, another dying cry rings over the plane, and looking down at the armies below, I begin to think that we might win.

I glance at Baza, who is floating higher, surrounded by his bodyguards, watching the battle below.

When his gaze meets mine, I know that the same thought had crossed his mind.

He narrows his gaze at me, and after holding it for a moment, he opens his mouth and begins calling the Old Sumerian words, chanting something, calling someone to his side, summoning someone.

"Sú-zu aru! Ba Ùri, šu-bur, gil-im!" Baza roars. "Ba Ùri, šu-bur, gil-im!"

His arms rise with the increasing force of his voice, and the more of these words he utters, the shiftier grow the grey bodies of the bodyguards around him. They turn their heads, shifting uncomfortably, checking the ground and horizon.

They are looking for something.

And looking at their alarm and discomfort, I know that something is coming, something I should fear as much as they do.

With the last spoken word, Baza grants me his soft grandfatherly smile and cocks his head to the side, and almost instantly, the deep rumbling vibrates from within the earth's core.

The noise rises up.

It's the unsettling sound of upset earth. It reverberates from somewhere deep, like a rumble of the ground before a volcano explosion. It rumbles and it increases.

The istana and grey malakhims have stopped fighting, glancing wearily at the ground under their feet. Only the lizards trudge around oblivious to the ominous sounds, continue swinging their tongues.

Half-heartedly, the "greys" throw their arms towards nearby lizards, skewing them with their angelic swords, but they are too preoccupied with the rising noise.

The pitch of the noise suddenly deepens, adding vibration to the ground, and whereas the vibration produced by the thousands of walking lizards was shallow, this one vibrates the entire ground, and it's everywhere.

"What is it?" I call down. I don't address anyone in particular. I don't know who would know.

But the confused faces of my angels on the ground betray that they don't know what to expect either.

I turn my head, spinning on the spot, trying to figure out how to neutralise the new danger. But for that I need to know what it is. I need to know what I am dealing with.

I turn and look at Baza.

His gleeful smile warns me of the upcoming impact of his surprise. It screams that I won't find it pleasant.

Holding my gaze and keeping his smile in place, he roars: "DAL!"

He throws his arms up, and following his call and his gesture, his malakhims, as one, take to the sky, leaving the ground.

Something is wrong with earth. Something is *within* it and it's coming for us.

It takes me another second to think, when suddenly the memory of the thick cold tubular body wrapped around me punches at my mind, the body that wanted my life and my soul, the tubular body that was strangling me, killing me, while flashing the images of the man into my mind.

I open my mouth, drawing breath.

"Up! UP!" I roar. "Everyone off the ground! Up! Immediately! Up!!"

I roar and following my command and after a glance at me, my angels open their wings and take to the sky, whilst confused and abandoned istana shuffle on the ground, their crowd peppered with lizards. They don't know what to do, where to go. They can't go up.

The sea of faces rise up towards me, looking at me, looking for my instruction, pleading to be saved by their mother, looking for their mother's help and care.

"Run!" I call to them. "Run!!" I roar.

"Into the buildings! On top of them! RUN!"

I roar, but my words are drowned by the ear-bleeding noise of the ripping of the millions shreds of fabric, the splitting tear of existence, surrounded by the sounds of hunger for essence and flesh of millions of voices.

Under my petrified gaze, the top layer of soil ripples, exploding with millions upon millions of the blind heads of huge earthworms.

The worms are brown and as big as a dolphin. They are the worms I've seen before. They are the worms Baza had paraded in front of me under the Gates of Uras.

The worms push their tubular bodies out of the ground, the brown rings on their bodies move through the soil, producing that rippling noise, and their muffled hungry cries ring above the plateau.

The worms are out of earth now. They are all over the top and there are millions of them. They cover the red ground to the horizon, turning it into a carpet of brown rippling sea. They are everywhere.

"Run!!" I roar to my istana below. "Run!!"

The istana are lifting their feet, stepping backwards, trying to avoid the brown bodies but the bodies are everywhere.

I look at a stupefied young istana below. The worms are between his feet. Their ringed bodies crawl along the ground, brushing against his legs. The nearby worms turn their heads towards him, zooming in on him.

Suddenly, with a surprised cry, a young istana boy falls, tripped by a brown tubular body.

While the boy's cry still ringing in the air, the tubular body rushes towards him, binding the boy's feet, and having him at his mercy, the creature begins a slow crawl on top of him, climbing higher and higher up the young and slim body until the entire weight and length of the brown worm lays on top of the boy.

The boy's scream rings in the air, but he is unable to break free from the worm.

The blind slimy face leans towards the istana, and almost as if listening to the boy's screams, it pauses there for a moment, before suddenly awakening, it rushes forward, closing the last few inches between their faces.

It attaches itself to the boy's face, swallowing it whole.

I don't breathe.

Shocked, I watch it. I am unable to draw my gaze away as the boy's new wave of agonising cries rings over the ground, now echoed by the cries of more istana from every corner, as more and more of them are taken hostage by the brown parasites.

"No!" I yell.

I dive towards the ground, aiming my long sword at the worm below, when under my gaze, the slimy tubular body morphs, turning into a... naked human.

I stop.

Unsteadily, the human scrambles to his feet, leaving behind him only a bundle of rags on the ground.

There's no sign of the istana anywhere. Nothing is left of the istana boy: no flesh, no bones, only a wad of dirty fabric, and it confuses me, playing with my feelings and my mind.

The worms crawl over the fallen bodies of the angels and istana, and every time a worm attaches its head to a face of a fallen fighter, the body of an angel or istana would dissolve and the worm would disappear, replaced by a human.

More naked humans rise off the ground below me, replacing the carpet of brown worms, fallen angels and istana.

The humans are young and old, males and females. Some begin to cry as they stand, while some stroke their bodies or turn their hands in front of their faces as they inspect their hands. Some drop to their knees to touch the ground, rubbing the sandy soil between their fingers. Younger girls and boys would cry, calling for their mums or dads.

I am confused.

I don't know what to do or who I am supposed to protect. I don't know if I still need to tell the remaining istana to run and hide or if this attack, as much as it was orchestrated by Baza, is a good thing and with it I am bringing humans back.

But the istana don't wait for further instructions.

Finally woken to the fate overtaking their kin, the remaining istana sprint to the nearest metal hangars, swinging their dark weapons at the worms under their feet, clearing their paths.

Some istana run into the sheds, while most climb over the face of the buildings and onto the roofs, as the tortured screams of their kin continue to ring over the plateau.

I am motionless. I don't know what to do. I don't understand this new magic. The human in me tells me that the appearance of the humans over the plateau can only be a good thing, whilst the angel in me reminds me that nothing that was masterminded by Baza is ever good.

The "Mother of Gods" chips in too, reminding me that I have responsibilities to my new people, people whom I've convinced to join me, to come with me, leading them into this slaughter.

On the ground, some worms climb over the fallen lizards.

But those worms don't turn into humans. They don't turn into anything. Unaffected by that magic, those worms progress their circular bodies along the ground, simply consuming the lizards' bodies, leaving behind loincloths, whips and thick gold necklaces.

The plane is now covered with the lost and weeping humans and the slimy brown bodies of worms.

No more than a hundred of the istana have managed to save themselves from the worms, now hiding inside and on top of the buildings.

"Now, this is as it was always meant to be", Baza's voice calls above the cries. "This is for the higher race to decide."

As I turn my gaze toward the voice, away from my "children", who have scrambled to safety, I see Baza's face above me, his malakhims hung in a solid grey cloud above my angels.

Jess!

I turn my head, looking for her but she is nowhere to be seen. She is not on the ground and she is not in the sky. I can't see Dumah either. I can't believe that I've lost a creature as large as her.

"With animals and slaves eating each other", Baza continues, calling to me past the wall of his bodyguards, "there's only one animal left for me to handle. Only one animal is left to be reminded of her place in this world, and once it's done, we will all go back to the way our worlds were."

He turns his head to my angels, who cluster mid-air, the males outside of the group with their weapons drawn.

"You will receive no clemency from me", he announces to them. "You chose your master. This will be the last time you see the sky. Be ready to meet your glorified Uriel in Udhad."

Suddenly, a high pitched shriek pierces the air. My ears hurt and my teeth gnash.

I turn my head towards the noise, in time to see the young man from earlier, the one who turned from the worm, standing on the ground with his head raised upwards as he produces this inhuman noise.

His head starts to shake on his shoulders and the speed of the shaking increases with every second, before with a dry pop, it explodes, revealing the blind earthworm's head.

The man drops to the ground like a sack. Slowly the brown earthworm body begins to wriggle from within the human shell, revealing one brown ring at a time.

It's not long before the shell of the human body is left on the ground behind the worm like a snake's old skin or a deflated costume. The human is truly gone and the worm is back.

Another shriek rings above the plane, followed by another, then by one more, and then one by one the dry popping sounds begin to resonate across the land, and soon the plateau is covered with a brown sea of worm bodies again, who are crawling over the ground and amongst the roaming lizards.

Although the earlier magic is reversed, it doesn't bring the istana back.

"That's it", Baza calls to me. "Whatever istana you had, are now gone like they were never born, and the ones that are still alive", he points to the ones sitting on the top of the buildings like pigeons, "won't be able to follow you anywhere. They will return where they belong, into their tunnels, to do their work, after a public flogging, of course."

He narrows his gaze on me.

"So you see, Ariel, you have nowhere to run and no one to take with you. You have failed everyone who has followed you. You've killed them all, just as I warned them you would. I've been at this far, far longer than you have, wardum."

CHAPTER 43

Suddenly, a bright white light bursts through the ground, shining between the lizards' feet and worms' bodies. It seeps through the layers of dirt as if the dirt is not a solid mass, but rather a fabric.

It shines from the depths, cutting the dust and the red light above.

Baza slams his mouth shut as his eyes fly open.

He is as surprised as I am.

The lizards mulling on the ground continue to shuffle aimlessly, disregarding the light, whilst the worms, who have returned to their original brown tubular form, begin to crawl faster, as if trying to get away from the light, and unable, they begin to twist and soon another, different wave of the high-pitched shrill descends over the plane.

The worms' wriggling grows faster, more urgent and erratic as if they're on a frying pan. Their desperate shrill rings higher, on one dying note, and suddenly, one by one the worms begin to pop, bursting with juicy snaps.

The worms explode over the plateau, leaving behind messy puddles of green goo.

The bursting of wet popcorn rings busy for a few minutes, but eventually it's done too and the stunned silence wraps over the dusty land.

My angels are watching the show and so are the "greys" above us.

I glance at Baza, calculating my next move, when the ground below explodes, raising a column of dust and dirt with clumps of flying soil, sending shockwave through the air.

I shield my face and close my eyes against the blast, managing to keep myself anchored to my spot in the air.

But some of mine and Baza's angels are pushed by the blast, tumbling arse over heels, which prompts a string of guttural cursing from Baza.

A few seconds later the dust settles enough to see a large crater in the ground, identical to the one I have found myself in.

Dšarael stands in the centre of the crater.

His large glass wings are open behind his back. His chin is raised and his stance is defiant.

"She doesn't need your permission to leave, none of us do", the god calls to Baza. "That is not your land and it never was. You have no right to it. I assert the claim over Arllu as mine. As the inheritor of Ishtar, as rightful ruler of this land, as the Father of all istana, I proclaim your rule false and erroneous. I pronounce Arllu under my authority again."

The god's voice is young, yet forceful and unyielding. His eyes are ablaze as he challenges Baza.

He doesn't look like the weak prisoner I rescued, although covered in dirt and worm goo, the god looks stronger and healthier than the last time I saw him.

Shana and Mitish come out from behind a nearby shed and I'm relieved to see those two alive.

Baza says nothing and I turn my head to him.

Baza's shocked gaze rakes the god, venturing to the crater and the surrounding debris of its explosion, darting to the green goo covering the ground.

It was a surprise Baza didn't see coming and he struggles to hide it.

"Down!" Rafe's voice calls, and as I turn my head, I watch my angels descending to the ground, following the wave of his sword.

"Ana sim-tim alanku!" I call from my vantage point to the animals left roaming the plateau. "Go away and be!"

With these few words, I dismiss the lizards.

The ground is ours again and as the feet of my angels touch it, the istana begin to crawl out and off the buildings.

"I don't think so!" Baza roars and I turn my head to him, watching his face growing red, then purple and blue.

"I don't know who freed you but I have a good suspicion", he growls.

Somewhere in my mind, Rage opens her eyes and pouts her mouth in a feigned shock, mouthing: *"Me?!"*

"Little wardum knows far more than she lets on", Baza bellows. "But that's fine too. That won't change a thing! I will kill her and then I will kill you."

Baza points at the god.

"Even if all of the istana die with you", Baza roars, and his eyes bulge, his spittle fly, his carefully cultivated manners discarded. "I will find myself different slaves, better, sturdier, more subservient, dumber. The worlds are big and infinite. The greed is everywhere and it's eternal. I don't need you or them."

Baza pushes his bodyguards out of the way.

He is crazed. Nothing is left of the refined and homely "Father Christmas", who kept his emotions and his world in check.

"You all are going to die, here, once and for all! All of you! The animals will die an animal's death, in your own blood and excrement, begging for forgiveness and mercy!"

"Tana-dassi!" Baza roars, pointing down at us, and following his call, the grey soldiers fold their wings behind their backs, and dive towards us.

But as the grey bodies begin to dive, arrows begin to fly through the air.

The white arrows whizz above our heads in a solid wall, cutting through Baza's army, and another fresh wave of cries pierces the land as the grey bodies begin to drop.

"Towards the Gates, everyone! Move, move! Everyone, forward, now!" I roar over the commotion which tolls above our heads, and the angels around me begin to fly and the istana turn and begin to run.

Baza screams something. Maybe trying to stop the rainfall of arrows, maybe giving instruction on how to stop us, maybe cursing this new play, god's arrival, me...

But I don't stop to listen.

I don't know what these arrows are. I don't know where they are flying from or who is responsible for this lethal shower. I don't have time to dwell on that, the Gates are near. They are almost in sight.

"Domiel! Lead the way!" I call.

I need to save as many as I can, leading them through the doors and into the promised freedom, but I can't see Dumah or my sister. I don't know where they are.

My angels land on the ground around me, sprinting in the direction of the Gates with the istana.

Domiel runs past me, and raising his sword above his head, he yells: "Follow me, geelshtar-naa, brothers and sisters!"

Suddenly, the grey body drops to the ground in front of me and I jump sideways in time out of its way.

The body is sealed in Baza's grey uniform and its face is covered by the familiar grey mask, with a white arrow protruding from the side of its head.

I don't stop to inspect the body, but I need a weapon. I've lost my sword.

I lean in and tug the long sword out of the body's grip, and when the sword's hilt lays into my palm, I turn around, bursting into a run, into the opposite direction to my small army.

The arrows are flying through the air, yet the grey army has descended too.

"God!" I call to Dšarael as I sprint around the edge of his crater, where he is rooted in the middle of the bowl.

"Do you need personal invitation? Move! Follow Domiel! Get out of here!"

Mitish and Shana have reached the edge of the crater too, stopping there, unsure if they need to follow the flow of their people or remain by the god's side.

"Move!" I yell, pushing them both in the direction of the Gates. "Run! Now!"

Shana turns and runs.

"I'm not going anywhere", the god says, glaring at me from the bottom of the crater, and I hit the brakes.

"This is my land", he bristles.

"And you will be *dead* on your land if you don't move!" I yell. "Mitish, get him out!"

"Jess!" I call, returning to a sprint. "Dumah!"

I can't leave without her.

The shower of the arrows above my head has finally stopped.

I run towards the nearest hangar, calling my sister's name, when something jumps out from around the corner.

On instinct, I swing my sword, slicing the air, and with it aiming to cleave any danger ahead.

"Beyelai Sar! Uriel!" The familiar voice calls. "'Tis me! Sabrael!"

I blink through fear and dust, and the bearded face of Sabrael comes into focus, with his brother standing behind him. Their dark hair and faces are covered in dirt and red dust.

Sabrael holds a white crossbow in his arms with a bag of white bows strapped to his hip. His brother is outfitted with a crossbow too, but it's not all the weapons they have. Both are strapped with long and short swords, with axes and other ammunition, most of them of the black rippling fire, but amongst them, the two weapons shine with the white fiery light.

"It was you", I exhale, realising the source of the shower of arrows. "Thank you."

I touch his arm.

"Have you seen my sister?" I ask. "I mean", I shake my head, "have you seen the adar?"

"Adar?" his eyes open wider. "Where? Here?"

"Nay, Beyelai", he answers under my expectant gaze and shakes his head.

"Follow everyone to the Gates", I say, waving my hand towards the direction I came from.

"Your brothers would be happy to see you", I add over my shoulder as I am about to return to my running.

But he grabs my arm and I grind to a halt, looking at him, my eyebrows raised.

"These wee swords must be yours", Sabrael says, pulling my two swords of white fire from his belt.

"Thank you", I mumble.

I reach out, taking the swords from him, stuffing them into the loops in my belt.

"You must go!" I tell him. "Find your brothers and give the weapons to the istana. Make sure everyone's armed."

Behind me, over the plateau, the sound of fighting has escalated.

"Please go!" I ask him once again.

But before I resume my running, I spin around and, stretching my neck, scan the plateau and the horizon, assessing the latest development over the battlefield.

The sky is clear of "greys" as the fighting has moved onto the slippery ground. Judging by the ringing sounds of clashing swords, my twenty angels, plus the hundred or so surviving istana, have begun cutting their way through the grey army blocking their path.

From this angle and at this distance I can't tell what is Baza's army's advantage or if there's any. But I hope that the shock tactics of the air assault that Sabrael and his brother brought with their arrows, have killed plenty of the grey angels, balancing the scales just a bit.

"Go!" I call to Sabrael.

I turn and I run.

I glance again towards the plateau as I round the metal hangar. Unobstructed by its metal skeleton, I spot Baza and a few of his guards at the edge of the god's crater, their weapons raised as they're looking to annihilate the god.

But as much as I want to help the god, I need to find my sister first.

"Jess!" I roar. "Jess!!"

I sprint between the buildings, darting between the bodies of lizards shuffling away from the battlefield, screaming my sister's name over and over again.

"Here!" A deep male voice cuts in.

"She is here."

The voice is unfamiliar, and fearing that it might be a trap, yet needing to check every possibility, I pull out one of my short swords and armed with it in one hand and the black long sword in the other, I take a few cautious steps closer to the place where the voice is calling from.

"Jess?" I call again.

"She is here, Beyelai Sar."

I turn the corner of another metal hangar.

My sister's large animal form lies on the red ground and the puddle of red blood underneath her is even redder. Dumah kneels next to her, holding her head on his lap.

"Hurry, Beyelai."

Dumah's voice is deep and velvety. It's the first time I hear him speak.

I run the last few steps, dropping to my knees in front of my sister.

I touch her body, stroking her fur.

"What's happened?" I ask, but I can guess myself, as I watch blood streaming from my sister's side where the sword of the grey soldier had wounded her, and the sword lying nearby, painted red.

My sister doesn't move. She doesn't whimper, doesn't make a sound. The rising of her furry side is barely visible.

"We need to move her!" I roar at Dumah. "Now! We need to take her into Uras. We need to help her! Move her. Help me!"

I grab hold of the fur on her neck, trying to lift her, but her heavy body won't budge.

I yank and I pull but to no avail.

"Come on, baby", I mumble. "Come on. I need you to move. We need to move. We need to go. Come on, Jess!"

I grab her leathery wing, pulling at it as I grind my teeth.

My feet slip on the sandy ground and my tears spill down my cheeks.

I let go of her withers, coming around towards her face.

"Come on, baby, come on", I mumble as I stroke her face and pink snout, but my voice is rising. "I can't leave you here and you can't leave me. You can't! You hear me? You can't leave me! Get it out of your head. You're not leaving me! You are stuck with me, Jessie-boo, stuck forever", I scream as I shake her head.

"You can't leave me, please, baby, please!" I mumble again. "Don't leave me. Please, not you."

I swallow and I wipe my face with the back of my hand.

I push at her body, but my feet are sliding on the dusty soil, yet her body remains on the same spot.

"You have to wake up, Jessie! You must! Hear me? You must! What I will do without you? How am I going to live without you? You can't leave me, baby. You can't. You are all I have!"

I feel Dumah's body next to mine, tugging at my sister's body, and I can feel it beginning to slide along the stony ground, but after a while it stops again.

I push with my legs at the ground. I pull with my arms until it hurts, but her large body refuses to move again.

She is stuck. She is too heavy.

"Jess!" I roar.

I strengthen, letting go of her wing.

The tears are running down my face and I have to bite inside my mouth, hard, to stem their flow and to wake up my anger and my Rage.

I wipe my face with my sleeve. I wipe my eyes, and bending over, I grab my swords.

"Stay here!" I bark at Dumah.

The plan, viable only a second ago, to make a run towards and through the Gates, leaving Baza behind in Arllu, and come back and deal with him later is no longer an option.

I can't outrun him, not while pulling the heavy body of my sister along the ground, and I am not leaving her behind.

Yet I need to move her fast, taking her into the sanctuary of Uras and under Amy's care.

She is not going to die. I am not going to be responsible for my sister's death. I can't be.

"Stay with her!" I repeat to Dumah, carving out each word.

He nods at me, and looking into his eyes, I don't think he even contemplated leaving her.

I turn around and run. I run towards the battlefield, towards the grey barrier that is blocking me from the Gates and Uras, the barrier that stands between my sister and healing hands of Amy and the energy of the orb and universe above.

I run forward, looking for Baza. I need to find and kill him and I need to do it now.

I need to finish it.

CHAPTER 44

The fight is spilling over the plateau. The grunts and screams of the fighters and the cries of the dying filled the air.

My attempts at reducing the size of Baza's army has paid off as his army of grey malakhims has been slashed, with only half left standing.

But even their half is larger than what is left of my army.

Baza's grey army have moved along the plateau, blocking my army's escape. Access to the Gates is closed off once again.

I roar as I run.

I don't have time for Baza's games. I will be coming through these Gates, I will and nothing will stop me. *No one* will stop me, otherwise I might as well die here.

"Sabrael", I bellow, lifting my head to the sky. "Arrows!"

I don't know where he is. I can't see him. He must be fighting somewhere within this mess of bodies.

I call and roar his name a few more times but my calls are left unanswered as no arrows fly.

I run into the heat of the battle, scooping up a few istana along the way.

"Move it!" I roar at them. "Today you either die or you live. Fight, if you want to live!"

I nudge them forward. I shove the long black sword into someone's hand.

I open my wings, lifting myself above their heads as I launch myself into the crowd of grey soldiers.

My short swords dance in my hands.

The blood explodes.

A voice cries and a body drops.

Someone flies above me, but I dive to the ground then. I fall, and scooping someone's long sword off the ground, I spin, drawing circles around me.

More bodies drop, more final cries resonate, but it's not enough.

It's far too many of them, too many standing, with Baza alive somewhere.

With my sister bleeding out past this field, my plan of the attack has changed.

I no longer have time for slow progression towards the Gates. I don't have time for games, protecting the lives of my fighters or my own. Now I need to enlist the help of everyone and everything I can.

"Alka ngen. Haal-dih, pulhu-nasu. Haal-dih", I roar, flying up.

"ALL of you! All come! Return to your mother!" I bellow, throwing my head up. But I am not summoning the ones I sent away earlier, oh, no. They are not the ones I want.

The Gates are not far.

During the earlier push and with the support of Sabrael's assault, my army significantly progressed forward and now I can see the rippling of the air in the horizon where the fabric of this world is thinnest, where the Gates stand, waiting for my command, ready to open.

The Gates are so close yet so far. We are blocked from them by the grey army.

But I can open the Gates from here. I hope I can.

"Peta!" I scream, as I rise above the heads. "Peta babkama luruba!"

"Open, damn you!" I roar. "Open! NOW!"

And I follow that summon with another one: "Alka ngen. Haal-dih, pulhu-nasu. Haal-dih."

I need to finish it now. I have to.

My sister might not have these few minutes.

I must save her. She's all I have. Somewhere deep I know, and fear, that the end of her might be the end of me.

The assault on the remainder of Baza's army must be escalated. I need to be through the Gates.

I fall down, into the depths of the fight. I need to clear the area around me. I need to get my bearings and to find the angels I need.

I twist and I slash. I turn and I dive.

My wings are folded tightly behind my back but they are not in the way.

With my wings, I sense the two istana's essences around me and slowly we find each other, covering each other's backs.

With sharp cries the bodies drop around me, and when I glance over my shoulder next time, I notice that both istana are no longer standing behind me.

I am exposed again.

But they've bought me the needed space, and rising on my wings, above the ground, I turn, looking for Rafe.

His purple wings bounce a hundred yards away.

"Rafe!" I roar. "Rafe!"

And when he turns his head to me, I yell: "Chamuel flies! Now!"

I hope he understands what I am asking of him.

But his gaze stays on me for a second, before he nods his head.

I hope he understood.

I don't have the power to keep the Gates open and to summon the flesh eating flies at the same time. The halved essence doesn't hold that much power, especially as I am already calling on other creatures.

The call on the flesh eating flies is risky. They are wild, hungry parasites and hard to control. In the conditions of the battle, with so many moving bodies, in a confusing smelling pot of so many different essences, I don't know if I or Rafe would be able to manipulate them.

I turn, looking for the other angel I need.

The bright blue wings dot the dark crowd of fighting bodies. My gaze slides from one blue dot to the next, until I find the large form I need.

Luckily, he is not far.

I fight my way through the crowd towards Sabrael.

"Sabrael", I call as I reach him after slashing at a few "greys" along the way. "Sabrael!"

He spins to me, his sword flies with him, stopping a millimetre away from my neck.

His crazed eyes relax and he exhales. The istana and his brothers around him come closer, fighting around us.

"I need arrows!" I call. "Find help, find cover. I need you to cover the sky. Malakhims are about to fly!"

"Aye, Beyelai", he barks without further question, his military training is apparent.

He roars his instructions to someone nearby but I am not listening. I am busy with my summoning.

"Peta babkama luruba!" I mumble, calling on the Gates to open.

"Alka ngen. Haal-dih, pulhu-nasu", I mumble as I turn and dive, fighting the dark swords around me, summoning another army.

The arrival of that army will be the poetic justice to Baza's end.

Suddenly I feel a ripple and a tug in the distance, like a draft from an open door.

The Gates have opened.

I know that the angels around me feel it too as I see the heads and glances turn towards the Gates amidst the battle.

"Alka ngen. Haal-dih, pulhu-nasu", I mumble, repeating it like a prayer, and finally I feel the answering pull and the movement past the open door.

They are here.

I kick at the nearby grey angel then open my wings and take to the sky.

The feet march and shuffle past the Gates. The steps resonate with different strides of bodies of different sizes and heights, and soon through the dust and rippling veil of the Gate, humans appear.

But I know what they really are, and soon everyone else will.

These creatures have nothing in common with humans, apart from their stolen skins. They are even less human than Baza or me.

They are the lizards Baza had placed into Apkallu realm. It's them he trusted with controlling humans, harvesting their souls. It's them he outfitted with larger brains, granting them use of angelic weapons.

He had created them as means to help his malakhims to harvest, as his trusted dogs and whips, but now I will use them against him. I am going to use these lizards against their creator.

The "greys" begin to shuffle, unsure about the new arrival.

They know that they are on the same side, or at least they used to be, but the lizards were not declared in the entertainment programme for this evening, and most certainly they were not supposed to come from this side.

Baza roars something near the Gates. He roars at the new arrivals, calling them to his heel but they don't respond to him. They have changed their allegiance.

These dogs don't belong to him anymore, they don't obey his command, and I even spot the Scouser amongst the crowd, his large frame towering above the heads.

The creatures stagger through, pressing forward, pushing the army of grey malakhims against us, as their shuffling steps raise dust higher on the flanks as they begin to close the circle.

The grey army is squeezed against us, encircled, and as the lizards in human skins force the situation and come closer. They draw their angelic weapons that Baza so kindly had supplied to them, and begin to slash at the nearby "greys".

The shock and surprise ring with the first cries.

The collision of weapons echoes past our little group.

The "greys" fight, chopping and slashing, desperate to block the advance of their former colleagues, but one by one they give up and, opening their wings, they take to the sky.

I open my mouth and draw breath about to call Sabrael, but that's not required.

As the first "greys" begin to rise, white arrows begin to fly.

There's a shift in the domination in the battle and this time it is tangible.

Baza roars, swearing, spitting out profanities in many languages.

At some point, he calls the words of power, summoning his upgraded lizards back into his fold, but my reverse was final.

I took control over them. I took back what was mine all along and I am not going to release them from their servitude to me. Not now, not ever.

A few more grey angels soar to the sky, but every one of them is shot down by an arrow.

I fly low, conscious of Sabrael's whizzing onslaught.

From this height, I can finally see that we have turned the corner in this battle and we finally were granted a chance.

I see the struggle of Baza's army on the ground, as more and more of his angels drop, skewed by the weapons of the lizards in human skins, and at some point I think I spot the familiar little boy from the clearing around my mother's house, but it's probably not him, as I remember destroying those.

My angels and istana are holding their side, fighting the pressing "greys", but the ongoing raging battle begins to take its toll. My army is slow in reacting. Exhausted, my followers trip over their own feet, the dance of their swords grows lethargic.

"Move out!" I yell towards the ground. "Get out of there!"

And following my command, my army begin to retreat, giving way to the lizards, who press the advantage and start to close the circle around the remainder of the grey army.

Baza's army grows smaller with every minute when Baza's voice rings above the plateau, issuing another instruction.

Busy, fighting at the front, refusing to retreat with the istana, I don't pay attention to his call until suddenly the attack of the arrows stops and the entirety of the grey flock opens their wings and takes to the sky.

With their prey lost, the lizards in human skins aimlessly swing their weapons, until they herd together like zombies, shuffling in the middle of the plateau, their heads drawn up, as the centre of their circle grows empty and smaller, with all "greys" now in the sky.

Shit! Sabrael!

But I can't leave my command.

My sister needs me and I need my istana and the angels to move her through the Gate. I can no longer run through the Gates, leaving Baza alive, and I have minutes to finish it all.

"Rafe!" I roar "Rafe! Now!"

CHAPTER 45

The familiar pulsating noise begins to rise in the distance, seeping through the veil dividing the worlds.

The pulse grows stronger and soon the veil ripples and the first dots of the dark stick insects begin to push through, filling the sky.

Their number grows with every second, prompting a scuffling response from the grey army in the sky.

The "greys" are sandwiched between the armed lizards on the ground and the swarm of the flesh-eating insects in the sky.

But so are we.

My angels float in the sky, below the greys, while the istana shuffle on the ground.

"Rafe! Let's do it!"

And following my call, the insects congregate tighter and their shrilling song with the promise of pain begins.

The cloud begins to pulsate and vibrate until it falls down, covering faces and bodies with a brown blanket, bringing with it the familiar sepia colour.

Agonising screams pierce the air and the mutilated bodies begin to drop.

Some bodies are only a collection of bones while the others are still alive, crying in pain, pleading for help, and while I pause for a moment, thinking of what to do with them, the nearby istana and the lizards skew the fallen with their swords.

In the heat of the battle, led by their hate, or maybe instinct, they have made the decision for me.

But some grey angels are trying to fly away, to put distance between them and the lethal cloud, and then the gaps in the layer of the "greys" appear and the bloodthirsty sticks drop one level lower, looking for more bodies and more food, and lower down are my angels.

I need to end it, fast.

"Attack!" I call, and opening my wings, I fly into the scuffle above, swinging my swords at the bodies the colour of sepia.

I swing my swords, I turn, I slash, ending their miseries and granting them peace.

Their cries break and their bodies drop.

I fly, slashing more.

I need to finish it soon, but I am looking for Baza. It's he whom I need.

I feel the tiny bites pierce my wings and my body, and I begin to cry out too, echoing the cries of the angels around me. I don't know how long I will manage before I am covered in a layer of parasites, how long before *my* angels will fall with the grey army.

I have played a dangerous card. I know that.

I will weed out the grey army, I might annihilate it, but with it I might kill mine. I am risking the lives of my angels, and with every minute I am not calling the brown sticks off, I'm risking loss of more lives, of the lives that matter to me.

"A bit more", I mumble to myself, "just a bit more."

I need more time. I can see the gap in their number, I can feel victory.

"Just a bit more", I say to myself as dozens of new teeth sink into me, pulling my flesh apart.

A female voice cries out to the right of me.

I turn my head in time to see beautiful Sablo, dropping to the ground, her entire body coated with the insects.

"Enough!" I roar. "No more! Alaku Situ! Disappear! All of you, be gone!"

"Rafe!" I cry out. I need the help of his essence to push them out. The left over shard of mine won't manage it all, keeping the Gates open, commanding the herd and halting the insects' ravaging party.

With the call of the Old Sumerian words, the Gates open and the cloud of the brown bodies lifts off their victims, a few at a time and sluggish at first, but as the pressure increases, their bodies are ripped off their victims, and accompanied by the pained bellows of victims, who are missing chunks of flesh, the swarm of the brown plague is syphoned into the red sky and out, through the veil, repeating their arrival in reverse.

My body, damaged by the insects, protest, crying at my every move, but the sky is almost free of the insects and the grey army. The horizon is finally clear.

A few grey angels continue to float above the ground, but their moves are weary and their bodies are damaged.

But there's a small cluster of the grey angels in the sky ahead.

They are moving away, and under the cover of bodyguards barely holding afloat, I spot Baza's stout body.

I grind my teeth and I push at my screaming wings, as pain pierces every part of my body and my head swims.

My blood soaks my clothing and I can feel the sand and wind brushing over my bared muscles, under missing and eaten feathers, but it's all unimportant.

I must end it, once and for all. I must, and then move on.

I hear the guttural swearing of the brothers behind me as they chase and finish off the last of the grey soldiers. I hear the dying cries and the cries of the injured on the ground.

But I see only the one ahead.

He is surrounded by six grey bodies and as I narrow the distance between us, one of the bodies cries out and drops.

"Baza plus five", Rage vocalises in my head the easy math.

But I don't care how many are around him, I will kill them all.

I manage to catch up with them in a dozen or so wings flaps, and as an announcement of my arrival, I swing my long sword, slashing at the body of the nearest grey.

He cries out and drops, exposing Baza.

But the circle closes before I have a chance to wedge my long sword inside it, and again, as many times before, I use my aerobatic skills, banking on my wings, sliding under the group, drawing the circles with my sword.

But I am tired and my moves are no longer lithe, failing to reach my target.

My sword finds the next victim and another grey body falls, but not before a sword cuts at my shoulder and my wing.

I cry out, releasing my long sword, which drops to the ground, clanking far below against the stony ground.

My blood, mixed with dust and picked by the wind, dances around me, the large droplets morph in front of my eyes, spinning a crazy dance, taunting my attempts and my mortality, yet reminding me of my sister's metamorphosis.

And that's whips me forward, pushing me, as I grind my teeth, looking for another weapon at my corset.

The beating of approaching wings cuts the air, and as a dog afraid to lose its prey, I rush at Baza and his bodyguards.

I rip the last of my white shining swords from my corset and a black slaves' dagger. One of them won't kill the "greys" but both of them should get the bodies out of my way.

I glide around the group, and on one of those turns, I sink both dark dagger and the short sword into two necks.

Two cries ring but only one body falls.

The approaching beating of wings is upon me.

I turn around, throwing my hand out with the white sword of mine... narrowly, by an inch missing Sam.

His eyes fly open and so do mine.

"Go", he says, nudging his head to Baza. "Finish it. I'll deal with them."

He throws himself into the midst of the floating bodies, colliding with a few, swinging his black swords.

A few feathers are missing off his wings and blood seeps from the shallow cuts over his body, but he doesn't look bad, taking into account how he looked in the tunnels and the fight we just had.

The bodies disperse, following his erratic flying, leaving only one bodyguard next to Baza.

Mine and Baza's gazes meet, and for the first time I see concern in it, and holding his gaze, I hurl my short dagger at his black leather clad chest, as the smile blossoms on my lips.

The dagger tumbles while flying through the air, but the second before it should find its target and sink into Baza's chest, a grey body darts in front of it, catching the dagger in his chest.

The voice cries and the body drops, leaving behind an exposed and unarmed Baza.

He is alone and, like a Christmas turkey, ready for my slaughter.

My hand dives to my corset, looking for weapons, finding the last sword.

I don't say a word to him as I tug the sword free, I have nothing to say. I've said it all before. There's nothing more to add. Nothing will change my mind or will affect his sentence.

* * *

"Check this out", Yofiel calls to me when my feet touch the ground. "It's Nanael."

He holds a grey mask in his hand, as he stares at the body on the ground.

"Probably the rest of them are here too", he muses, as he trudges along, grinding his teeth against the pain.

"Istana! Angels!" I call. "We've won!"

I push at my sore wings as I fly up.

"Our way into Uras is wide open and no one will stop us now! Come with me!" I call. "We are ready to go home. Uras is waiting for us. But before we go, please, come and help me to bring my sister with us, to the home where she belongs too."

The last standing istana and the angels follow me. Against the pain in their broken and damaged bodies, they follow me to collect my sister because now they will follow me to the end of the worlds. They will die for me and fight for me past the veil.

There's nothing they won't do for me now.

We collect Jess' body and I promise them to come back later, to collect the bodies of their fallen kin, before they are led past the ripping veil of the Gates and into the promised land of Uras, into their forever home in the sky, into the promised and free Heaven.

CHAPTER 46

I stand in the room in the high tower, watching my sister's large brown body lying in the middle of the white square in the centre of Uras.

The new arrival of istana is congregating around her and Dumah is standing watch.

A couple of the old angels, who refused to come and fight with me and didn't want her in Uras, are nearby, whispering to each other.

"Amy said she is dying", I say, keeping my gaze on my sister. "She said that because she is adar it takes longer for the magic of angelic swords to work, but either way it's only a matter of time before my sister will be dead.... dead, gone, like she was never born."

I watch the square.

Steeled by the battle the istana are not the submissive and scared bunch I found in the tunnels. The males and females of the istana in the central square were drenched in the blood of their kin and in the blood of angels. They carry the weapons of angels and they killed a few angels too. They no longer look with veneration at the angels bright and full wings. Now they know that angels die the same way as them. Slaves are gone.

"When I asked Amy if my sister will be reborn", I continue without turning to Rafe, "if her soul will be saved, Amy said she doesn't know for sure, but she thinks it's unlikely. She said that the adar and the shard of essence would pull her into Udhad, blocking her from entering the rebirth cycle."

I fall quiet.

"Can you imagine, to be born, to live, knowing very little joy but plenty of suffering, every day for eleven years of your life, only to be dead by the end of that road? Without any real life, without knowing enjoyment, without knowing any love apart from mine. Was she born only to suffer? Was she born for nothing? Was her life a punishment to her and if so, what for, why? Don't you think it's unfair?"

I turn to Rafe. There are only two of us here.

He takes a few steps closer. His footsteps echo in the bright empty room.

"Ariel, I promise you, we'll think of something. We will figure this one out. But even if we don't, you need to remember that there's a reason for every birth and death under An's sun. There's a reason for everything that happens to us. Maybe the reason for her life was to make you *you*? To help you to become the strong leader that you are now? Maybe she was born *for* you?"

I know he's trying. He thinks he is helping.

But it's irrelevant what he says.

The decision has already been made.

"I've sent Pronoia into the tunnels", I say, turning towards the window. "I want all of the istana freed and brought here. I promised them home and I'm going to give it to them. I am going to keep my promise. I'll be going into the tunnels of Arllu myself soon too. I want to speak to every imprisoned angel that's still there. I need to know what they've done to piss Baza off and then I will carry out *my* justice. I plan to give them a fair hearing that they never had before offering them to pledge to me and join my army."

I'm not telling Rafe that I am building a new empire, a different empire to anything that the angelic world has ever seen. My plans are big and they go into the future for many GA. My empire will be operating under different rules to anything that was in their world before.

I don't tell him that he won't be part of it, that he won't be around to see it grow. The future is no longer his. It's mine.

"The enemy of my enemy is my friend", I recite absentmindedly.

"Mik'hael is coming", I say, bringing myself back to the topic. "I know it. After Baza's defeat I bet he would think long and hard on it, but sooner or later he'll come and I must be ready. I *will* be ready."

I sigh.

I don't know why I'm telling him all this, although if I am completely honest with myself, I have to admit that I'm telling him this to delay the moment, to find the strength to push through with my decision.

"The god doesn't want to return to Arllu", I say. "He wants to stay here for a while, said his place is with his children, before he decides what to do next. Apparently Ishtar has many more worlds elsewhere, and he is thinking to go there. It must be nice to be a child to a god, float from world to world, pick and choose a residence", I huff.

I fall silent again.

"I'm sending Sam to rule Arllu for me", I say.

"He will go", Rafe answers behind my back. "He loves you."

I turn, glancing at him. It's strange to hear him admitting it, instead of his usual lecture.

"Love has very little to do with anything", I cut him off. "I know he will do what I order him to do and the reasoning for it is entirely up to him. I will command him to rule Arllu in my name, after I demand his sworn fealty to me. I will be ruling that land by his proxy and he can do it either out of his love for me or out of fear", I clip.

"If he does, it's because he wants to be the second in charge of the rising dynasty, I'm okay with that too. I don't care of his motives. All I want from him is his servitude and I intend to receive it. He will subject himself to me and to my rule, and I am happy to pay him in the currency of his choosing."

I will control Sam and my feeling for him the way I intend to control everything around me, the way I will rule my domain. I will use his weaknesses, whilst killing mine. I will utilise his strength for my gain. His powers, his past, his love will serve the new empire and me, and he doesn't necessarily need to be briefed on it.

And my feelings? They mean nothing, they don't matter. They are irrelevant in the larger scheme of things. They will be weeded out over time, plucked out together with every memory of him, of his every scent and his every taste. One by one they will be abandoned, ignored and starved until nothing is left in my heart and my mind but the burnt landscape of Arllu.

"Dumah is so gentle with Jess", I say, smiling, as I watch the large angel sitting cross-legged on the stone floor, while Jess' large head rests on his lap as he strokes her fur, barking at the occasional istana, whom he deems came too close.

"Maybe he can be her guardian angel. We all need one, especially if we continue our lives on earth. We need someone to look after us, to have our back, and I won't be there for her anymore. But with him watching over her, I know she'll be alright. Maybe for once she will enjoy and love her life, maybe then her life will become the happy life she deserves."

"She will be fine wherever she goes next", Rafe mutters behind me.

"She will", I say. "She absolutely will."

"I will make sure of it", I mumble, feeling the handle of one of my short swords at my corset.

I turn to face Rafe.

I look at his beautiful face, washed by the light streaming through the window. His brown eyes are on me and the soft smile is on his lips.

I swallow and take a step closer.

"I want to say thank you for everything you've done for me, Rafael, for every little thing you did. I know I wouldn't have made it that far without you."

I breathe out, coming closer.

"I'm sorry, Rafael", I say quietly.

"What for?" he asks and smiles, his eyebrows fly up. "There's nothing to apologise for. I know you are only a human and I wasn't expecting any more than that from you."

"Human", I mumble.

"Human", I repeat, nodding my head and keeping his gaze.

"But I was an animal to many, a dirty animal, a wardum. I am still seen as an animal by some, an animal not worthy to be here, let alone to lead, not worthy to have such a great essence inside. I saw how far you were prepared to go to save the essence of the one you love. I saw what her essence meant to you. It's the only thing that is left of Uriel in this world, the last piece of her. That is the only pure thing in me, the only thing that makes me somewhat godly. I saw what you were prepared to do for it. You were prepared to court the animal for the Qal of your loved one, to save her essence and her legacy. You were prepared to do whatever it took to keep Uriel, and anything that is left of her, pure and holy."

Rafe's face drops the longer I talk and his smile varnishes.

I am a few inches away from him and the scent of tropical fruits is strong.

"That's love. That's true love", I murmur. "I wish someone loved me even half as much as you love her."

"Oh no, don't worry", I say and I shake my head and smile at his narrowing gaze. "I understand. I totally understand. I understand you completely and I understand your motives. I understand more than you think, Rafe. You haven't given me enough credit, I understood a lot. I understand about doing absolutely anything for a loved one, for the one who is your whole life. In this respect we have more in common than you might think. I too would do absolutely anything for the love of my life, for the one who means the world to me, with whom the sun rises and sets. And I am sorry, Rafael. I really am."

The deep wrinkles carve between his eyebrows, his gaze affixed to me.

My hand flies away from my corset and the white short sword sinks into Rafe's neck.

His eyes snap open in surprise as he begins to gurgle.

"You courted the animal to save your wife's essence. Can you imagine what I do to save the life of the only one I love, the one who means the world to me?" I say as I push the sword deeper.

"I will do absolutely anything for her. She needs to live, live her life and mine, live for the both of us. Her story can't be only the story of abuse, suffering and death. Her happiness is more important to me than my own, and it will remain like that forever. She will live a happy life for both of us, and I hope you understand that. I hope you do."

Rafe's body is about to fall, so I grab hold of him, laying him gently on the white marble floor.

"Maybe I am not that different from you after all. Maybe I am an angel", I whisper to him.

Rafe's wide open eyes stare at me as he tries to speak.

"Soon you'll see your wife", I say softly, as I stroke his hair. "You will be together again and the half of Uriel's essence will return to Udhad where it belongs. It will free my sister too and Dumah will take her to earth, where she'll be able to live, live as she should, without the rotting shards of angelic essence inside her. She will have her life back and this time I will make sure it's a good life.

"I am sorry, Rafael, for this, but I hope you understand, and I think you do. But I always will be grateful to you for everything you've done for me. I promise to keep Uriel's teachings going. I promise to protect the human kind as your wife did, and I promise to be fair to everyone. I will make sure that everyone who seeks refuge will be granted it. I will protect these people. I will protect the free will. I will make Uriel proud of my rule. I will make sure to leave the legacy behind when I'm gone, but it will be the legacy that was formed by your wife and refined by me."

Rafe's throat gurgles and blood trickles out of a corner of his mouth.

His blood pulsated around the sword's blade and the sword's handle dances in my grip.

With the last rise of his chest, the last breath leaves him. His glazed eyes freeze on the window behind me.

I pull the sword out, wiping the blood on my trousers before sliding it into the sheath.

"I know you understand", I murmur before I rise to my feet.

I come to the window and with another glance at my sister's body, I march across the large white room to save the one I love.

Throwing the heavy door open, I walk out of the room.

But I don't manage to go far.

The moment I put my feet on the cobblestone floor of the corridor, fire erupts in my wing, followed by a familiar noise of a long sword cutting the air.

The whizz of a sword slashing the air is the recognisable sound.

I listen to it as I turn to my attacker, when the slashing noise is followed by another, the bursts of flames sear my wing and I scream.

I fall to my knees, raising my gaze upward, to the face of the attacker.

Yofiel towers above me.

Rafe's long sword with the purple and golden handle is in his hand and my blood drips off its tip.

"Why?" I rasp, looking up at him.

"Uriel's essence should reside only in Uriel or in her Arcanum", he booms. "Rafael was right, you don't deserve to lead. You should never have been given this right. The essence should never have woken in you, in a human. That was Ophanims' mistake that I will correct now. With Uriel gone, Rafael is the only one who should lead Uriel's Erimnate."

"I saved you", I wheeze, breathing through pain.

"No. Rafael came to rescue us from Arllu, to fix our mistake of giving the essence of his Arcanum to a human."

He spits at the floor.

"If Rafael is ready to lead", Yofiel says, "I am happy to follow. He has promised to us to be the true leader of Uras, the *real, angelic* leader, and he is right, you are a liability that needs to be eliminated once and for all, and I am happy to take it on myself to fix my mistake. I will prove to Rafael that I am serious about his reign. I will prove to Rafael that I am worthy. If he wants the mistake eliminated, I will do it for him!"

I huff and smile.

"You are too late to pave the way for your leader", I say. "Rafael is dead."

"What?!" Yofiel's voice rustles. His eyes open wide, the hand holding his long sword shakes and falls.

"No, no", he stammers. "How could it be?"

"The unworthy animal has killed him", I huff, calling myself the name they have assigned to me. "The animal, who has been learning your games and now outplaying you all."

And I begin to laugh.

"You've made a mistake alright", I say. "You've underestimated me."

My hand slides to my corset, looking for the handles of my weapons, when suddenly a black blade of a sword penetrates Yofiel's chest.

His eyes fly open, his gaze drops to the blade of black rippling fire sticking out of him, then to me, and when the blade slides out, his body falls.

Dumah stands in front of me.
The sword in his hand is drenched in Yofiel's blood.
Without a word, he reaches to me, offering his hand.

CHAPTER 47

The network of dark corridors looks and smells as before. The familiar claustrophobic tomb, filled with the scent of mushrooms spores and mildew, growing under a constant song of dripping water and rustles of blind worms and beetles.

I walk alone. I've left everyone behind, only Sam and I know that I am here.

There will be a few more junctions, a few more turns before I will reach my destination, but I don't rush. There's no need.

The one I am about to see is not going anywhere. He will be there for as long as I will it and I've decided it won't be much longer.

His life means nothing to me, it is worthless, whereas his death will change everything, and not just for me.

The last of his life's value lies in his death. His death will be a precious gift to me.

But I won't be asking anyone's permission to take it. I don't need anyone gifting it to me. I will take it because I want it and because it is the spoils of war, a war that he lost and I won.

His life became mine the moment my blunt black daggers sliced off his wings. The moment he fell to the ground, wingless, exiled from the sky and begun to crawl in the dirt with the rest of us, that moment he lost the sky and with it, his kingdom.

He lost and I've won.

His fall has reversed our roles, changing with it the lives of everyone in Dingir-Ki and other worlds.

With no army, no slaves or followers, he became another broken "fallen", abandoned and soon to be forgotten.

The tip of the fire from the torch in my hand licks the low ceiling.

I know this route. I took it before.

I walk past the barred wall of a locked section and my torch illuminates empty carved niches past it, free of prisoners or shady oily snakes.

My trainers splash the water when I step into puddles, dirty droplets fly, spraying the bottoms of my white trousers.

With another turn, the light from many torches fills the air and with a few extra longer strides I come to stand by the familiar wall of metal bars, and as if of its own volition, my gaze jumps to the cell to the left, which was occupied by me not so long ago.

The section is well lit yet quiet.

Jamming the black ring into the metal wall births the familiar sizzling sound, drawing me into the past, but I blink it away, resisting its pull.

I swing the door and step inside, onto the pressed earth.

"Did you find it alright?" Sam's voice asks in the distance, his footsteps grow, marching forward, until he comes to stand in the pool of light, in front of me.

His body is sealed in a black tunic and trousers of angelic fashion underneath a heavy vest of padded leather with a skirt. He looks medieval and merciless. The backdrop of his white wings reminds me that he is ancient after all.

I huff.

"Of course, how could I forget?"

"I thought so, that's why I chose it."

He comes closer, laying his hands on my waist and pulling me closer, and taking a step forward, I lift my head to him, ready for his kiss.

"You look beautiful today, my Beyelai", he whispers, smiling against my lips before sharing with me the taste of blackberries.

But I don't let it linger for too long nor do I forget why I am here, and after a brisk second, and by far earlier than he expected, I pull away, licking the taste of wild blackberries away.

"He is here", I say and it sounds almost like a question, although I know that he must be here.

"He is", Sam answers, taking step back, adapting a restrained business tone, reminded by my distance and the question why we are both here.

"Where?"

"This way, at the end."

Sam waves his hand toward the farthest end of the corridor, which unlike the rest of the area, is shrouded in shadows.

I take a few steps in that direction.

"How do you find your new job?" I ask him, without glancing at him.

"It's fine", he answers behind my back and I almost feel the indifferent shrug of his shoulders.

As Rafe predicted, Sam has agreed to take the command of Arllu, to rule the land in my name, but the moment my request came in, I could read in his eyes that it was not what he had hoped I would ask of him, and it wasn't the job he wanted.

But irrespective of that, he agreed. He bowed to me, and while kneeling in front of me on one knee, he confirmed that he will do anything I command, always, and then he said the sacred vows.

I stop and turn to him.

"Thank you, Sam, for everything", I whisper, gazing into his eyes, and although not sure if feeling it, yet knowing that it what he wants to hear and what will help me with him, what will keep him near, what will ensure his ongoing cooperation, I add, "I love you."

I take his large hand into mine and, holding his gaze, I bring his hand to my face, resting it against my cheek, and close my eyes.

I open my eyes to the confronting, smouldering gaze of his, and I repeat, "Thank you", and pulling his hand away from my cheek, I kiss his warm palm.

His pine and moss scent bursts around me, riding high notes of the intensity of his emotions.

"I need to do it", I whisper and he nods.

I turn and walk away, glancing into each cell as I walk by. The light from my torch illuminates the corridor and each cubicle.

The cells are empty, yet as promised, the last one is occupied.

The familiar stout figure hangs in the centre, suspended off the damp earthy ceiling, swinging slightly. The large four wings brush the ground.

Baza's head is slumped on his chest soaked in his blood and a fat black oily parasite is wrapped around his wrists.

Sam comes behind me, and feeling his presence, I turn around, handing him the torch, which he takes without a word.

"I was wondering when you'd come", Baza's low yet coarse baritone suddenly utters.

I come closer to Baza's body.

We are a few inches from each other and my head is filled with the stench of his blood, the dark scent of the parasite above and a faint scent of river water, which must be the scent of Baza's essence.

I reach out, and pinching his chin, I lift his head.

I take a clean cloth from my corset and wipe his eyes glued by the dried blood, and when his eyes open and his gaze narrows on me, I glance over my shoulder at Sam and say: "Can you please wait past the wall, Sam?"

I can feel Baza's clever gaze on me.

"Ariel", Sam begins, but stops himself and just adds: "Are you sure?"

"Yes. Please, Sam."

"Light..." he starts.

"No, I don't need anything", I interrupt, "thank you, Sam."

Following my dismissal, the light gradually disappears with Sam's footsteps, leaving me and Baza alone within the grey shadows.

"Finally, our formidable Uriel is here", he says and his gaze moves over me. I don't know what he sees in the darkness but he adds with a huff: "You've changed. Although I'm not surprised, victory and power can do that to the unprepared."

I don't know what he is talking about or what he sees. I can't see anything but the glowing of his eye whites in the dark and a bit of the right side of his face.

I don't know where he is going with his subtle dig, so I stay quiet.

"What took you so long, child? I would've thought you'd come the following day to gloat. Where is your entourage?"

His gaze jumps behind my shoulder.

"Aren't you here to instantiate your victory, to show everyone how low you have brought the Lord of Arllu, to demonstrate where you are now and where I am, and what happens to anyone who crosses you?"

His gaze jumps back to me.

"I'm not here for that", I say and shrug my shoulders. "I don't need an entourage or a speech, in fact, turning everything into a spectacle is more your speciality."

His chest rumbles with a quiet laugh.

"So why are you here, Ariel?" he huffs, sobering. "Came to threaten me with eternity spent here?"

"Nope. Wrong again, Baza. Do you think I'd lock you in and keep you alive, leaving you even the smallest chance of escape? To keep your name alive, keep those embers going? Why would I, Baza? Huh? Why would I keep you alive? You showed me that any serious threat should be eliminated, and pronto, and I've watched you, Baza. I watched and I've learnt."

"But what about your humanity, Ariel?" he chuckles. "What about precious life, second chances, forgiveness? Isn't that what you were about? Isn't that what your weak gods preach? Not to kill, dirtying one's hands, not to take that "sin on your soul" or however it goes?"

I don't answer.

"It's not you, Ariel. You don't have it in you and you're not one of us", he huffs, narrowing his gaze on me.

"Again, Baza, you are working on old information and because of that, you're wrong. You're making your proclamation about the girl you once knew. Who told you that I'm still the same person?" I ask, shrugging my shoulders. "Maybe once upon a time I was human, with humanity, forgiveness and all the things you're talking about, but it was long time ago, before all this."

I swing my free hand around me.

"...And there was fear too back then, but now things have changed. Since then, I've learned a thing or two from you, then Lis and Chamuel taught me a few extra lessons and finally, I realised that I'm doing it all wrong. I thought to myself, "Why am I trying to live by my old principles, acting like a human when I am no longer one? Who am I trying to convince, you or myself?" Then, I remembered that I am immortal now, with a different set of needs, and if I'm an angel now, then I had better start acting like one, following angelic rules, and who better to show me those if not Baza? So I figured I'd follow the rules from your playbook."

"Ah", he stretches and his face lightens, "so you came here for advice?"

I laugh and my laugh comes out so easy and naturally, that it takes Baza by surprise and he stops, furrowing his eyebrows at me.

"I don't need your advice, Baza", I continue. "What did you think? That I'd lock you up here and will be visiting you daily, looking for advice, consulting you on my every ruling decision? Or you think that I'd appoint you as my moral compass in Hell?"

I laugh.

"That proposition is even funnier", I add.

"Why are you here then?" he asks, "to kill me? Then here's my advice to you, child, freely given advice. You should have done it back then, in Arllu, in front of your army, to demonstrate your powers. Moving and slaughtering such important figure as me in silence, behind closed doors is highly illogical and wasteful, child. There is no point, only your time was wasted. Maybe you do need to keep me as your advisor after all, as you have wasted a great fear inducing opportunity."

"If I needed your life, Baza, or your public execution, then dragging you here would've been stupid, agreed. But the thing is..." I pause. "I don't want either of those. I don't need your advice or your life... There's something else I'm going to take from you."

His soft baritone laughs, absorbed swiftly by the soil.

"Child, I have nothing left. You have taken everything from me, my people, my land, my rule. My life is the only thing that is left to me."

"Not only", I whisper as I lean closer to him. "Your life is not the only thing. You have something else, something that I want, something very precious. Not only I want it, but that is the reason why I've brought you here and why I have attached you to your little pet."

I smile at him and then I push his head upwards so his gaze can take in the whole glory of the black snake.

After a moment I bring his head down and his gaze turns back on me.

He is looking at me, but doesn't say a word, and I don't rush him either. I want him to figure out this one on his own.

Slowly, the confused gaze of Baza changes, his eyes open wider, his face, grey within the shadows, contorts and he begins to struggle, wishing his chin out of my hold.

He understood.

But the snake's control over one's body is absolute, I know it. Baza's struggle is futile and my hand won't leave his chin.

"No, no, no", he mumbles. "No! Ariel, no! Please, don't do it!"

His words grow louder and heated, more urgent and... scared.

"For everything that is sacred in Dingir-Ki, for everything that you hold sacred, please no. Please don't do it, please don't. Don't take my Qal from me, please. I beg of you, Ariel, in the name of anything that you hold dear, please don't do it to me. Please! Please, leave me this, leave me my Qal. Please allow me to die and enter the cycle, don't banish me from it. Please, Ariel. It's not really you. You are not that cruel. You don't need my Qal, you don't need it. I know I've hurt you, but no one deserves this, no one! Ariel, please! Leave me my soul..."

But I don't listen to him anymore.

I lean into him, my lips brush over his neck with old wrinkly skin over it, and I open my mouth, my teeth sinking into his flesh as they sunk once into Lis', drawing his blood, bringing with it his essence into me, making me the strongest and the most powerful archangel in their world, stronger than Uriel ever was, stronger than Mik'hael is, stronger than any ruler Dingir-Ki has seen.

EPILOGUE

"Thank you, Dumah, for doing this. I will never forget it. I trust you to keep my sister safe until her last breath on this Earth. Your guardian duties may cease once her essence has left her body and has entered the cycle of rebirth. Until then, I trust you'll look after her as your own kin."

Dumah touches his four fingers to his head and bows low. But as if it's not enough to show how much he honours this duty, he falls to his knees.

He raises his gaze to me.

"I know you would", I say and I lay my hand on his shoulder. "I trust you would."

The three girls, *my* girls, stand in the distance, chatting and laughing.

From here they look like average teenagers, with Tabby and Jess being younger friends of Shana.

Tabby is back to her eccentric fashion choices.

Upon her arrival in Uras, she scooped the entire selection of angelic clothing from her wardrobe, dumped it outside her door, swiftly replacing it with her psychedelic, crazy Goth ballerina attire.

Amitiel had approached me, complaining about Tabby's choice of clothing, but after I've suggested that if the choice of clothing creates so much split in our otherwise united Erimnate, I should bring Uras back to the time of Eden, and following Adam and Eve's lead, ban all clothing, Amy closed her mouth, agreeing that some clothing is better than none and had bowed out.

351

Now, Goth ballerina tells something to Jess and Shana, and after listening for a moment, both burst out laughing.

I watch Jess. I can't draw my eyes away from her, can't stop watching her.

It's the last time I'll see her. It's the last time she'd know who I am to her, and where she and I came from.

These are the last moments of her knowing and remembering her sister, the last time her memories of me will live in her, good and bad, along with memories of our mother and father, memories of our step-dad, her memories of his death, memories of Uras, of her and me flying above its white castle and over the red terrain of Arllu.

Soon it all will be gone, erased like it had never existed.

Her memories instead would be replaced with memories of a loving single father, who would dote on her, who would love her, keeping her safe, the father who would give her the world and a future.

My gaze darts to Shana, who jumps up and gives my sister a tight hug.

Shana's hair grew, moving with the evening breeze. Unlike Tabby, she was very pleased with angelic fashion the moment she laid her eyes on it. Now she stands at the edge of the park, wearing all white tunic and trousers, copying mine. She adores me, wanting to be like me.

The fashion of blue colours had slowly dissipated, replaced with the pure white colours I wear. I had refused any stitching and decoration over my tunic. The Council had begun insisting on it, saying that it would show everyone who I am and what I have achieved as Uriel, but after a few pushbacks from me, they waved their hands and finally let it go.

After Yofiel's attack, I exiled the rest of Ophanims out of Uras.

I don't know where they went. Maybe Mik'hael had welcomed them back into his fold, maybe they went somewhere else, but Uras and Arllu are closed for them now.

Sam was arguing that I had made a mistake by not killing the co-conspirators, but I didn't want continue with revenge killings, with the bloodshed. I didn't want any more deaths.

Sam has agreed to take responsibility of governing Arllu in my name. We've agreed that he'd keep the lizards in Arllu, to help with Arllu's day-to-day running, but swore that the animals would join my banners the moment I call upon them. He will join me too.

He loves me, at least he says so, it is quite possible that he does, but I don't trust anyone now.

The rest of the angels have settled well too, and once the brothers' period of mourning for their fallen had ended, they have embraced their new home and the leader, and their laughter has begun to boom in the halls of Uras rather often.

Tabby has decided to divide her time between Uras and Sam's headquarters in Arllu, and she too seems to be happier now.

The god had settled into Uras and doesn't appear to have any desires to leave anytime soon. Mitish's love and adoration has finally found the way into Dšarael's heart and I begin to see the signs of an answering love blossoming there.

I turn to Dumah.

"If you ever need anything, please let me know straight away, and please remember to send me your memories of her."

Dumah bows again.

I walk to my sisters.

"Guys, if that's okay, can I please have a moment with Jess."

Tabby and Shana turn their heads to me when I speak. They can read my face well and they know what is coming, they were warned before we left.

To cram in as many memories as possible into the last few hours with my sister, we spent all day yesterday on the pier. The girls loved every minute of it and their laughter and excited shrills rang above seagulls' squawks, music, laughter and chatter of the pier's visitors.

We arrived earlier this summer morning and the five of us sat at the top of the hill, watching the sunrise as it painted rooftops of the town bronze, bringing with it my memories.

So much has happened since then.

I can't believe that once I was running down that street at sunrise, wanting to end the pain.

That girl is long gone. She is now dead.

Her wish to stop being herself came bearing fruit.

Now, I have nothing in common with the girl I once was, and sending my sister away will cut the final tie with my human life.

I'm no longer human and no longer a child. I am the archangel Uriel: the most feared of archangels, the archangel who holds the largest army in the memory of Sarukh and whose essence is vast. I've brought both istana and lizards into my fold, whilst starting the release of the imprisoned in Arllu angels, who will soon stand under my banners too.

Mik'hael has backed out for now, but I doubt it will remain like that forever, he doesn't strike me as an angel who accepts defeat. I bet he'll be knocking, but that's okay too, as I'll be waiting.

"Jessie-boo", I whisper. I reach out and take her hands in mine. "I have to go, baby. It's time."

I can't push any more words past the tears and closing of my throat.

I want to tell her so much.

I want to tell her how much I love her, how much I will miss her, how lost I will be without her, how empty my life will become, how much I regret my decision already, how much I need to fight with myself to let her go, how slowly I am dying on the inside, how much it hurts...

But I don't tell her that. I never will.

For once in her life, she will be protected and loved. She will live as a carefree child, even if it will kill me.

I swallow my tears, pushing the selfish pain down my throat too.

"I love you, Jessie-boo", I croak.

It's all I can manage.

But my sister doesn't need any words. She knows me well. She knows me better than anyone ever would.

She jumps up at me, hugging me tight, and begins to cry, her body starts to shake and childish cries float into the golden air around us, rising into inconsolable wails of pain of the one I love the most.

And before I change my mind, I lift my wet face to Dumah and I nod.

"Cushu-ndi-go", I whisper above her head, stroking her soft hair for the last time. "I love you, baby. Forever. Cushu-ndi-go."

"No, Ariel. No!" she screams and sobs into my chest. Her fists are full of my tunic, her arms strangling me, her tears soaking through fabric and I begin to feel its wetness on my skin.

Suddenly I feel lightheaded.

Before the magic takes hold, I pry her arms open, listening to the ripping of the fabric, as I wriggle out of her tight grip.

My fingers sink into her shoulders, digging deep into her flesh as I wrestle with my own hands, which scream at me of their own need to bring her closer, hug her tight and never let her go.

And before I crumble, I turn her away, pushing her towards Dumah's ready embrace, and once his arms close around her, her heart wrenching cries disappear, evaporated as if they never existed, replaced by soft playful giggles.

"Caught you!" Dumah's deep voice booms above her head as he holds her close. His gaze finds and locks to mine, and he gives me a small nod.

"That's not fair!" Jess protests, laughing and wriggling in his hold. "You're faster than me."

"We can go again", he offers.

"Okay, dad, but you have to give me more of a head start", Jess begins negotiations, "like twice longer than the one before."

"Alright", Dumah answers and without a pause he begins to count: "One, two, three..."

Jess squeals with delight, spins on the spot and sprints away from him, her laughter ringing silver bells of happiness and content in the summer air.

THE BOOKS IN THE "CELESTIAL CREATURES" SERIES:

THE BOOKS ARE AVAILABLE VIA ALL MAJOR PLATFORMS & BEST RETAILERS!

"HEAVENWARD", BOOK 1: https://books2read.com/u/bWzWlx

"HALLOW", BOOK 2: https://books2read.com/u/m2vkw6

"HARBINGER", BOOK 3: https://books2read.com/u/bx8n1l

"HALO", BOOK 4 (AND FINAL): https://books2read.com/u/3nvW56

www.ingramcontent.com/pod-product-compliance
Lightning Source LLC
Chambersburg PA
CBHW051529250626
47156CB00001B/285